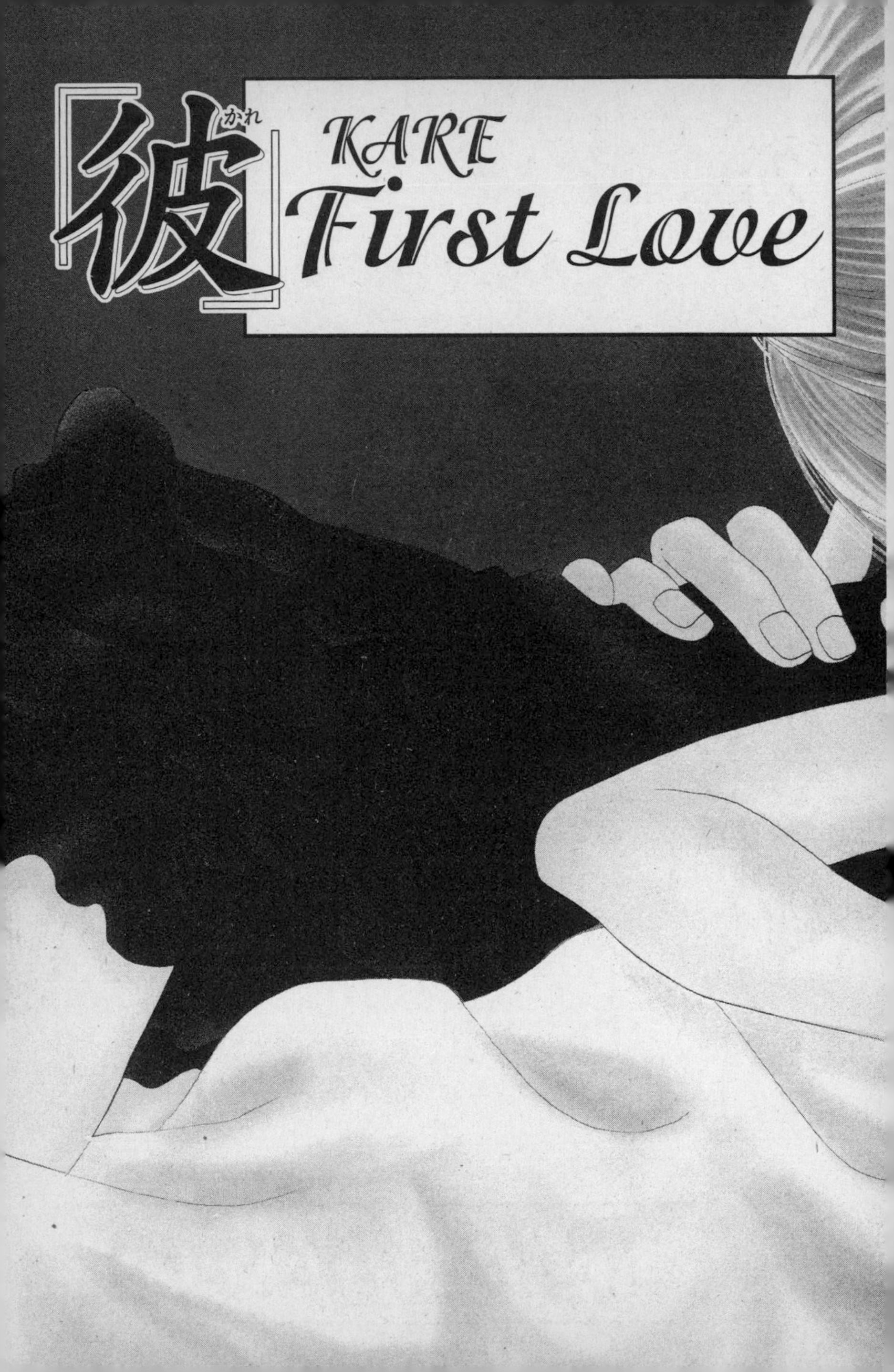
『彼』
かれ
KARE
First Love

Characters and Story Digest

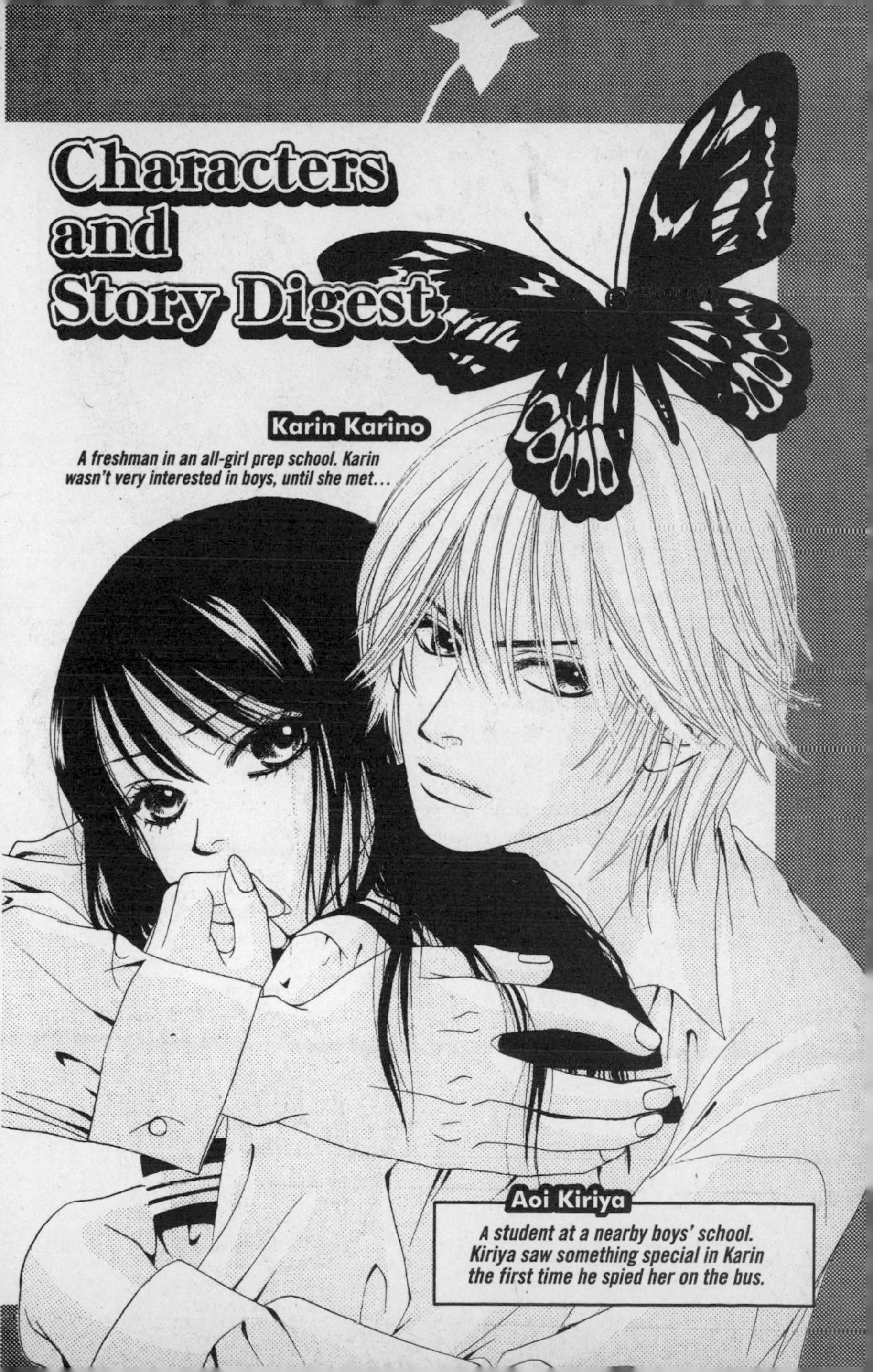

Karin Karino

A freshman in an all-girl prep school. Karin wasn't very interested in boys, until she met...

Aoi Kiriya

A student at a nearby boys' school. Kiriya saw something special in Karin the first time he spied her on the bus.

「彼」 KARE First Love

2

Karin opted to go to a girls' school in part because she was never comfortable around boys. It might not have been bliss, but she managed a quiet life and liked it.

Then she had an unfortunate run-in with a group of local boys on the morning bus. A fellow named Kiriya accidentally flipped up her skirt! Karin was embarrassed and wanted to put the whole thing behind her. No such luck. Her friend Yuka heard about the incident and, thinking the boys were cute, bullied Karin into arranging a group outing with Kiriya and his friends. Karin drank too much and passed out. When she came to, she found herself alone with Kiriya in his apartment! She scrambled out quickly—but not before Kiriya could steal a kiss and turn her world upside down. Now, just as Kiriya and Karin are starting to acknowledge their feelings for each other, Yuka has decided she wants Kiriya for herself. But Karin doesn't want any trouble with her friend. Will she risk her quiet life for love?

Yuka Ishikawa

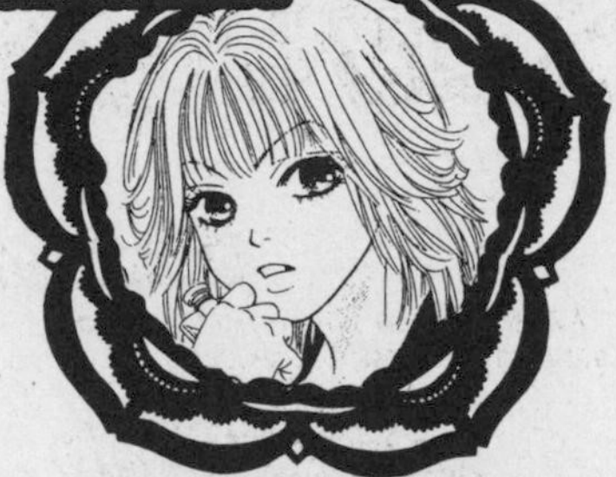

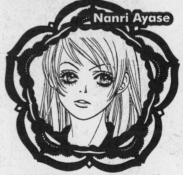

Karin's classmate. She wants Kiriya for herself.

Nanri Ayase

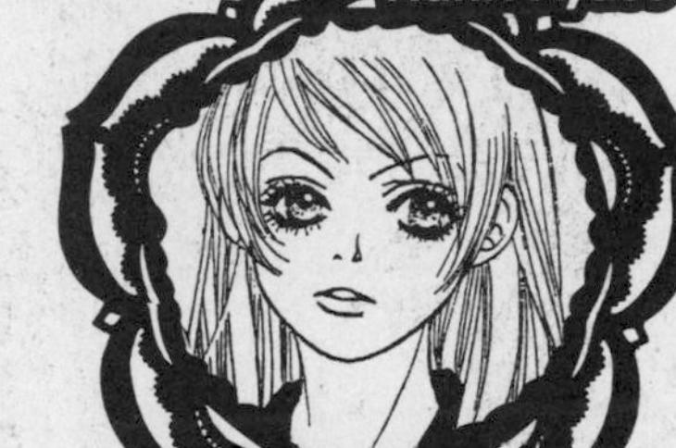

Karin's classmate. Nanri's an outsider at school, but she's nice to Karin.

Hiromu&Toru

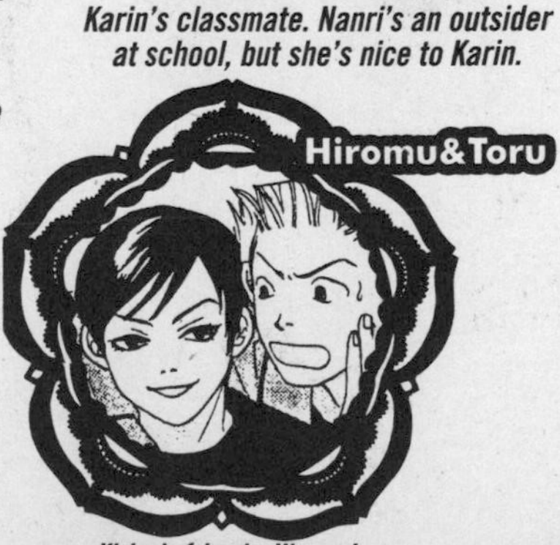

Kiriya's friends. Hiromu's cool. Tohru's girl-crazy.

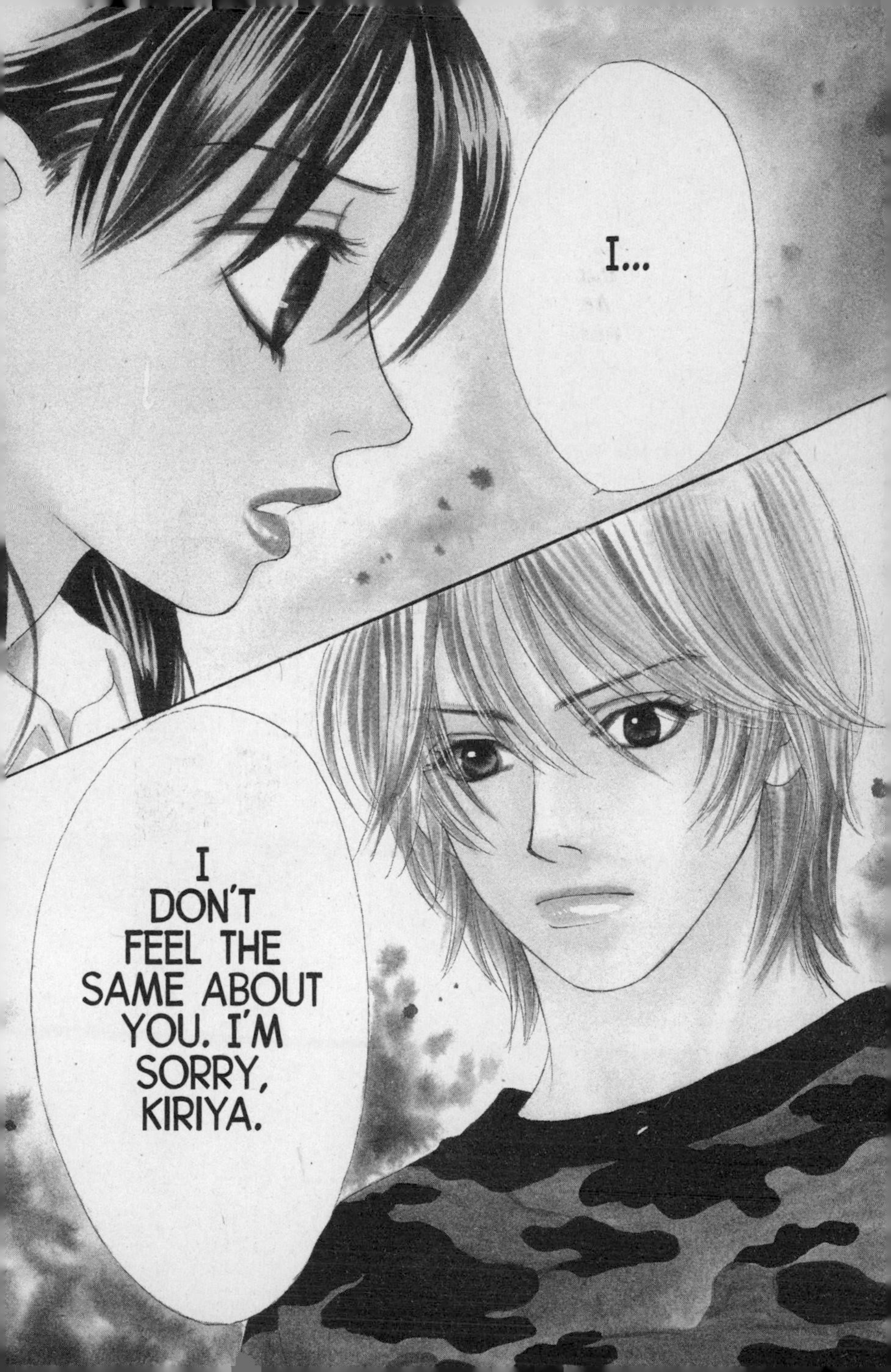
I...
I DON'T FEEL THE SAME ABOUT YOU. I'M SORRY, KIRIYA.

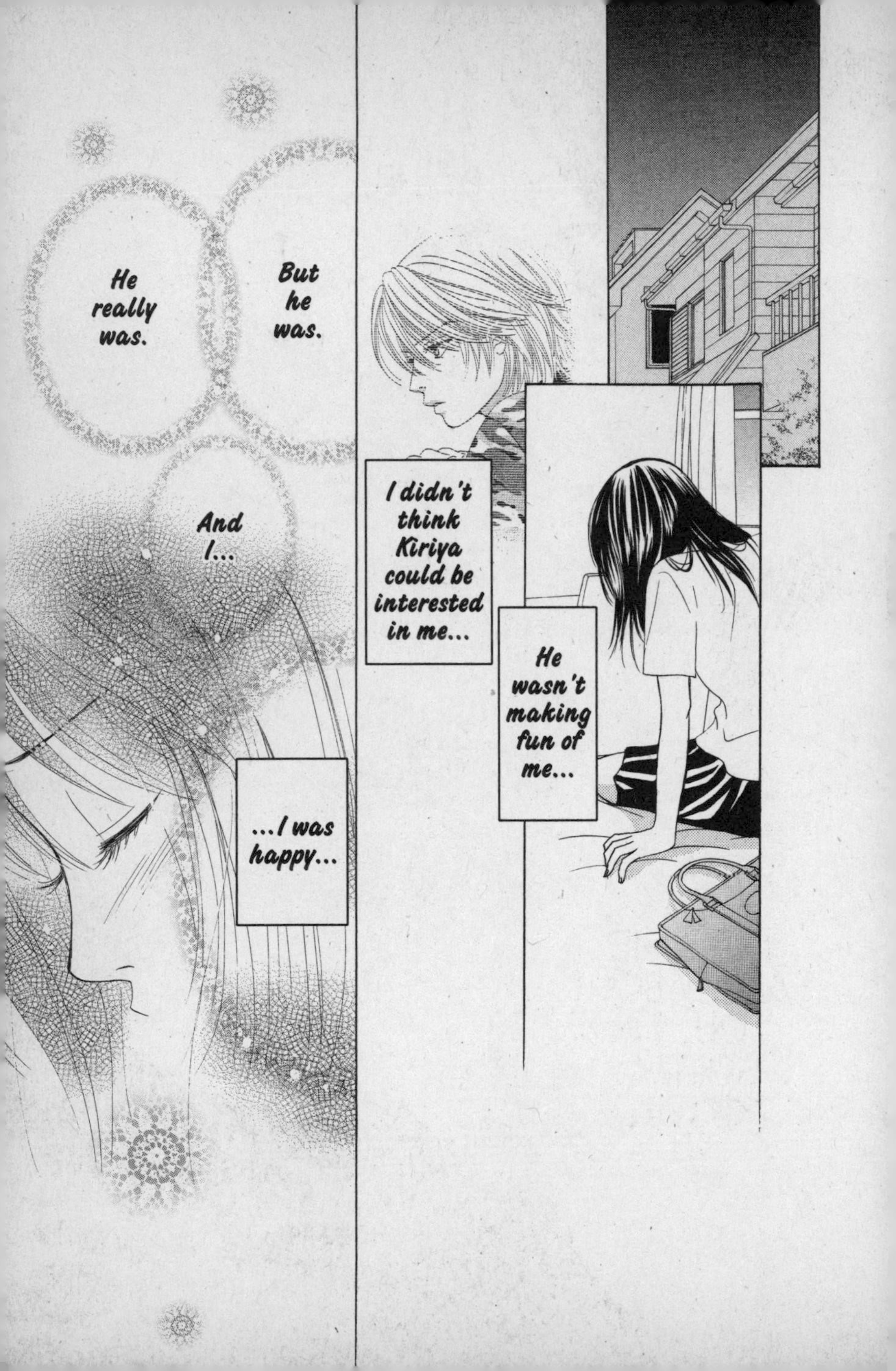
I didn't think Kiriya could be interested in me...
He wasn't making fun of me...
But he was.
He really was.
And I...
...I was happy...

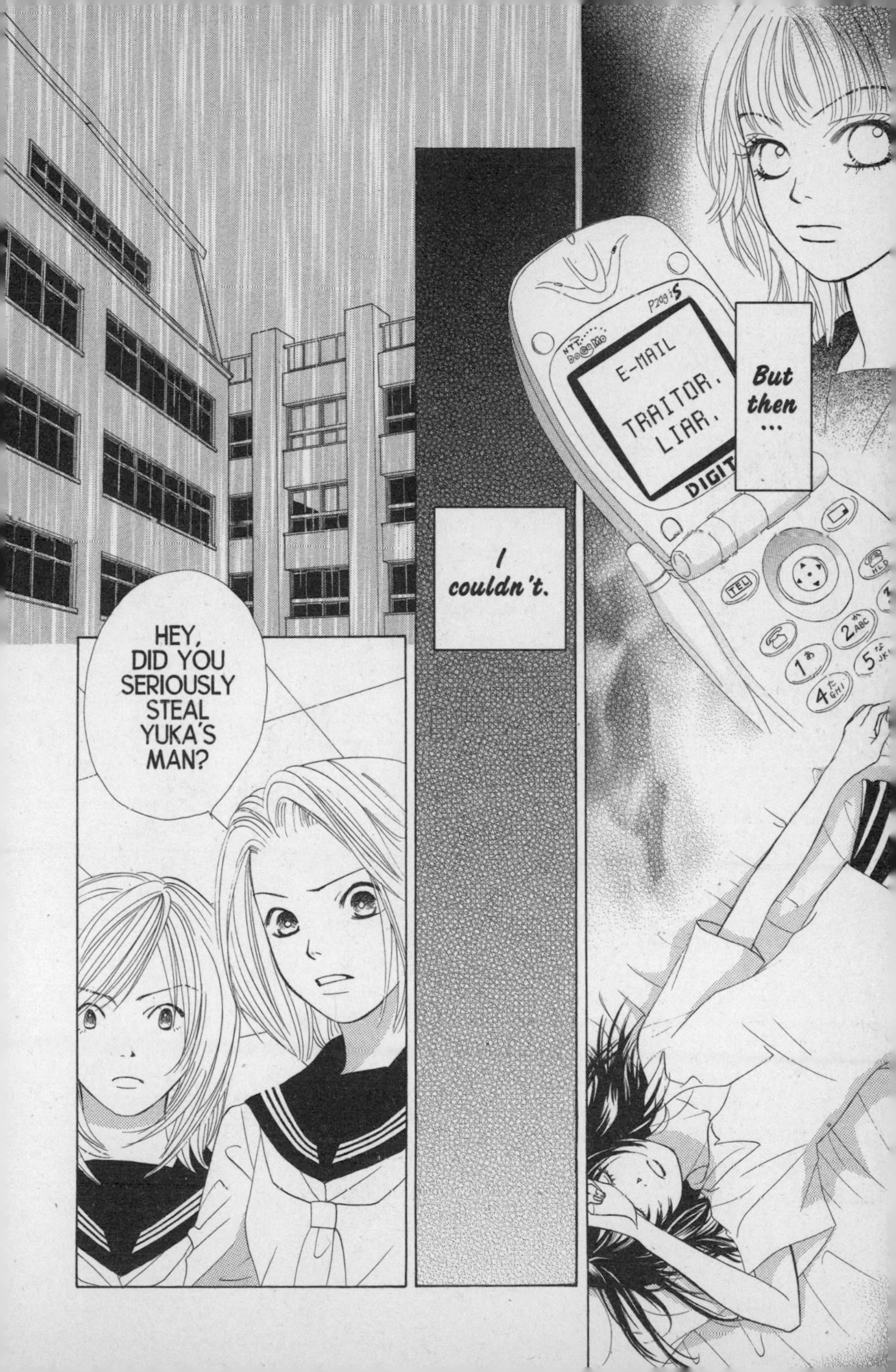
But then ...
E-MAIL
TRAITOR. LIAR.
I couldn't.
HEY, DID YOU SERIOUSLY STEAL YUKA'S MAN?

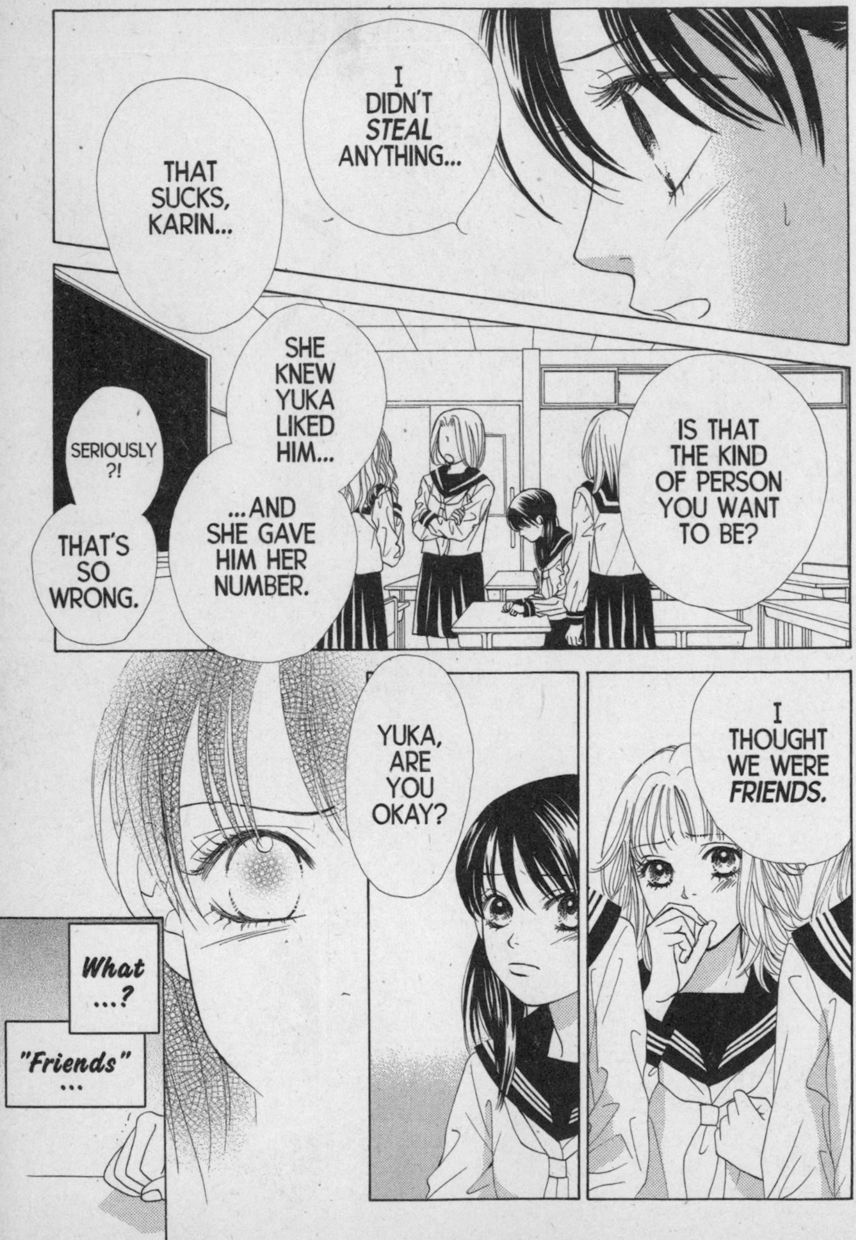
I DIDN'T *STEAL* ANYTHING...
IS THAT THE KIND OF PERSON YOU WANT TO BE?
THAT SUCKS, KARIN...
SHE KNEW YUKA LIKED HIM...
...AND SHE GAVE HIM HER NUMBER.
SERIOUSLY?!
THAT'S SO WRONG.
I THOUGHT WE WERE *FRIENDS.*
YUKA, ARE YOU OKAY?
What ...?
"Friends" ...

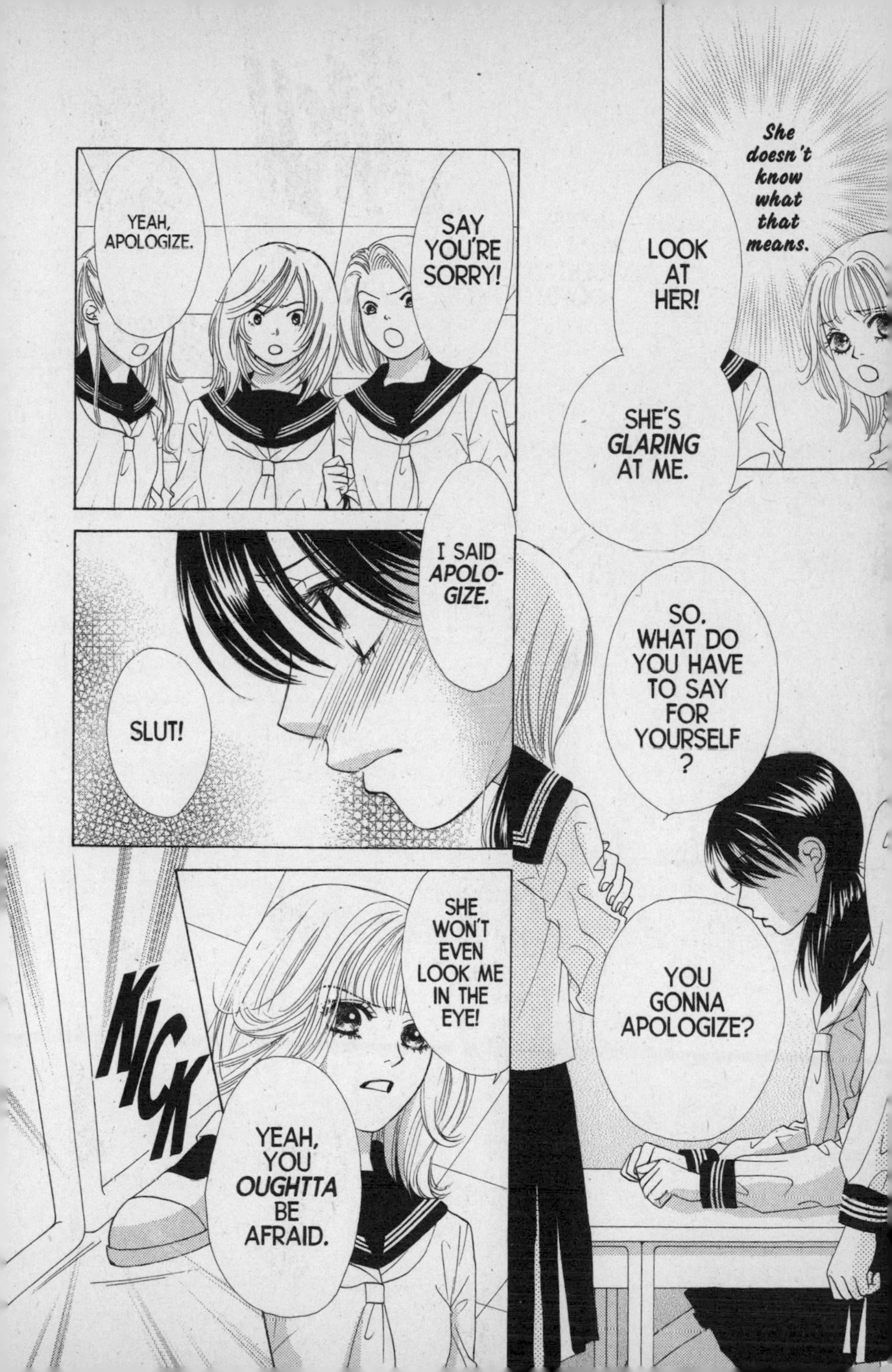
She doesn't know what that means.
LOOK AT HER!
SHE'S *GLARING* AT ME.
SO. WHAT DO YOU HAVE TO SAY FOR YOURSELF?
YOU GONNA APOLOGIZE?
SAY YOU'RE SORRY!
YEAH, APOLOGIZE.
I SAID *APOLOGIZE.*
SLUT!
SHE WON'T EVEN LOOK ME IN THE EYE!
KICK
YEAH, YOU *OUGHTTA* BE AFRAID.

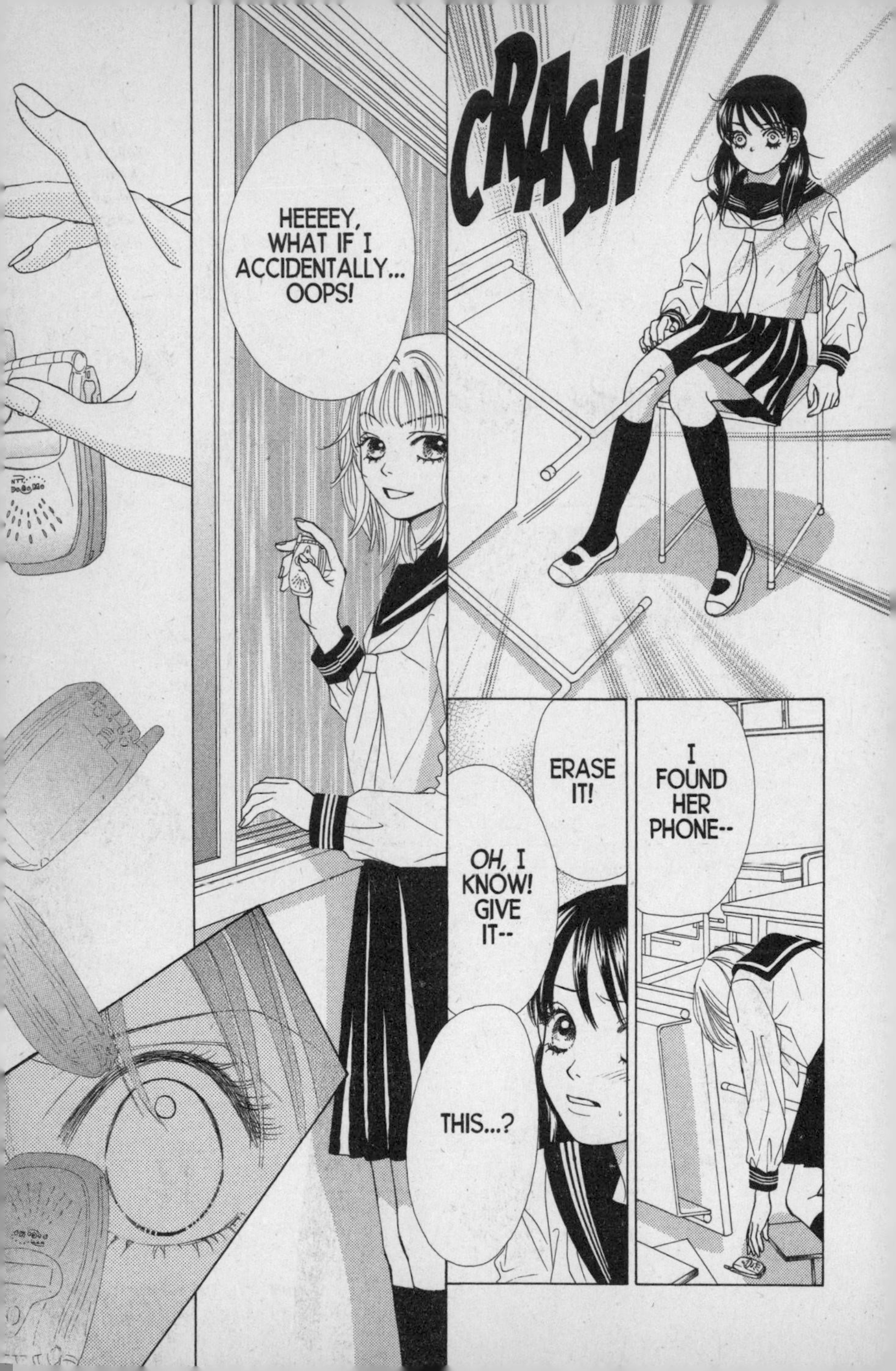
CRASH
I FOUND HER PHONE--
ERASE IT!
OH, I KNOW! GIVE IT--
THIS...?
HEEEEY, WHAT IF I ACCIDENTALLY... OOPS!

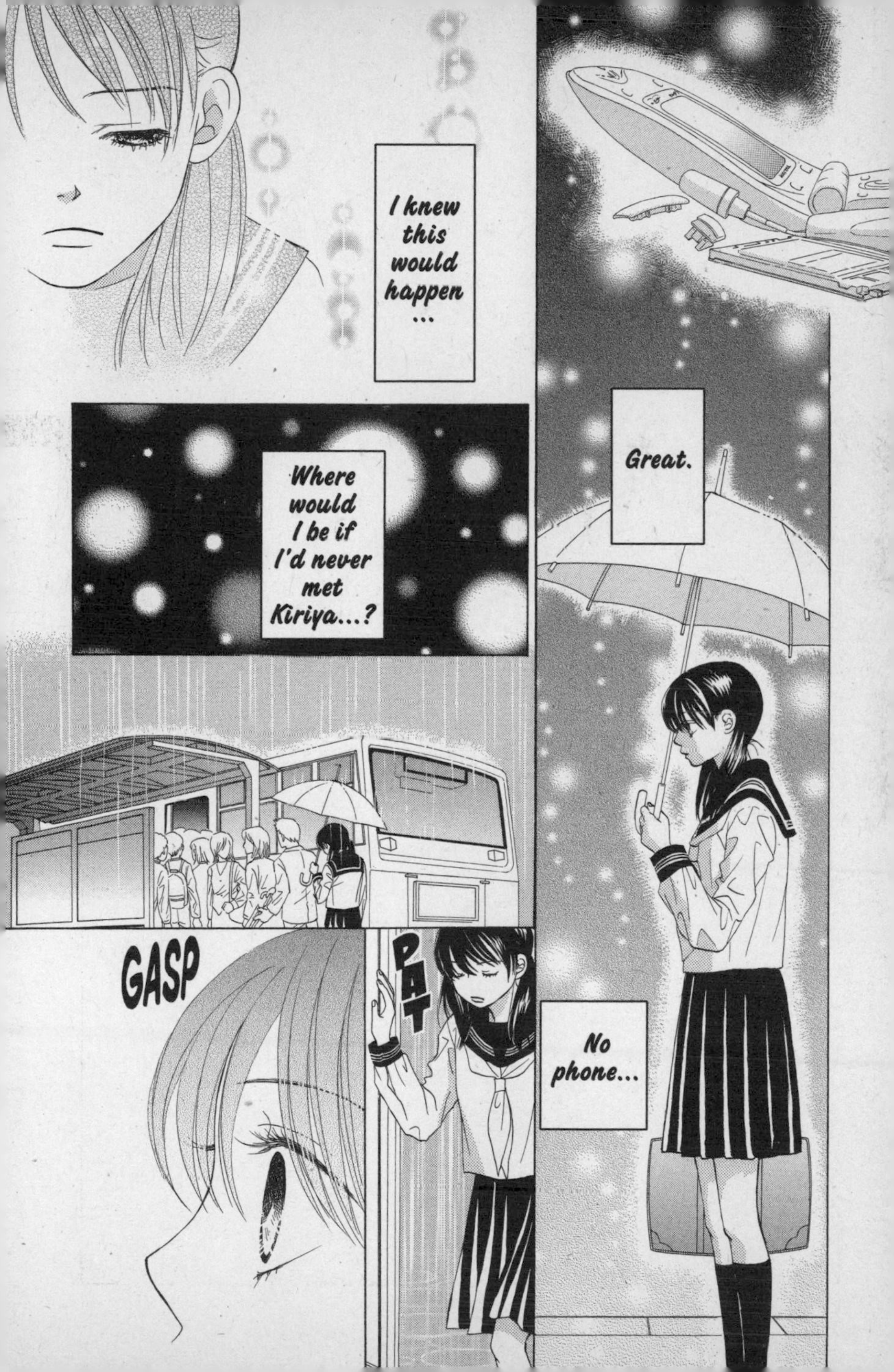
Great.
No phone...
I knew this would happen...
Where would I be if I'd never met Kiriya...?
PAT
GASP

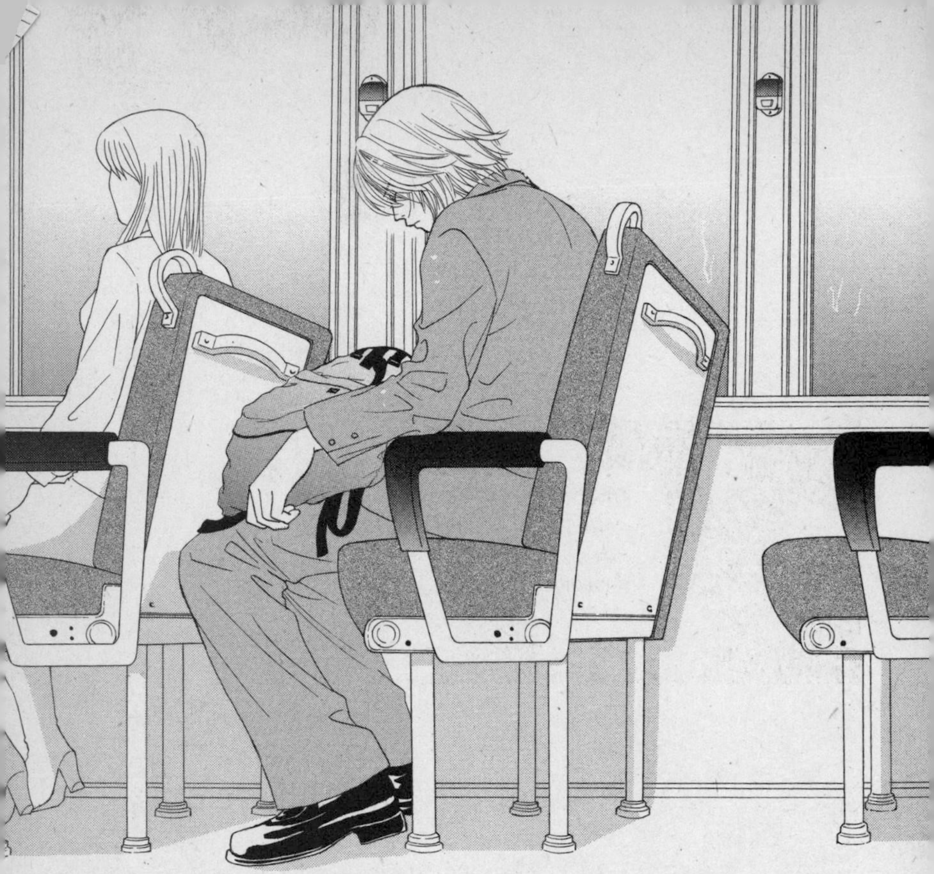

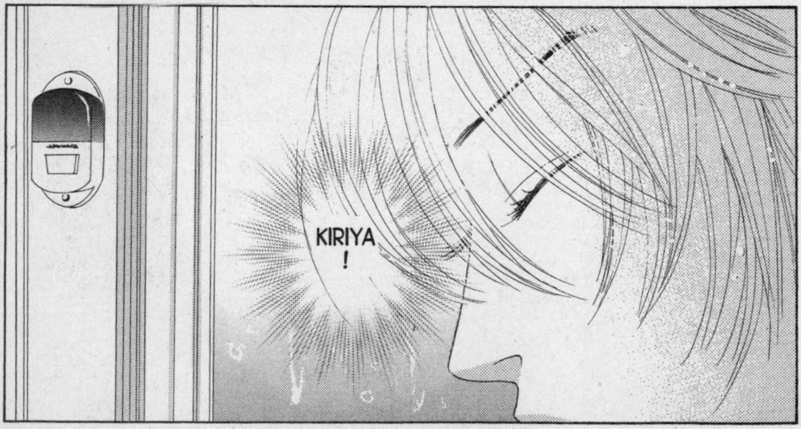
KIRIYA
!

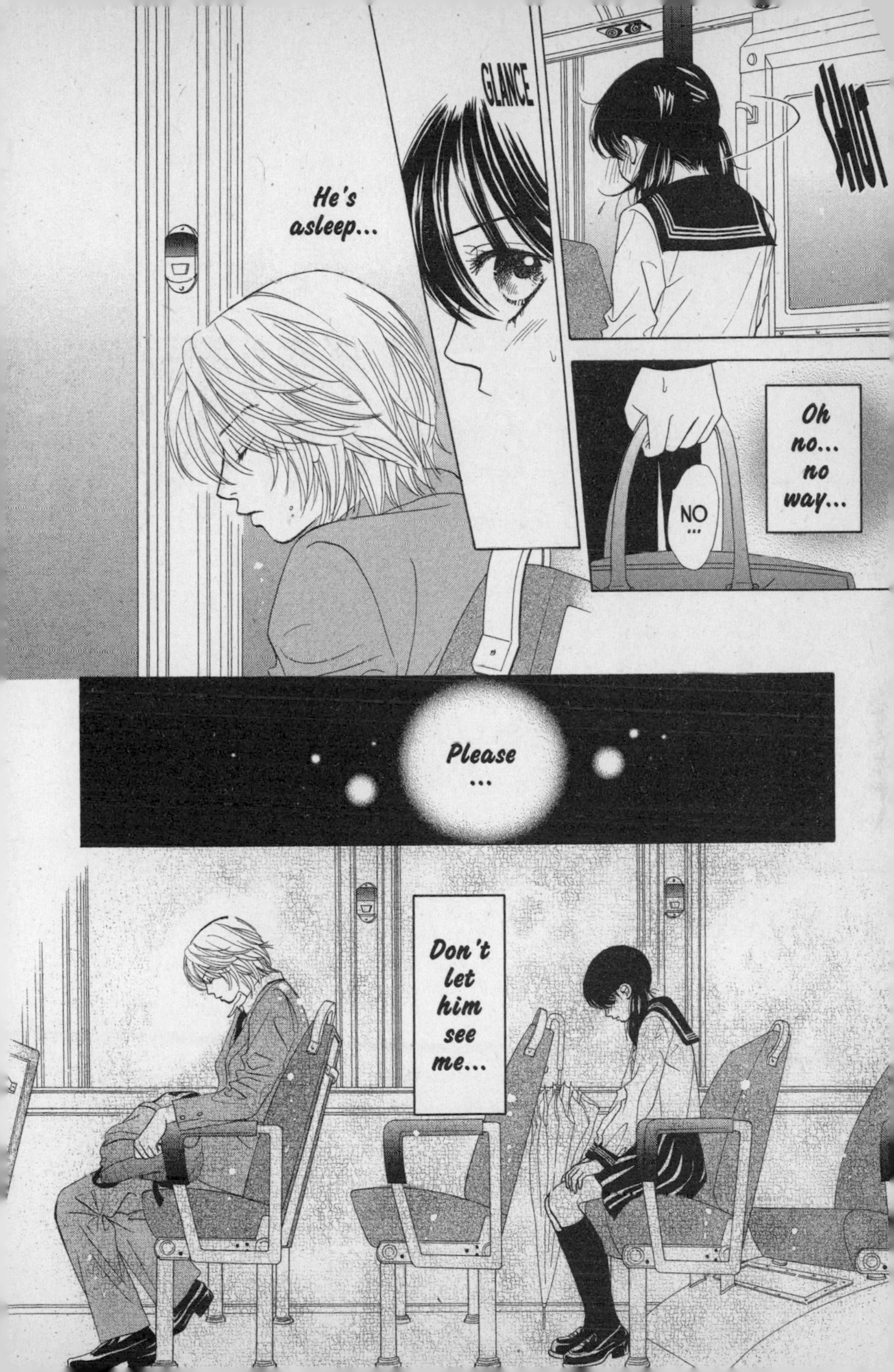
SHUT
Oh no... no way...
NO...
GLANCE
He's asleep...
Please...
Don't let him see me...

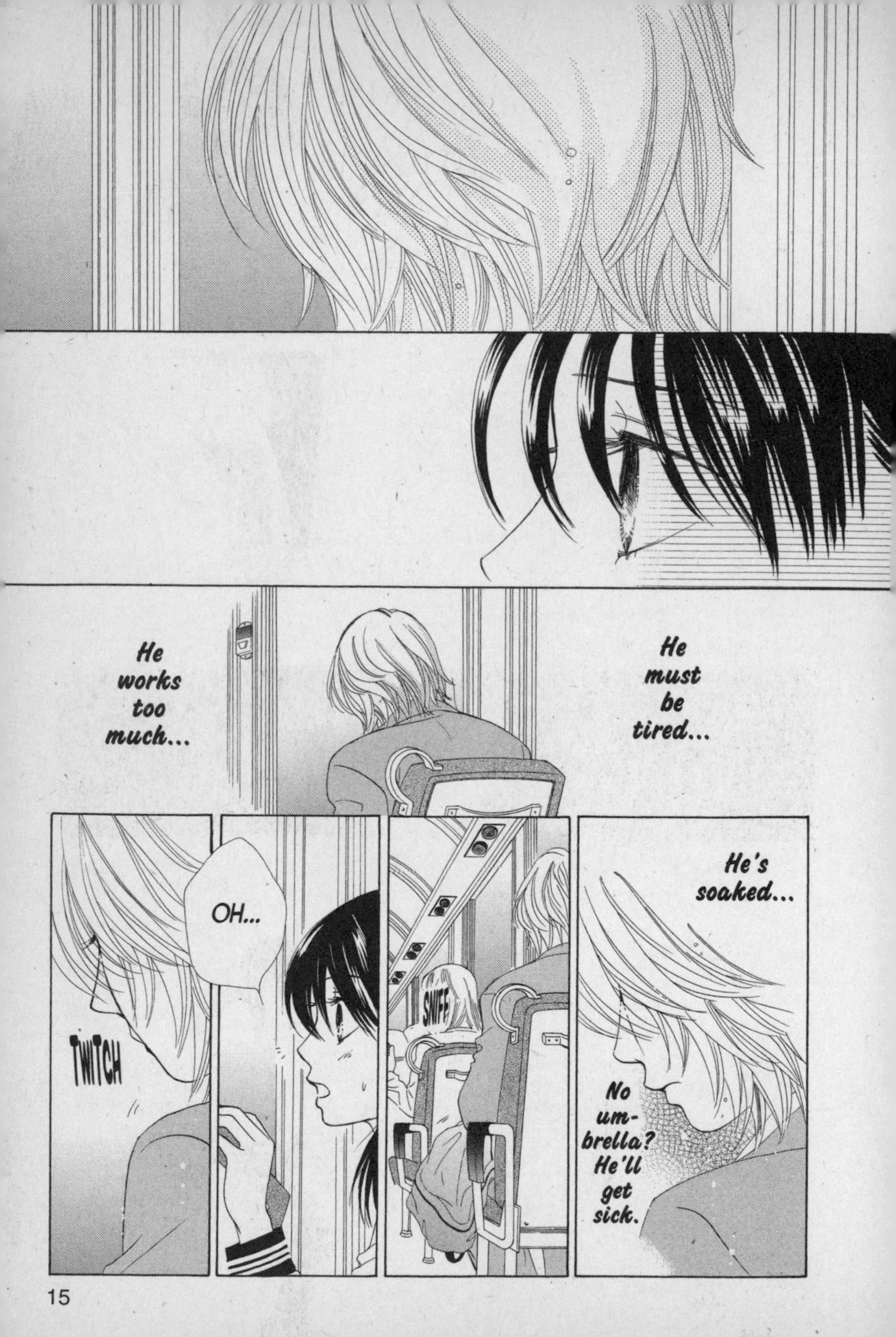
He must be tired...
He works too much...
He's soaked...
No um-brella? He'll get sick.
SNIFF
OH...
TWITCH

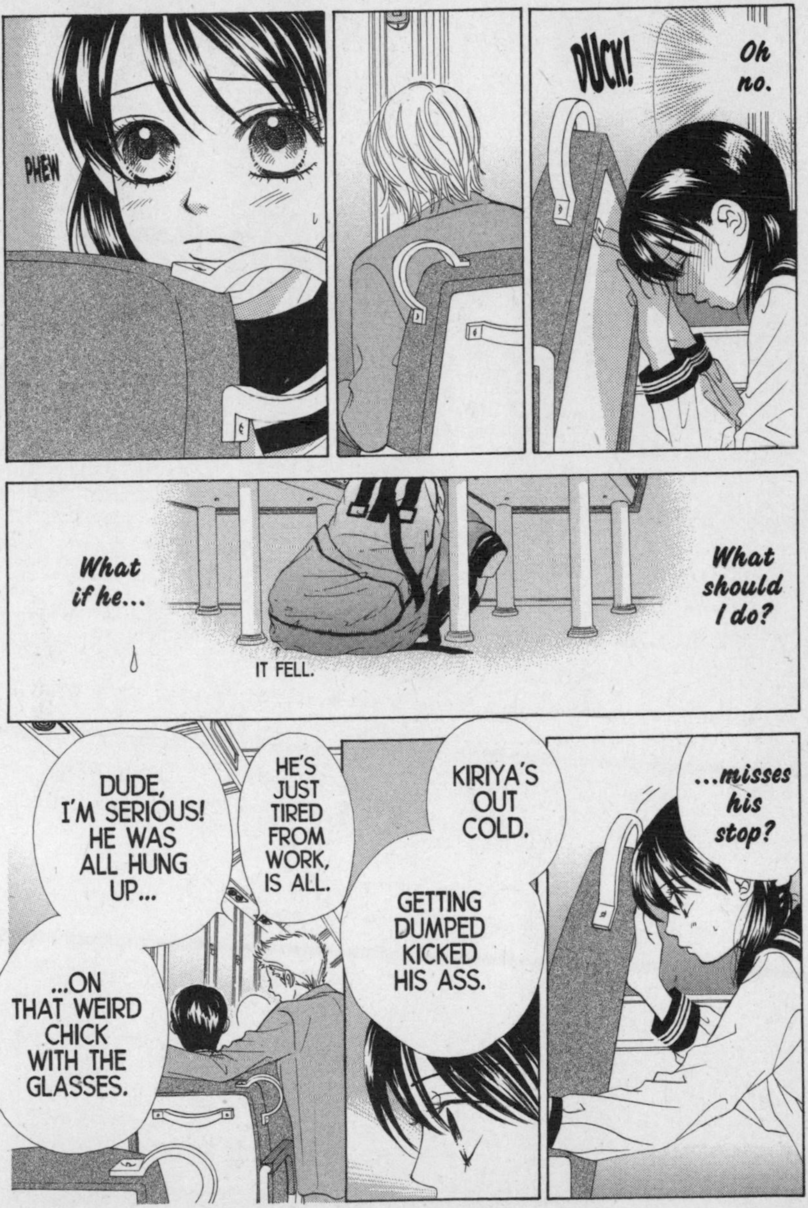

DUCK!
Oh no.
PHEW
What should I do?
What if he...
IT FELL.
...misses his stop?
KIRIYA'S OUT COLD.
HE'S JUST TIRED FROM WORK, IS ALL.
DUDE, I'M SERIOUS! HE WAS ALL HUNG UP...
GETTING DUMPED KICKED HIS ASS.
...ON THAT WEIRD CHICK WITH THE GLASSES.

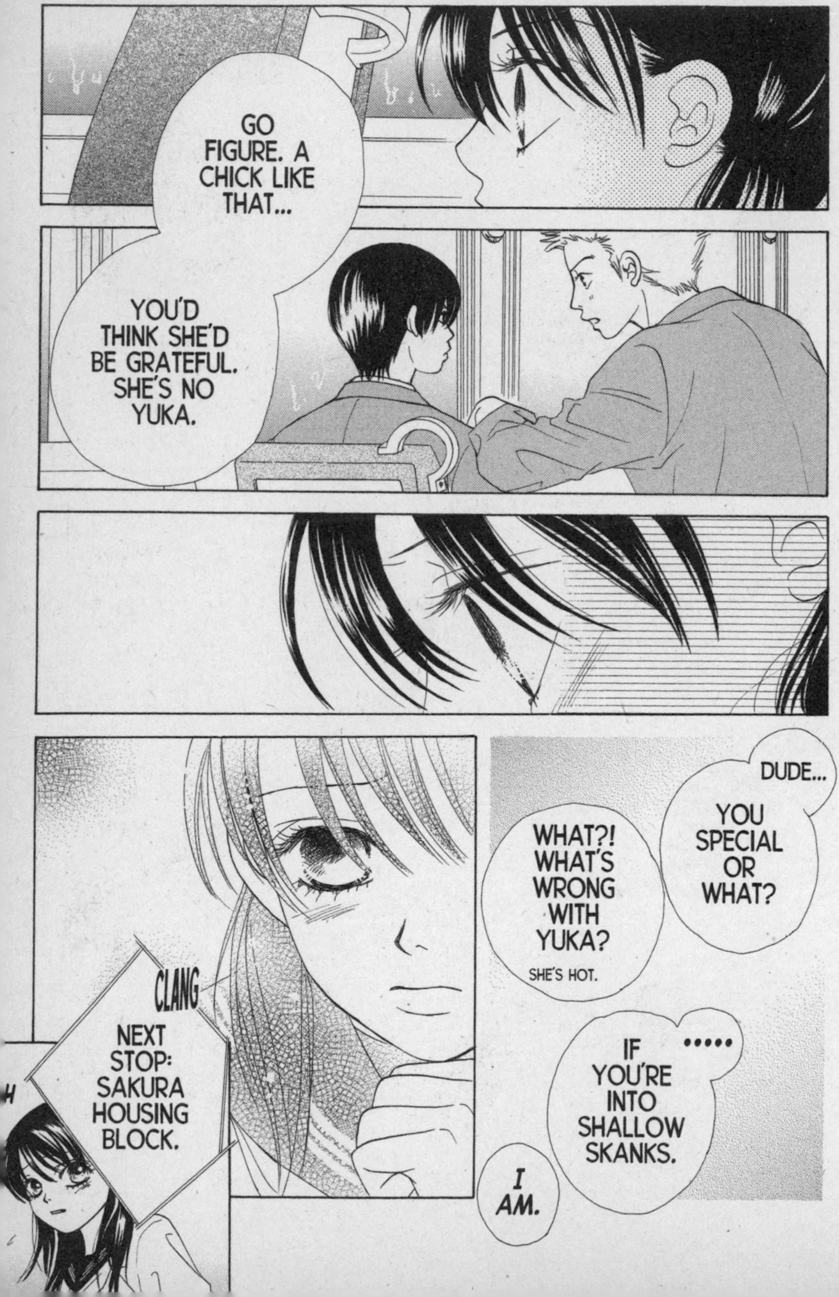
GO FIGURE. A CHICK LIKE THAT...
YOU'D THINK SHE'D BE GRATEFUL. SHE'S NO YUKA.
DUDE...
YOU SPECIAL OR WHAT?
WHAT?! WHAT'S WRONG WITH YUKA?
SHE'S HOT.
.....
IF YOU'RE INTO SHALLOW SKANKS.
I AM.
CLANG
NEXT STOP: SAKURA HOUSING BLOCK.

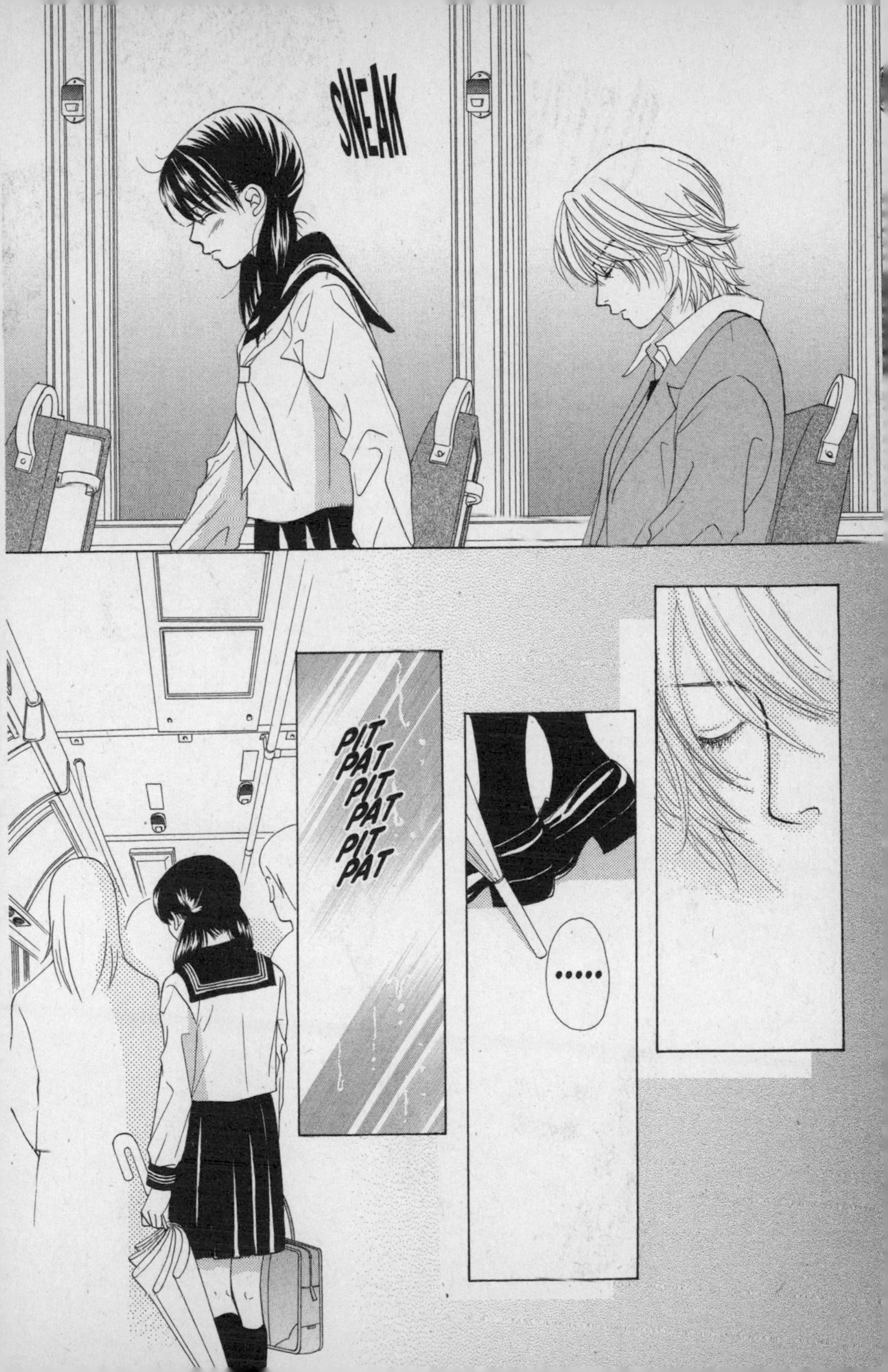
SNEAK
.....
PIT PAT PIT PAT PIT PAT

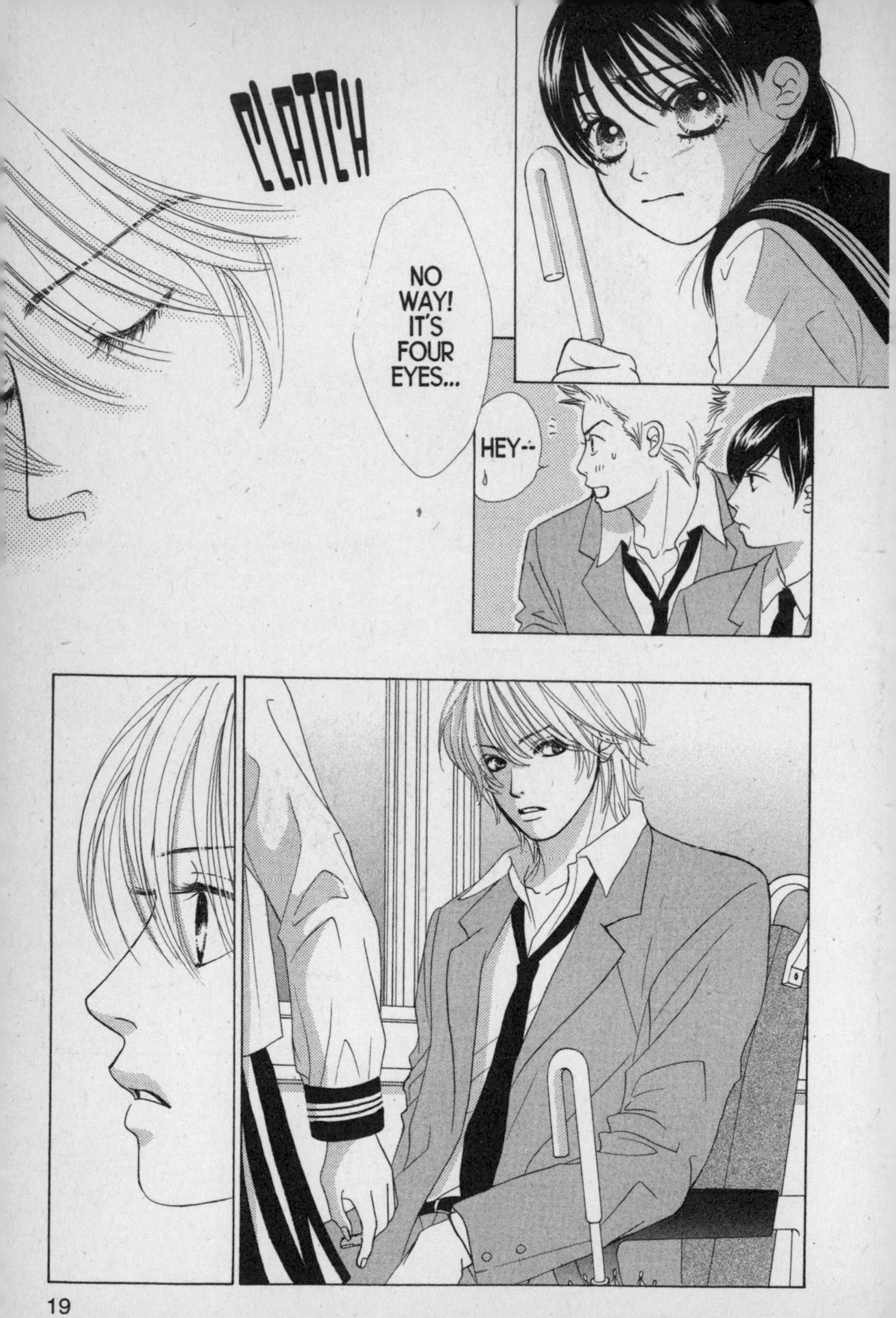
HEY--
CLATCH
NO WAY! IT'S FOUR EYES...

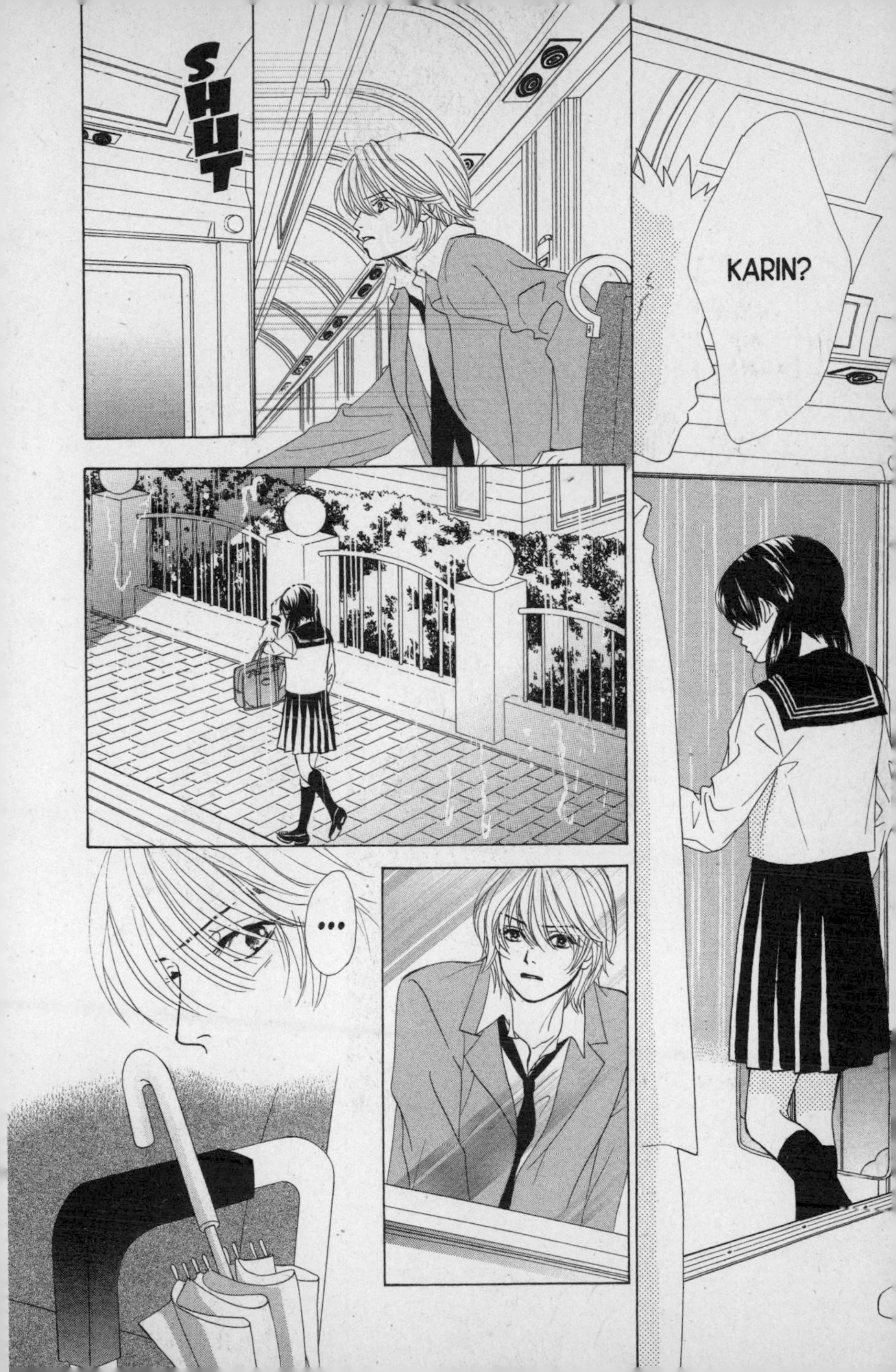
KARIN?
SHUT
...

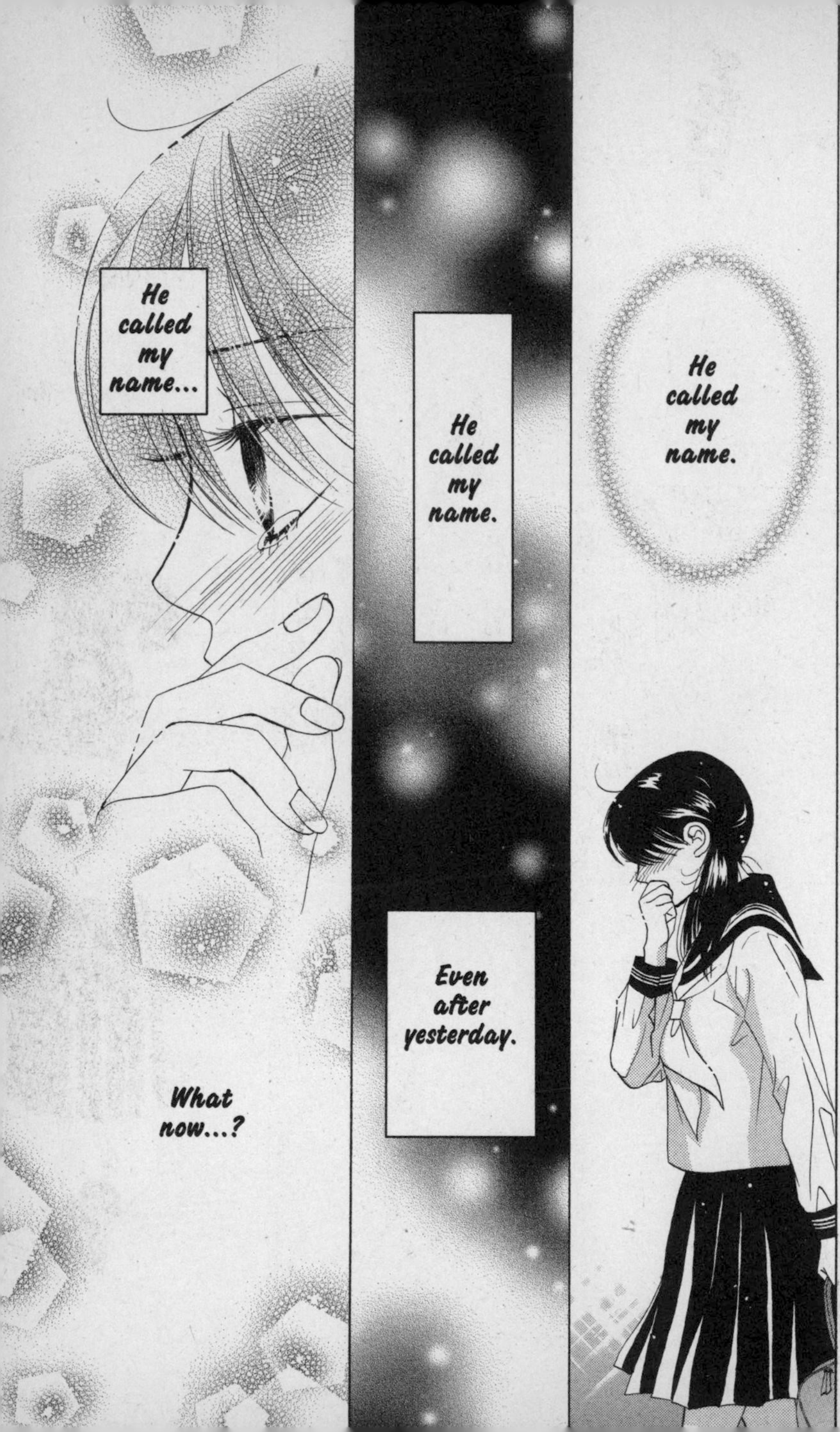
He called my name.
He called my name.
Even after yesterday.
He called my name...
What now...?

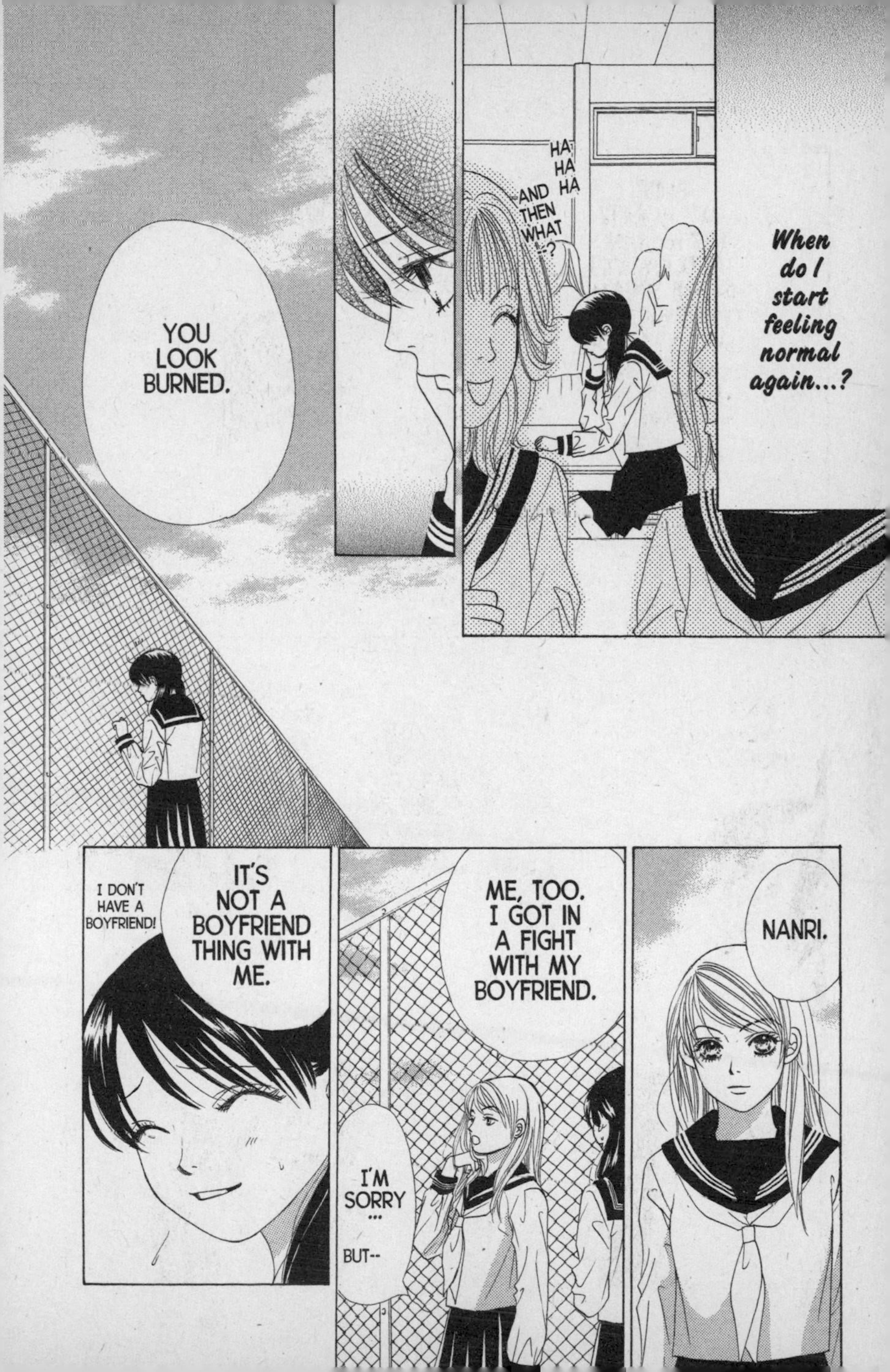
When do I start feeling normal again...?
HA HA HA HA
AND THEN WHAT --?
YOU LOOK BURNED.
NANRI.
ME, TOO. I GOT IN A FIGHT WITH MY BOYFRIEND.
I'M SORRY ... BUT--
IT'S NOT A BOYFRIEND THING WITH ME.
I DON'T HAVE A BOYFRIEND!

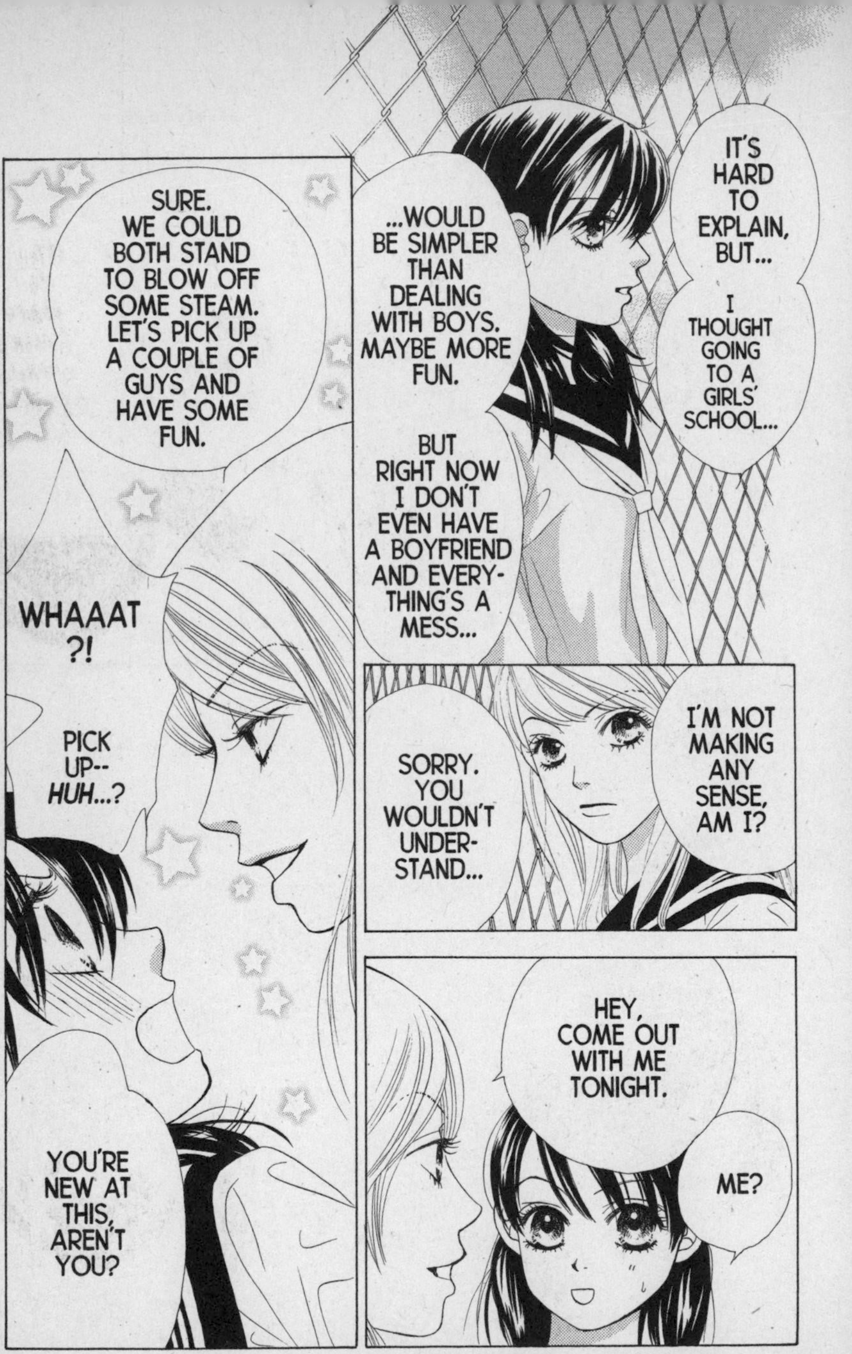

IT'S HARD TO EXPLAIN, BUT...
I THOUGHT GOING TO A GIRLS' SCHOOL...
...WOULD BE SIMPLER THAN DEALING WITH BOYS. MAYBE MORE FUN.
BUT RIGHT NOW I DON'T EVEN HAVE A BOYFRIEND AND EVERY-THING'S A MESS...
I'M NOT MAKING ANY SENSE, AM I?
SORRY. YOU WOULDN'T UNDER-STAND...
HEY, COME OUT WITH ME TONIGHT.
ME?
SURE. WE COULD BOTH STAND TO BLOW OFF SOME STEAM. LET'S PICK UP A COUPLE OF GUYS AND HAVE SOME FUN.
WHAAAT ?!
PICK UP-- *HUH*...?
YOU'RE NEW AT THIS, AREN'T YOU?

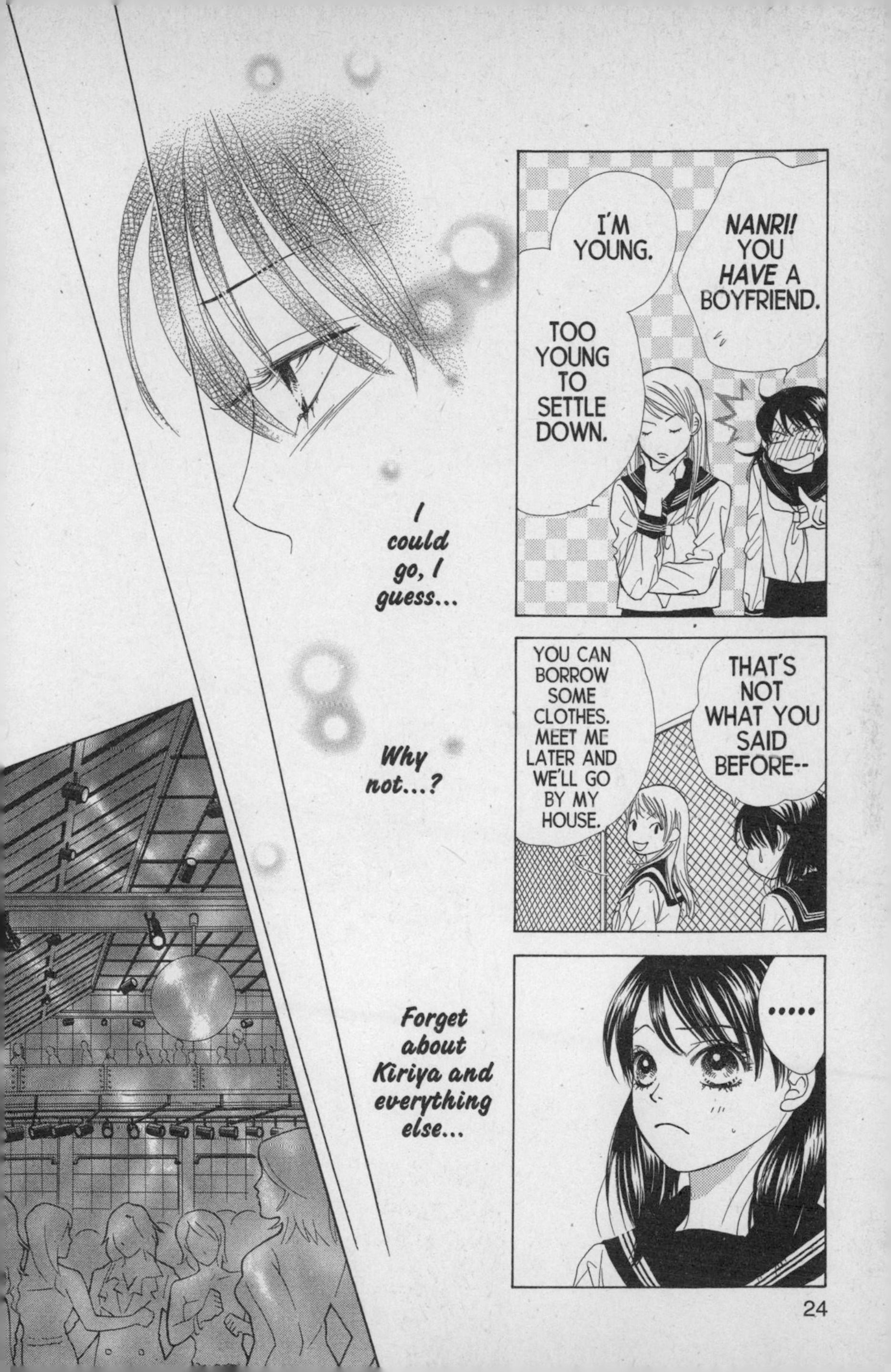
NANRI! YOU HAVE A BOYFRIEND.
I'M YOUNG.
TOO YOUNG TO SETTLE DOWN.
THAT'S NOT WHAT YOU SAID BEFORE--
YOU CAN BORROW SOME CLOTHES. MEET ME LATER AND WE'LL GO BY MY HOUSE.
.....
I could go, I guess...
Why not...?
Forget about Kiriya and everything else...

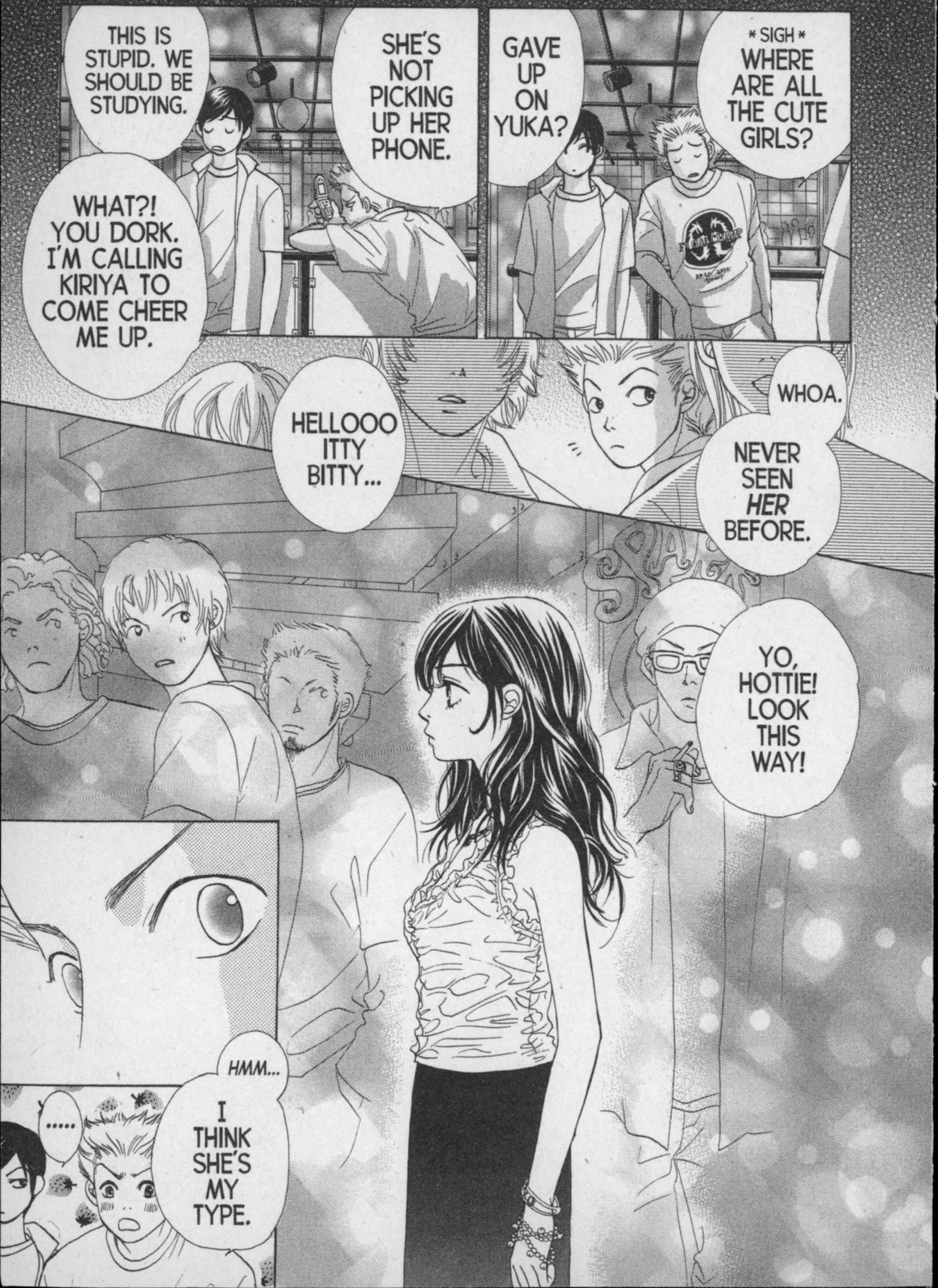
SIGH WHERE ARE ALL THE CUTE GIRLS?
GAVE UP ON YUKA?
SHE'S NOT PICKING UP HER PHONE.
THIS IS STUPID. WE SHOULD BE STUDYING.
WHAT?! YOU DORK. I'M CALLING KIRIYA TO COME CHEER ME UP.
WHOA.
NEVER SEEN *HER* BEFORE.
HELLOOO ITTY BITTY...
YO, HOTTIE! LOOK THIS WAY!
HMM...
I THINK SHE'S MY TYPE.
......

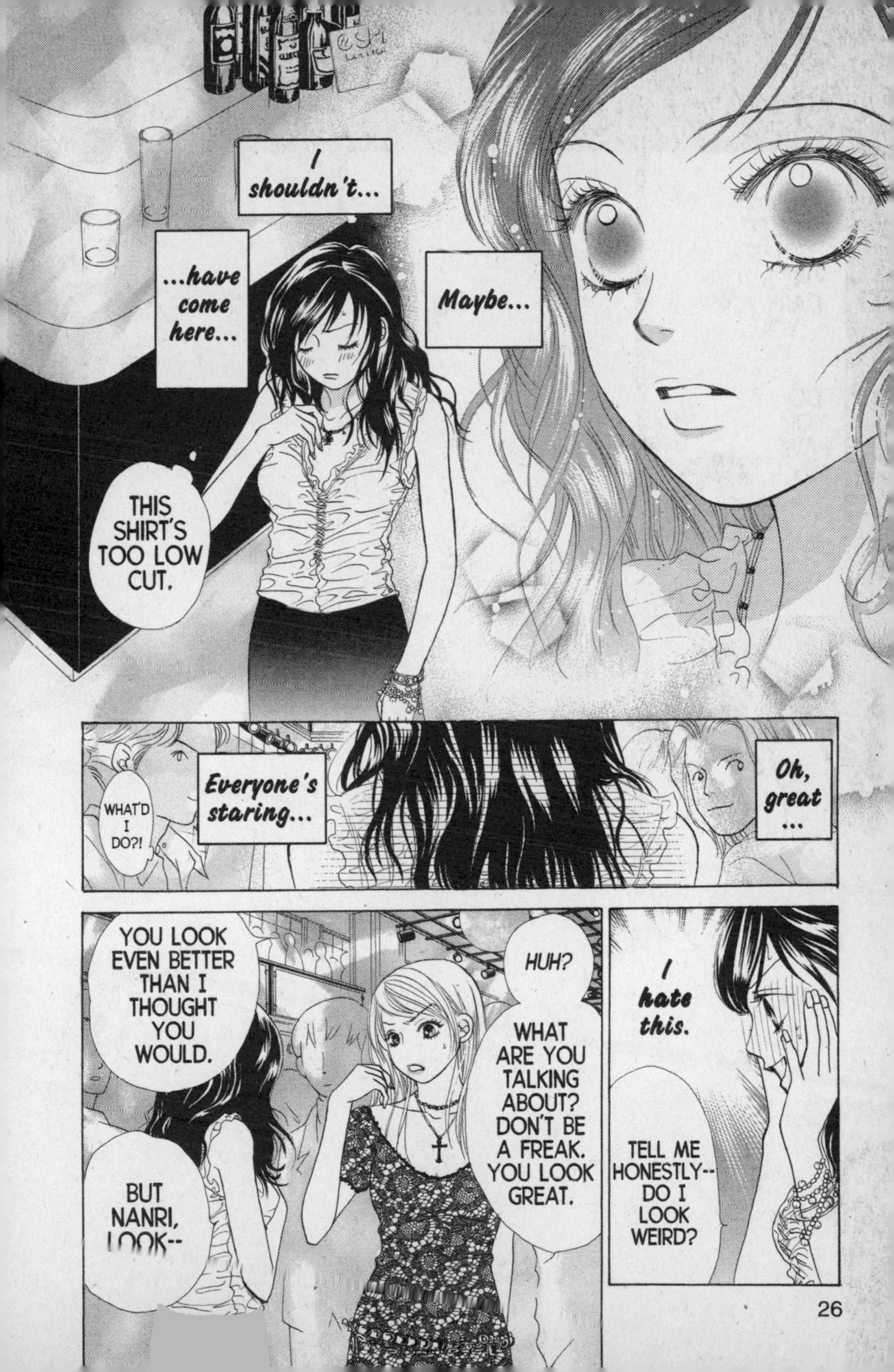
Maybe...
I shouldn't...
...have come here...
THIS SHIRT'S TOO LOW CUT.
Oh, great ...
Everyone's staring...
WHAT'D I DO?!
I hate this.
TELL ME HONESTLY-- DO I LOOK WEIRD?
HUH?
WHAT ARE YOU TALKING ABOUT? DON'T BE A FREAK. YOU LOOK GREAT.
YOU LOOK EVEN BETTER THAN I THOUGHT YOU WOULD.
BUT NANRI, LOOK--

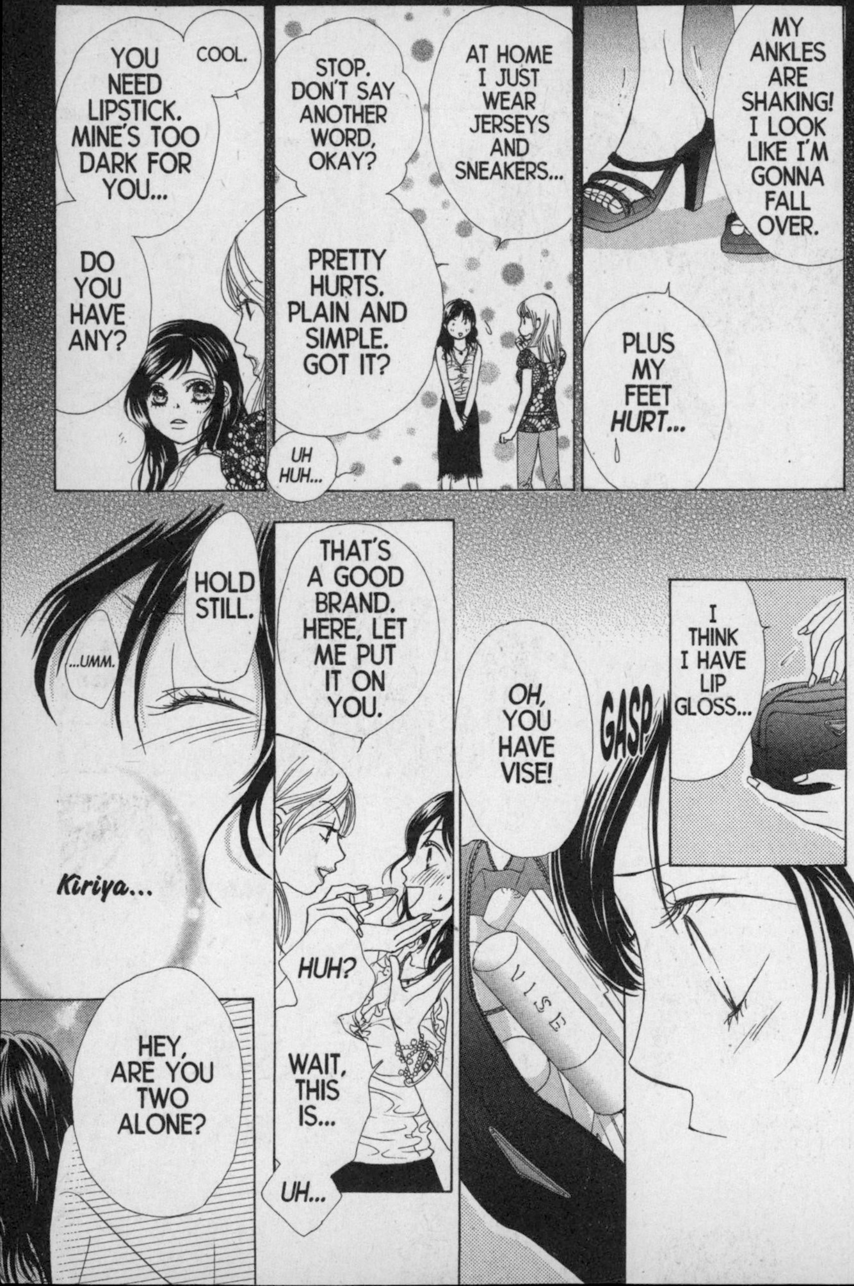
MY ANKLES ARE SHAKING! I LOOK LIKE I'M GONNA FALL OVER.
PLUS MY FEET *HURT*...
AT HOME I JUST WEAR JERSEYS AND SNEAKERS...
STOP. DON'T SAY ANOTHER WORD, OKAY?
PRETTY HURTS. PLAIN AND SIMPLE. GOT IT?
UH HUH...
COOL.
YOU NEED LIPSTICK. MINE'S TOO DARK FOR YOU...
DO YOU HAVE ANY?
I THINK I HAVE LIP GLOSS...
GASP
OH, YOU HAVE VISE!
VISE
THAT'S A GOOD BRAND. HERE, LET ME PUT IT ON YOU.
HUH?
WAIT, THIS IS...
UH...
HOLD STILL.
...UMM.
Kiriya...
HEY, ARE YOU TWO ALONE?

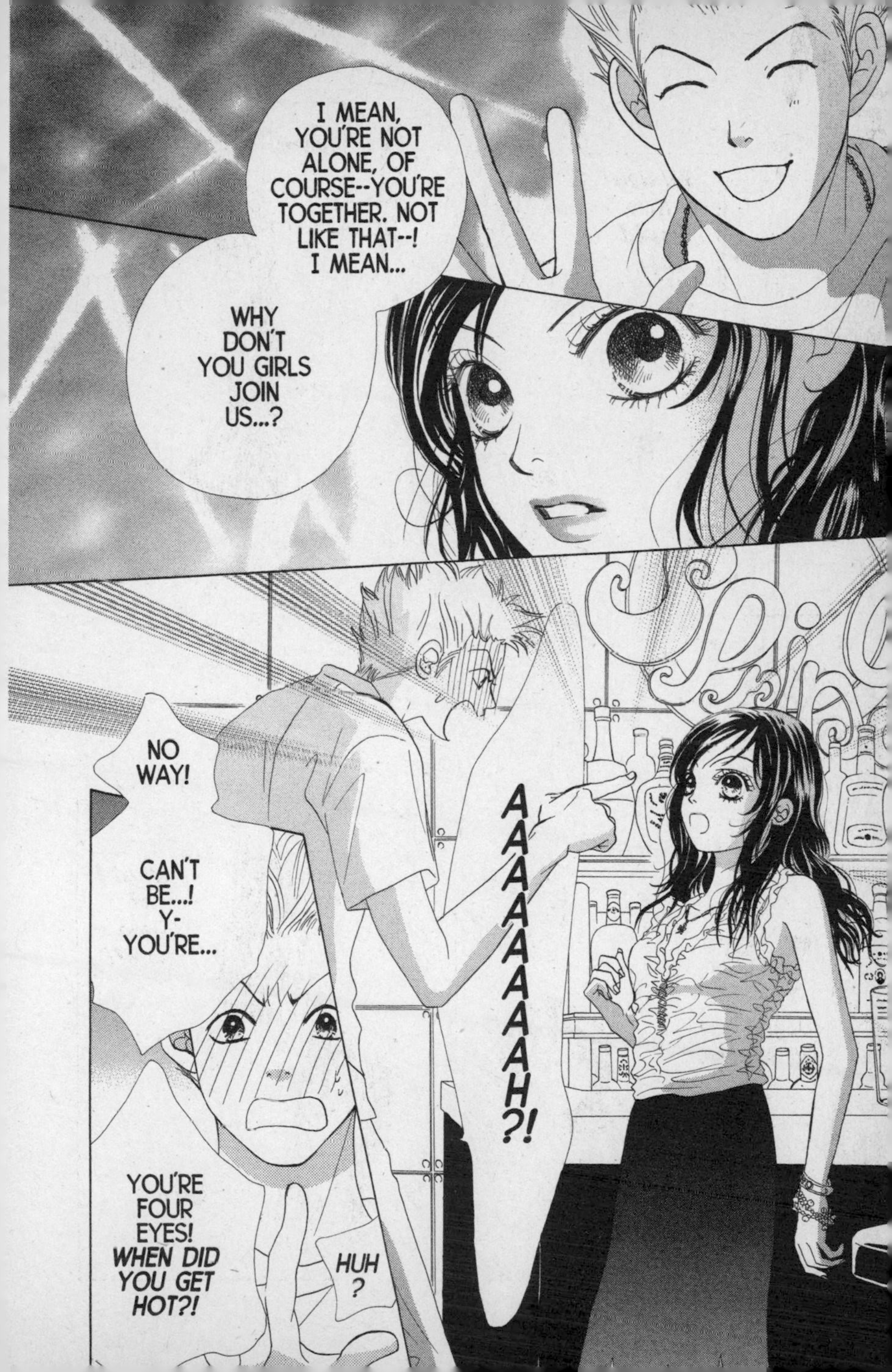
I MEAN, YOU'RE NOT ALONE, OF COURSE--YOU'RE TOGETHER. NOT LIKE THAT--! I MEAN...
WHY DON'T YOU GIRLS JOIN US...?
AAAAAAAAAAAH?!
NO WAY!
CAN'T BE...! Y-YOU'RE...
YOU'RE FOUR EYES! *WHEN DID YOU GET HOT?!*
HUH ?

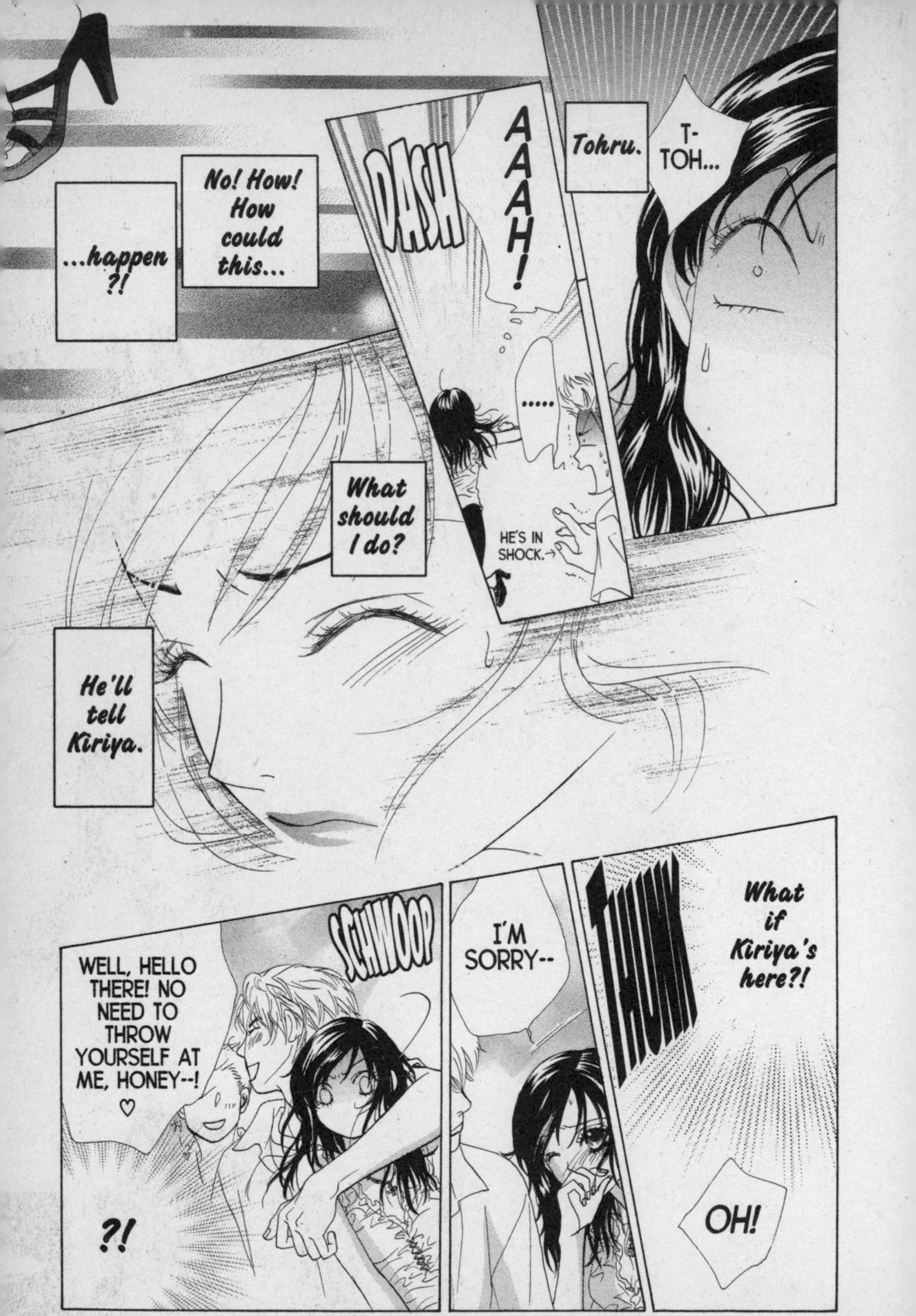

T-TOH...
Tohru.
AAAAH!
DASH
.....
HE'S IN SHOCK.
No! How! How could this...
...happen?!
What should I do?
He'll tell Kiriya.
What if Kiriya's here?!
THUNK
OH!
I'M SORRY--
SCHWOOP
WELL, HELLO THERE! NO NEED TO THROW YOURSELF AT ME, HONEY--! ♡
?!

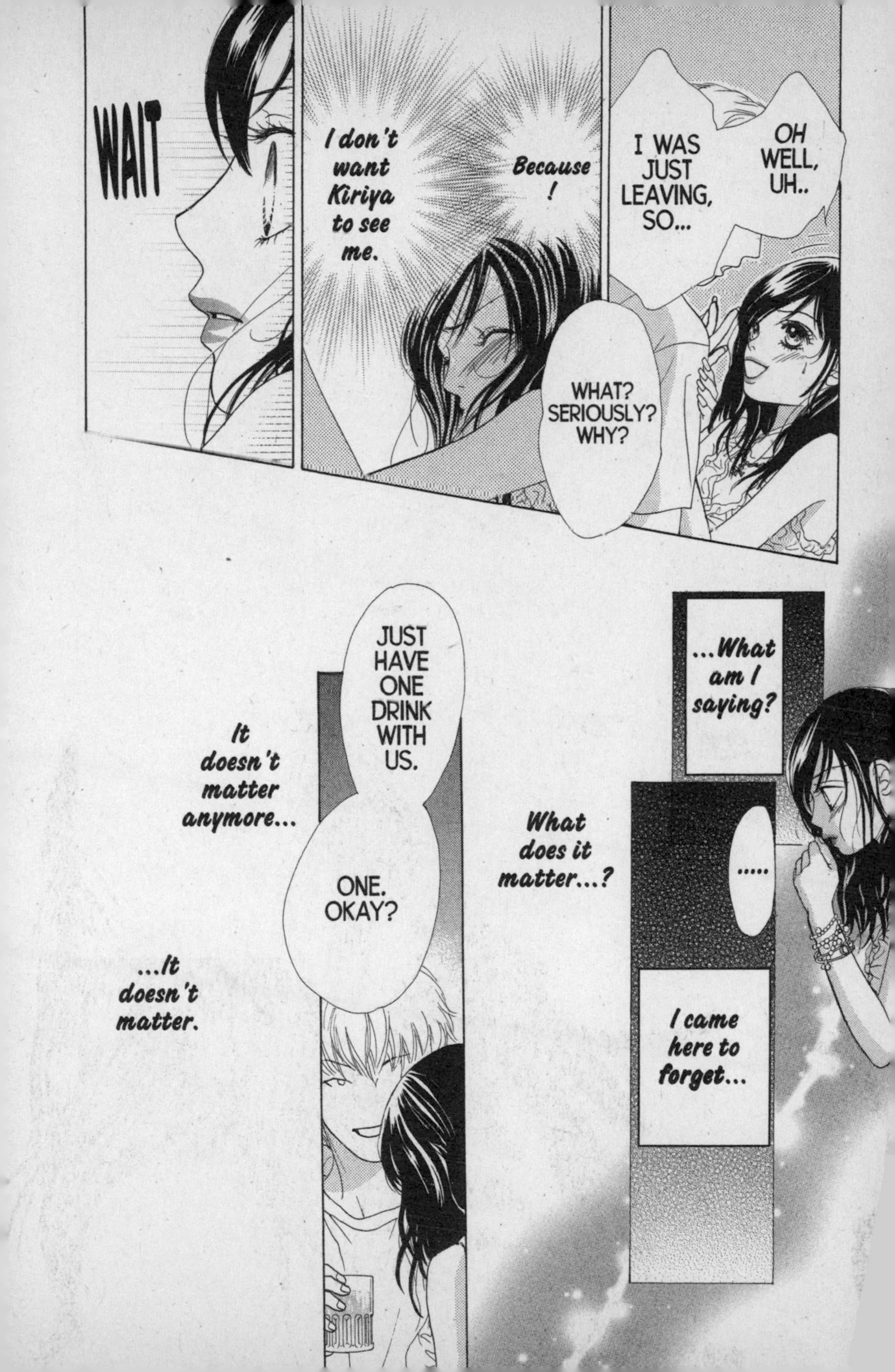

OH WELL, UH..
I WAS JUST LEAVING, SO...
WHAT? SERIOUSLY? WHY?
Because!
I don't want Kiriya to see me.
WAIT
...What am I saying?
.....
I came here to forget...
What does it matter...?
JUST HAVE ONE DRINK WITH US.
ONE. OKAY?
It doesn't matter anymore...
...It doesn't matter.

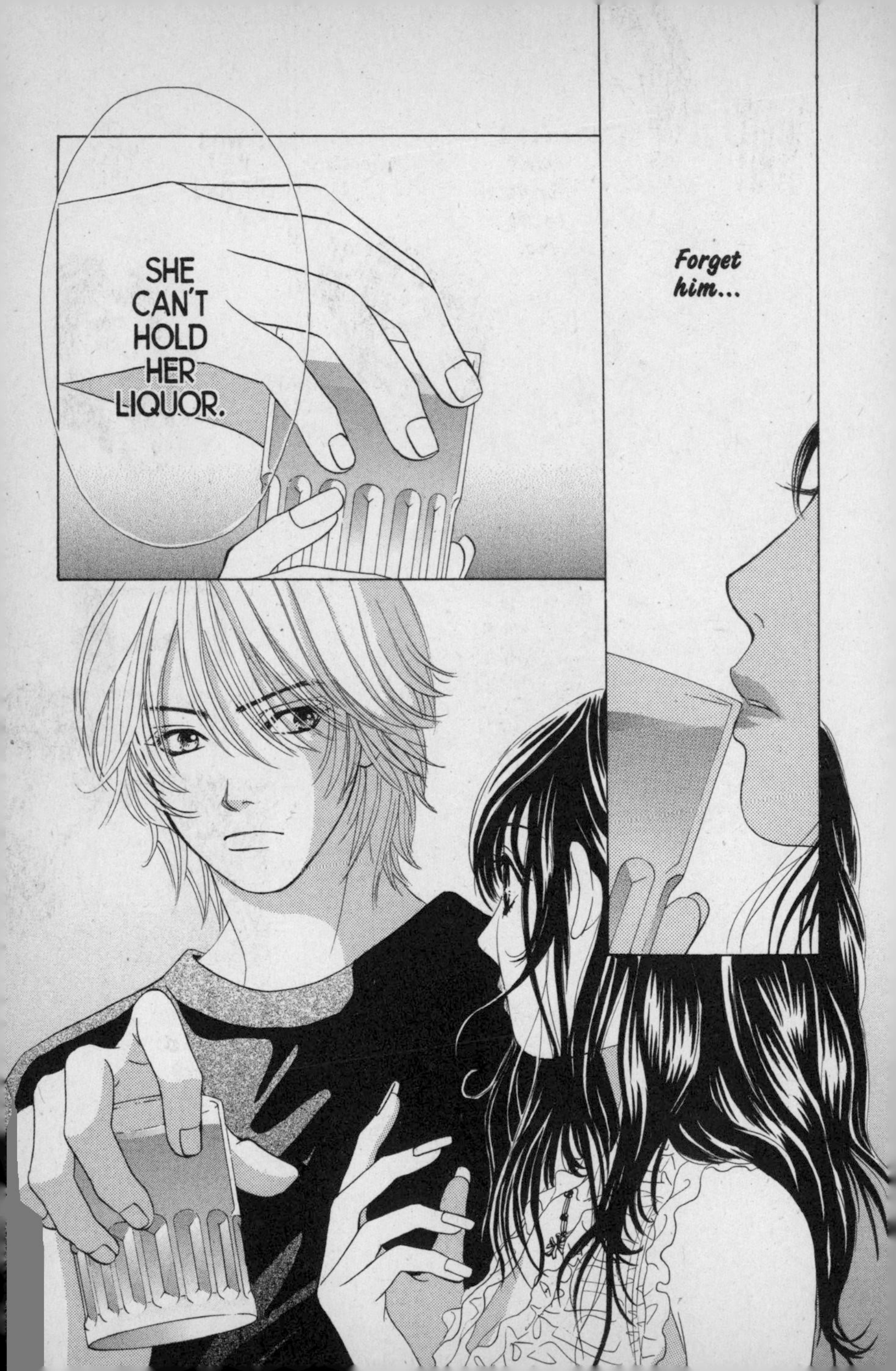
Forget him...
SHE CAN'T HOLD HER LIQUOR.

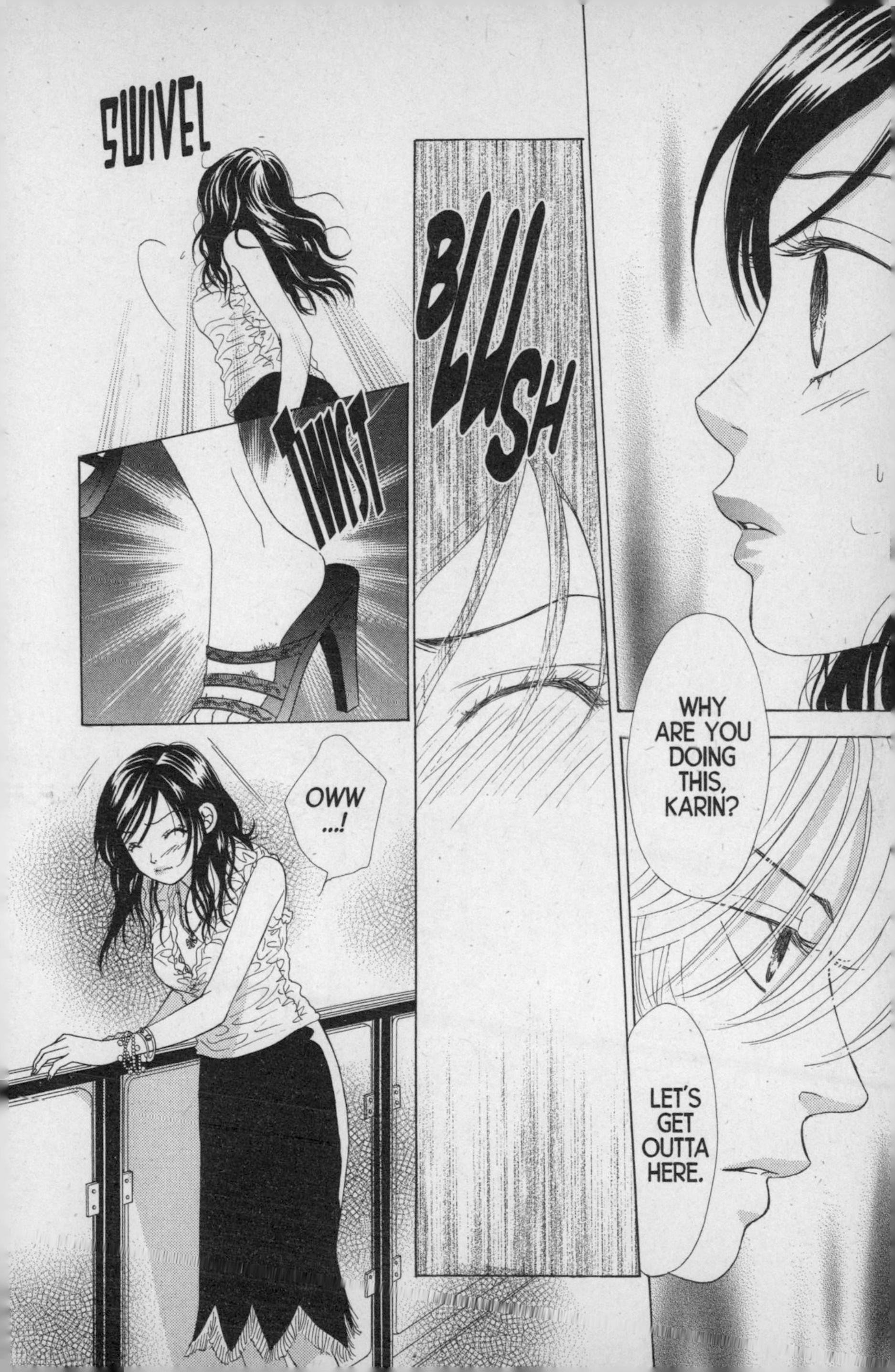
WHY ARE YOU DOING THIS, KARIN?
LET'S GET OUTTA HERE.
BLUSH
SWIVEL
TWIST
OWW ...!

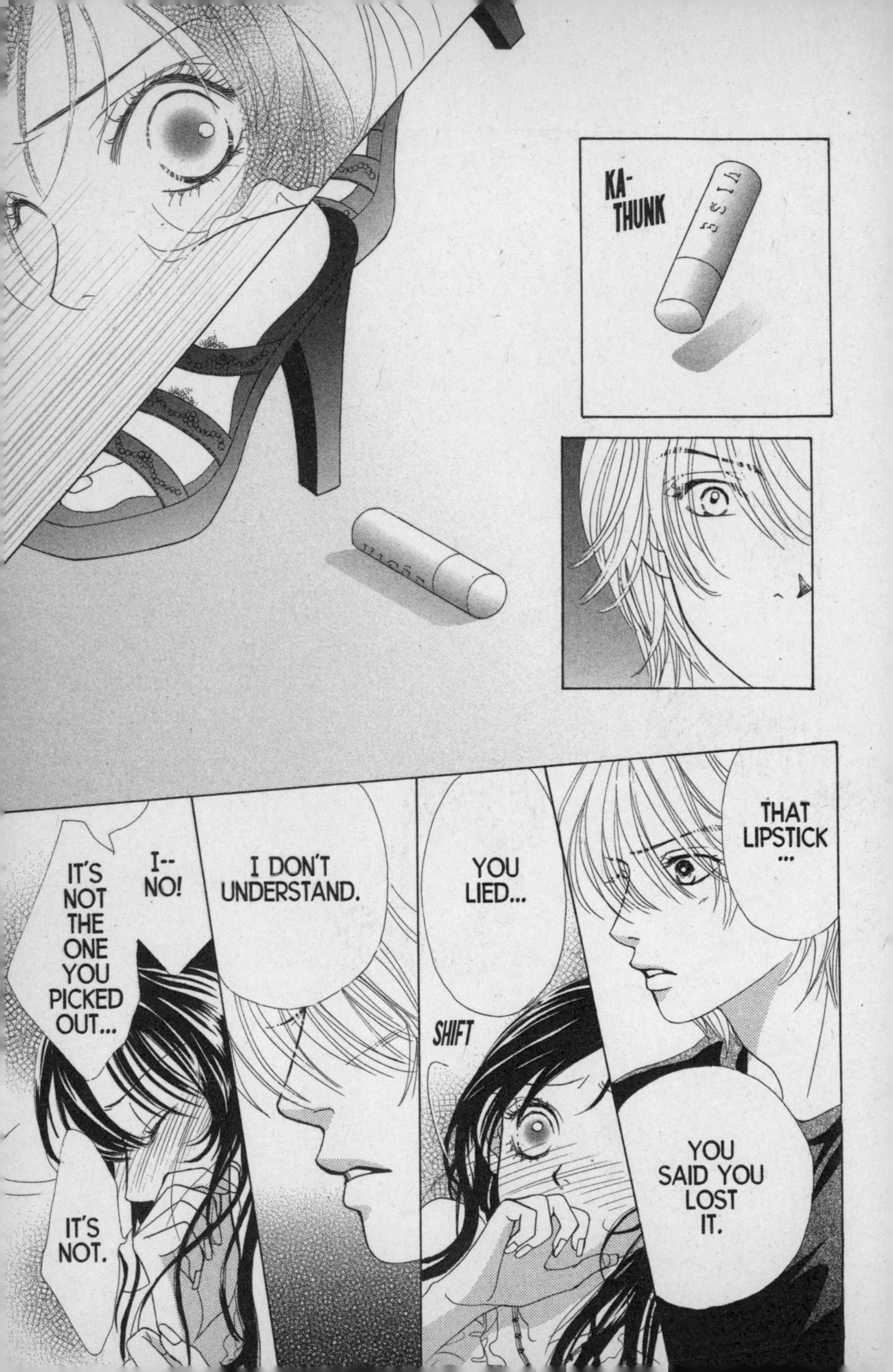
KA-THUNK
THAT LIPSTICK ...
YOU SAID YOU LOST IT.
YOU LIED...
SHIFT
I DON'T UNDERSTAND.
I-- NO!
IT'S NOT THE ONE YOU PICKED OUT...
IT'S NOT.

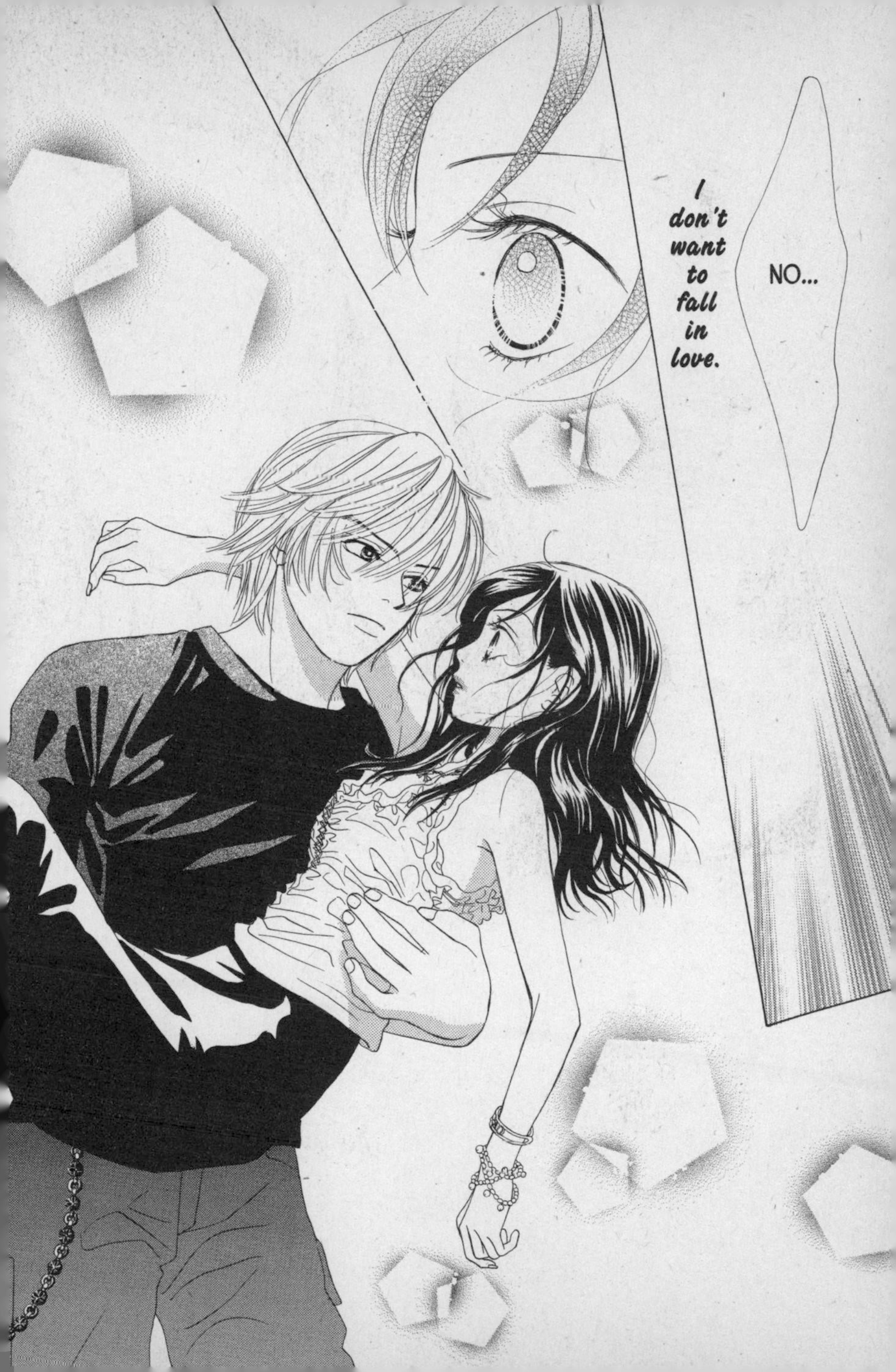
NO...
I don't want to fall in love.

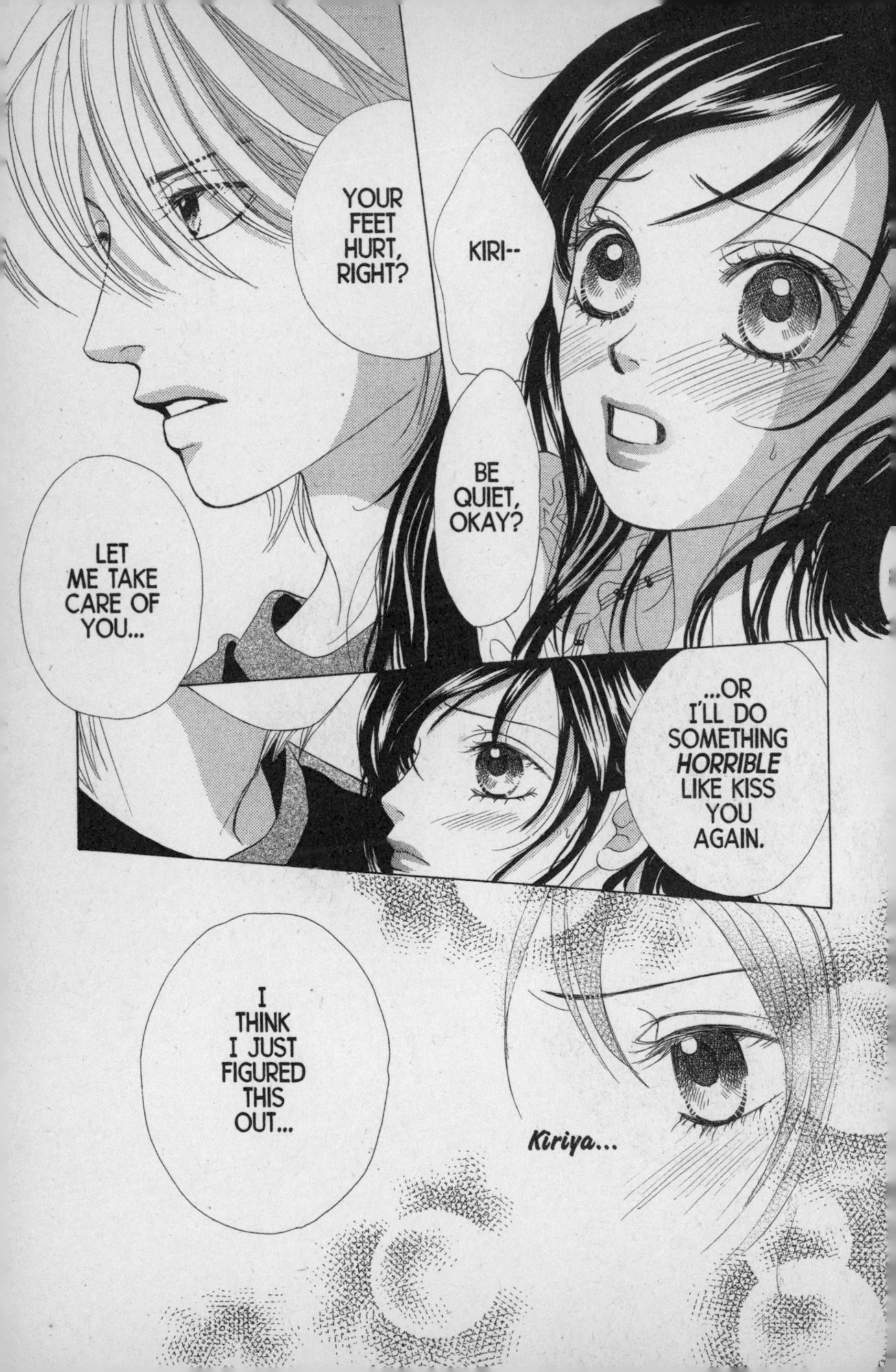
KIRI--
BE QUIET, OKAY?
YOUR FEET HURT, RIGHT?
LET ME TAKE CARE OF YOU...
...OR I'LL DO SOMETHING *HORRIBLE* LIKE KISS YOU AGAIN.
Kiriya...
I THINK I JUST FIGURED THIS OUT...

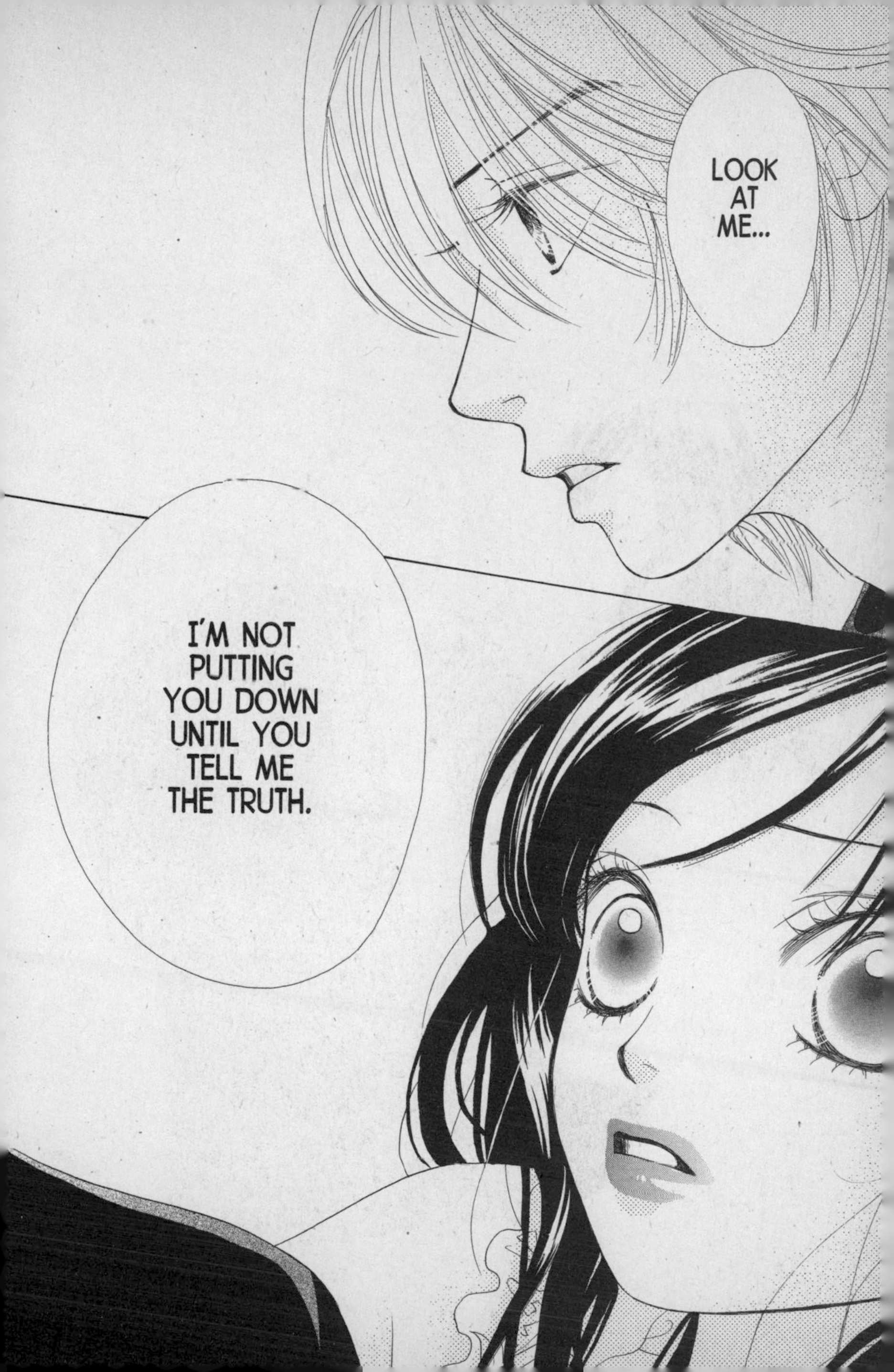
LOOK AT ME...
I'M NOT PUTTING YOU DOWN UNTIL YOU TELL ME THE TRUTH.

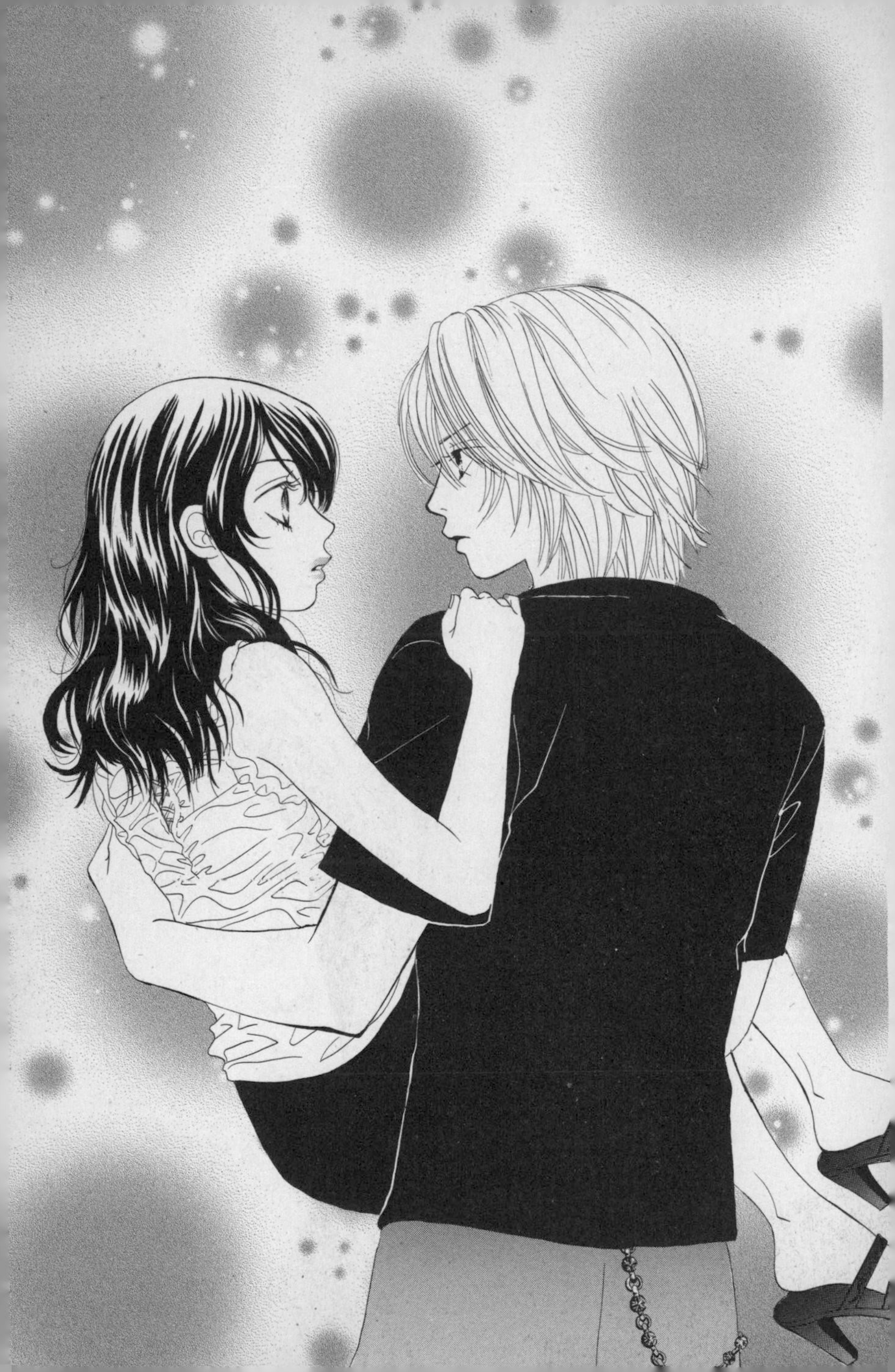

「彼」 KARE First Love

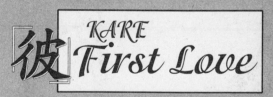

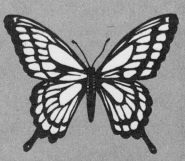

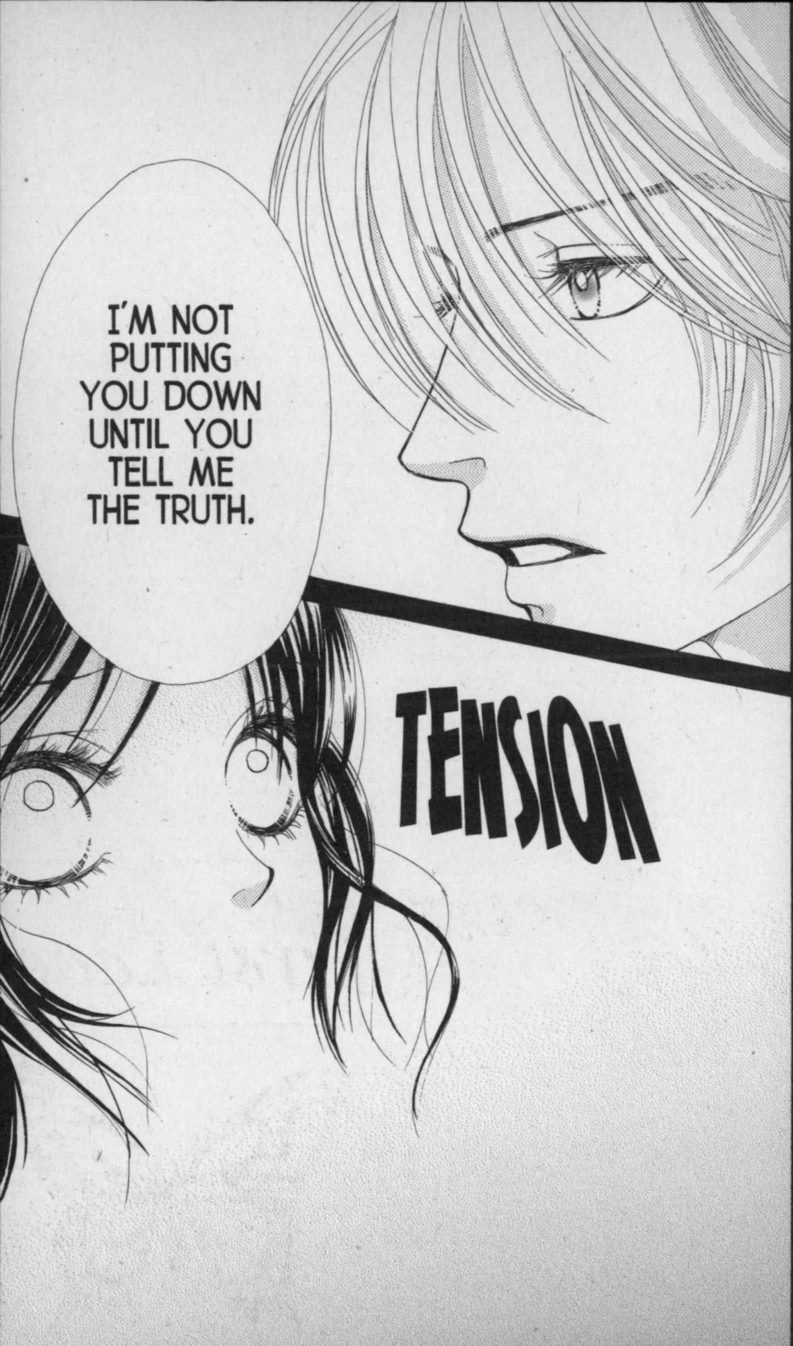
I'M NOT PUTTING YOU DOWN UNTIL YOU TELL ME THE TRUTH.
TENSION

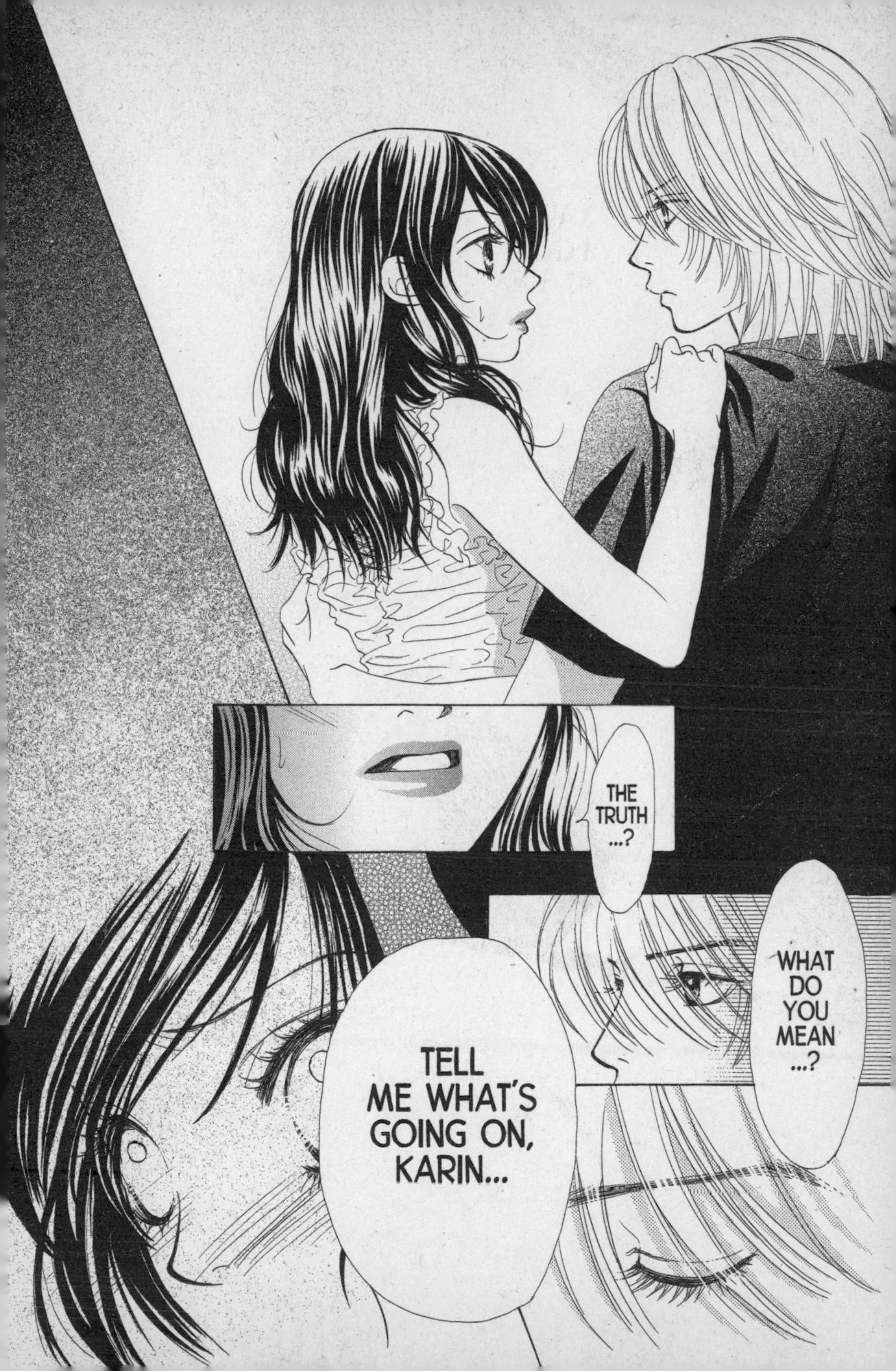
THE TRUTH ...?
WHAT DO YOU MEAN ...?
TELL ME WHAT'S GOING ON, KARIN...

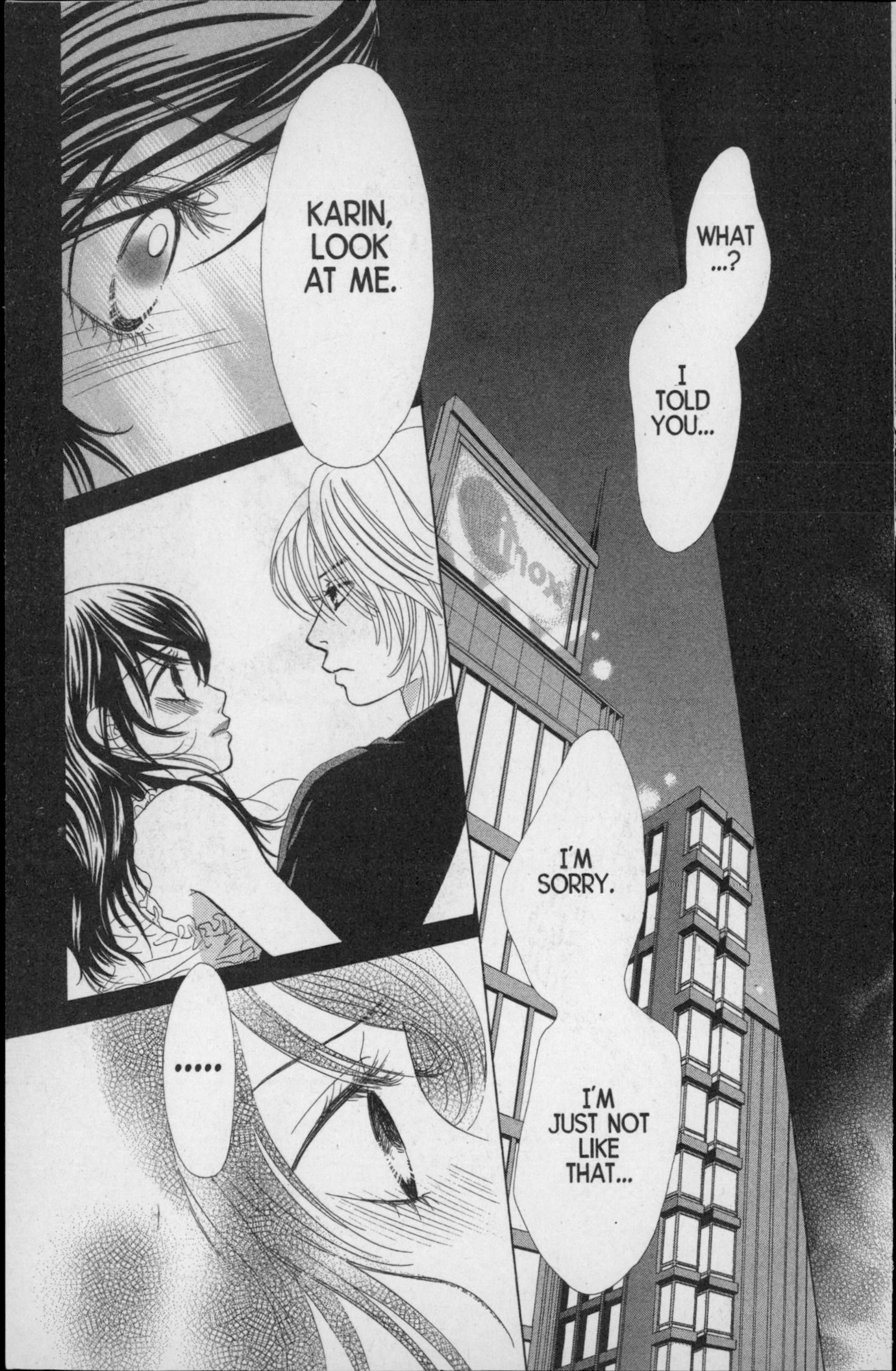
WHAT ...?
I TOLD YOU...
I'M SORRY.
I'M JUST NOT LIKE THAT...
KARIN, LOOK AT ME.
.....

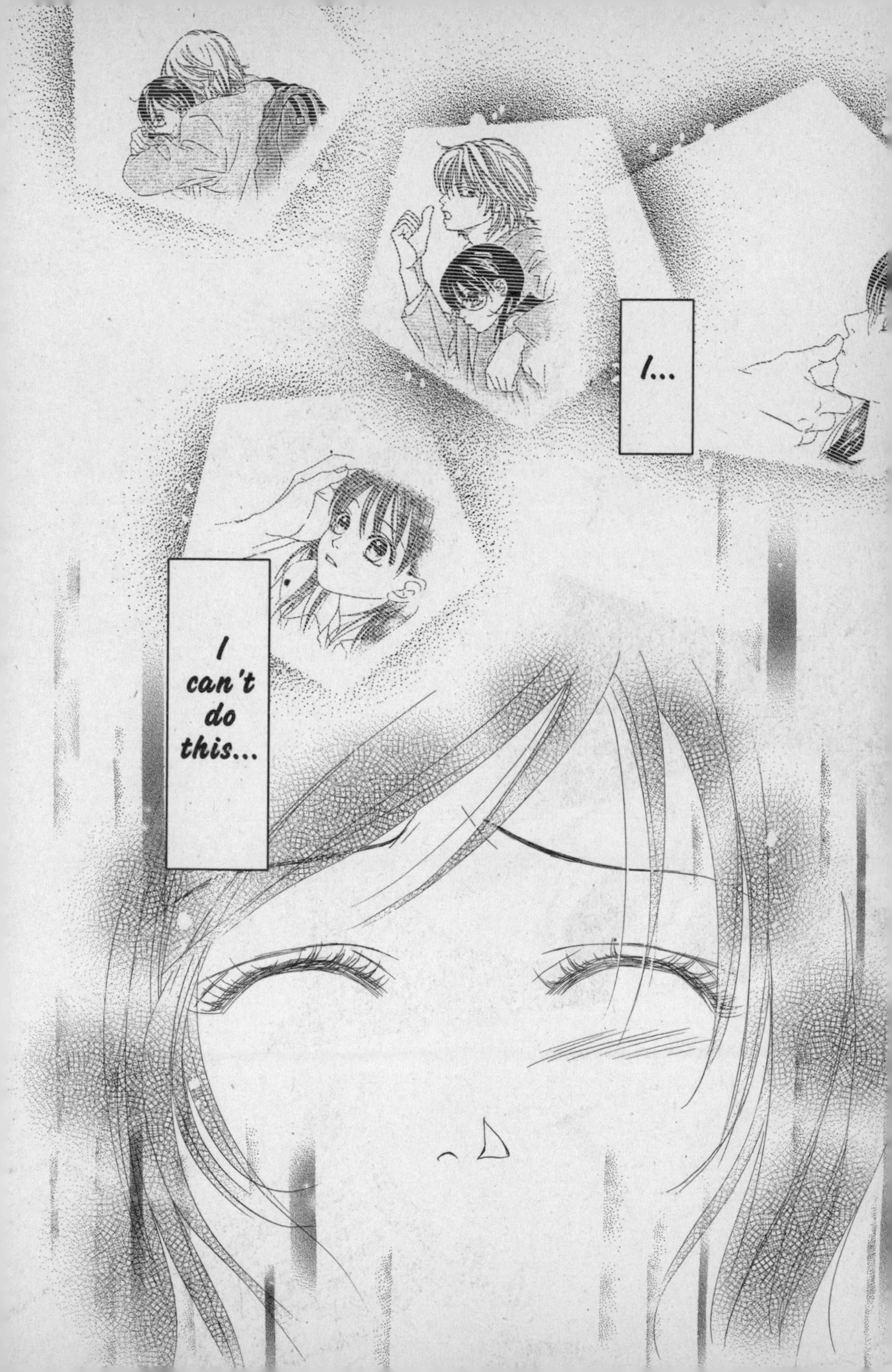
I...
I can't do this...

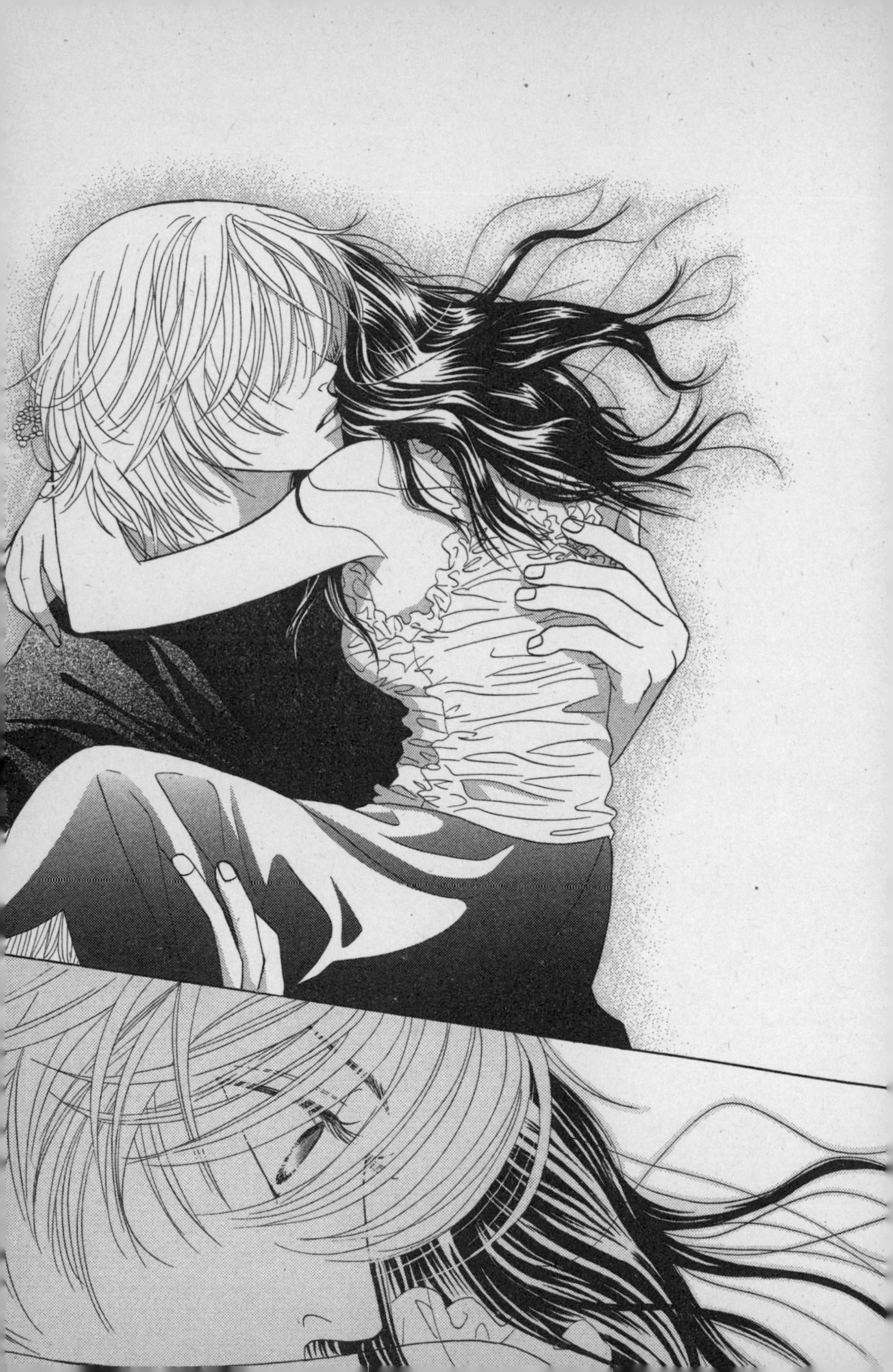

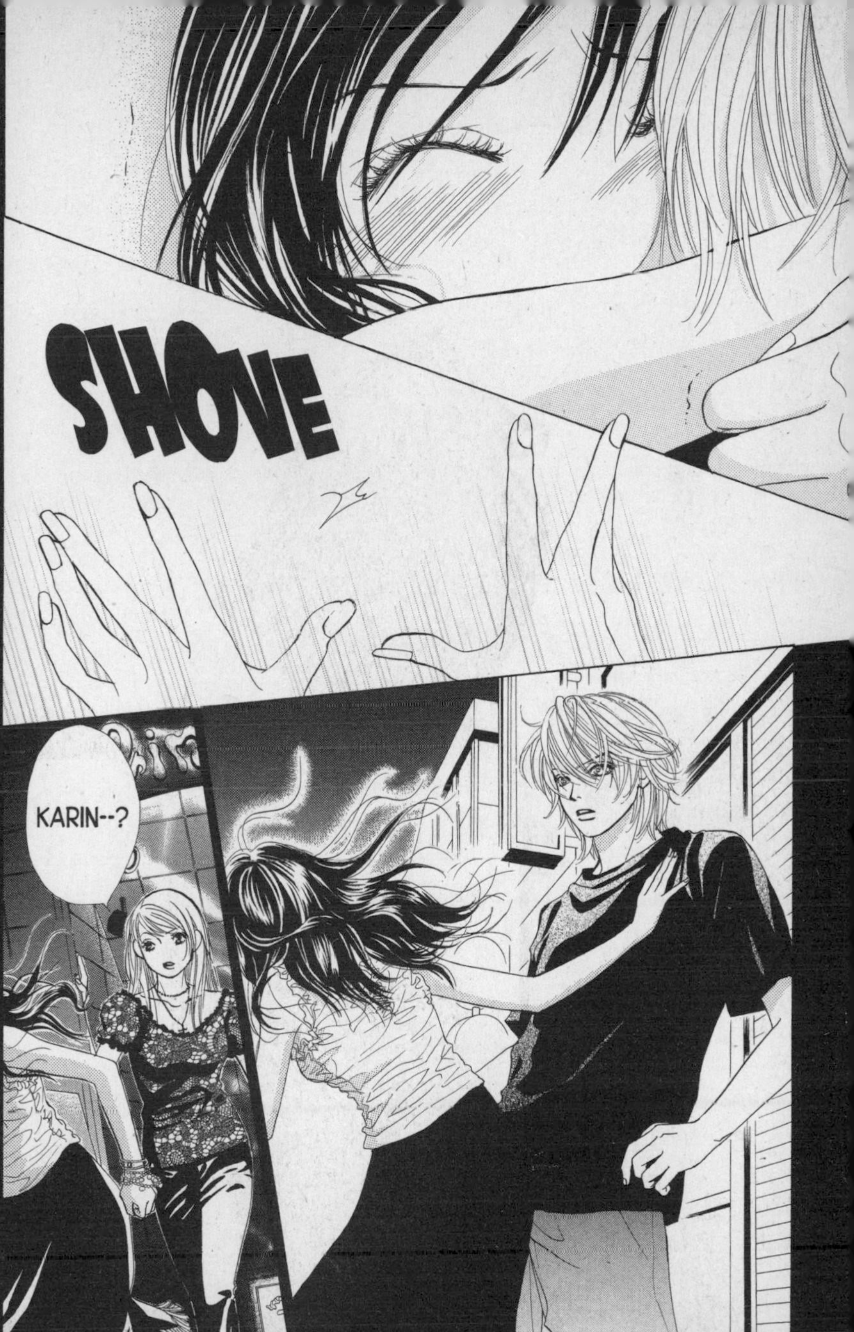
SHOVE
KARIN--?

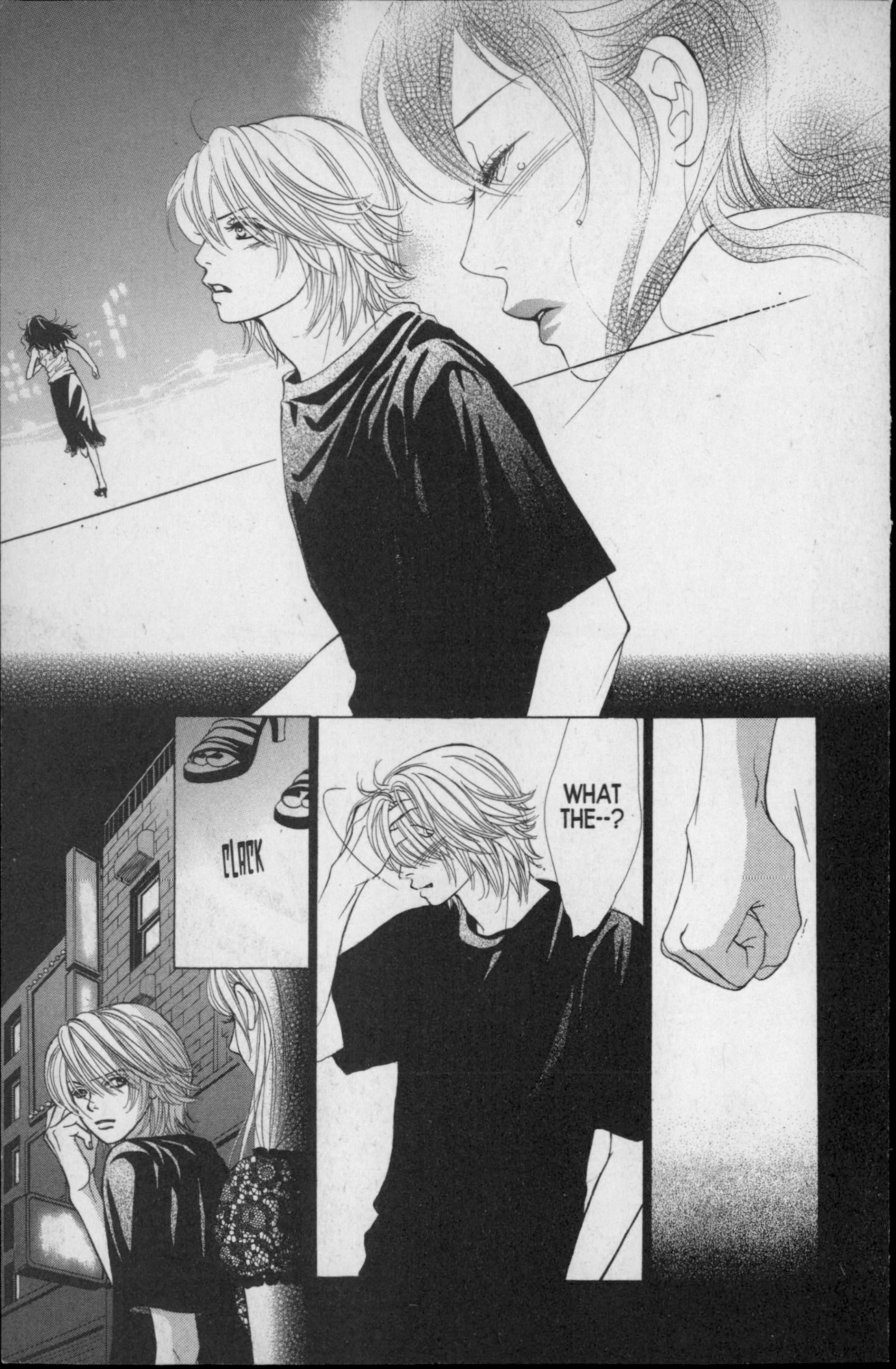
WHAT THE--?
CLACK

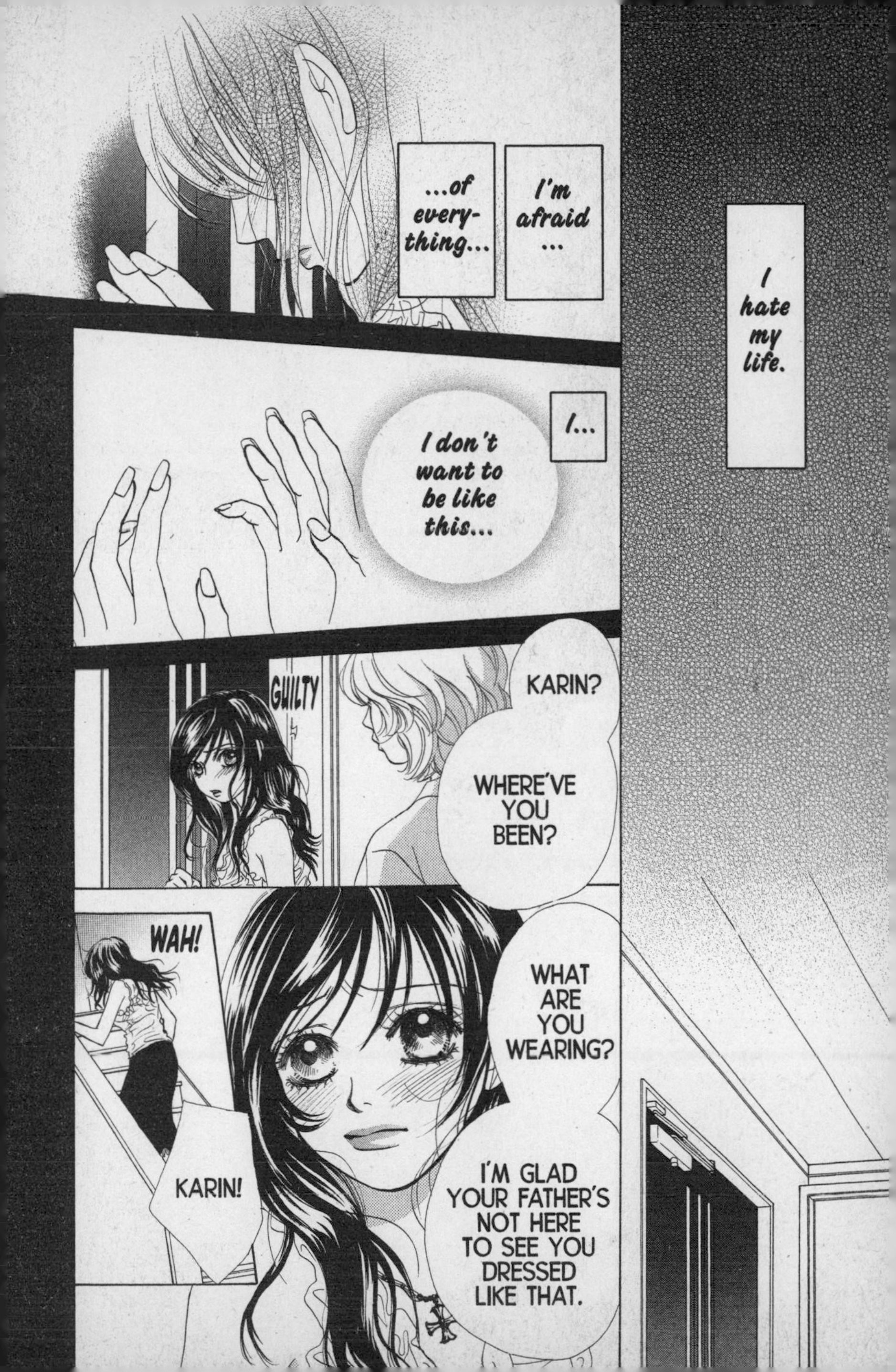
I hate my life.
I'm afraid ...
...of every-thing...
I...
I don't want to be like this...
GUILTY
KARIN?
WHERE'VE YOU BEEN?
WHAT ARE YOU WEARING?
I'M GLAD YOUR FATHER'S NOT HERE TO SEE YOU DRESSED LIKE THAT.
WAH!
KARIN!

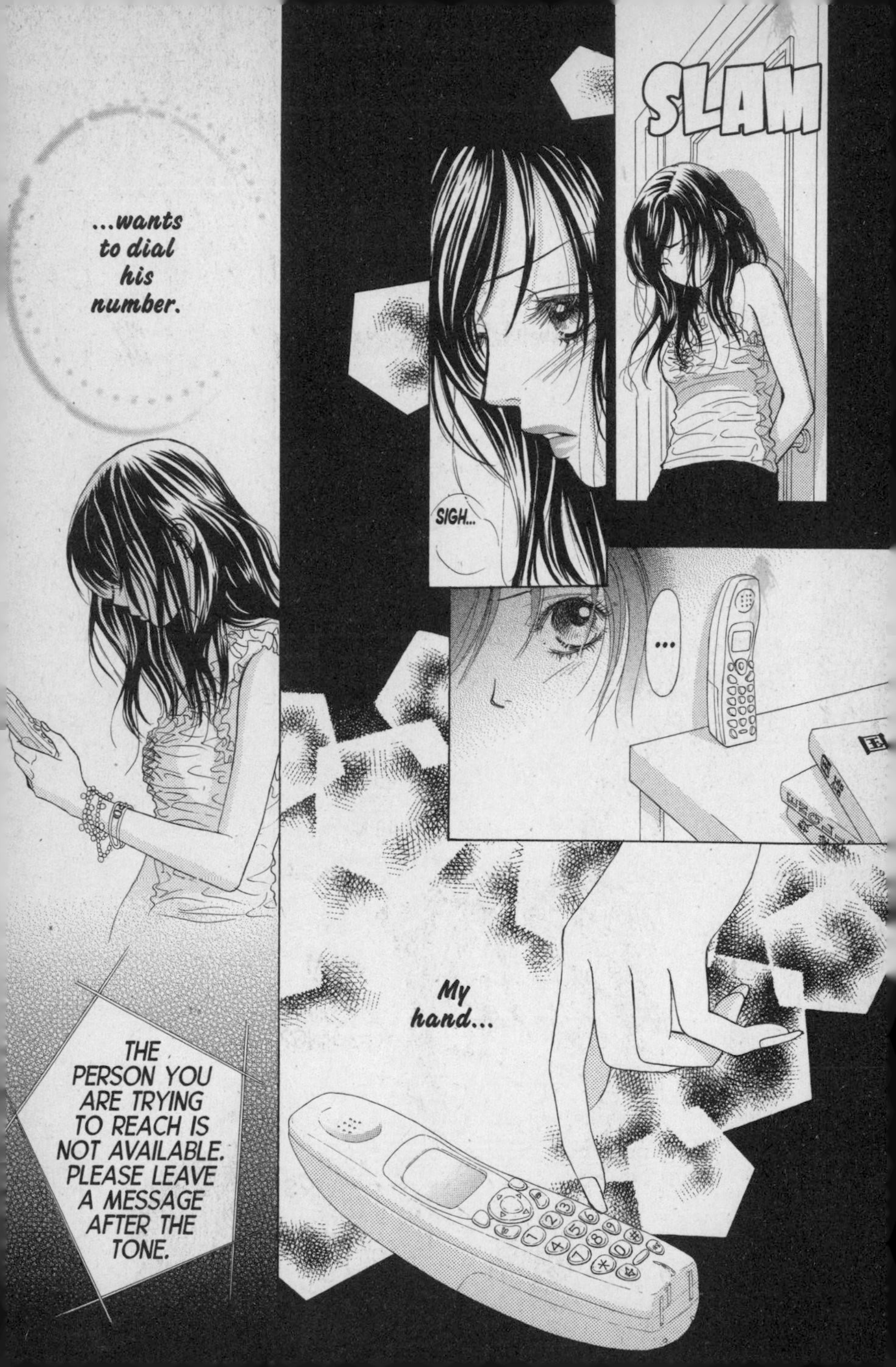
SLAM
SIGH...
...
My hand...
...wants to dial his number.
THE PERSON YOU ARE TRYING TO REACH IS NOT AVAILABLE. PLEASE LEAVE A MESSAGE AFTER THE TONE.

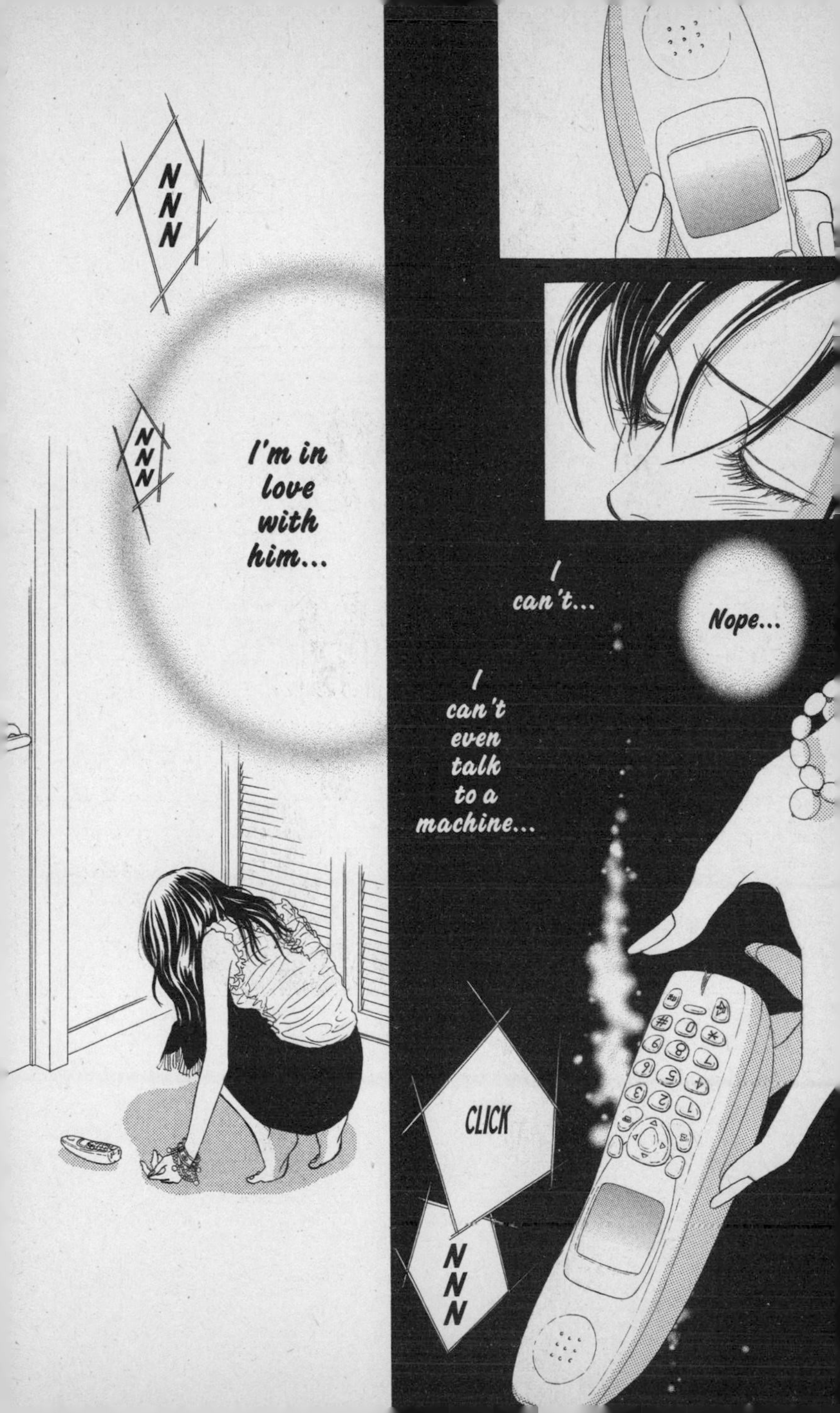
Nope...
I can't...
I can't even talk to a machine...
CLICK
NNN
NNN
NNN
I'm in love with him...

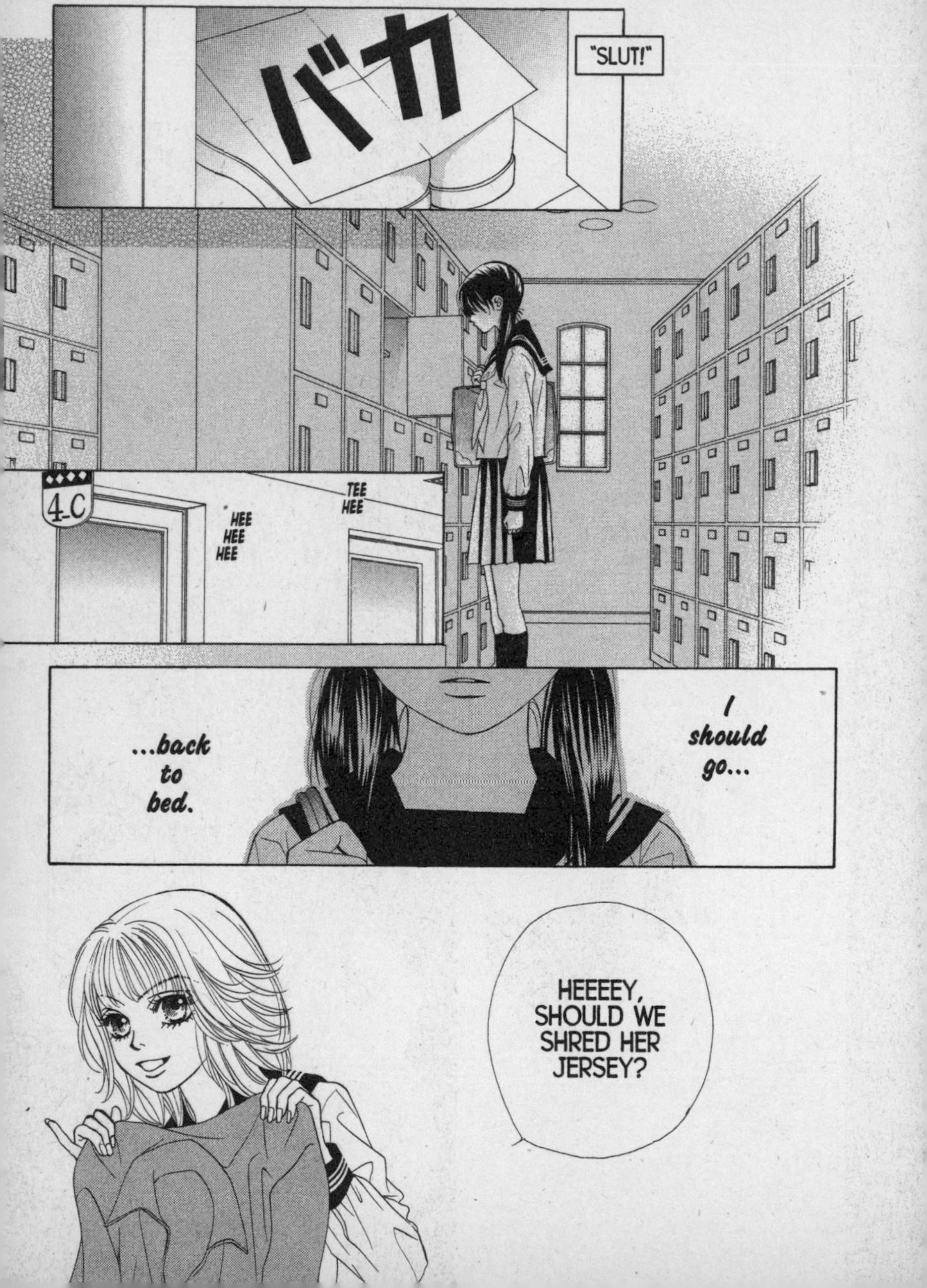
バカ
"SLUT!"
4-C
TEE HEE
HEE HEE HEE
I should go...
...back to bed.
HEEEEY, SHOULD WE SHRED HER JERSEY?

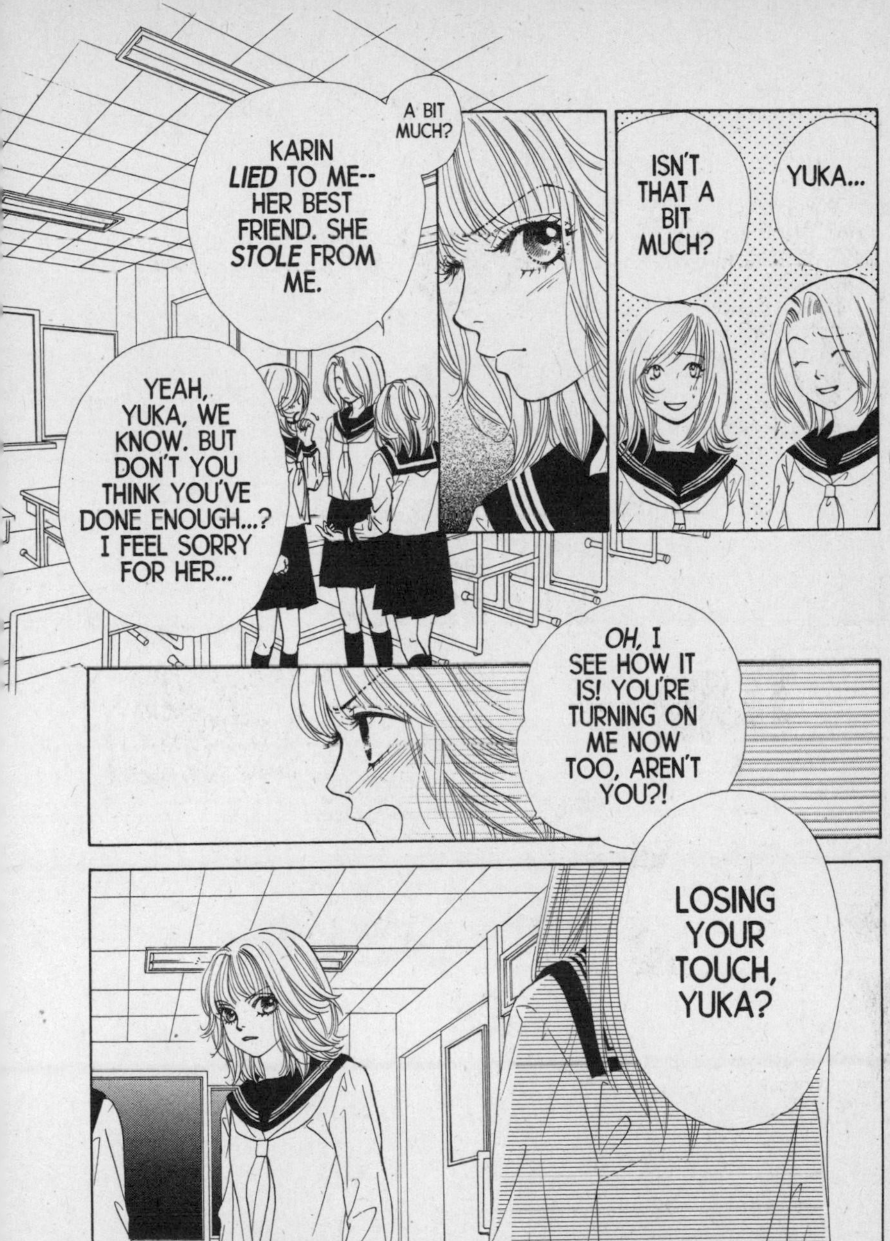

YUKA...
ISN'T THAT A BIT MUCH?
A BIT MUCH?
KARIN *LIED* TO ME-- HER BEST FRIEND. SHE *STOLE* FROM ME.
YEAH, YUKA, WE KNOW. BUT DON'T YOU THINK YOU'VE DONE ENOUGH...? I FEEL SORRY FOR HER...
OH, I SEE HOW IT IS! YOU'RE TURNING ON ME NOW TOO, AREN'T YOU?!
LOSING YOUR TOUCH, YUKA?

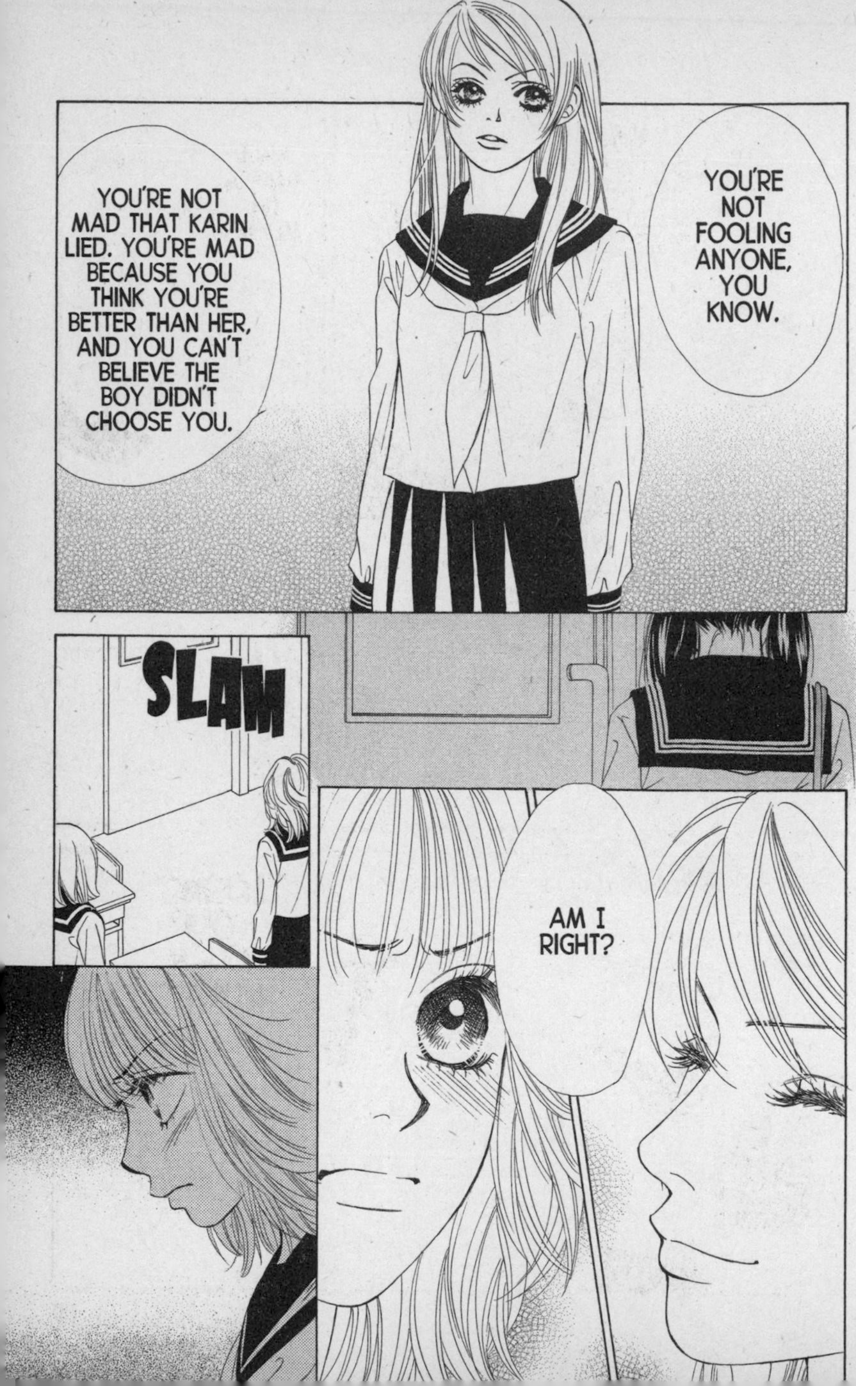
YOU'RE NOT FOOLING ANYONE, YOU KNOW.
YOU'RE NOT MAD THAT KARIN LIED. YOU'RE MAD BECAUSE YOU THINK YOU'RE BETTER THAN HER, AND YOU CAN'T BELIEVE THE BOY DIDN'T CHOOSE YOU.
SLAM
AM I RIGHT?

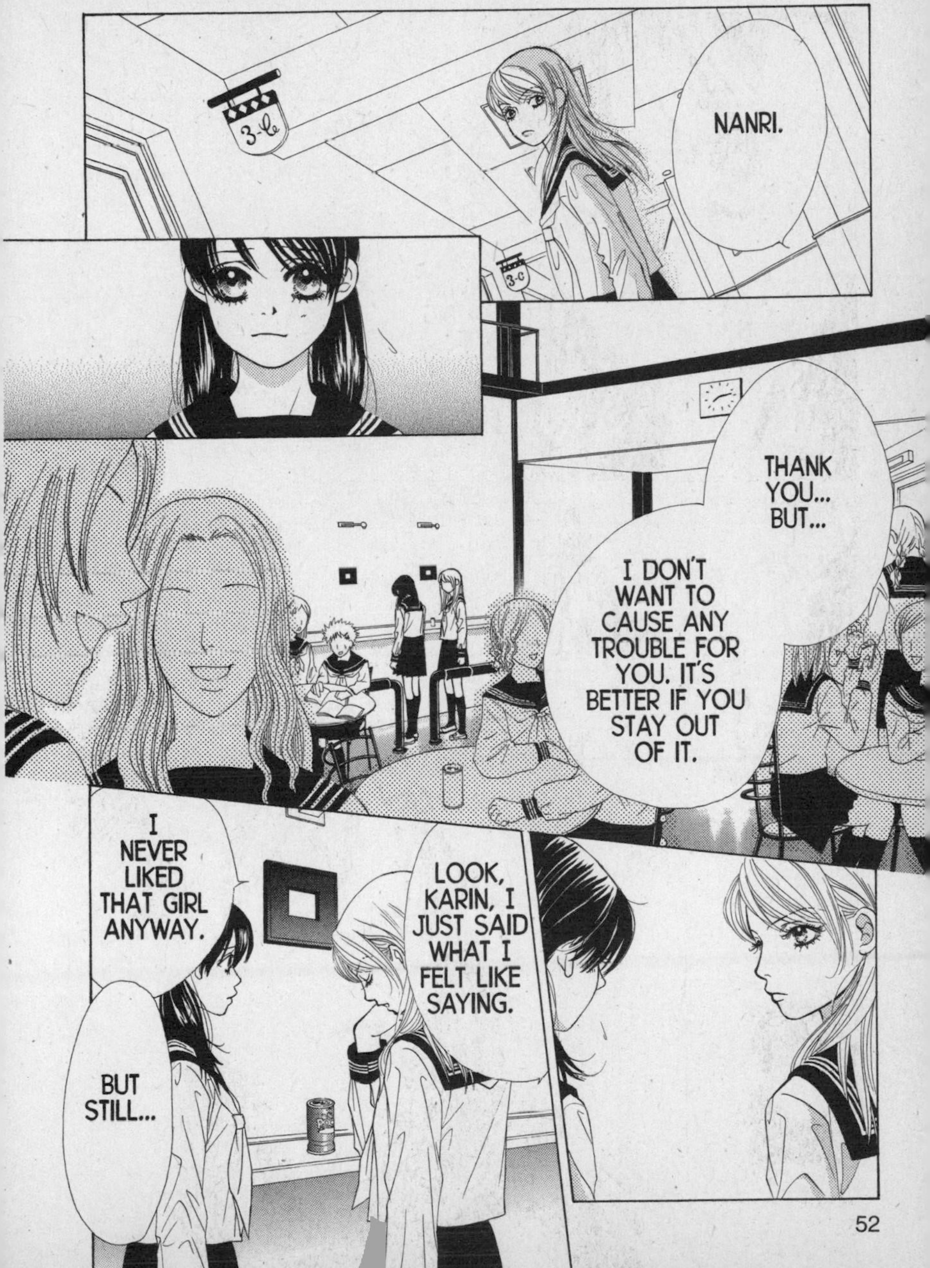
NANRI.
THANK YOU... BUT...
I DON'T WANT TO CAUSE ANY TROUBLE FOR YOU. IT'S BETTER IF YOU STAY OUT OF IT.
LOOK, KARIN, I JUST SAID WHAT I FELT LIKE SAYING.
I NEVER LIKED THAT GIRL ANYWAY.
BUT STILL...

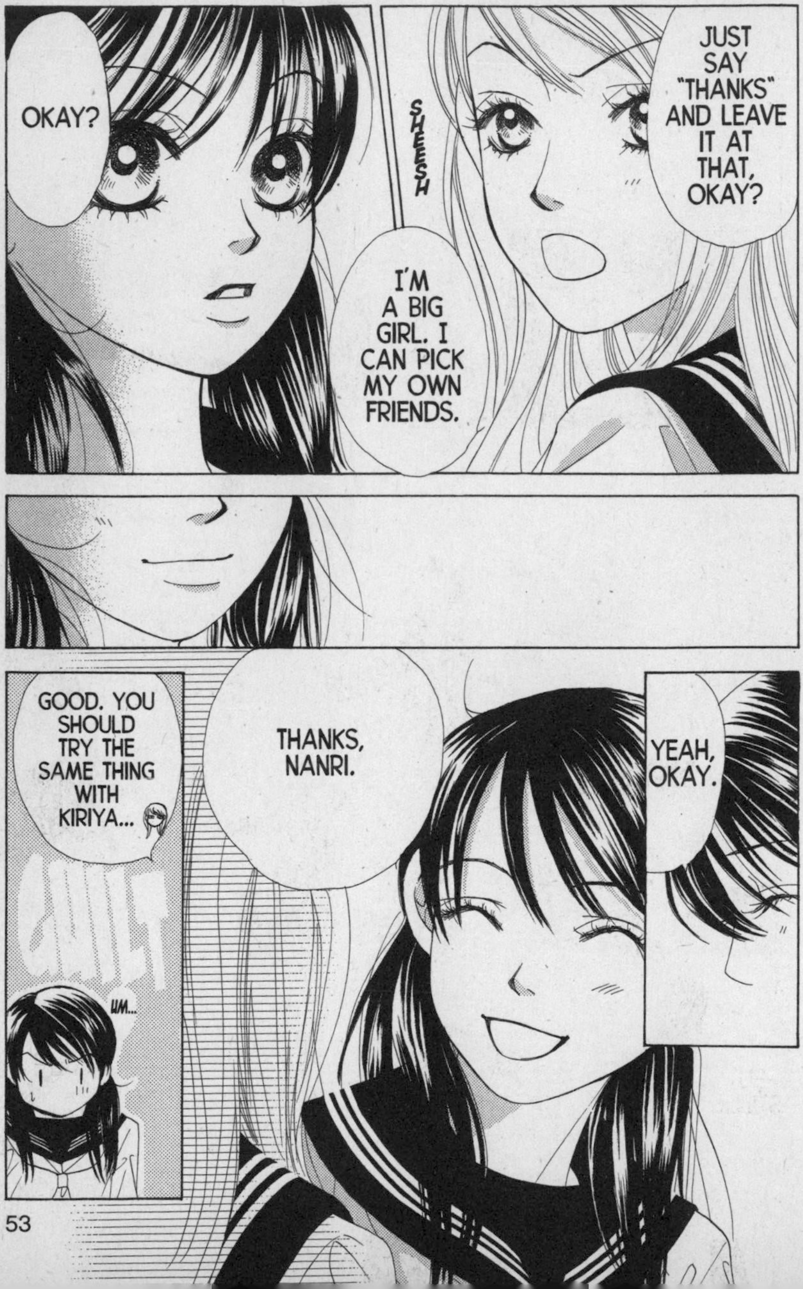
JUST SAY "THANKS" AND LEAVE IT AT THAT, OKAY?
SHEESH
I'M A BIG GIRL. I CAN PICK MY OWN FRIENDS.
OKAY?
YEAH, OKAY.
THANKS, NANRI.
GOOD. YOU SHOULD TRY THE SAME THING WITH KIRIYA...
GUILT
UM...

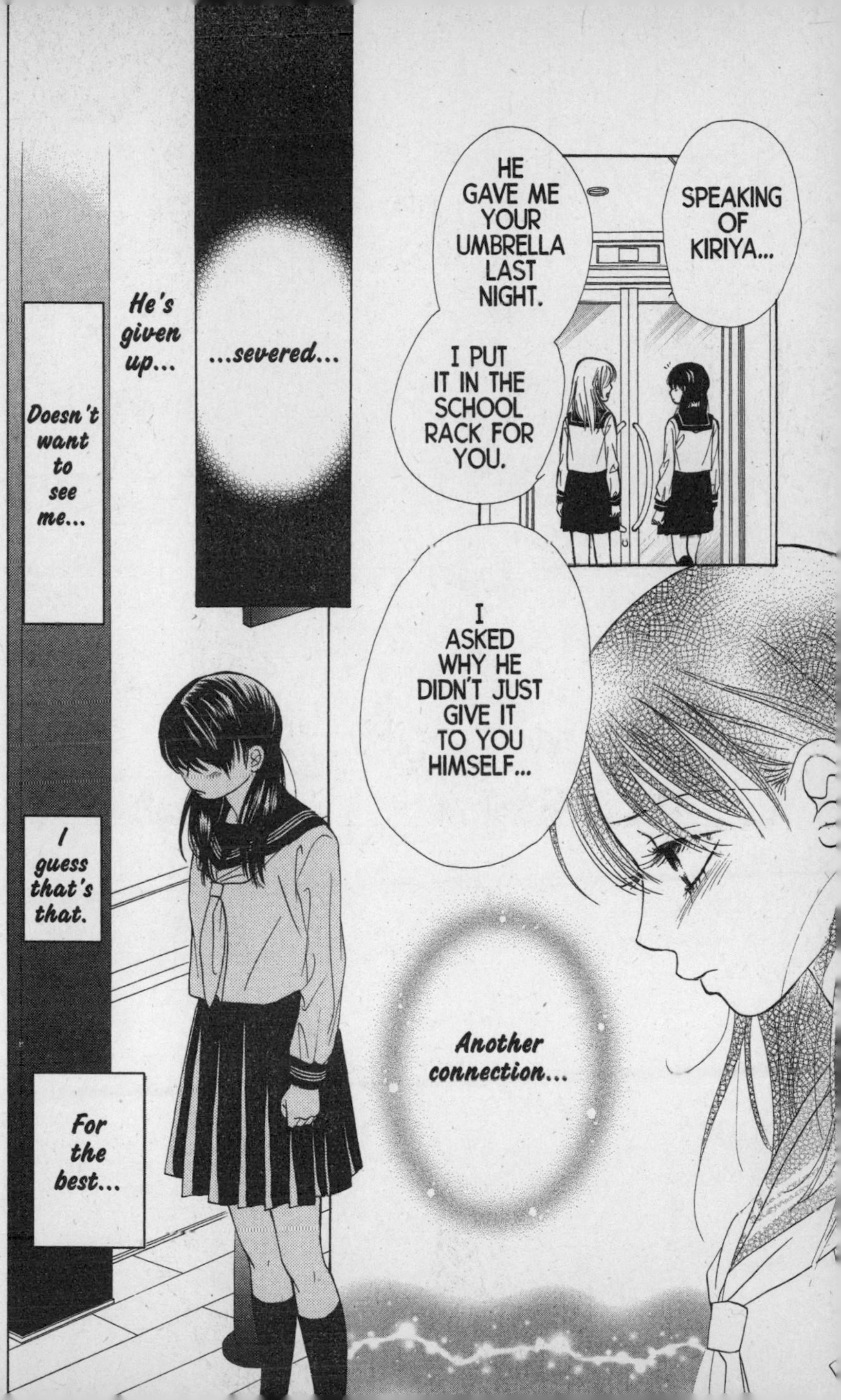
SPEAKING OF KIRIYA...
HE GAVE ME YOUR UMBRELLA LAST NIGHT.
I PUT IT IN THE SCHOOL RACK FOR YOU.
I ASKED WHY HE DIDN'T JUST GIVE IT TO YOU HIMSELF...
Another connection...
...severed...
He's given up...
Doesn't want to see me...
I guess that's that.
For the best...

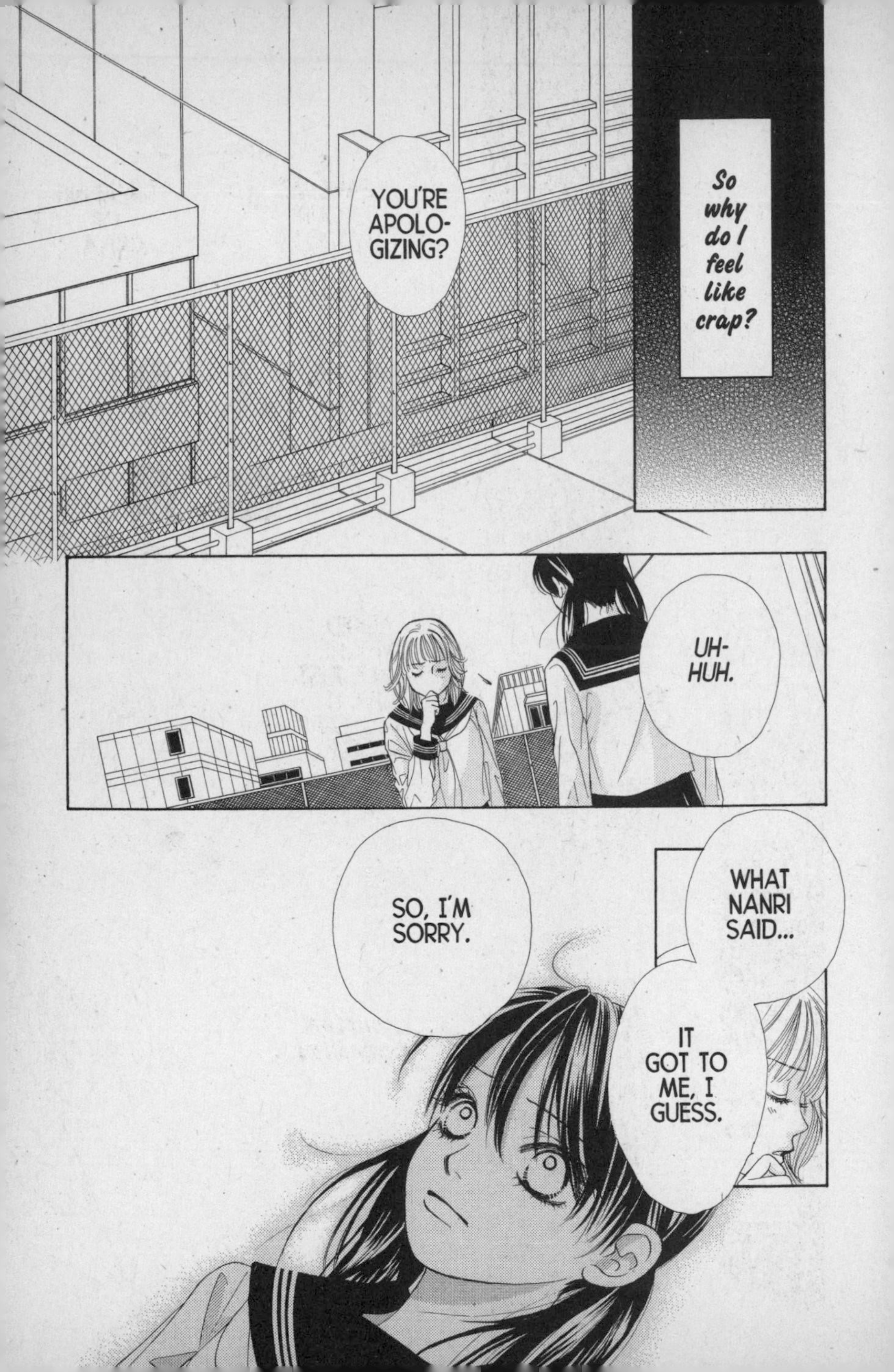
So why do I feel like crap?
YOU'RE APOLOGIZING?
UH-HUH.
WHAT NANRI SAID...
IT GOT TO ME, I GUESS.
SO, I'M SORRY.

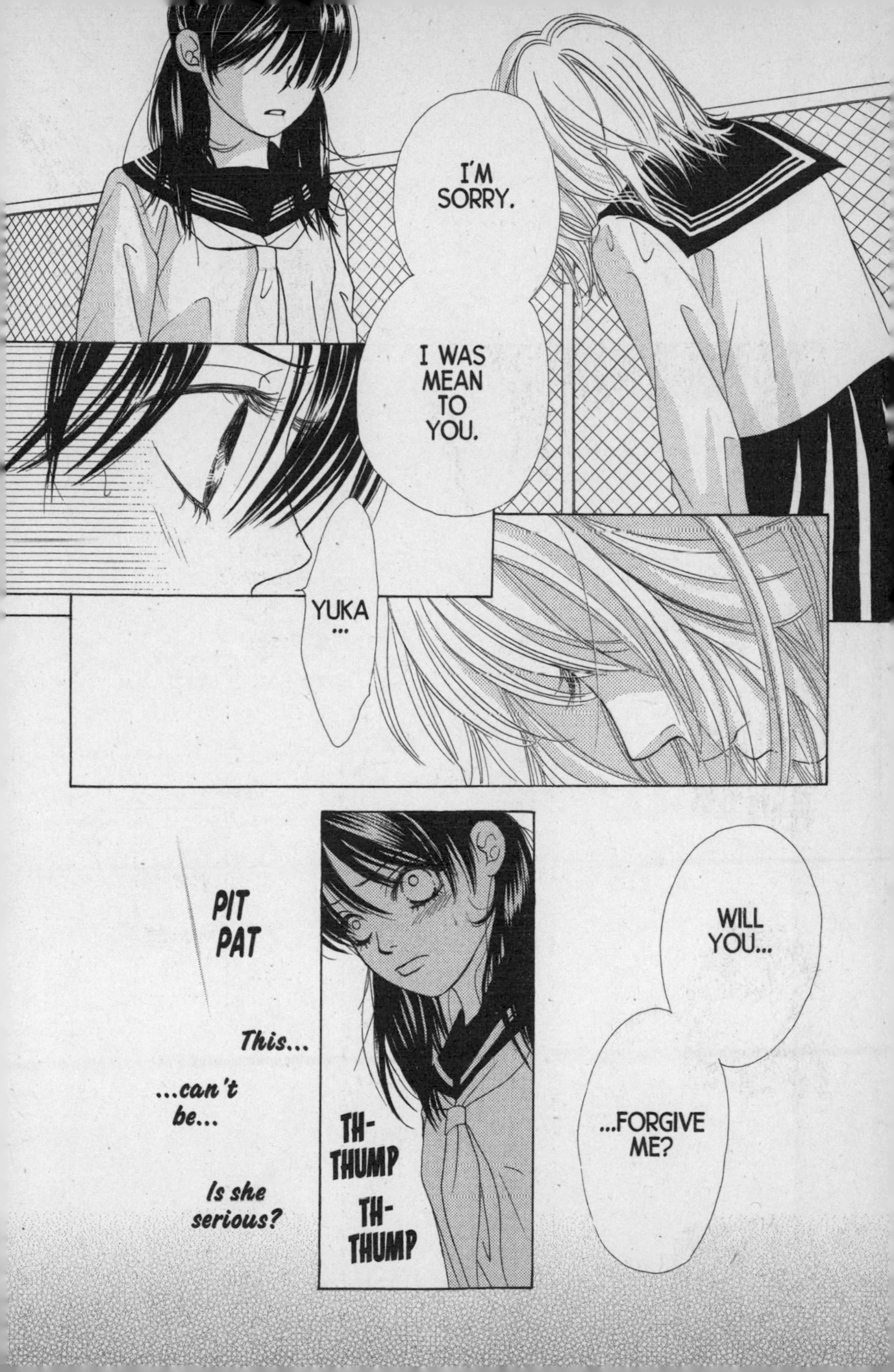
I'M SORRY.
I WAS MEAN TO YOU.
YUKA...
WILL YOU...
...FORGIVE ME?
TH-THUMP TH-THUMP
PIT PAT
This...
...can't be...
Is she serious?

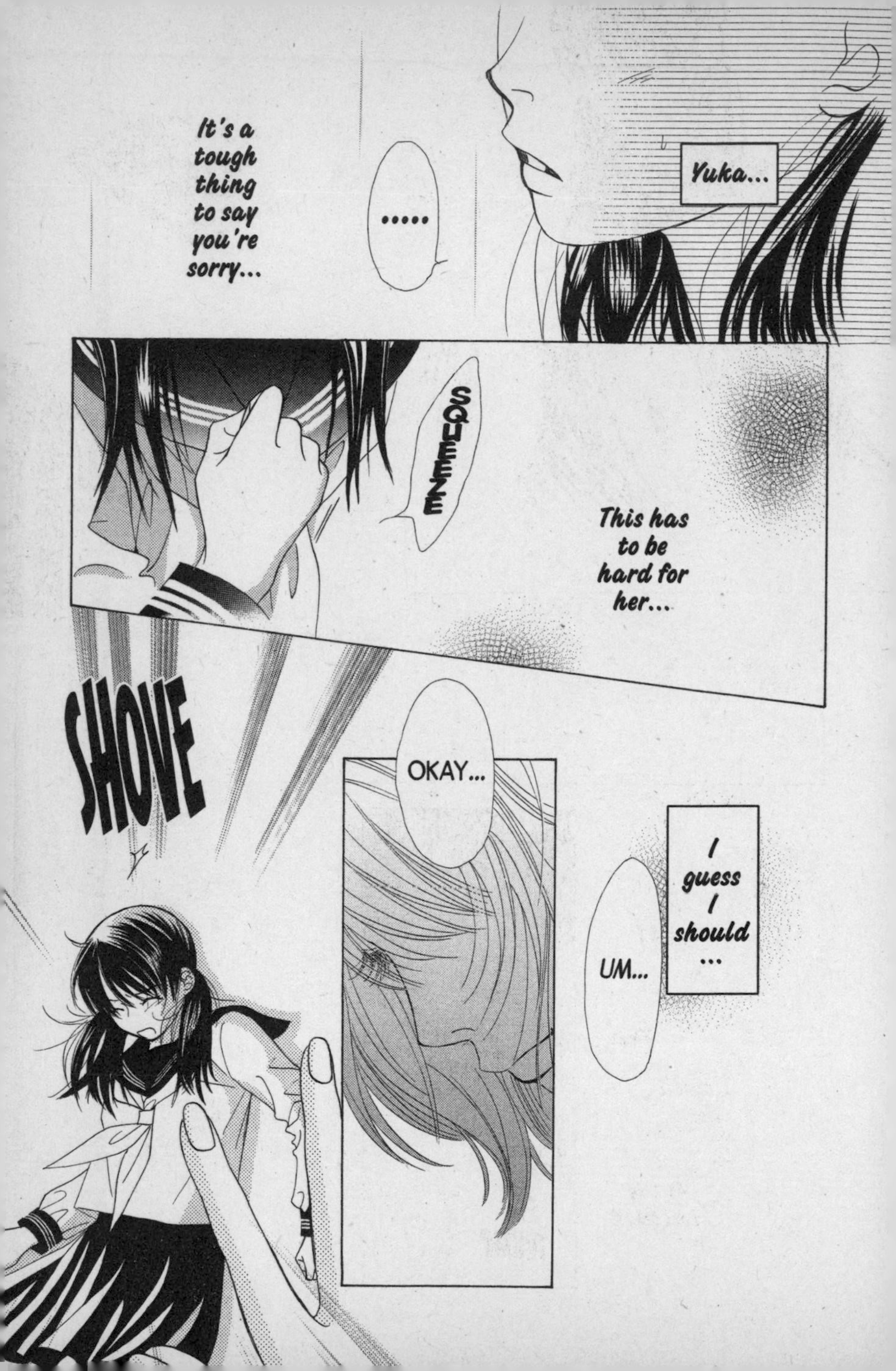

Yuka...
......
It's a tough thing to say you're sorry...
This has to be hard for her...
SQUEEZE
I guess I should...
UM...
OKAY...
SHOVE

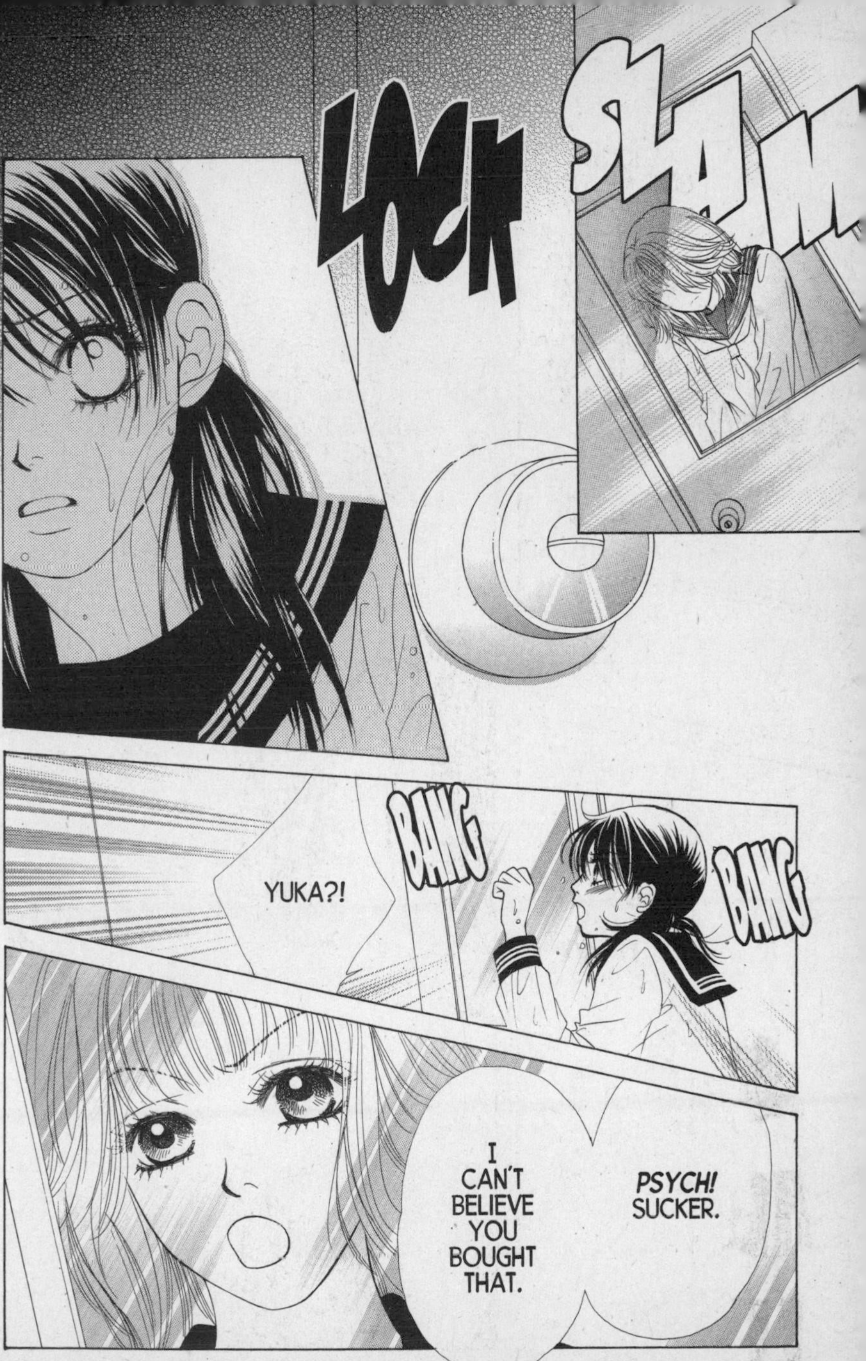
SLAM
LOCK
BANG
BANG
YUKA?!
PSYCH! SUCKER.
I CAN'T BELIEVE YOU BOUGHT THAT.

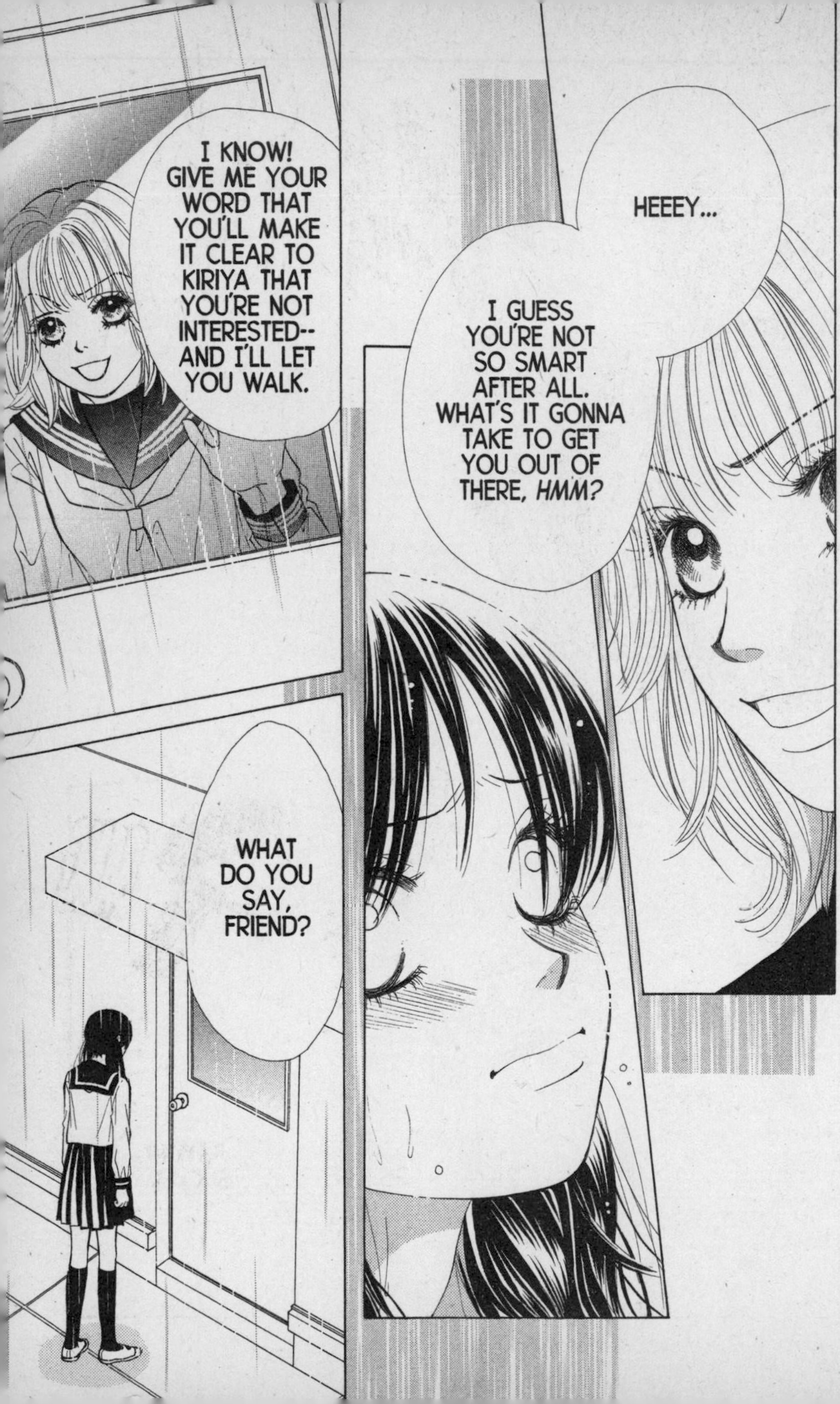
HEEEY...
I GUESS YOU'RE NOT SO SMART AFTER ALL. WHAT'S IT GONNA TAKE TO GET YOU OUT OF THERE, *HMM?*
I KNOW! GIVE ME YOUR WORD THAT YOU'LL MAKE IT CLEAR TO KIRIYA THAT YOU'RE NOT INTERESTED-- AND I'LL LET YOU WALK.
WHAT DO YOU SAY, FRIEND?

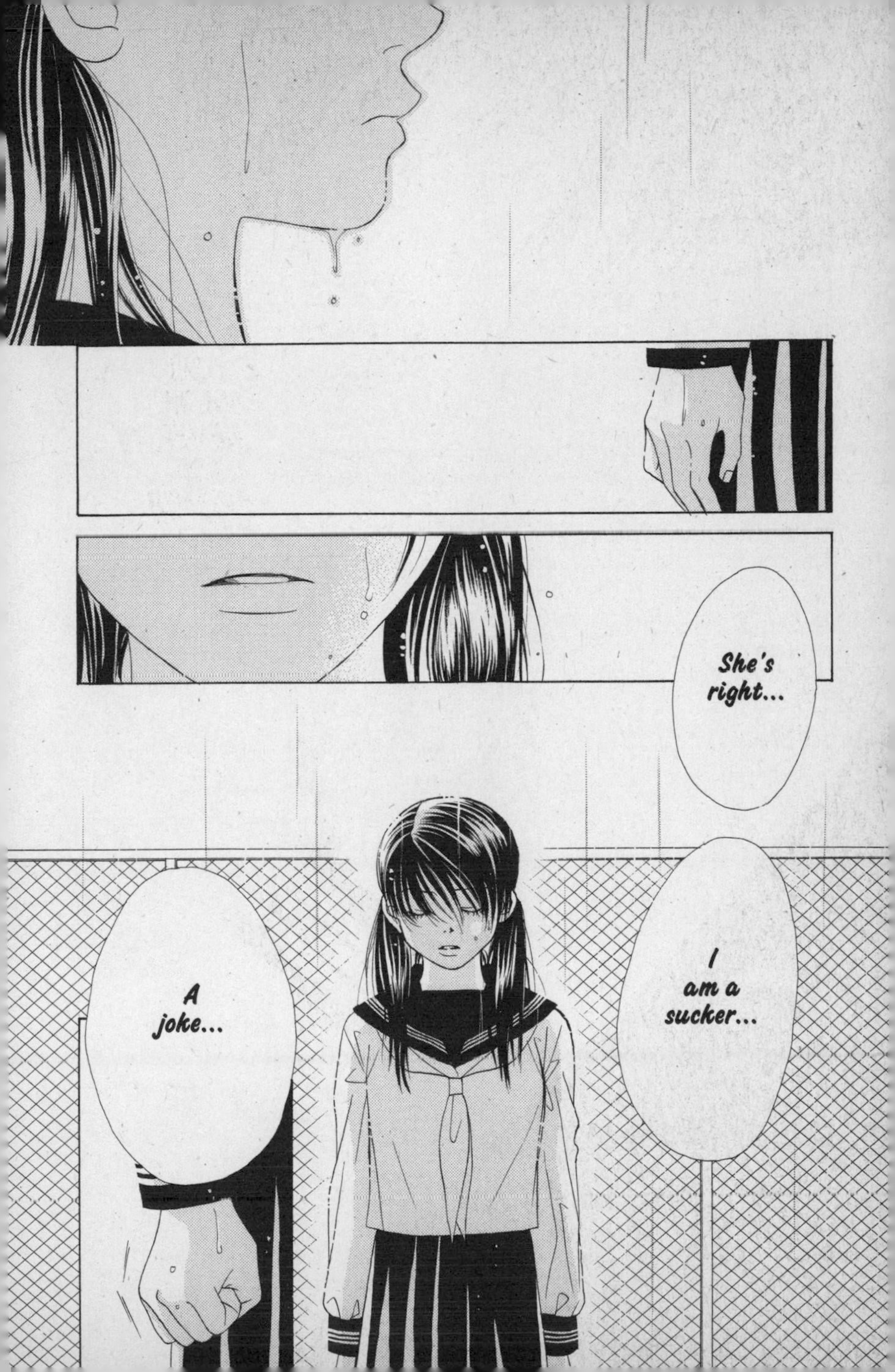
She's right...
I am a sucker...
A joke...

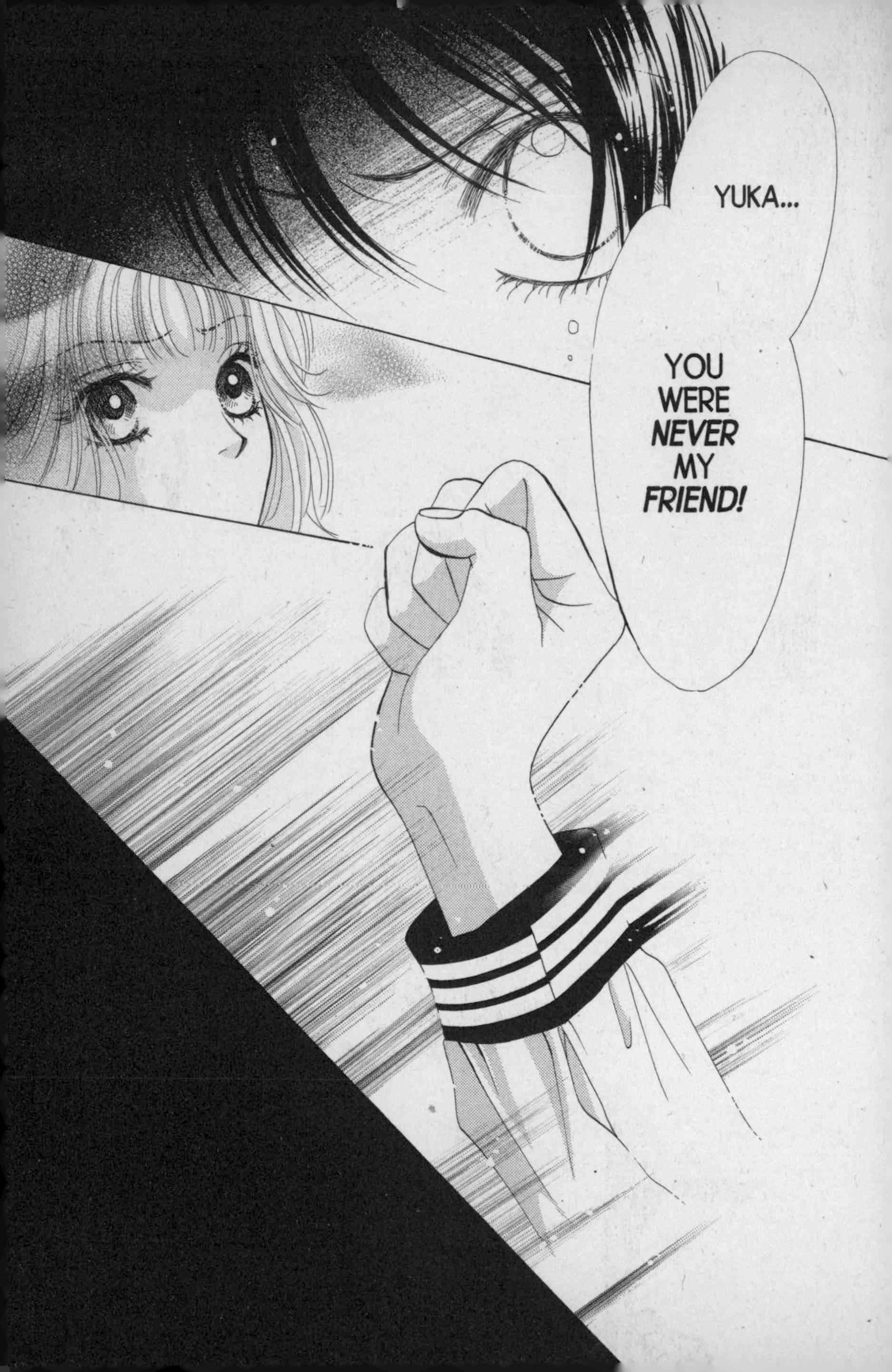
YUKA...
YOU WERE *NEVER* MY *FRIEND!*

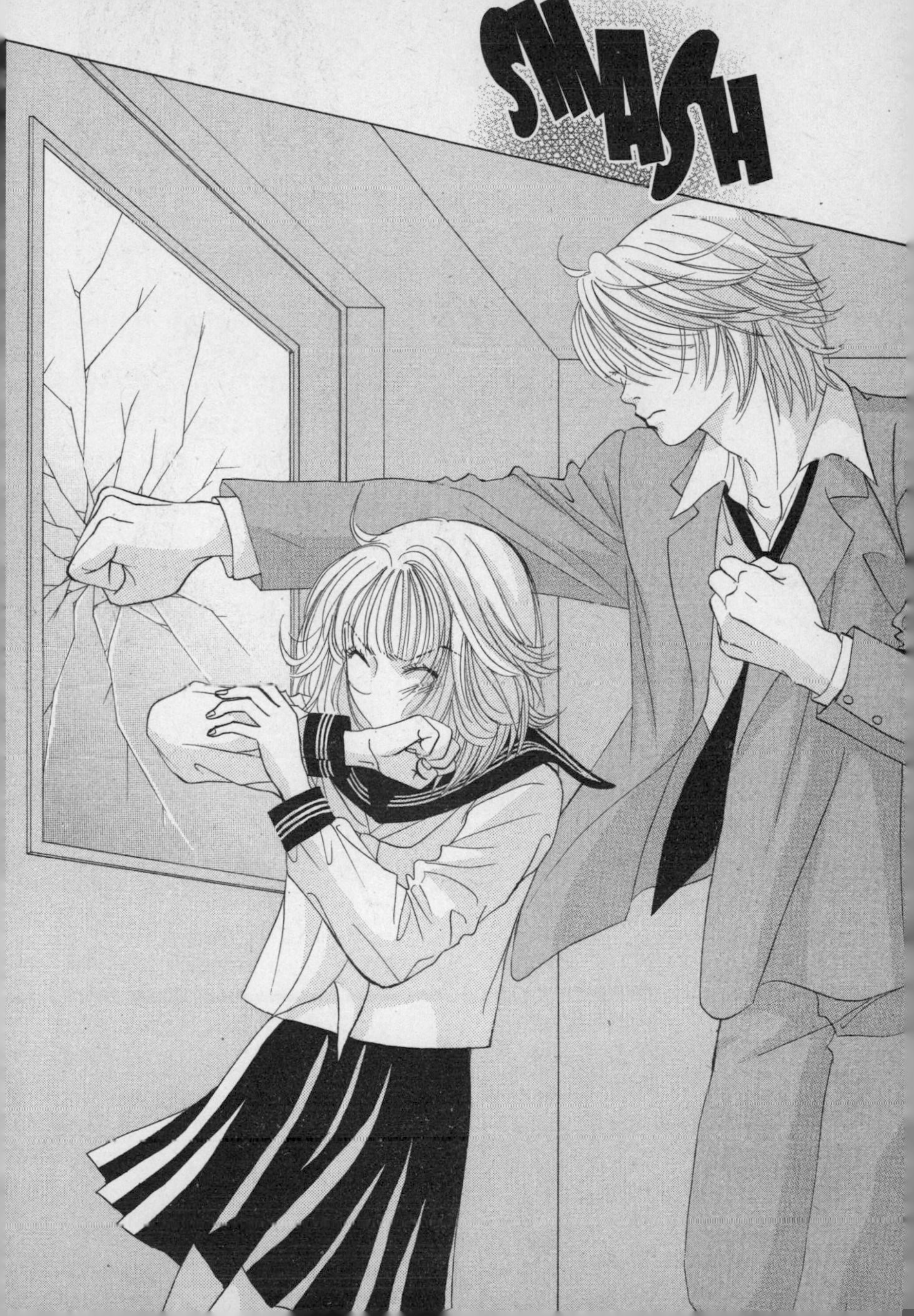
SMASH

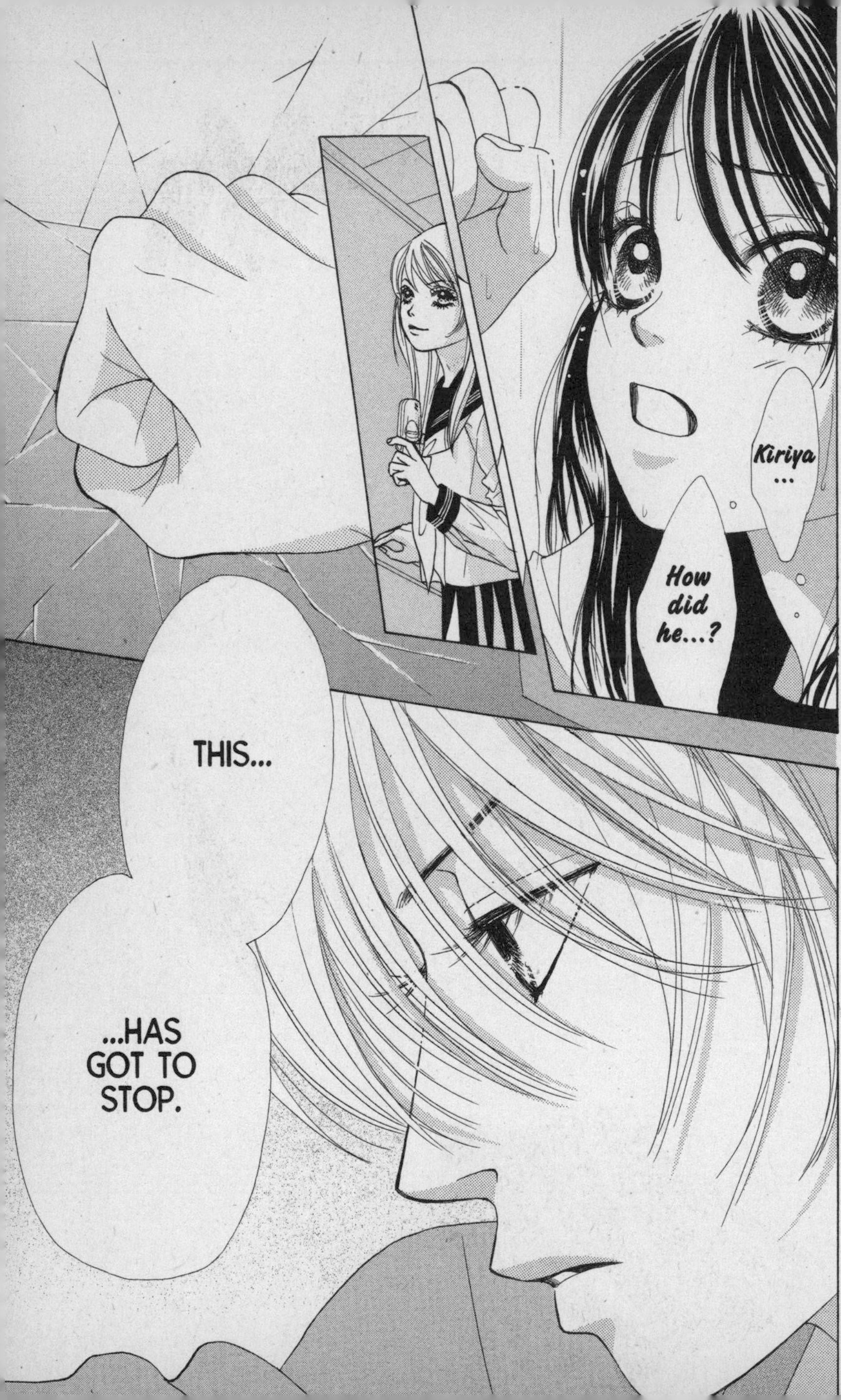
Kiriya...
How did he...?
THIS...
...HAS GOT TO STOP.

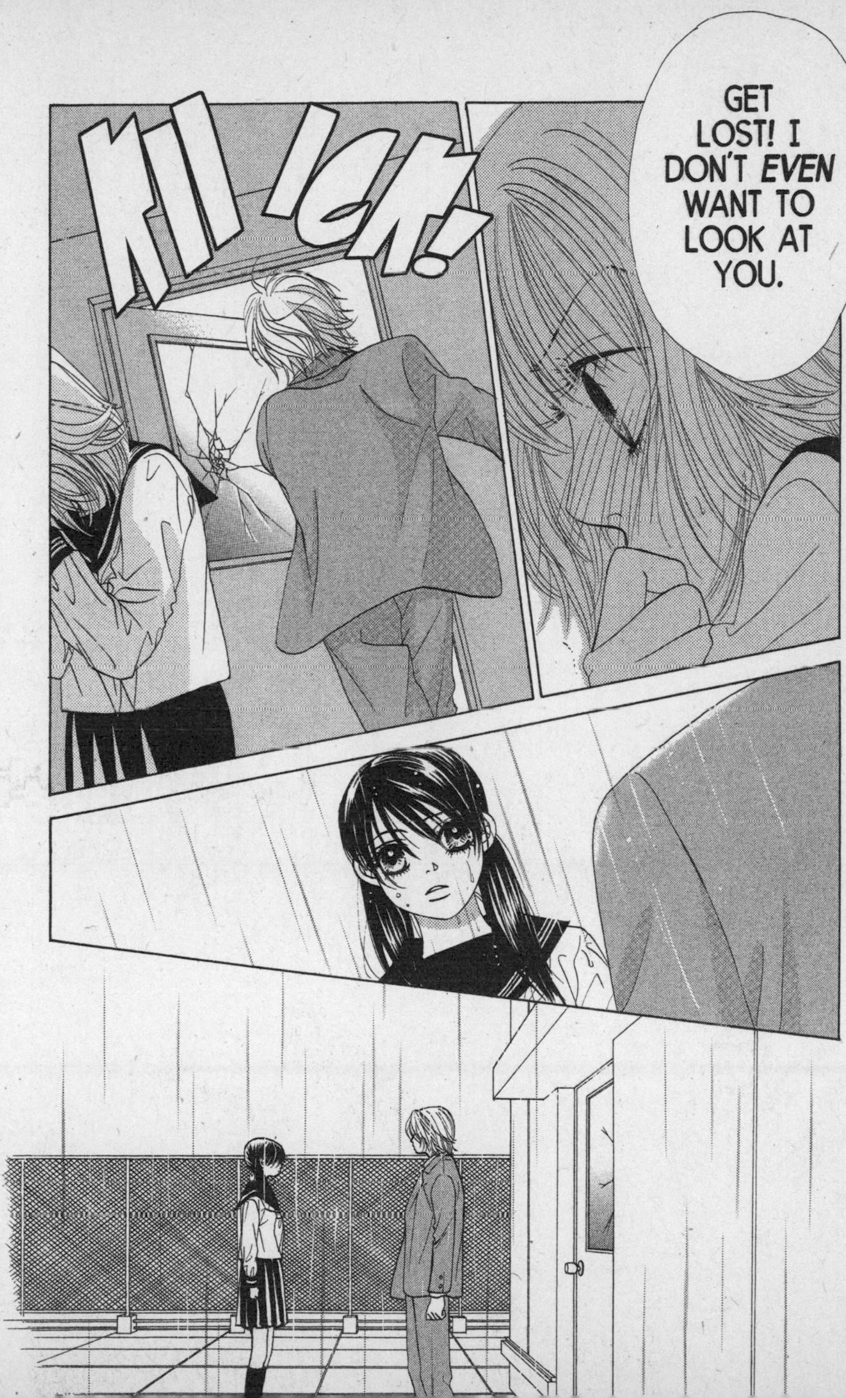
GET LOST! I DON'T *EVEN* WANT TO LOOK AT YOU.
KRR ICK!

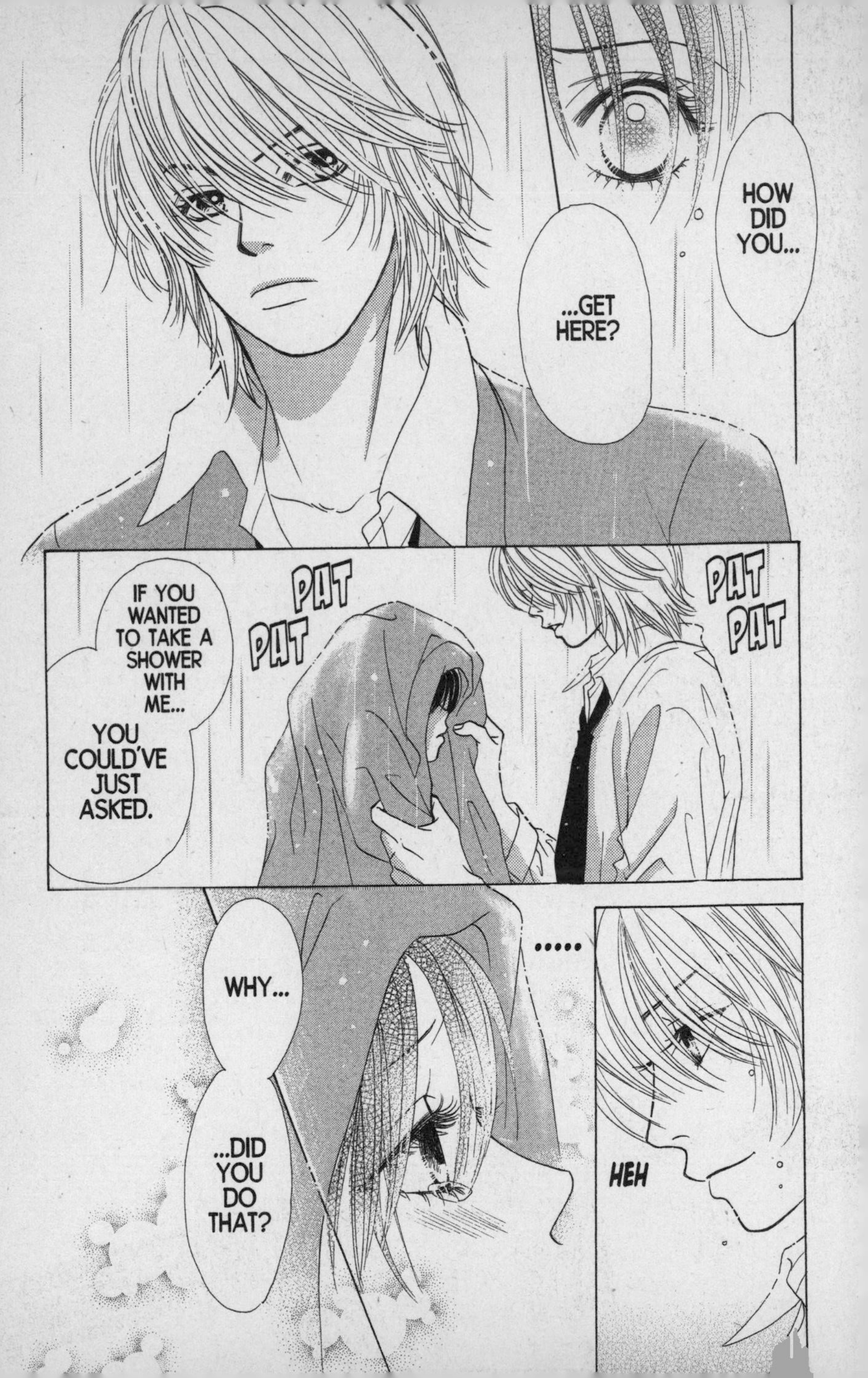
HOW DID YOU...
...GET HERE?
PAT PAT
PAT PAT
IF YOU WANTED TO TAKE A SHOWER WITH ME...
YOU COULD'VE JUST ASKED.
WHY...
...DID YOU DO THAT?
.....
HEH

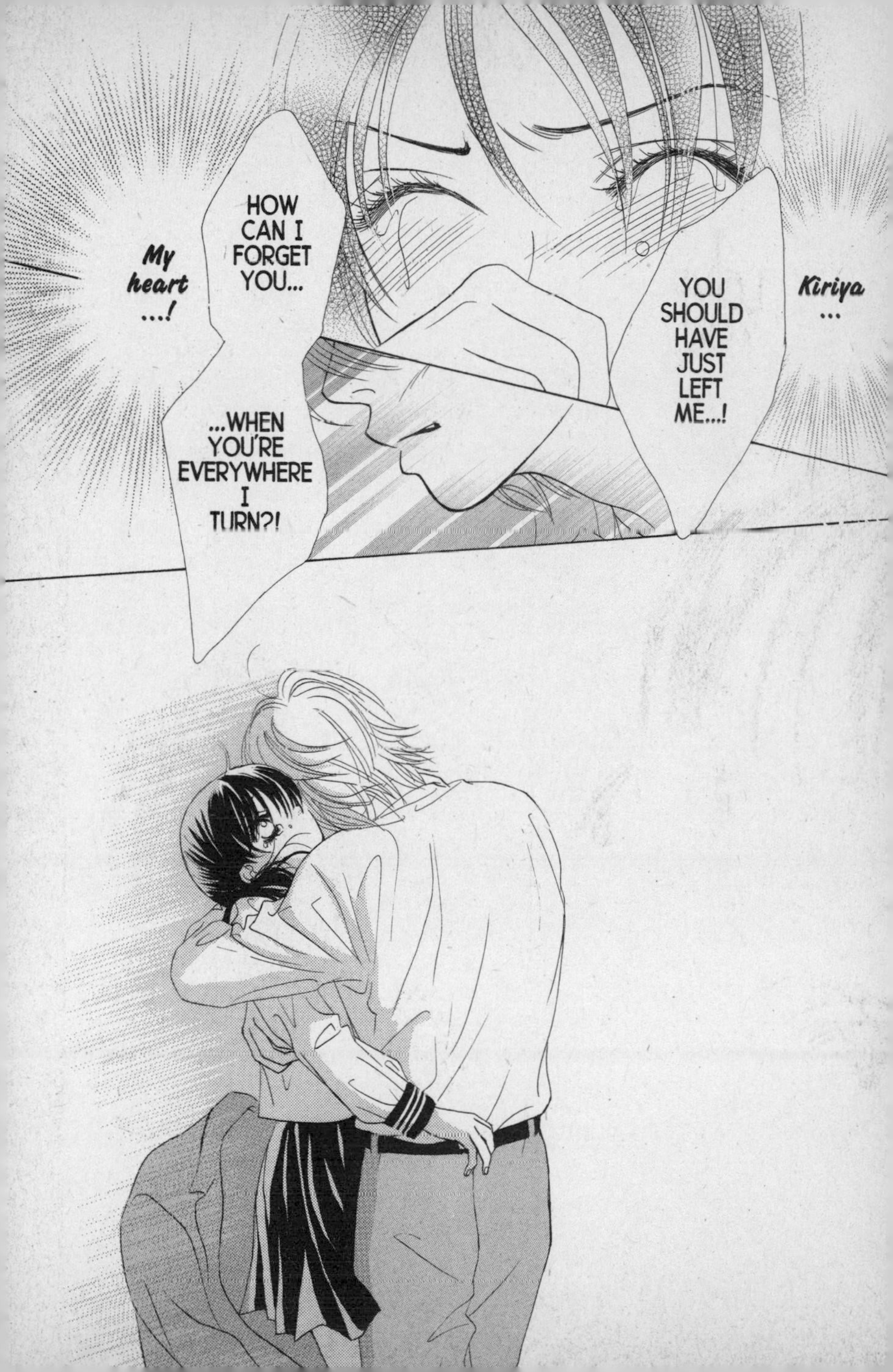
Kiriya...
YOU SHOULD HAVE JUST LEFT ME...!
HOW CAN I FORGET YOU...
My heart...!
...WHEN YOU'RE EVERYWHERE I TURN?!

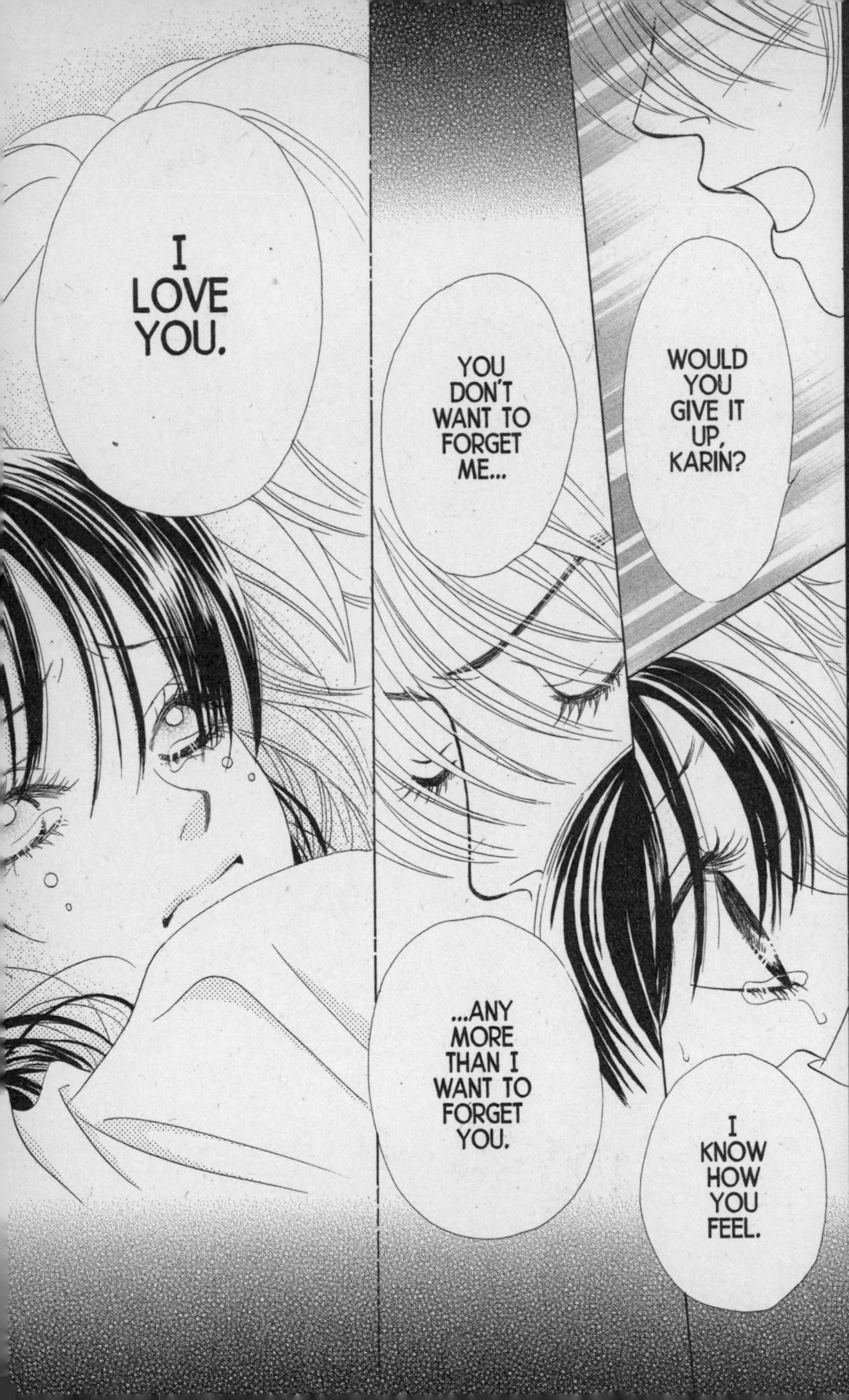
WOULD YOU GIVE IT UP, KARIN?
I KNOW HOW YOU FEEL.
YOU DON'T WANT TO FORGET ME...
...ANY MORE THAN I WANT TO FORGET YOU.
I LOVE YOU.

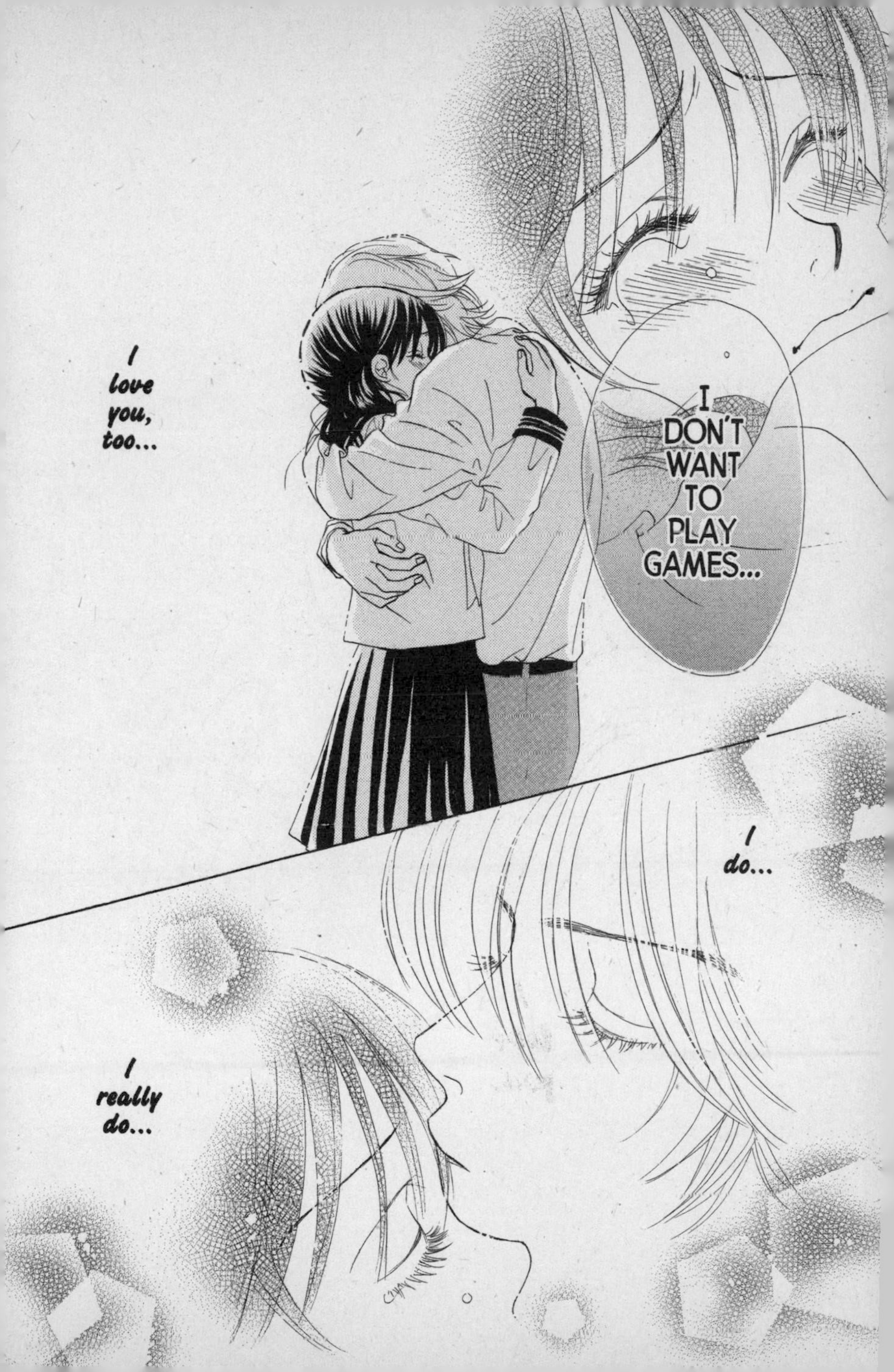
I DON'T WANT TO PLAY GAMES...
I love you, too...
I do...
I really do...

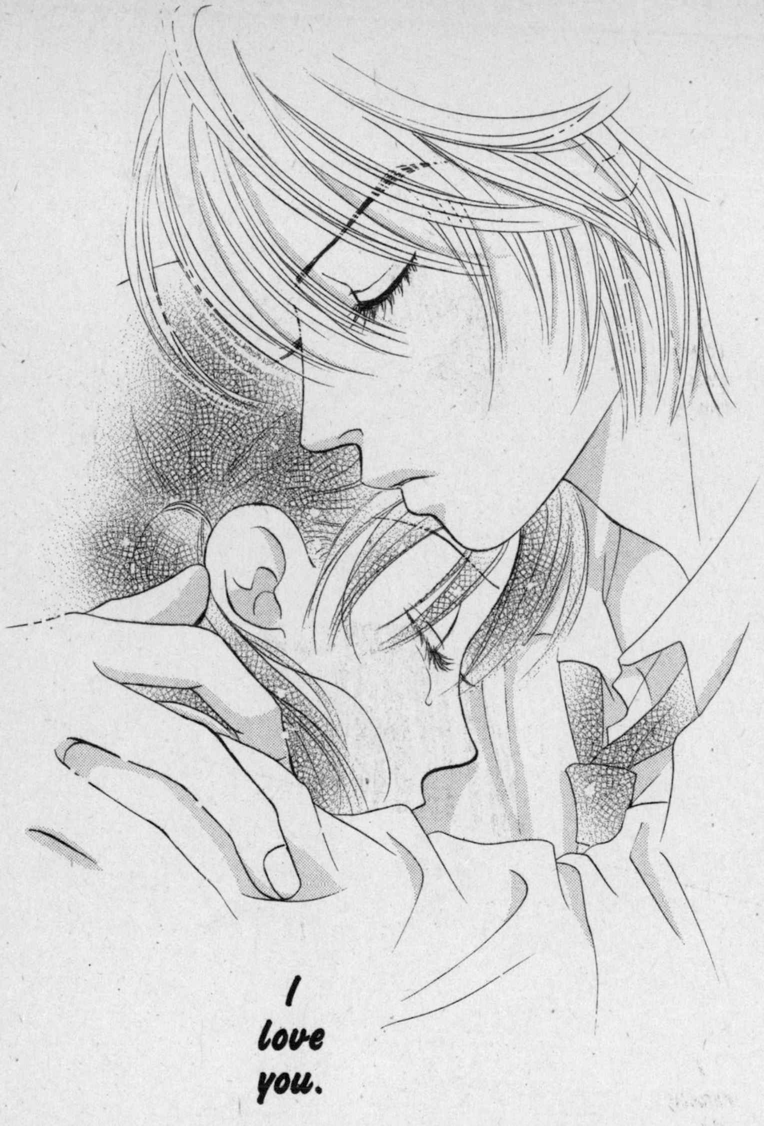
I love you.

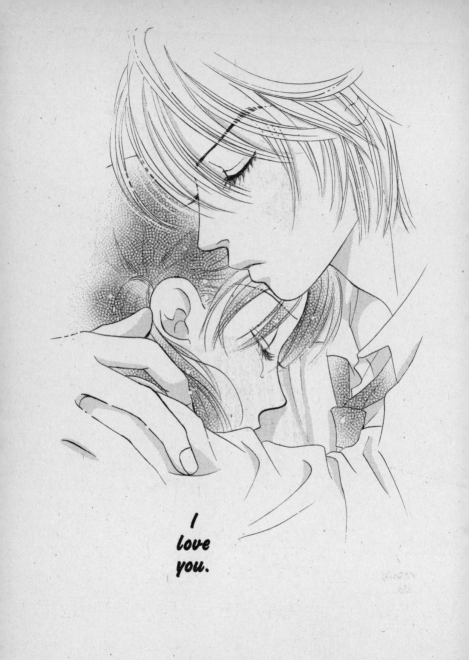

「彼」KARE First Love

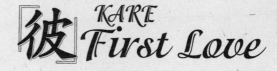

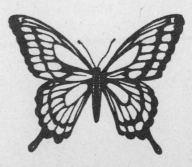

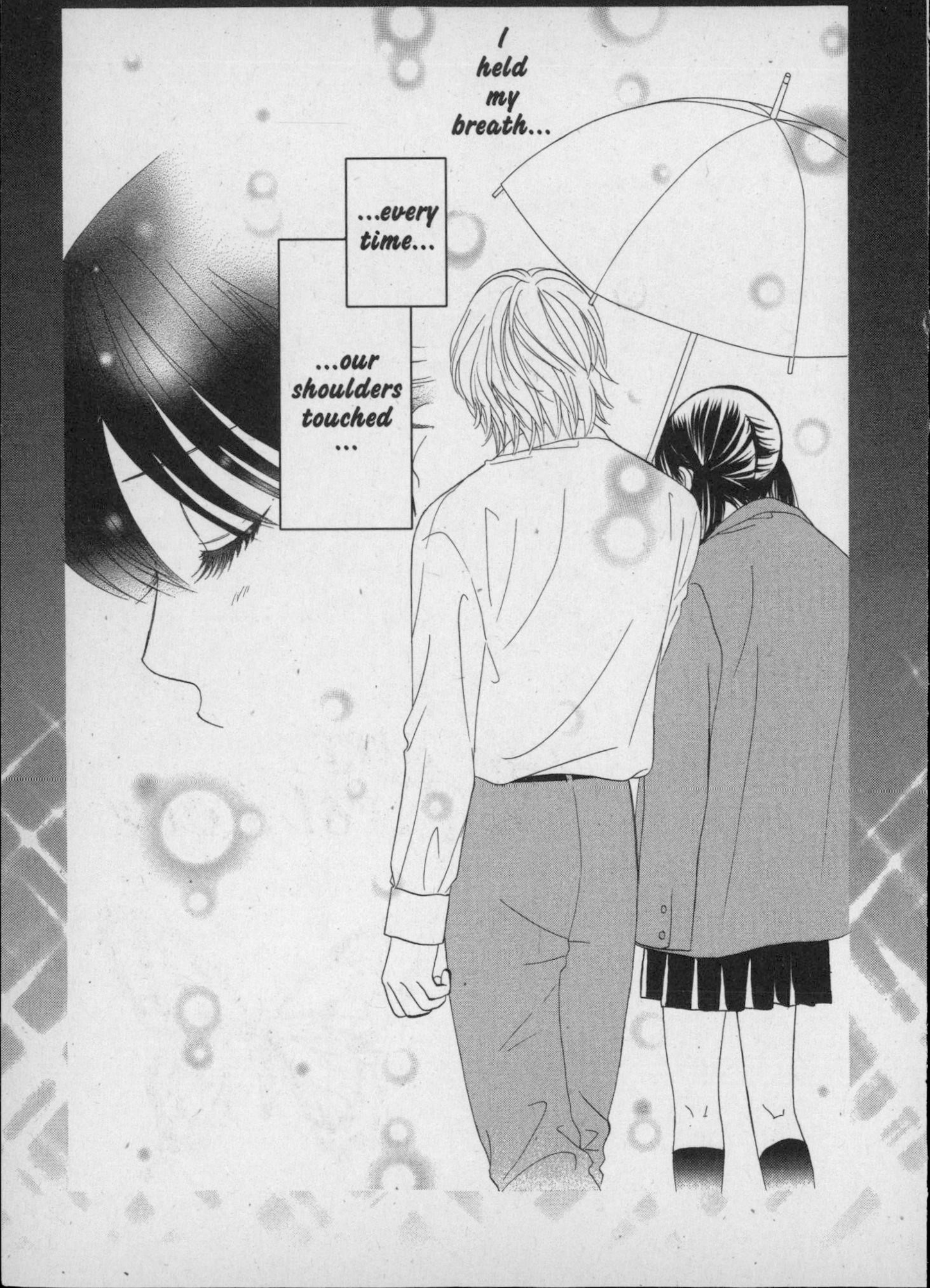
I held my breath...
...every time...
...our shoulders touched...

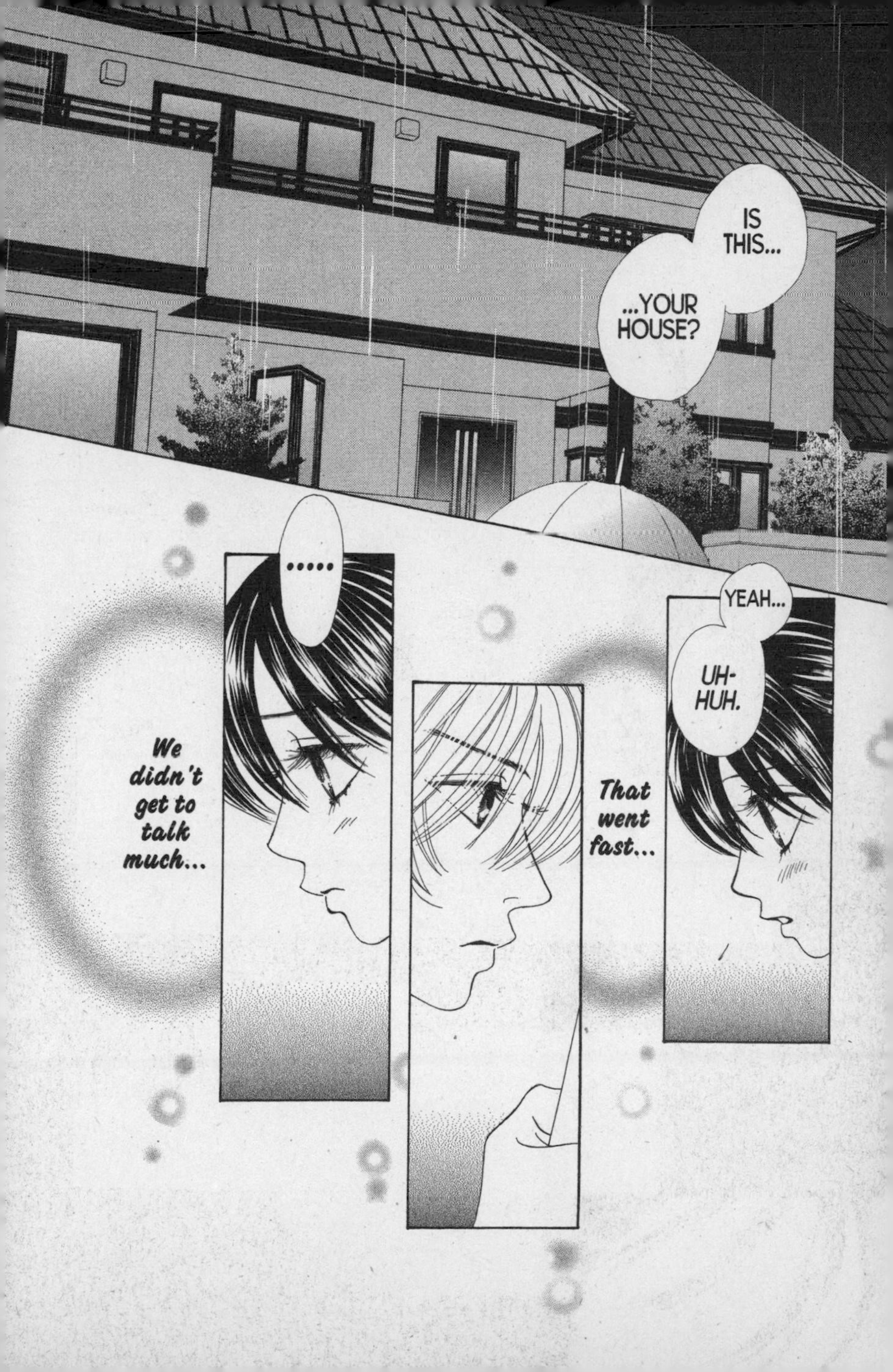
IS THIS...
...YOUR HOUSE?
YEAH...
UH-HUH.
That went fast...
.....
We didn't get to talk much...

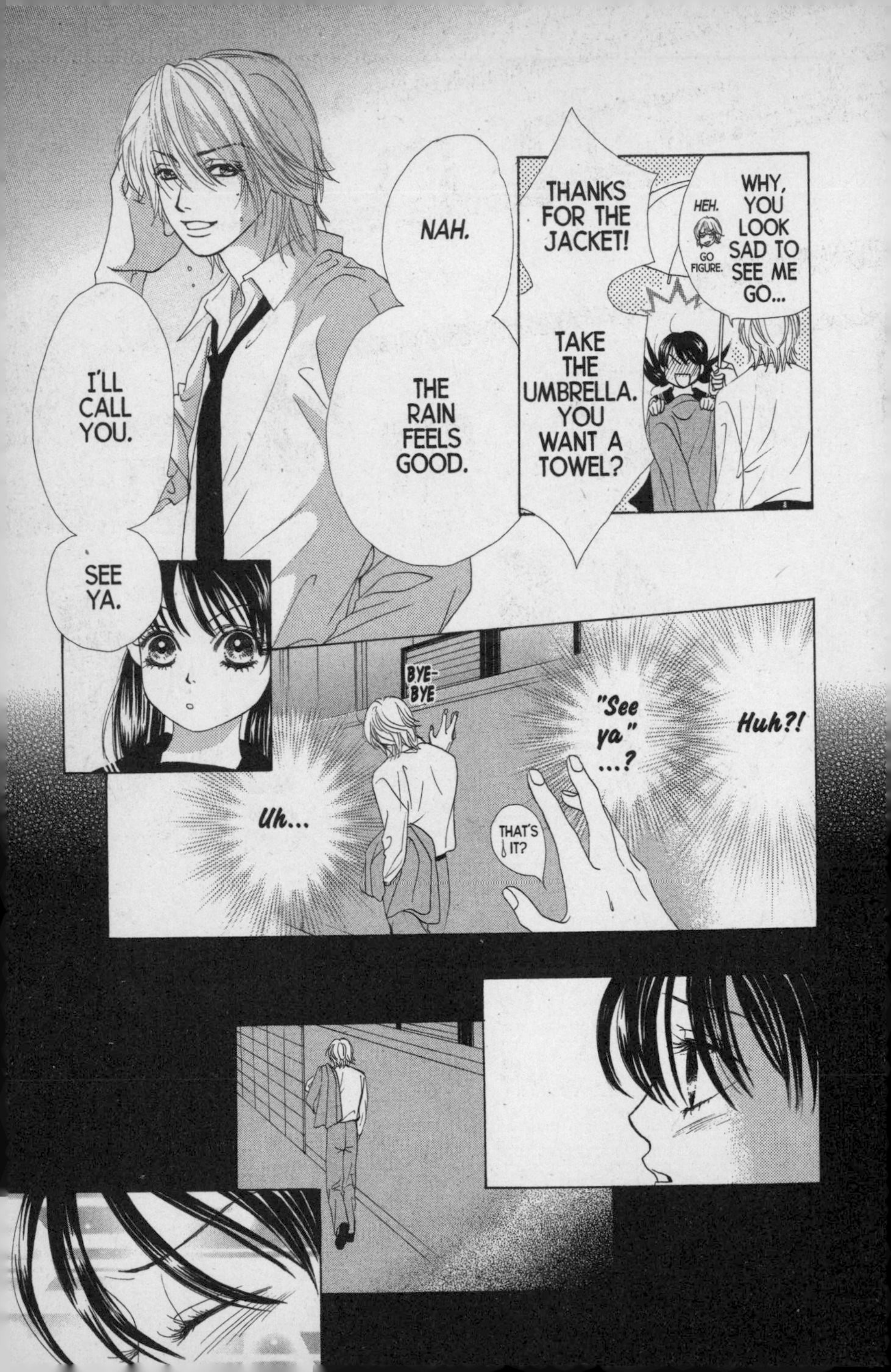
WHY, YOU LOOK SAD TO SEE ME GO...
HEH. GO FIGURE.
THANKS FOR THE JACKET!
TAKE THE UMBRELLA. YOU WANT A TOWEL?
NAH.
THE RAIN FEELS GOOD.
I'LL CALL YOU.
SEE YA.
Huh?!
"See ya" ...?
THAT'S IT?
BYE-BYE
Uh...

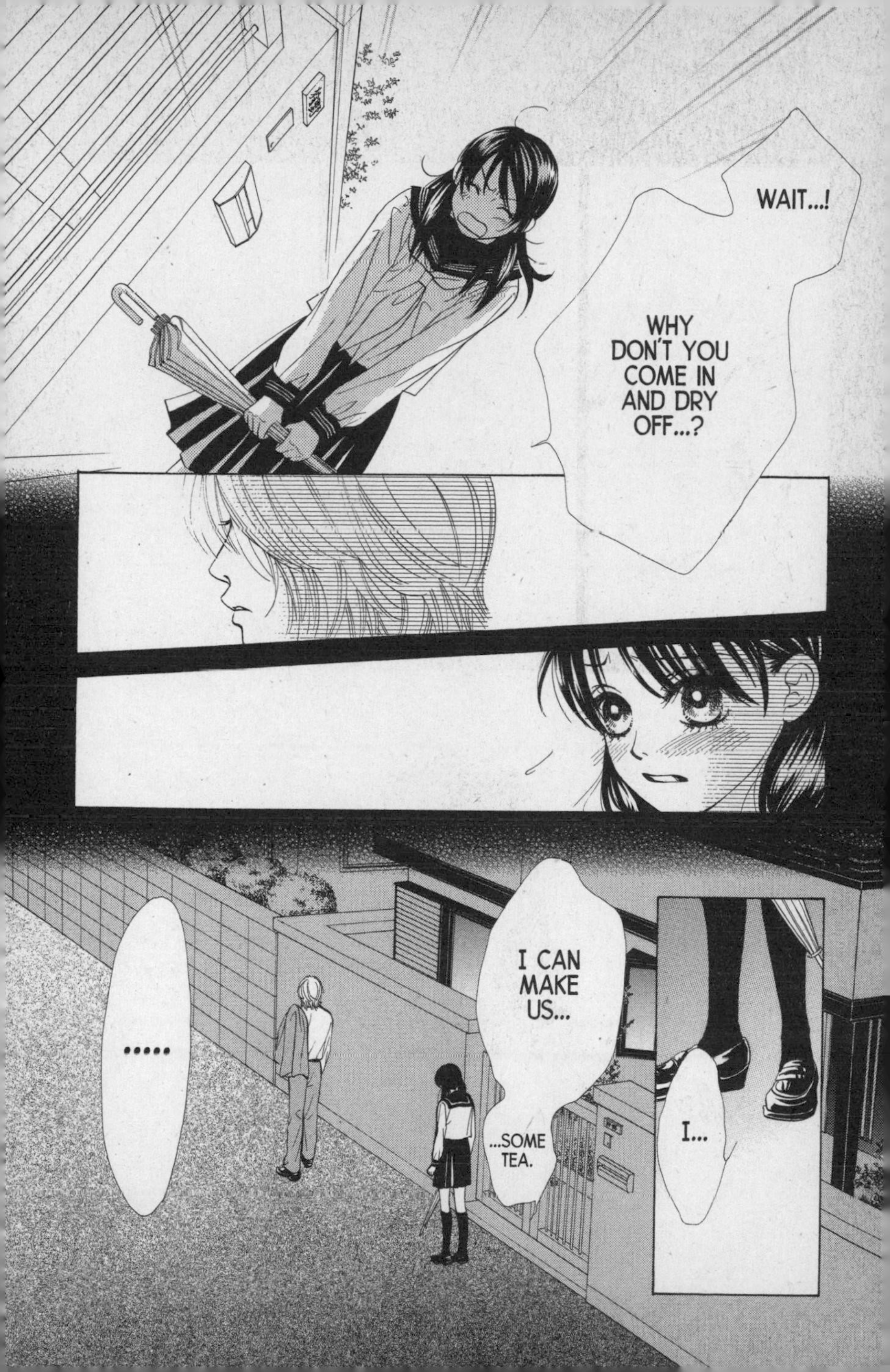

WAIT...!
WHY DON'T YOU COME IN AND DRY OFF...?
I...
I CAN MAKE US...
...SOME TEA.
.....

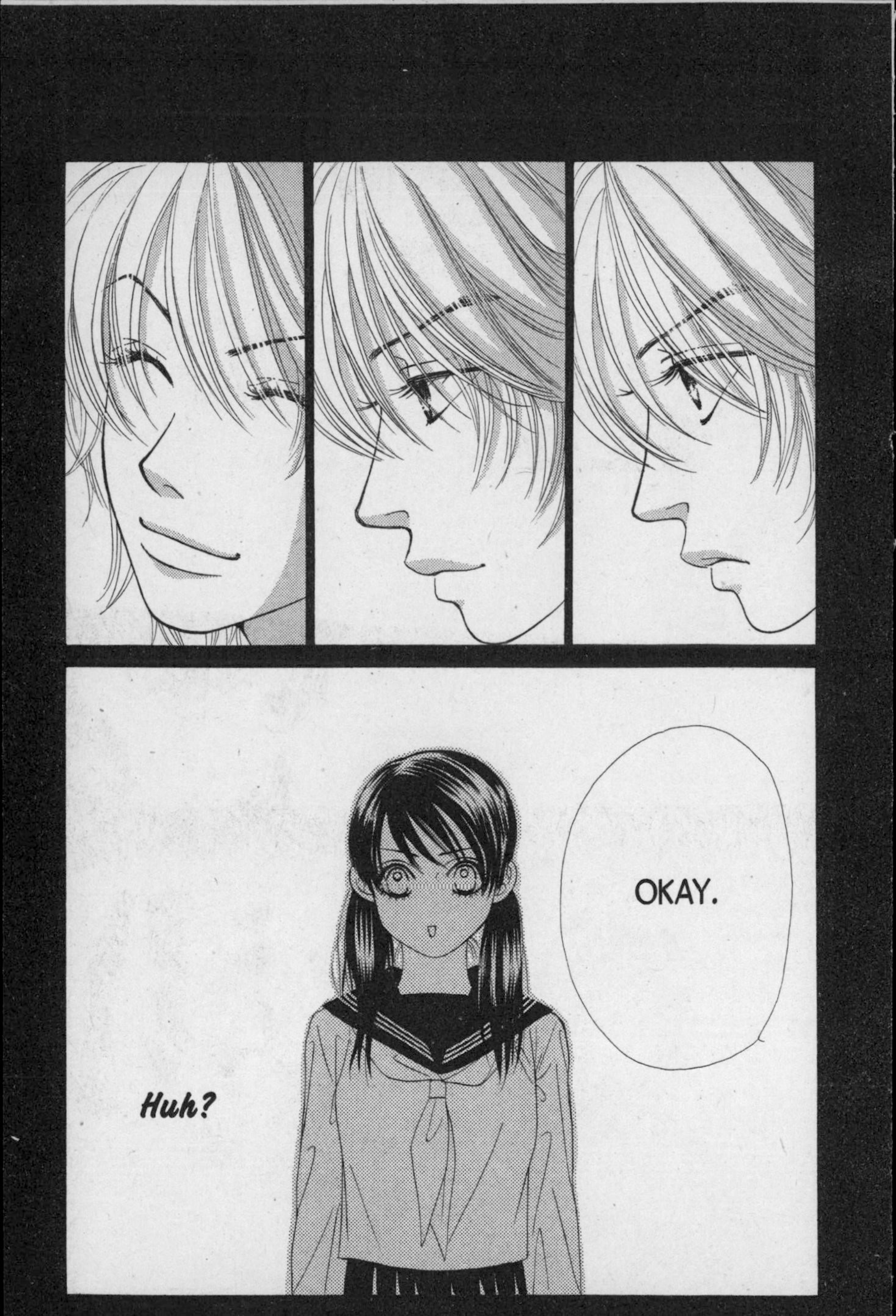
OKAY.
Huh?

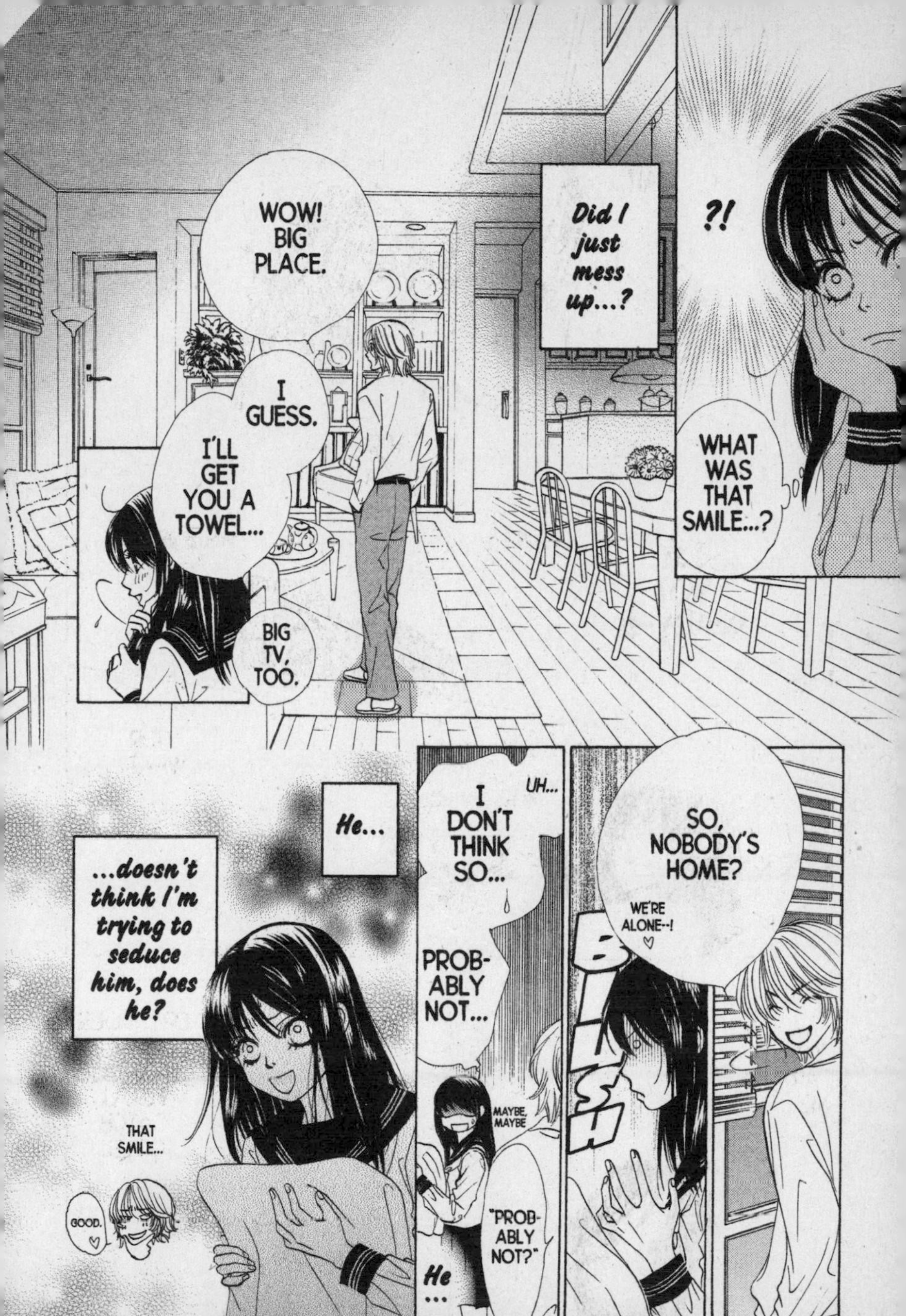
?!
Did I just mess up...?
WHAT WAS THAT SMILE...?
WOW! BIG PLACE.
I GUESS.
I'LL GET YOU A TOWEL...
BIG TV, TOO.
SO, NOBODY'S HOME?
WE'RE ALONE--! ♡
BSHH
UH...
I DON'T THINK SO...
PROB-ABLY NOT...
"PROB-ABLY NOT?"
MAYBE, MAYBE
He...
He...
...doesn't think I'm trying to seduce him, does he?
THAT SMILE...
GOOD. ♡

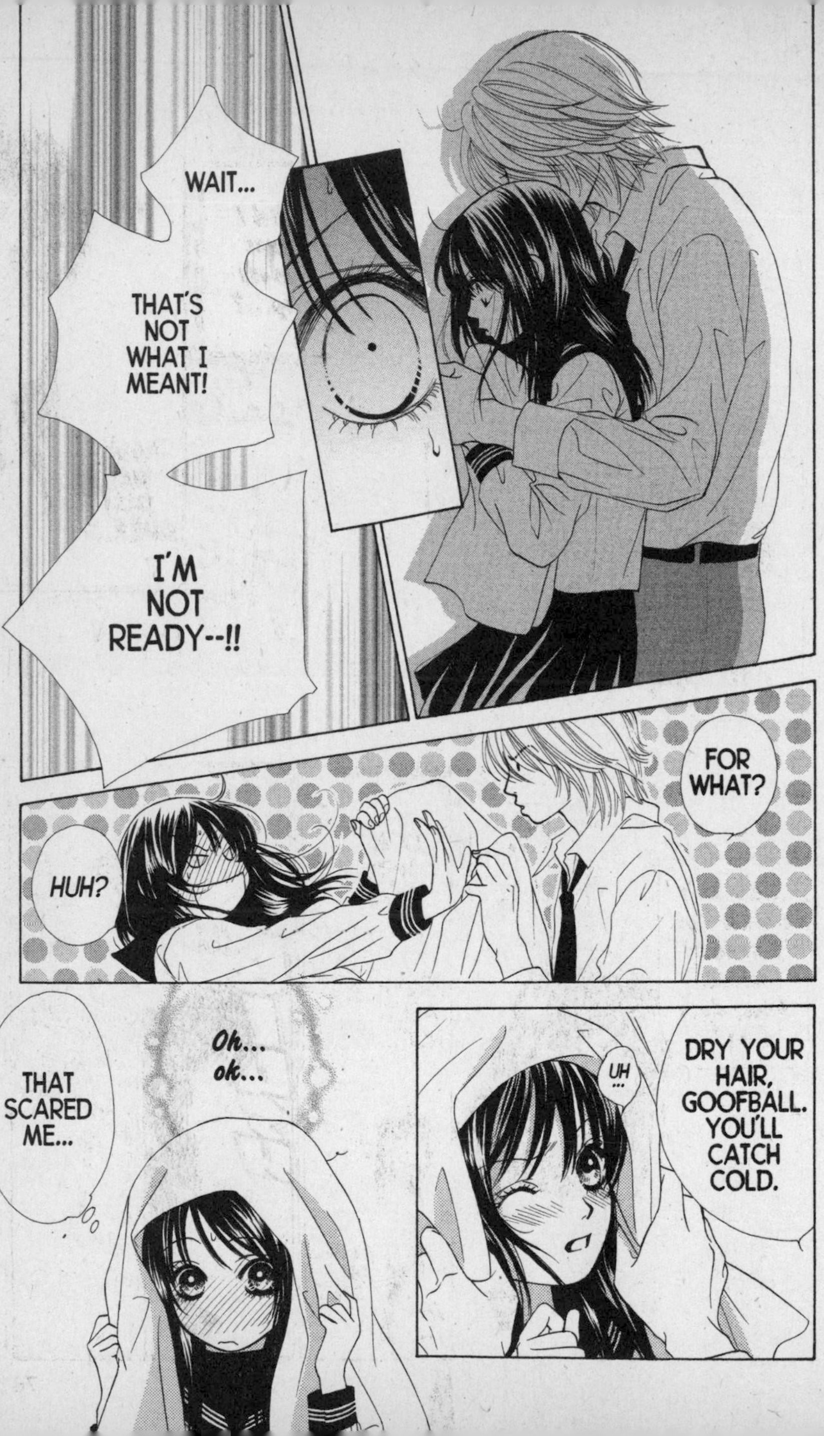
WAIT...
THAT'S NOT WHAT I MEANT!
I'M NOT READY--!!
FOR WHAT?
HUH?
DRY YOUR HAIR, GOOFBALL. YOU'LL CATCH COLD.
UH...
Oh... ok...
THAT SCARED ME...

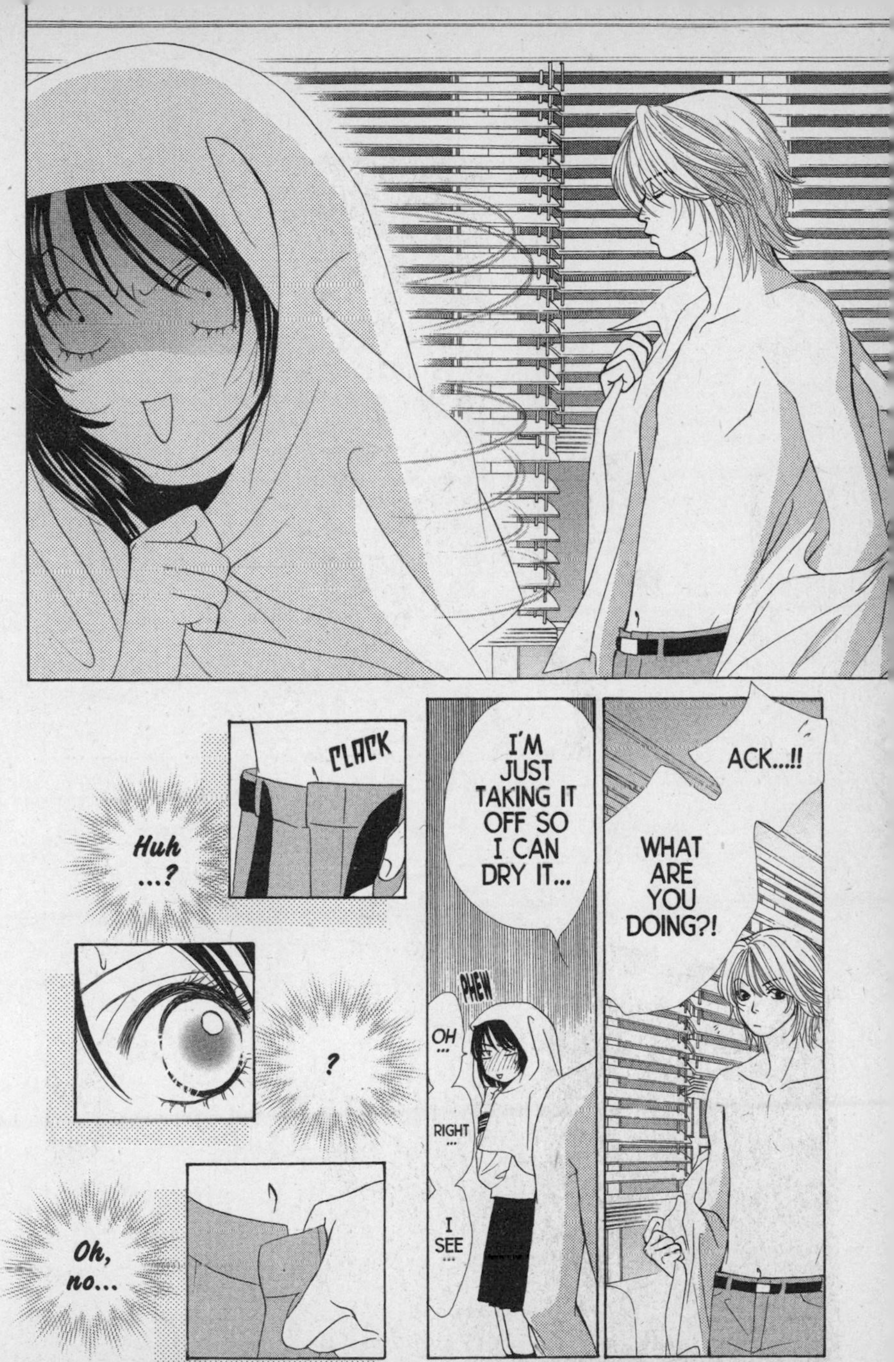
ACK...!!
WHAT ARE YOU DOING?!
I'M JUST TAKING IT OFF SO I CAN DRY IT...
PHEW
OH... RIGHT... I SEE...
CLACK
Huh...?
?
Oh, no...

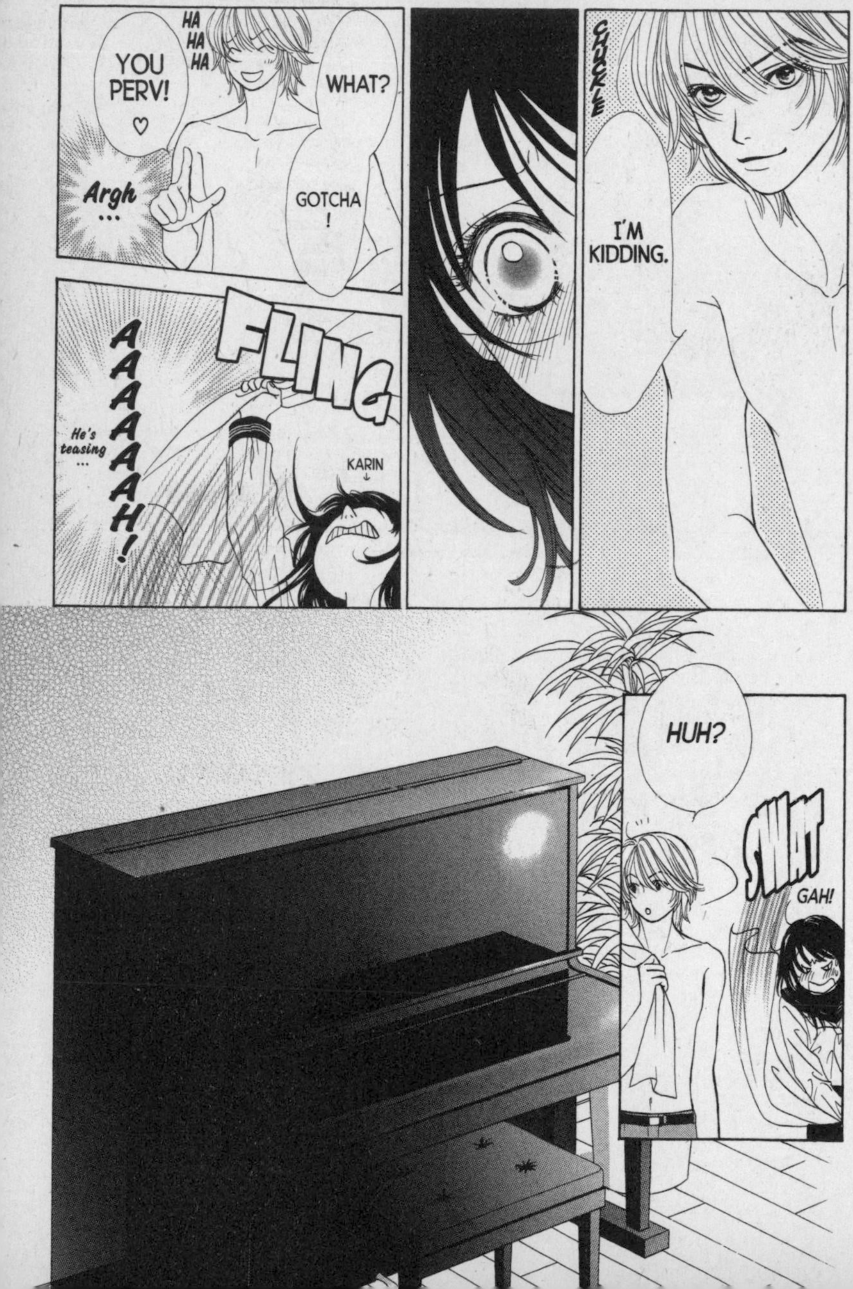
CHUCKLE
I'M KIDDING.
WHAT?
GOTCHA!
HA HA HA
YOU PERV! ♡
Argh...
FLING
AAAAAAAH!
He's teasing...
KARIN
HUH?
SWAT
GAH!

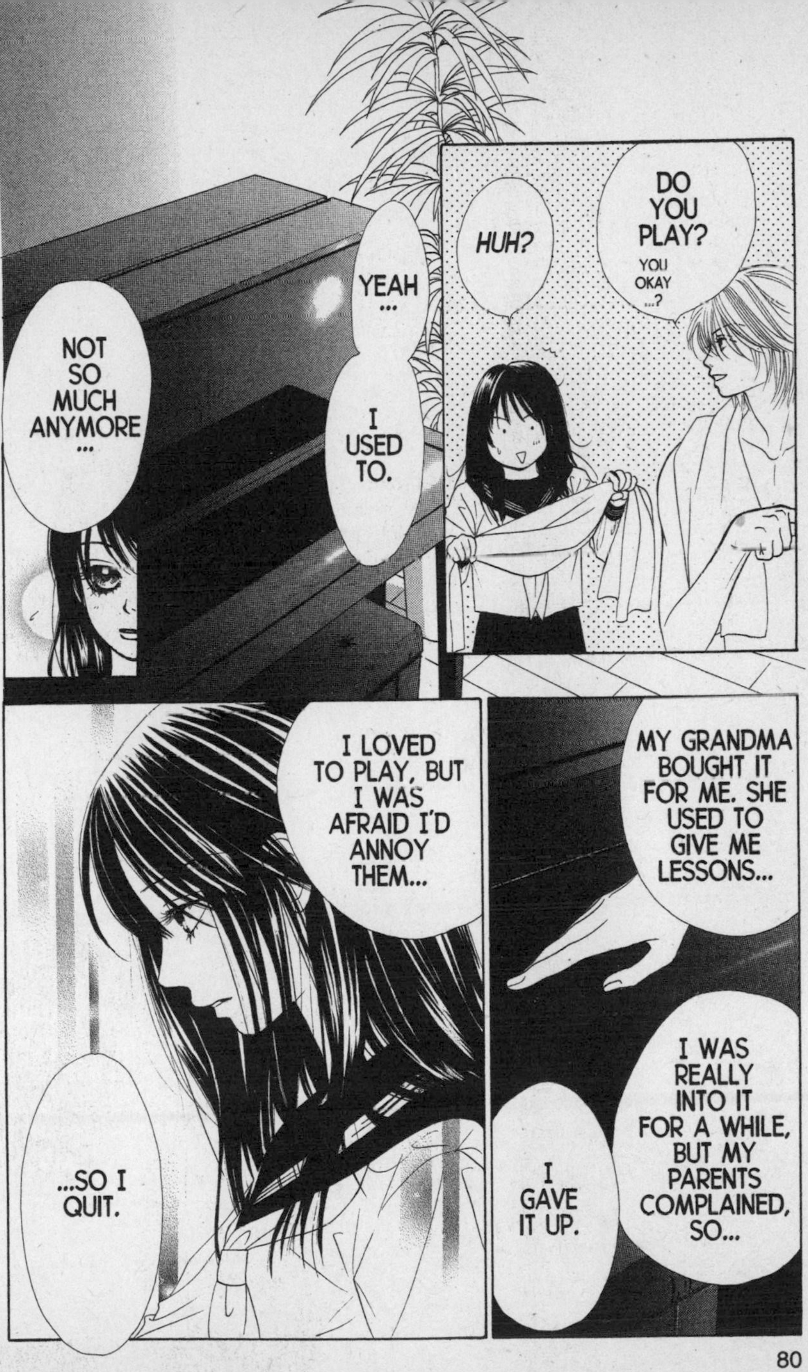
DO YOU PLAY?
YOU OKAY ...?
HUH?
YEAH ...
I USED TO.
NOT SO MUCH ANYMORE ...
MY GRANDMA BOUGHT IT FOR ME. SHE USED TO GIVE ME LESSONS...
I WAS REALLY INTO IT FOR A WHILE, BUT MY PARENTS COMPLAINED, SO...
I GAVE IT UP.
I LOVED TO PLAY, BUT I WAS AFRAID I'D ANNOY THEM...
...SO I QUIT.

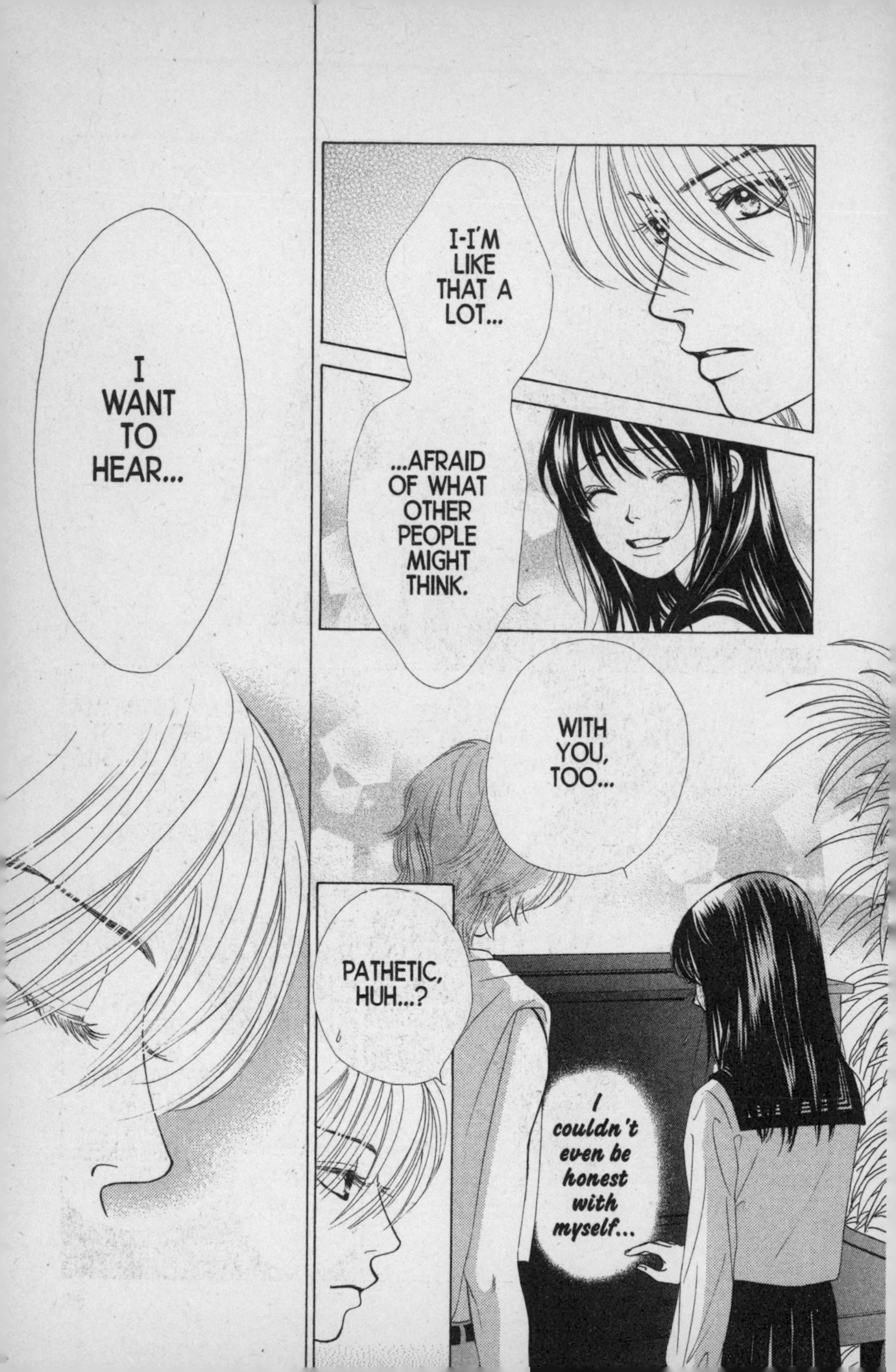

I-I'M LIKE THAT A LOT...
...AFRAID OF WHAT OTHER PEOPLE MIGHT THINK.
WITH YOU, TOO...
I couldn't even be honest with myself...
PATHETIC, HUH...?
I WANT TO HEAR...

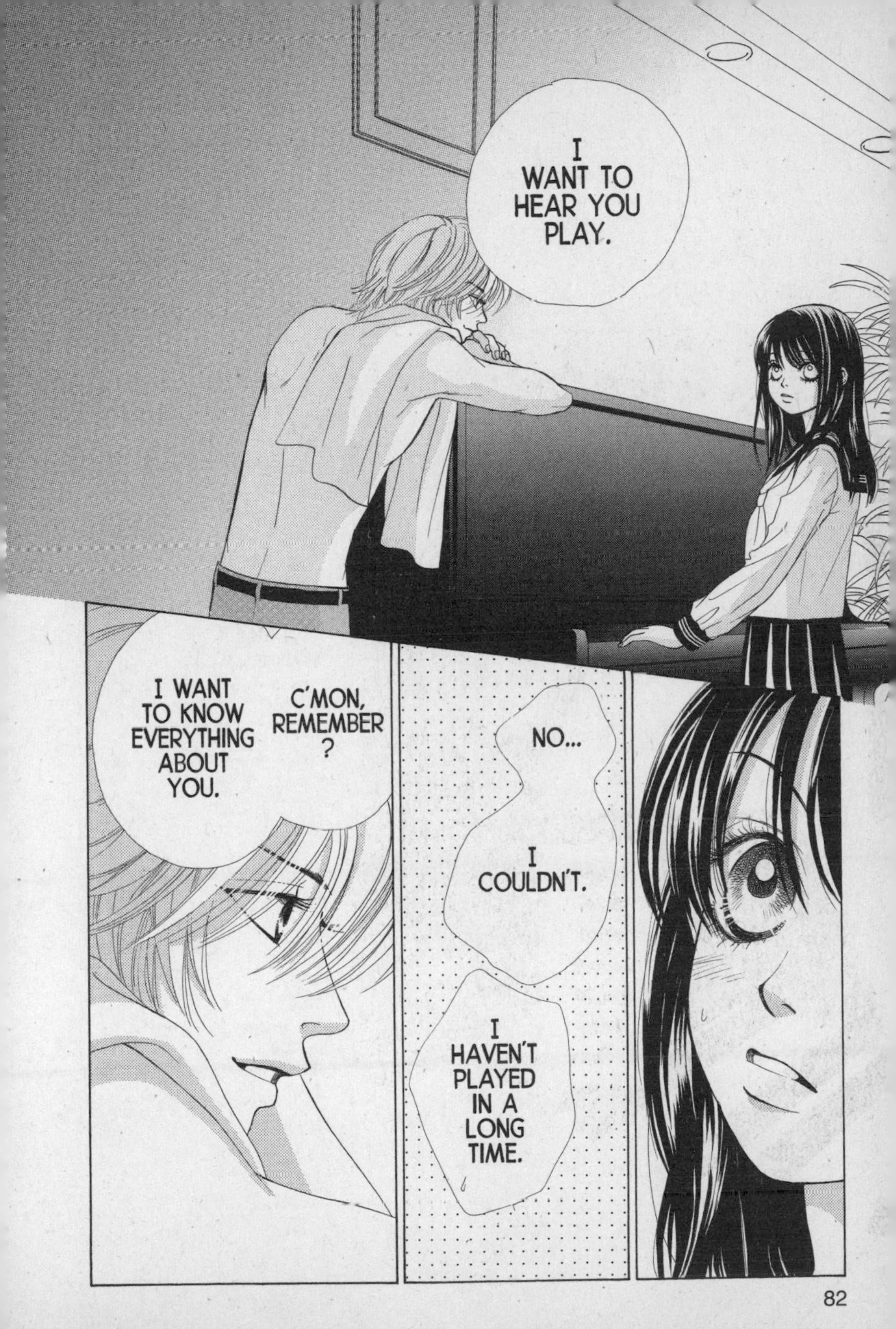
I WANT TO HEAR YOU PLAY.
NO...
I COULDN'T.
I HAVEN'T PLAYED IN A LONG TIME.
C'MON, REMEMBER?
I WANT TO KNOW EVERYTHING ABOUT YOU.

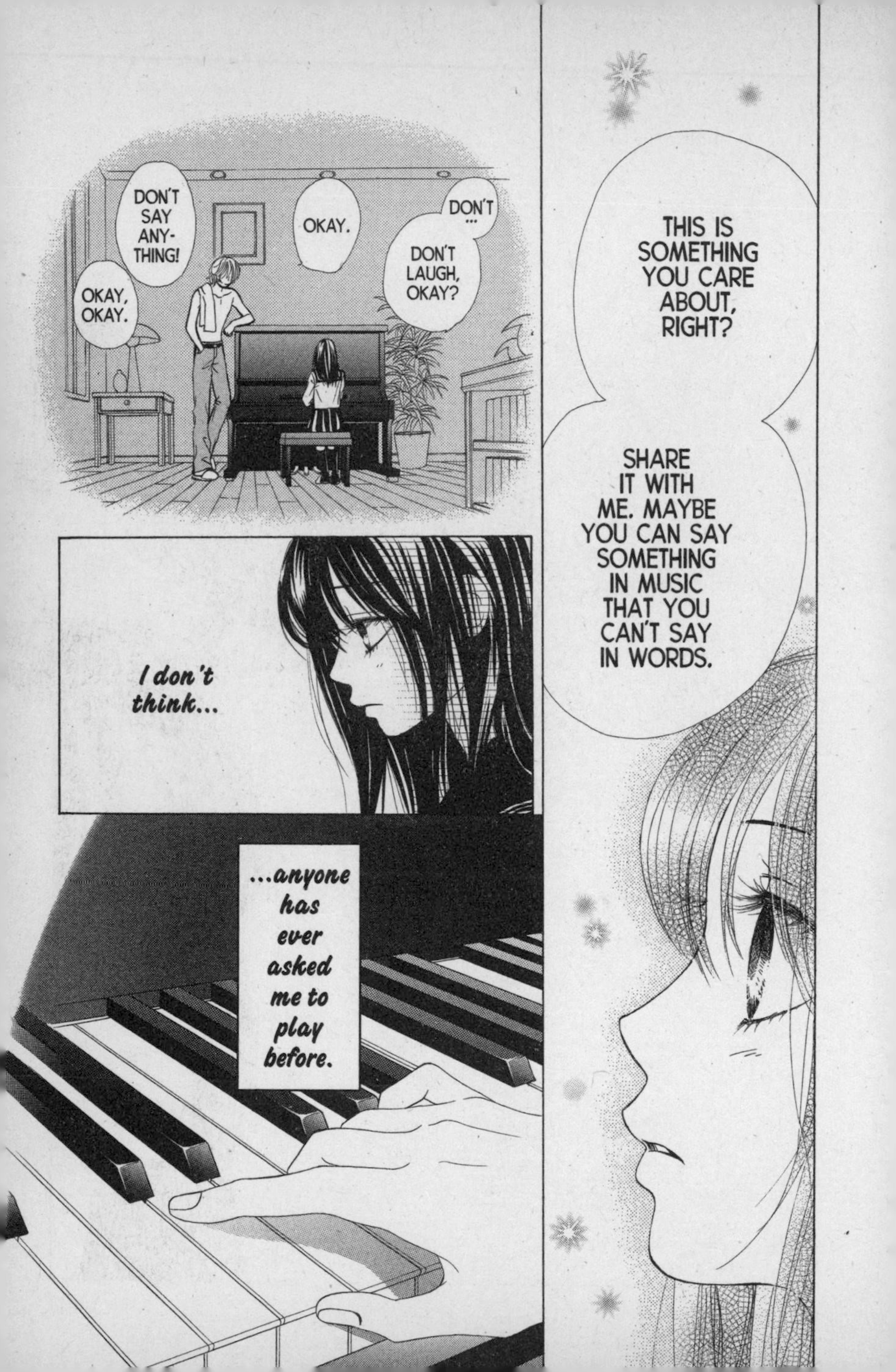
THIS IS SOMETHING YOU CARE ABOUT, RIGHT?
SHARE IT WITH ME. MAYBE YOU CAN SAY SOMETHING IN MUSIC THAT YOU CAN'T SAY IN WORDS.
DON'T ...
DON'T LAUGH, OKAY?
OKAY.
DON'T SAY ANY-THING!
OKAY, OKAY.
I don't think...
...anyone has ever asked me to play before.

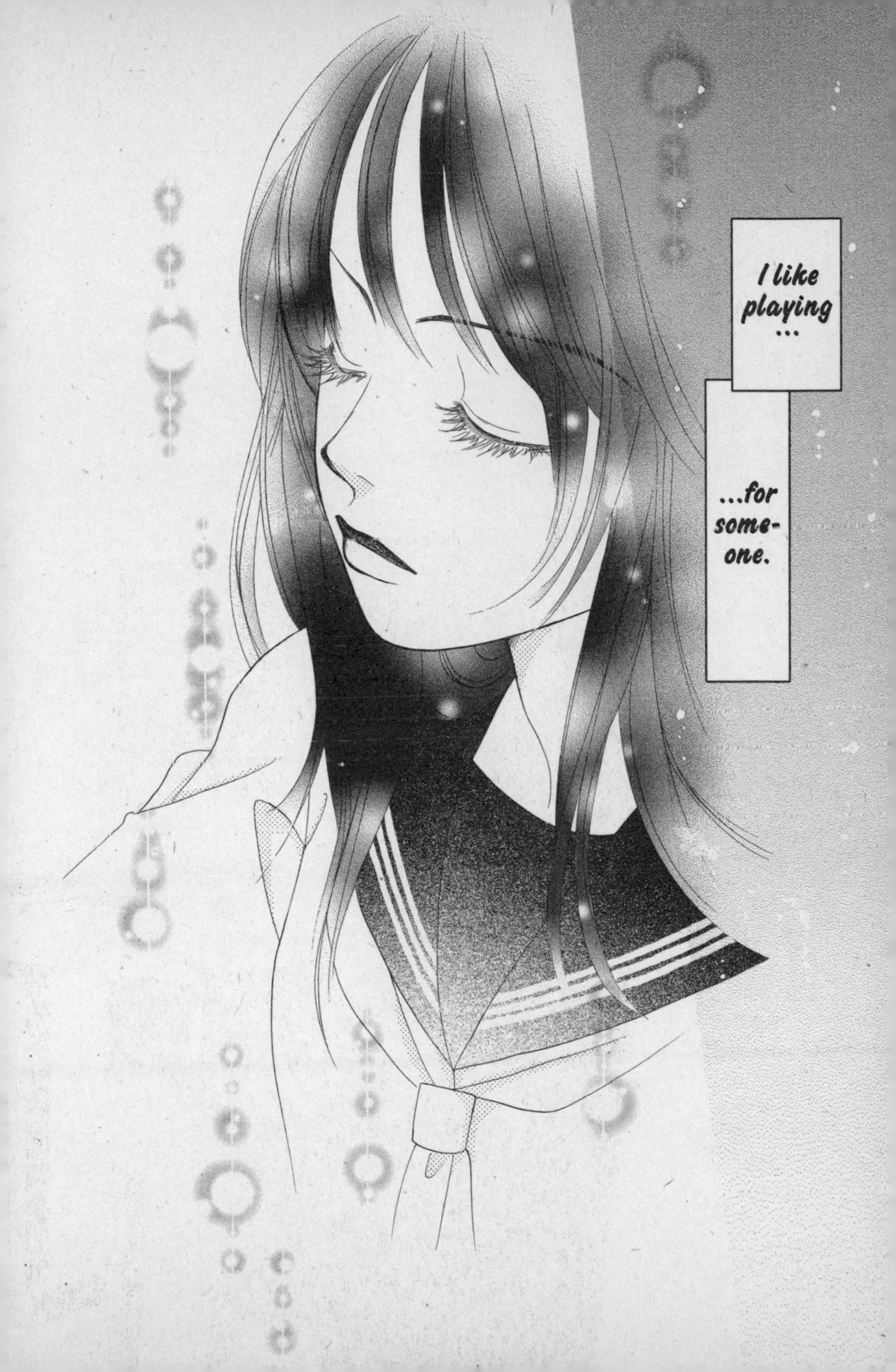
I like playing ...
...for some-one.

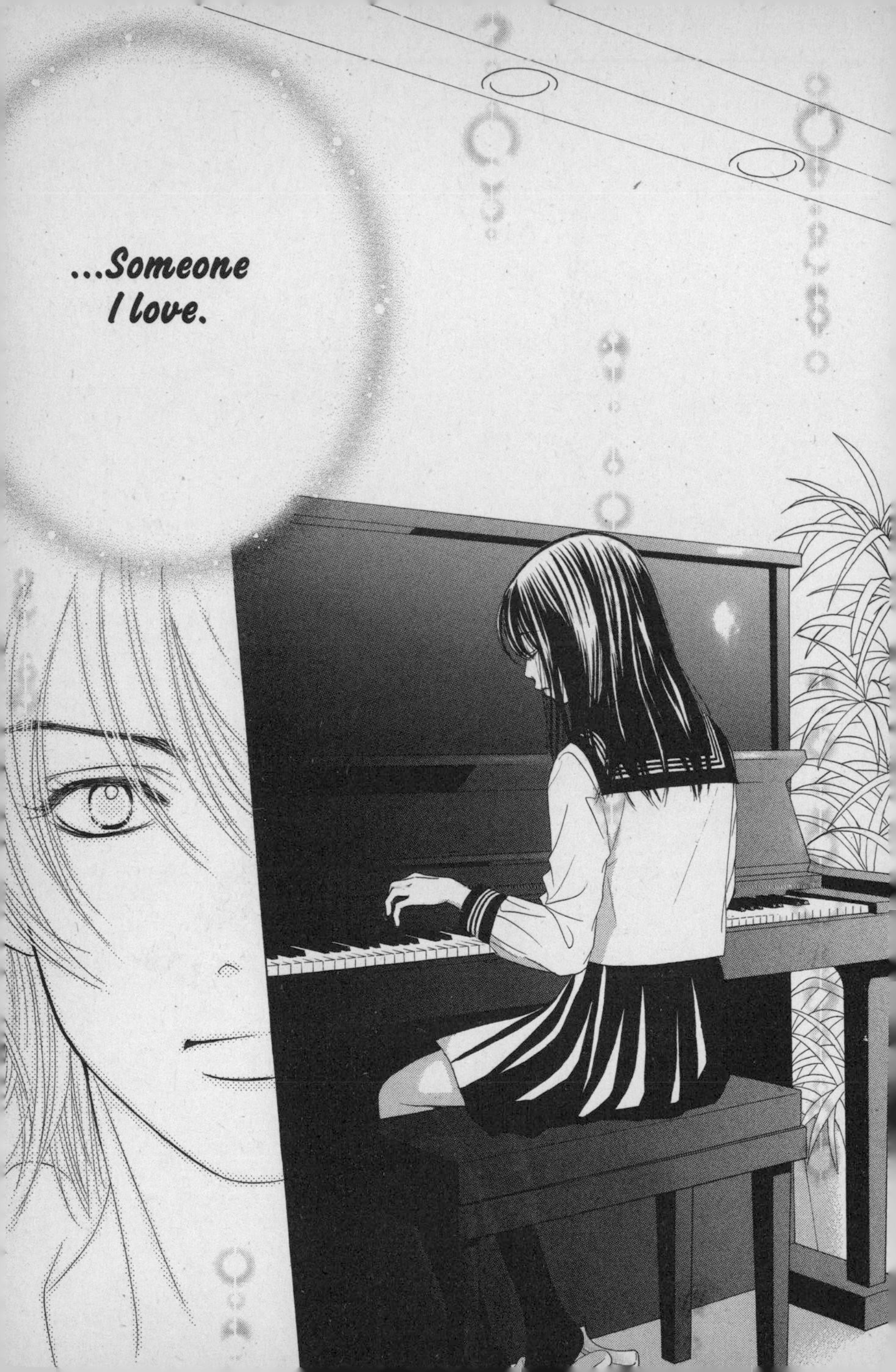
...Someone I love.

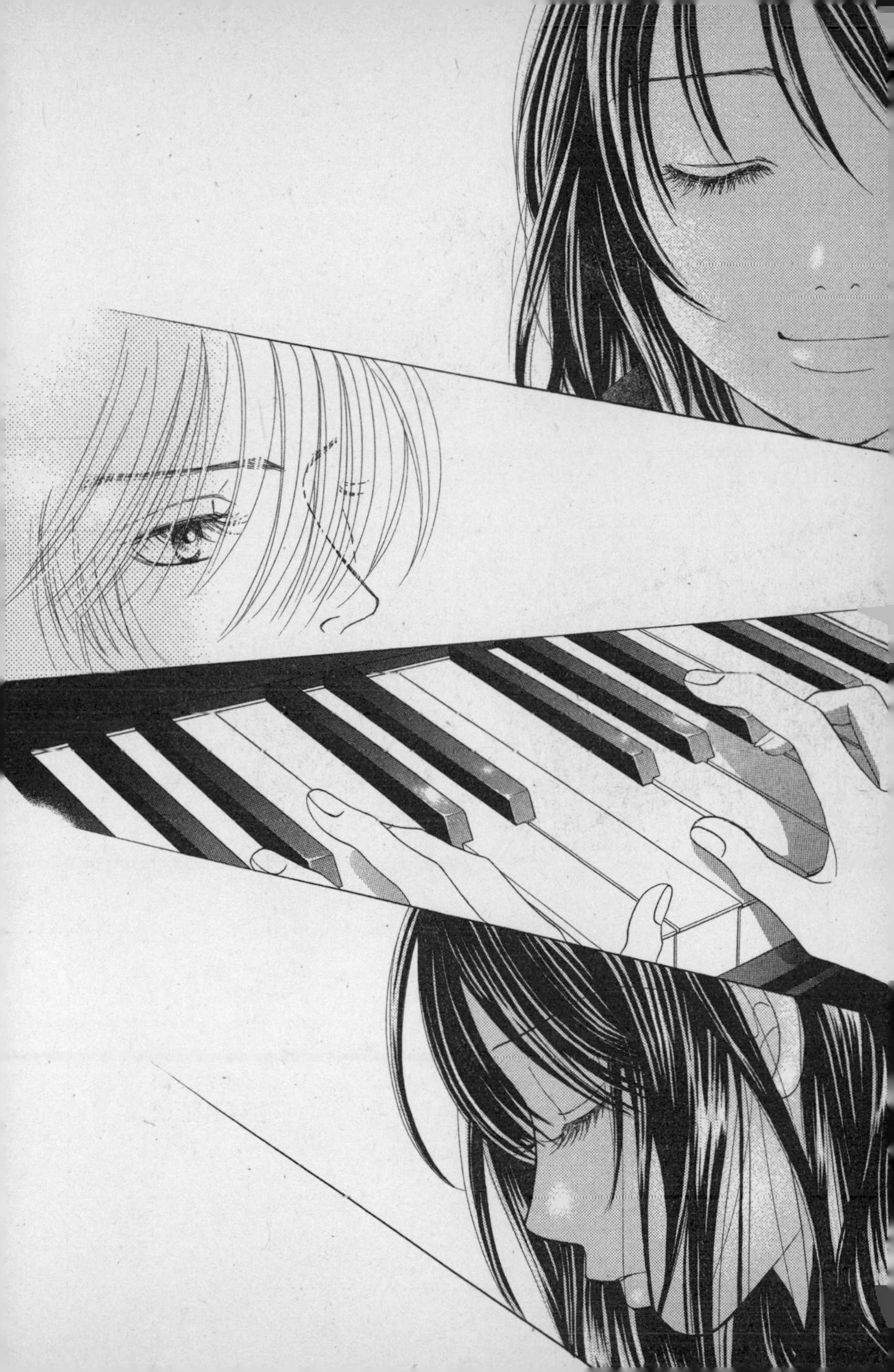

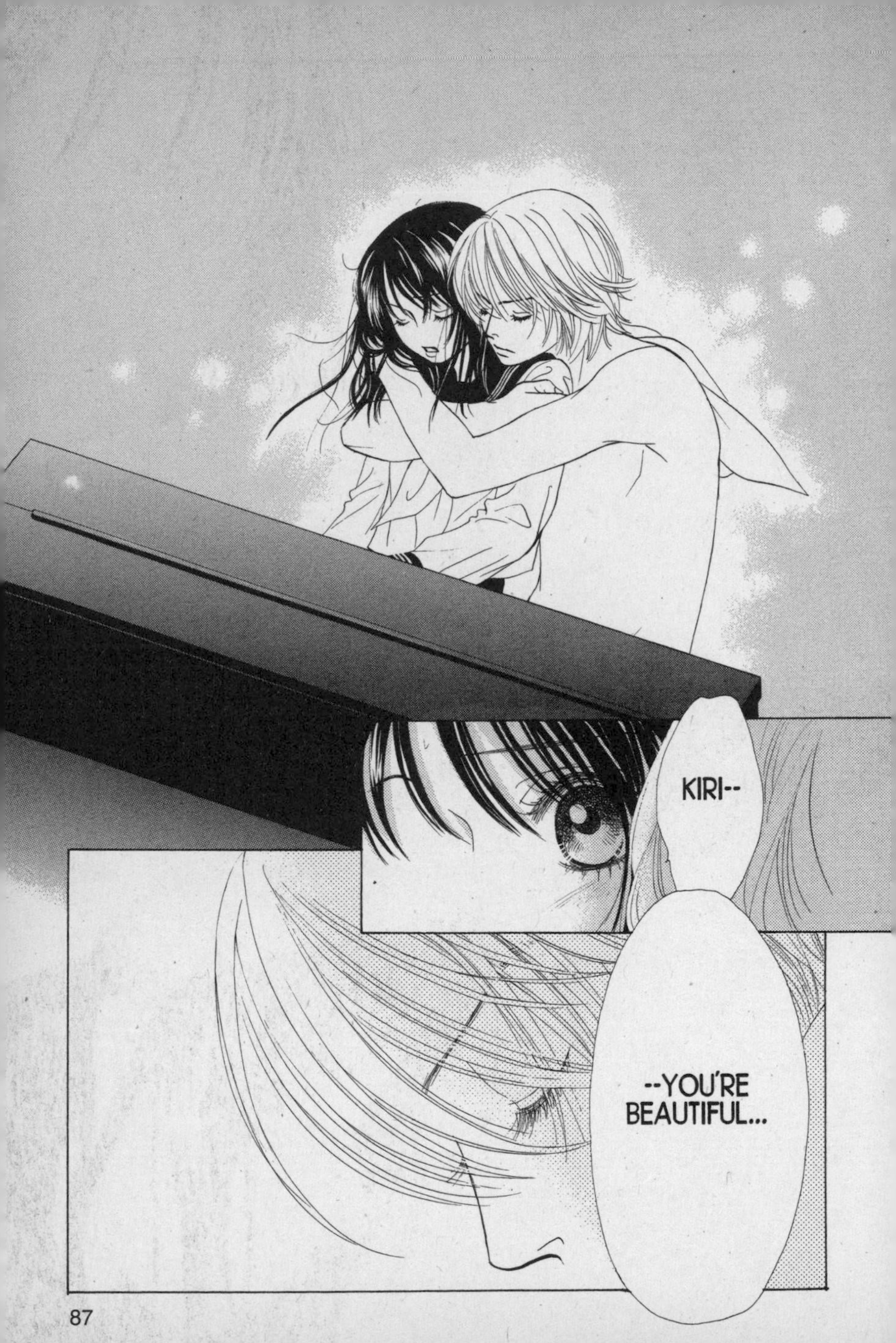
KIRI--
--YOU'RE BEAUTIFUL...

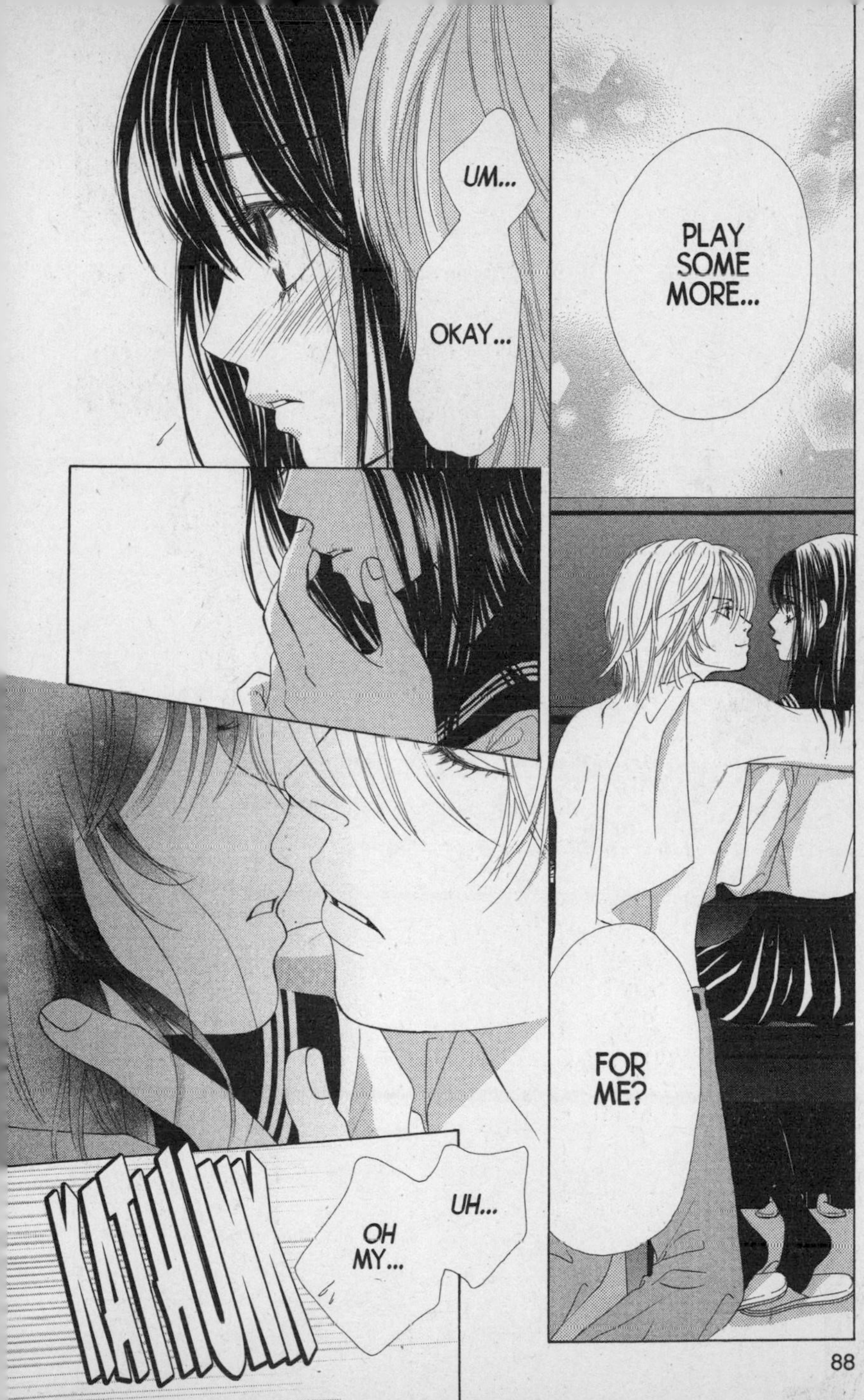
PLAY SOME MORE...
FOR ME?
UM...
OKAY...
KATHUNK
UH...
OH MY...

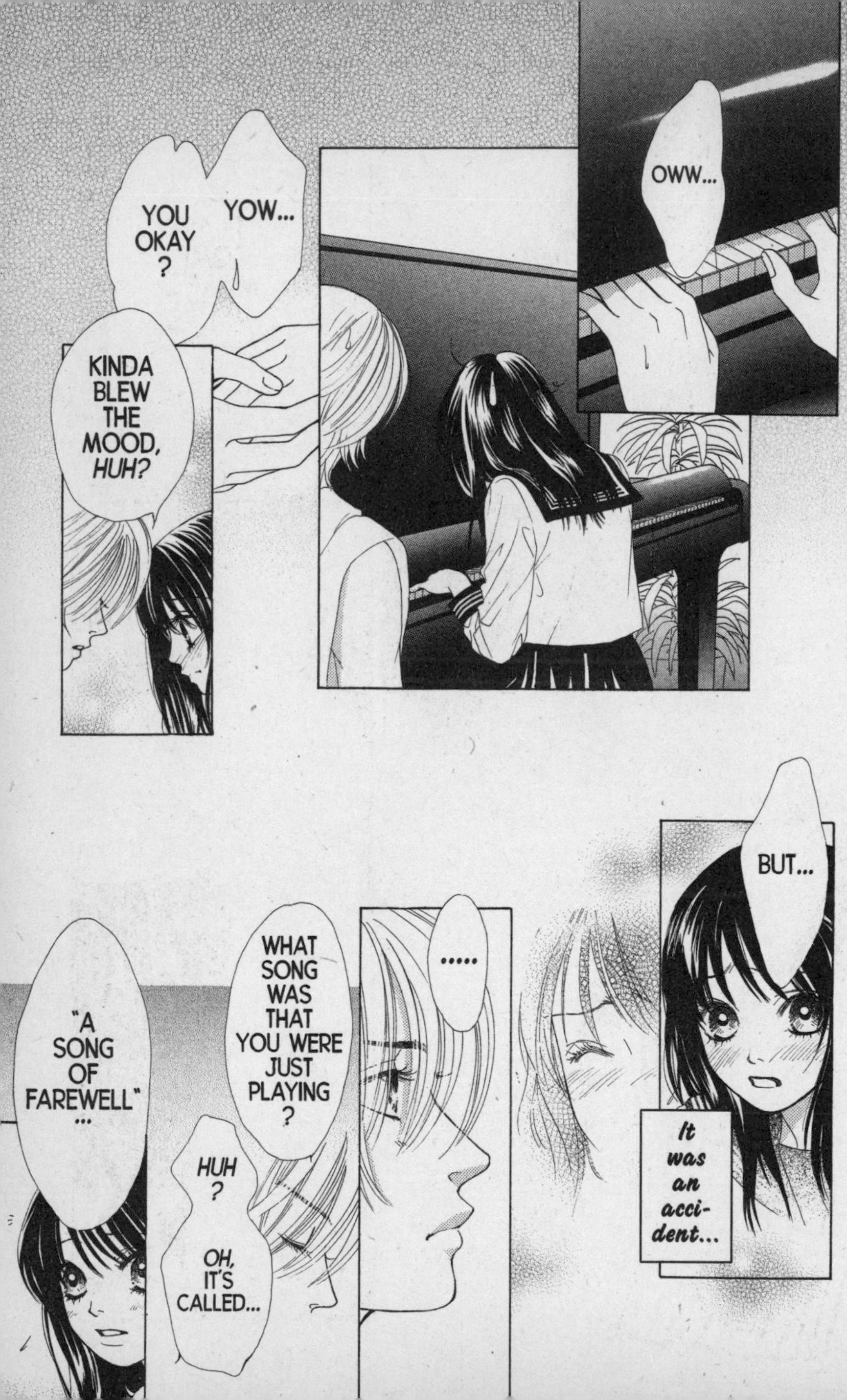
OWW...
YOW...
YOU OKAY?
KINDA BLEW THE MOOD, *HUH?*
BUT...
It was an accident...
......
WHAT SONG WAS THAT YOU WERE JUST PLAYING?
HUH?
OH, IT'S CALLED...
"A SONG OF FAREWELL"...

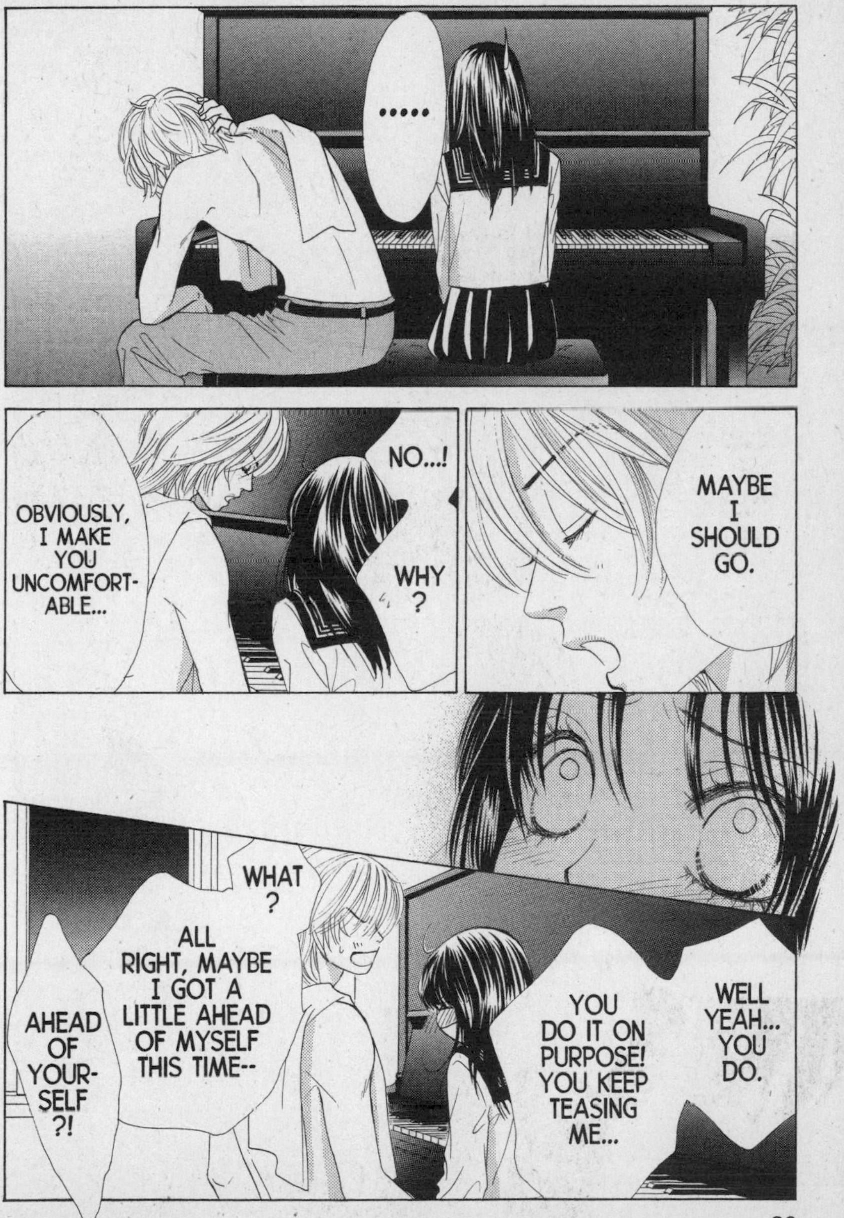
......
MAYBE I SHOULD GO.
NO...!
WHY?
OBVIOUSLY, I MAKE YOU UNCOMFORTABLE...
WELL YEAH... YOU DO.
YOU DO IT ON PURPOSE! YOU KEEP TEASING ME...
WHAT?
ALL RIGHT, MAYBE I GOT A LITTLE AHEAD OF MYSELF THIS TIME--
AHEAD OF YOURSELF?!

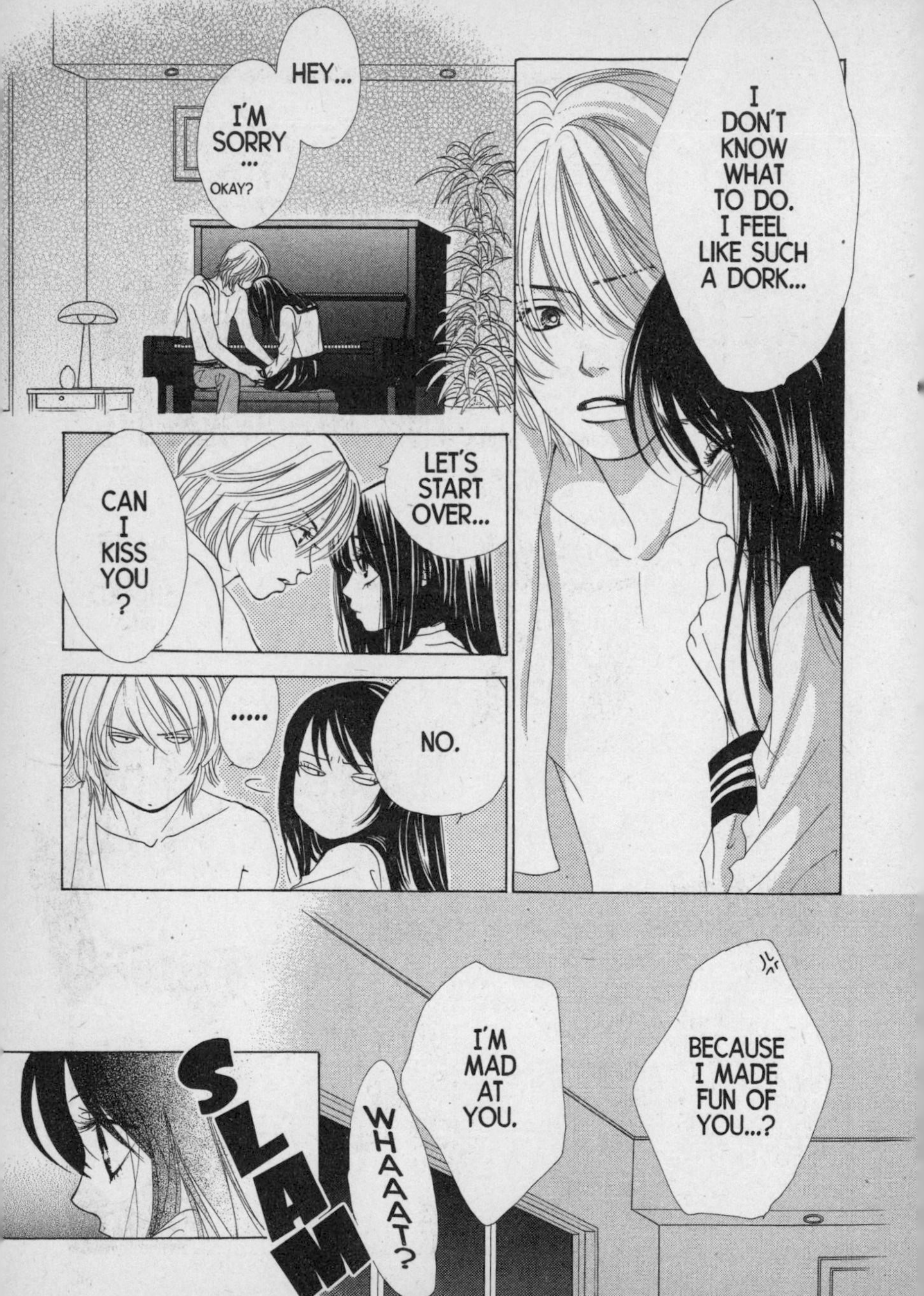
I DON'T KNOW WHAT TO DO. I FEEL LIKE SUCH A DORK...
HEY...
I'M SORRY...
OKAY?
LET'S START OVER...
CAN I KISS YOU?
NO.
.....
BECAUSE I MADE FUN OF YOU...?
I'M MAD AT YOU.
WHAAAT?
SLAM

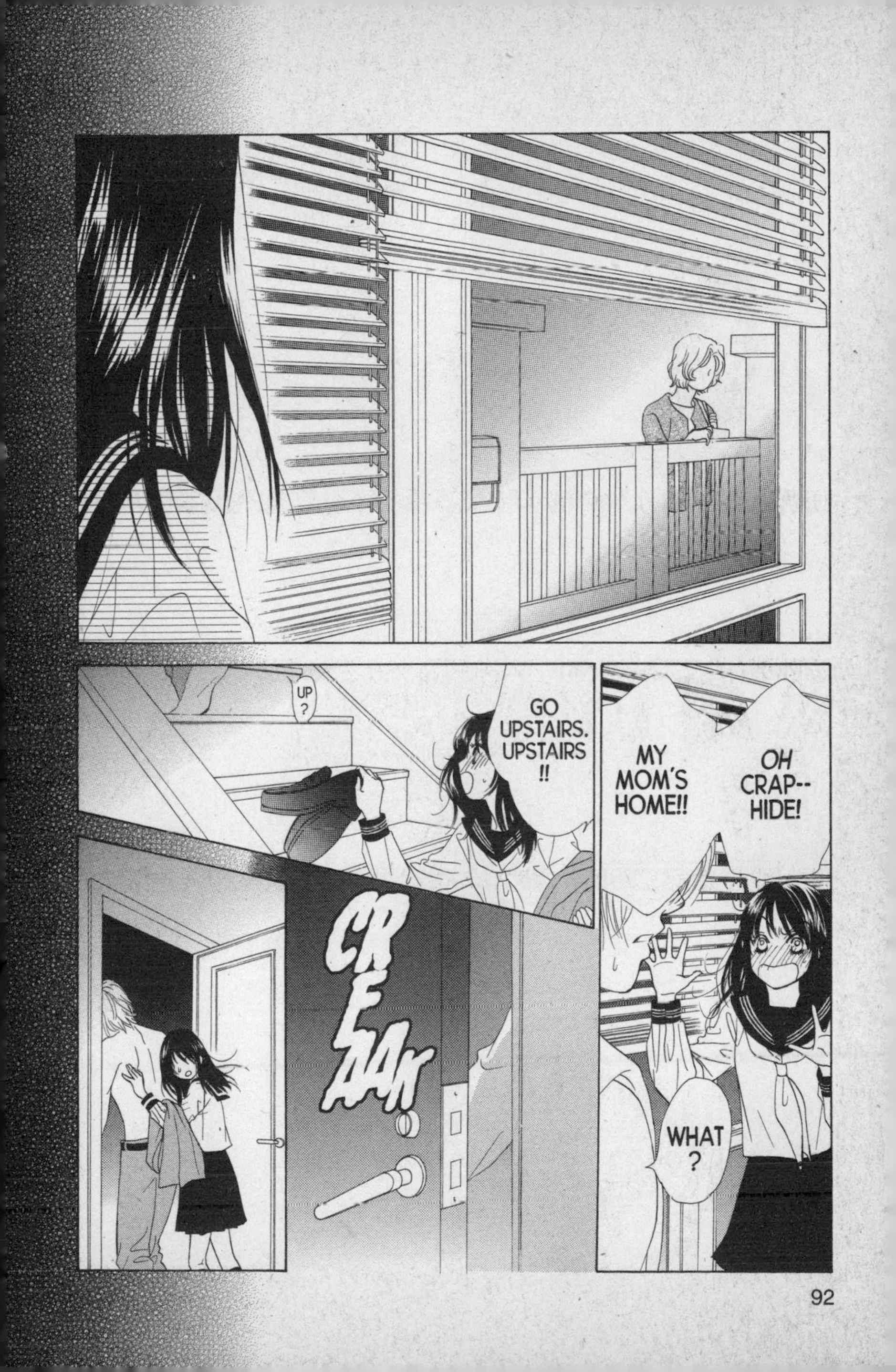
OH CRAP-- HIDE!
MY MOM'S HOME!!
WHAT ?
GO UPSTAIRS. UPSTAIRS !!
UP ?
CREAAK!

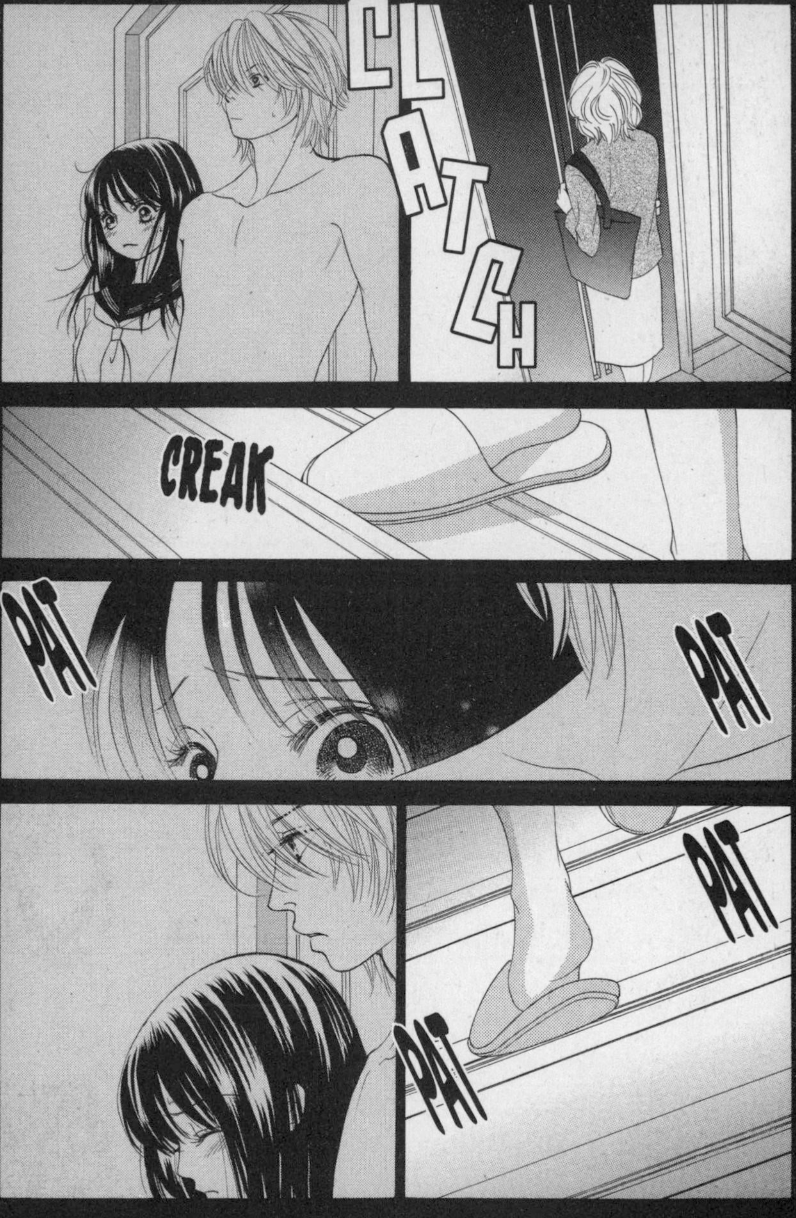
CLATCH
CREAK
PAT
PAT
PAT
PAT

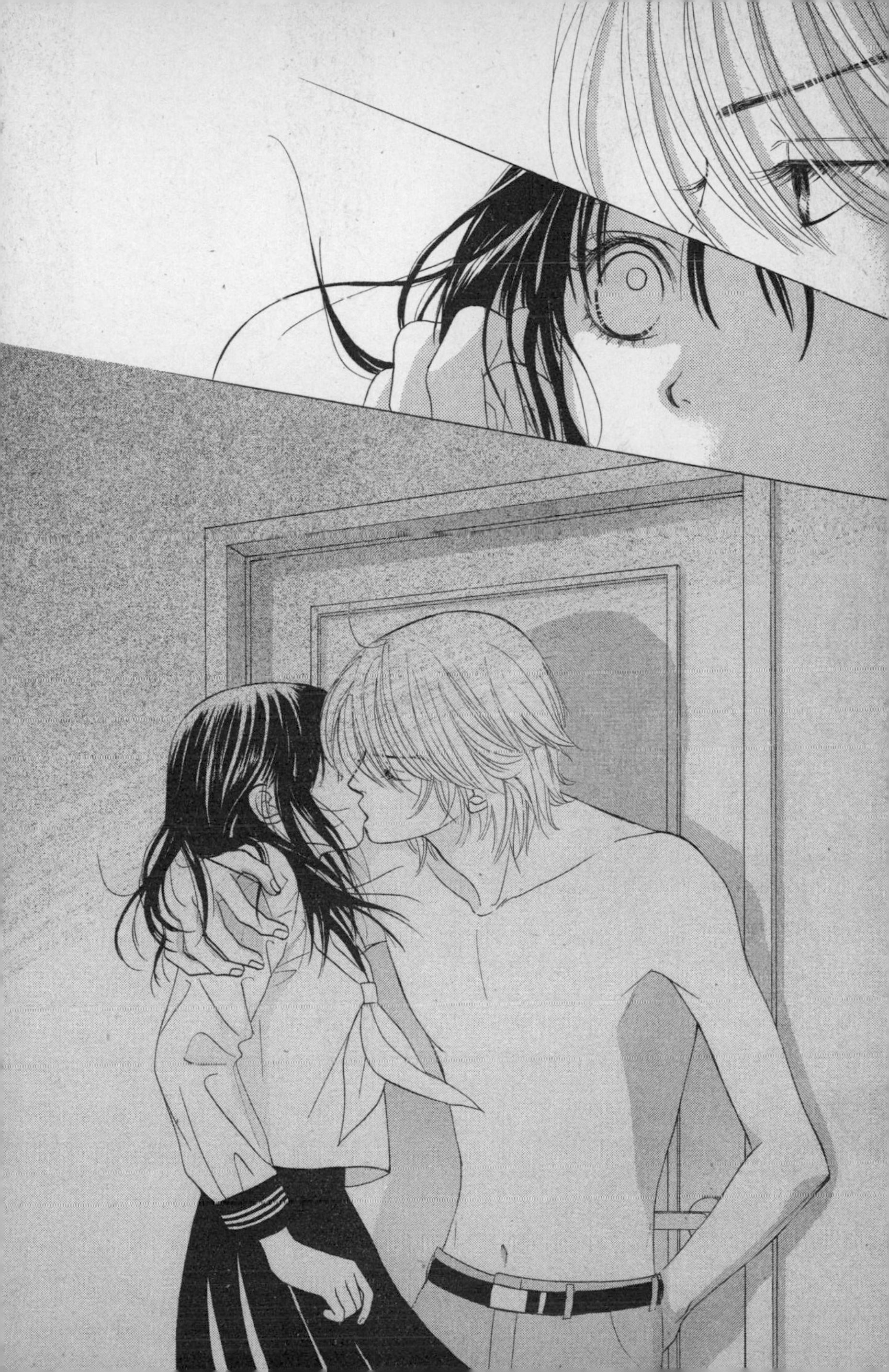

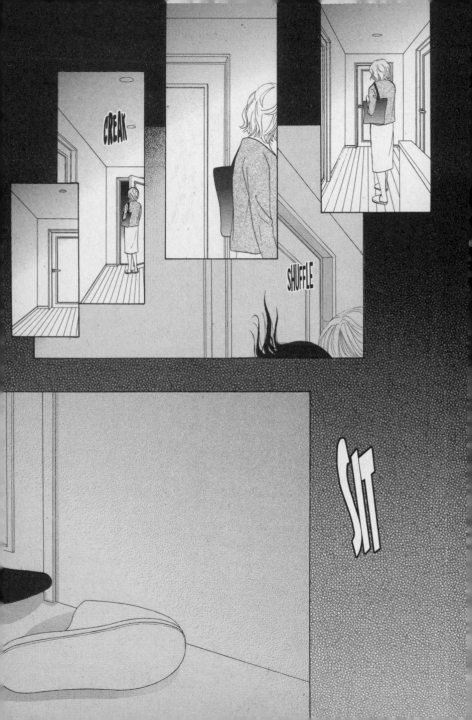

CREAK

SHUFFLE

SLT

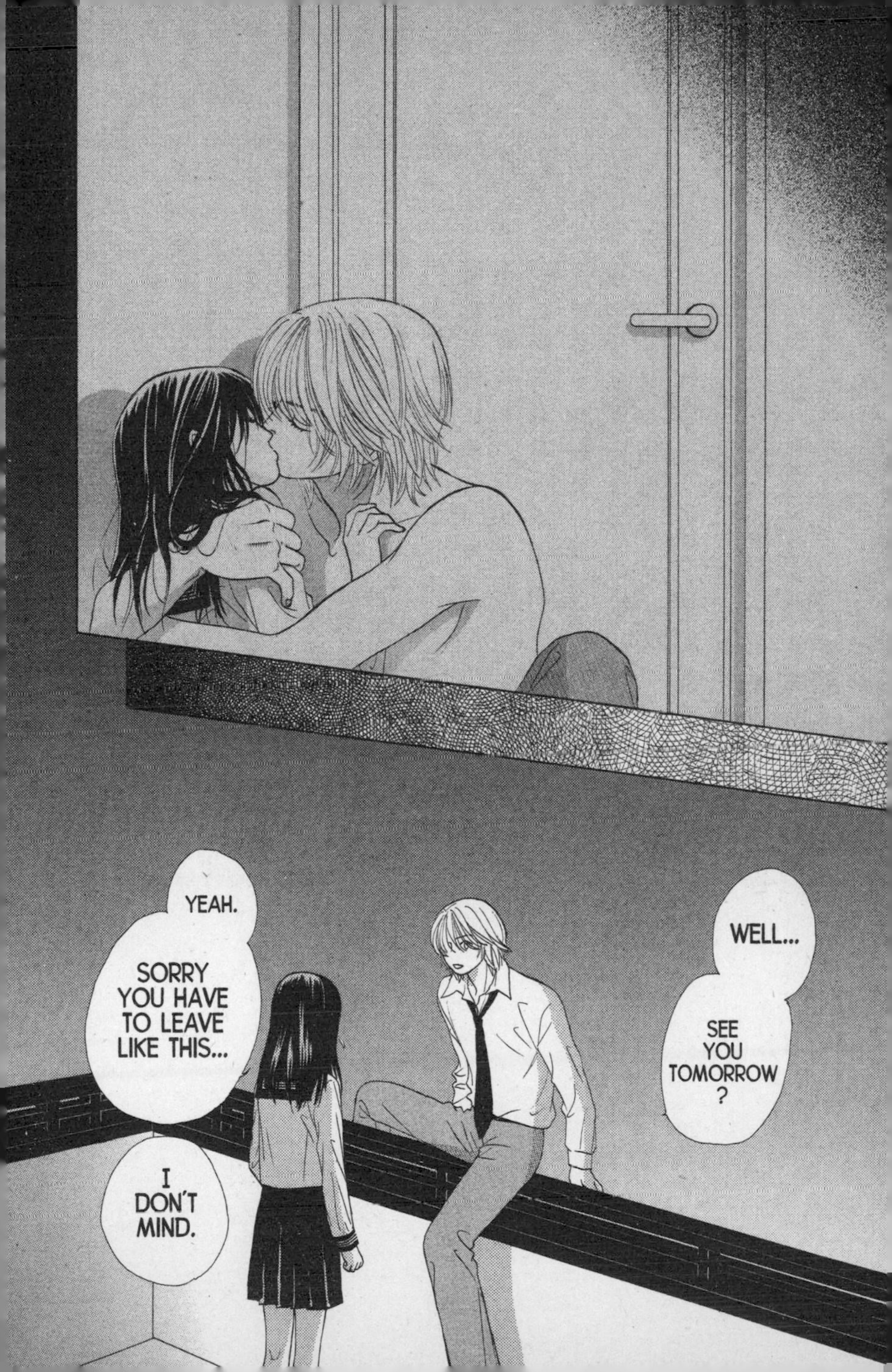
WELL...
SEE YOU TOMORROW?
YEAH.
SORRY YOU HAVE TO LEAVE LIKE THIS...
I DON'T MIND.

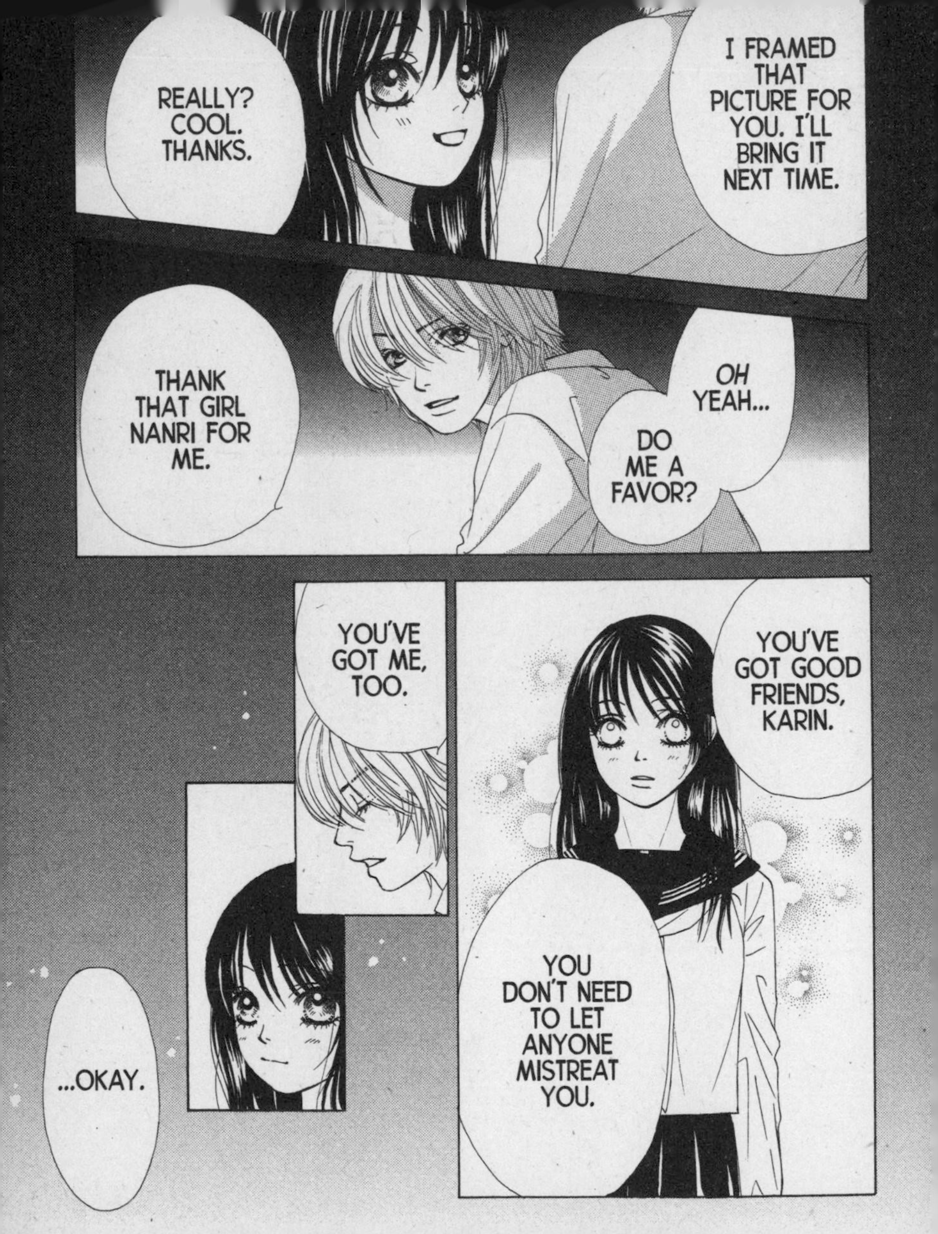
I FRAMED THAT PICTURE FOR YOU. I'LL BRING IT NEXT TIME.
REALLY? COOL. THANKS.
OH YEAH...
DO ME A FAVOR?
THANK THAT GIRL NANRI FOR ME.
YOU'VE GOT GOOD FRIENDS, KARIN.
YOU DON'T NEED TO LET ANYONE MISTREAT YOU.
YOU'VE GOT ME, TOO.
...OKAY.

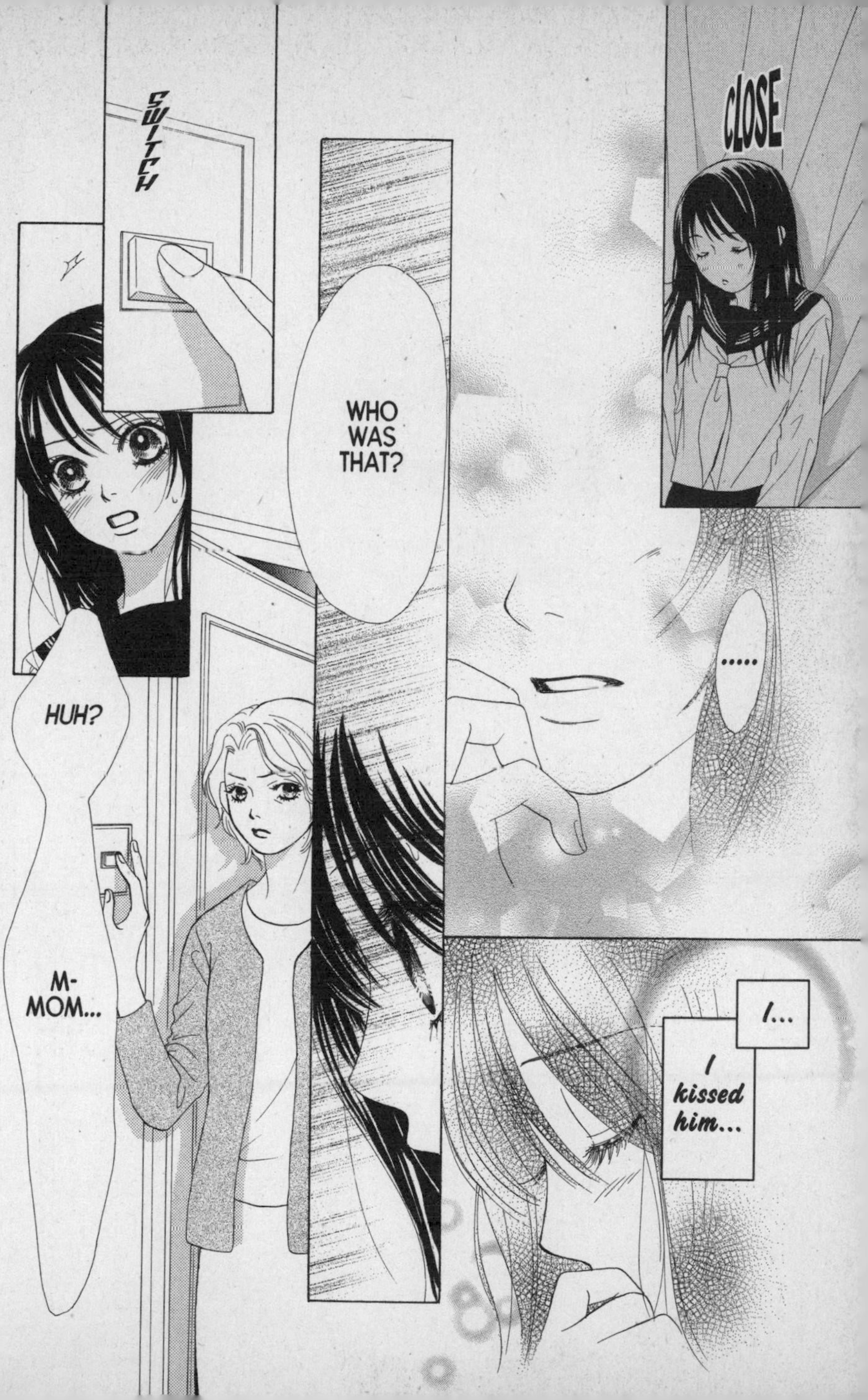
CLOSE
.....
I...
I kissed him...
WHO WAS THAT?
SWITCH
HUH?
M-MOM...

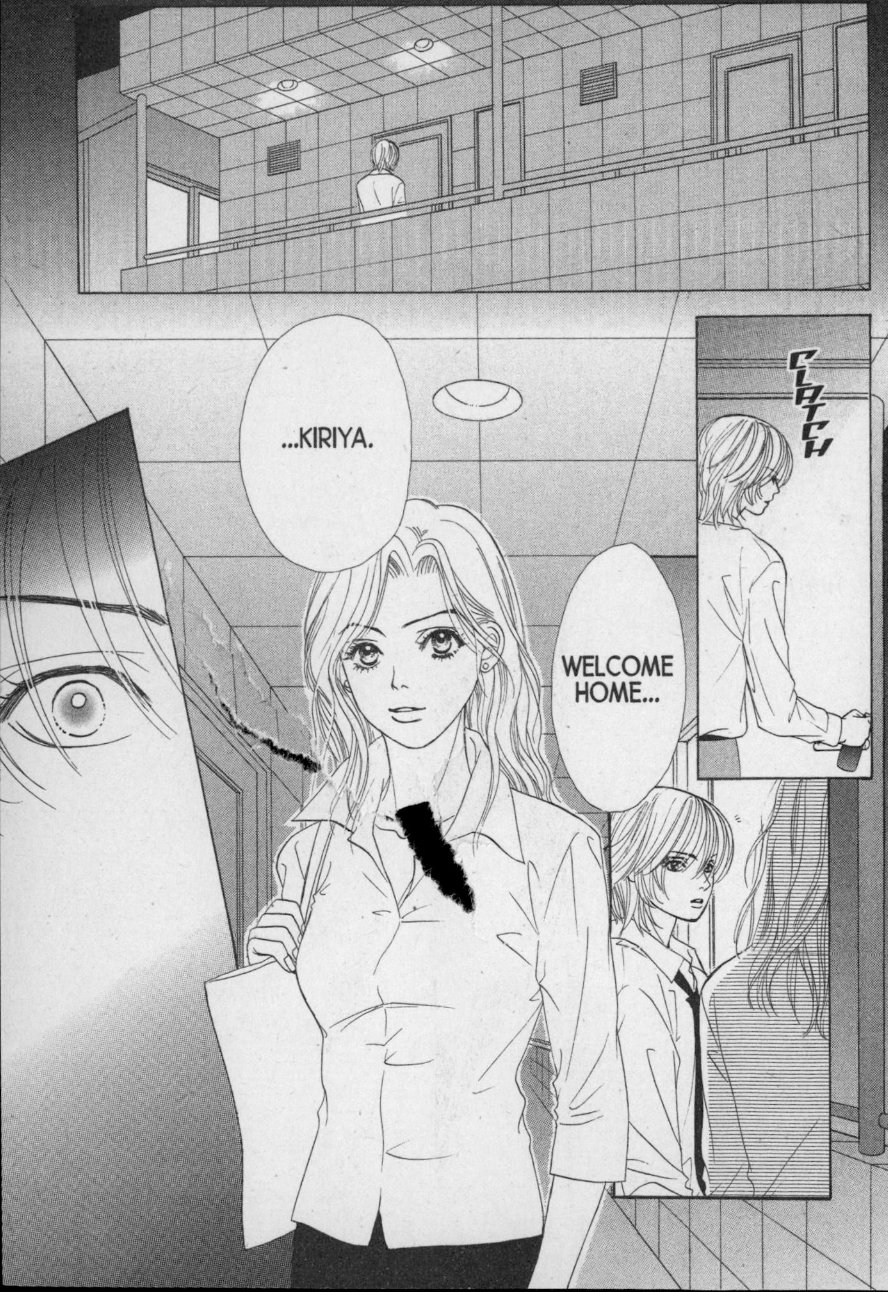
CLATCH
...KIRIYA.
WELCOME HOME...

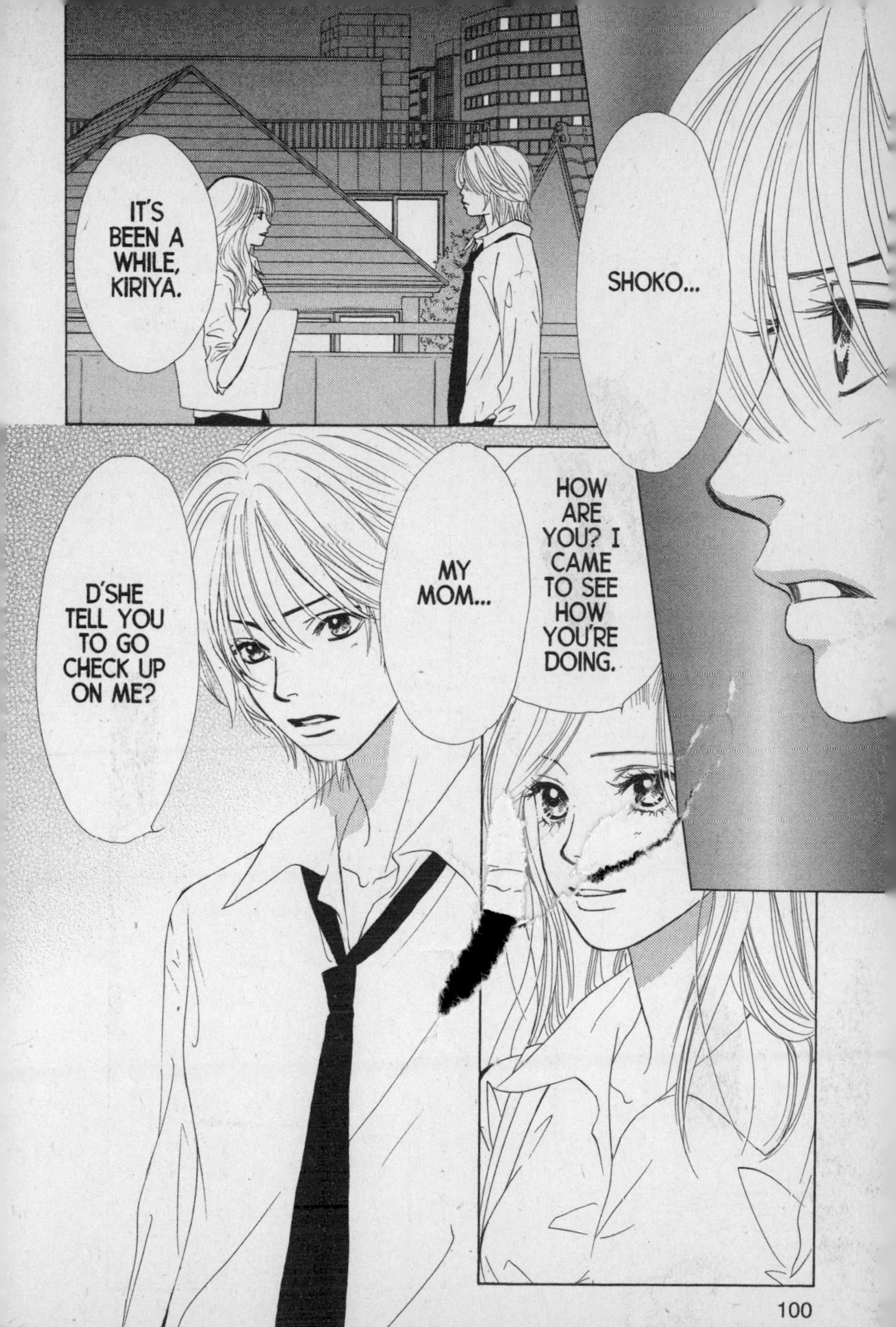
SHOKO...
IT'S BEEN A WHILE, KIRIYA.
HOW ARE YOU? I CAME TO SEE HOW YOU'RE DOING.
MY MOM...
D'SHE TELL YOU TO GO CHECK UP ON ME?

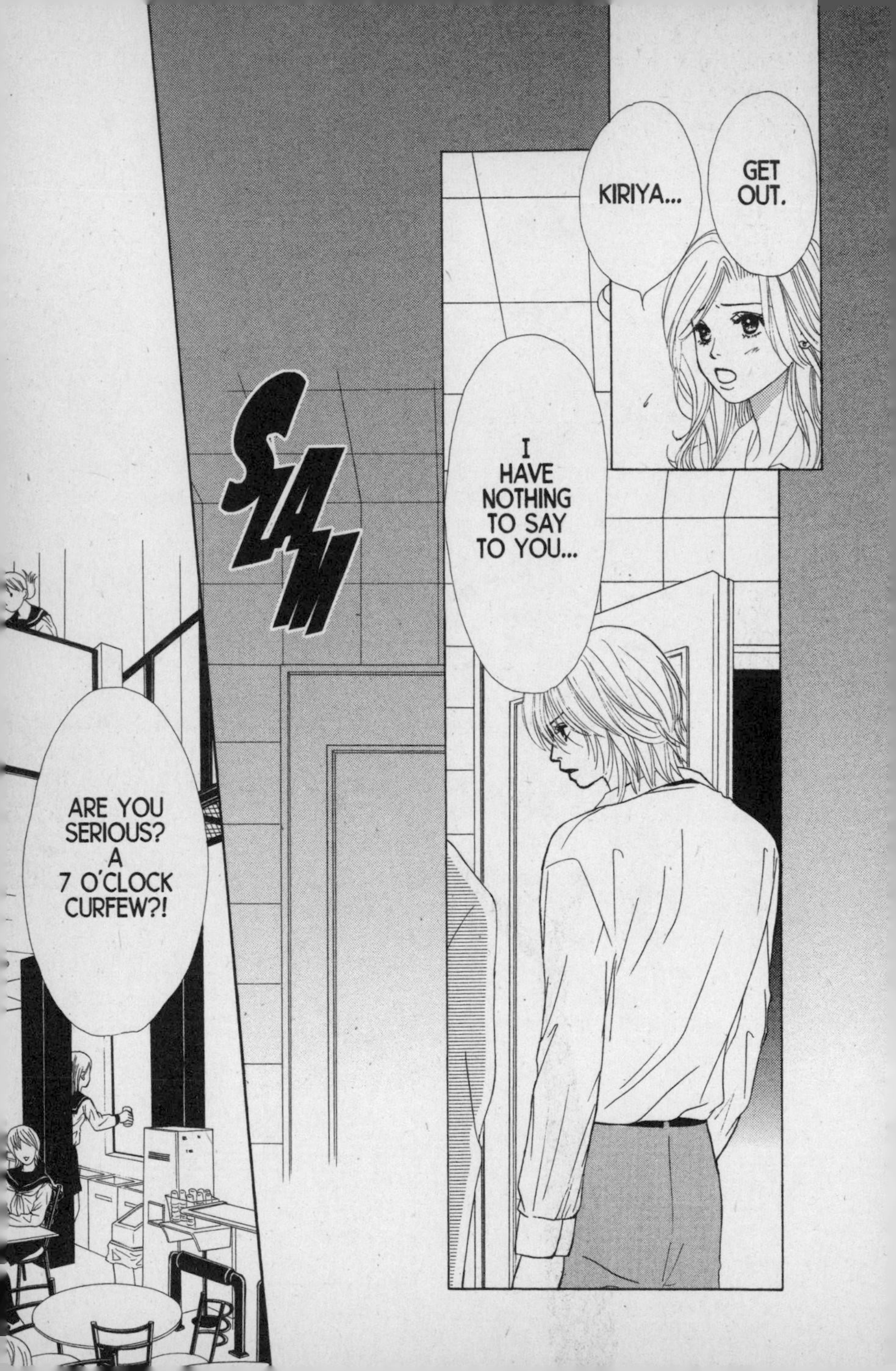
GET OUT.
KIRIYA...
I HAVE NOTHING TO SAY TO YOU...
SLAM
ARE YOU SERIOUS? A 7 O'CLOCK CURFEW?!

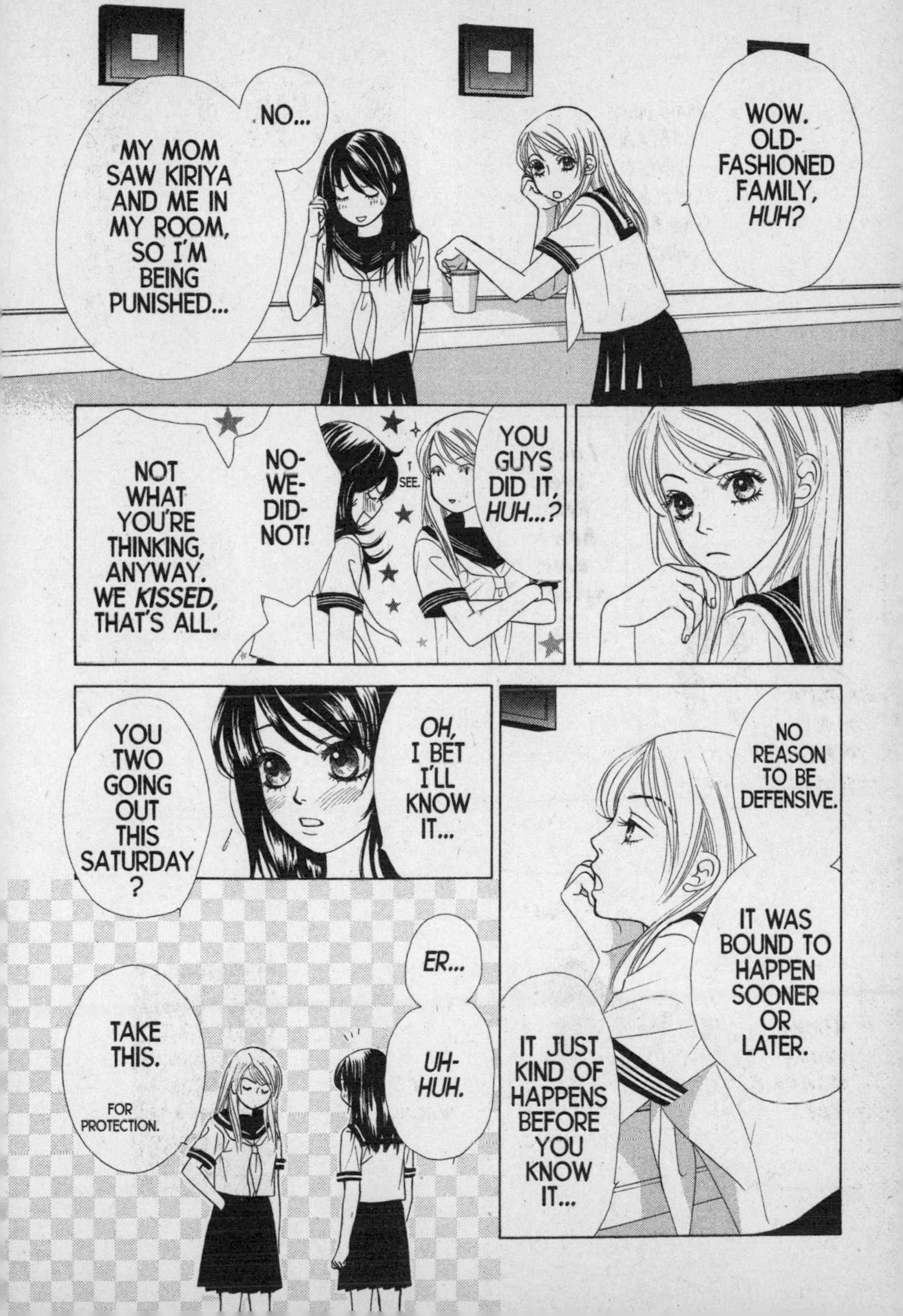
WOW. OLD-FASHIONED FAMILY, HUH?
NO...
MY MOM SAW KIRIYA AND ME IN MY ROOM, SO I'M BEING PUNISHED...
YOU GUYS DID IT, HUH...?
I SEE.
NO-WE-DID-NOT!
NOT WHAT YOU'RE THINKING, ANYWAY. WE KISSED, THAT'S ALL.
NO REASON TO BE DEFENSIVE.
IT WAS BOUND TO HAPPEN SOONER OR LATER.
IT JUST KIND OF HAPPENS BEFORE YOU KNOW IT...
OH, I BET I'LL KNOW IT...
YOU TWO GOING OUT THIS SATURDAY?
ER...
UH-HUH.
TAKE THIS.
FOR PROTECTION.

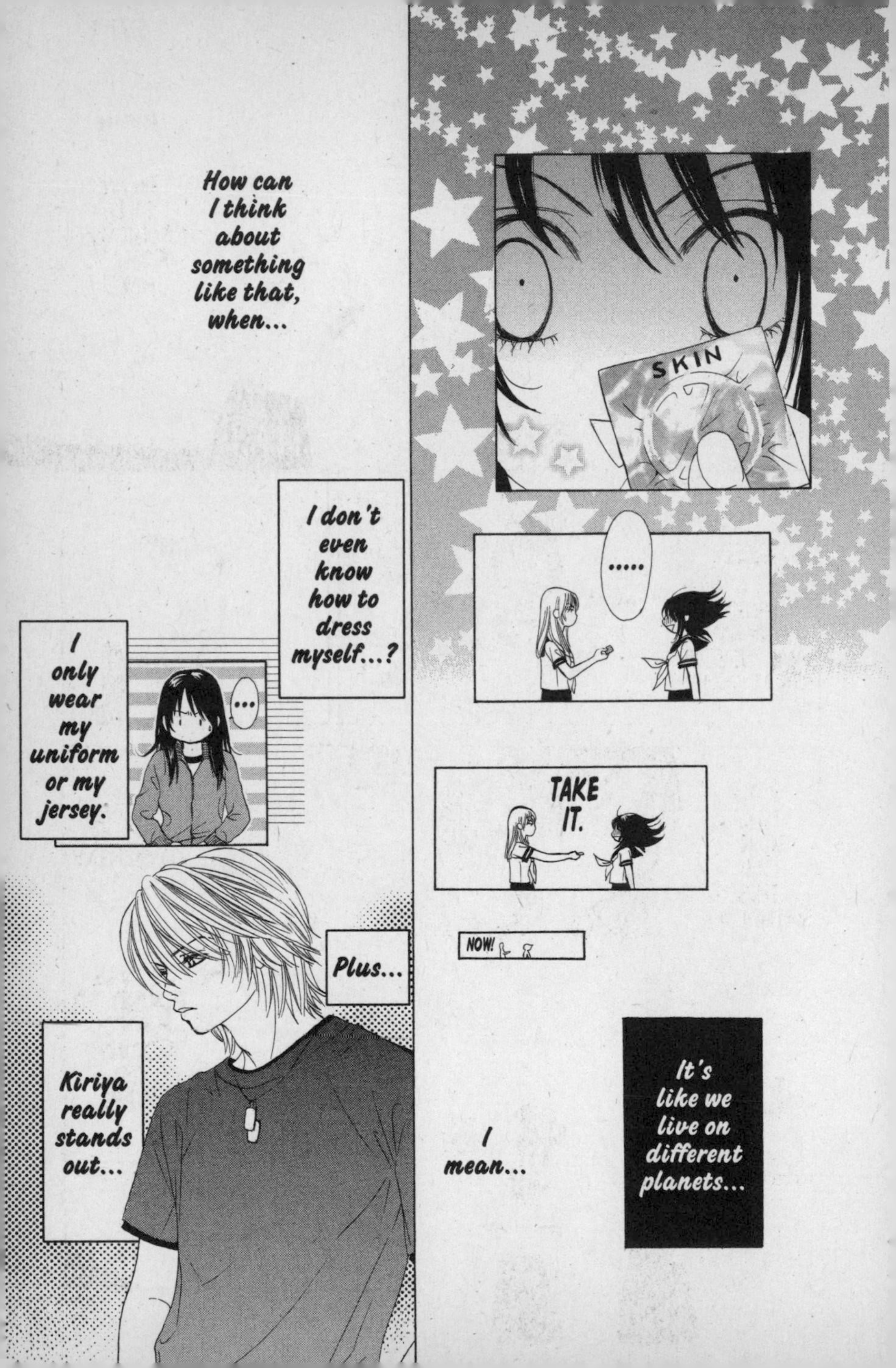
SKIN
.....
TAKE IT.
NOW!
I mean...
It's like we live on different planets...
How can I think about something like that, when...
I don't even know how to dress myself...?
I only wear my uniform or my jersey.
...
Plus...
Kiriya really stands out...

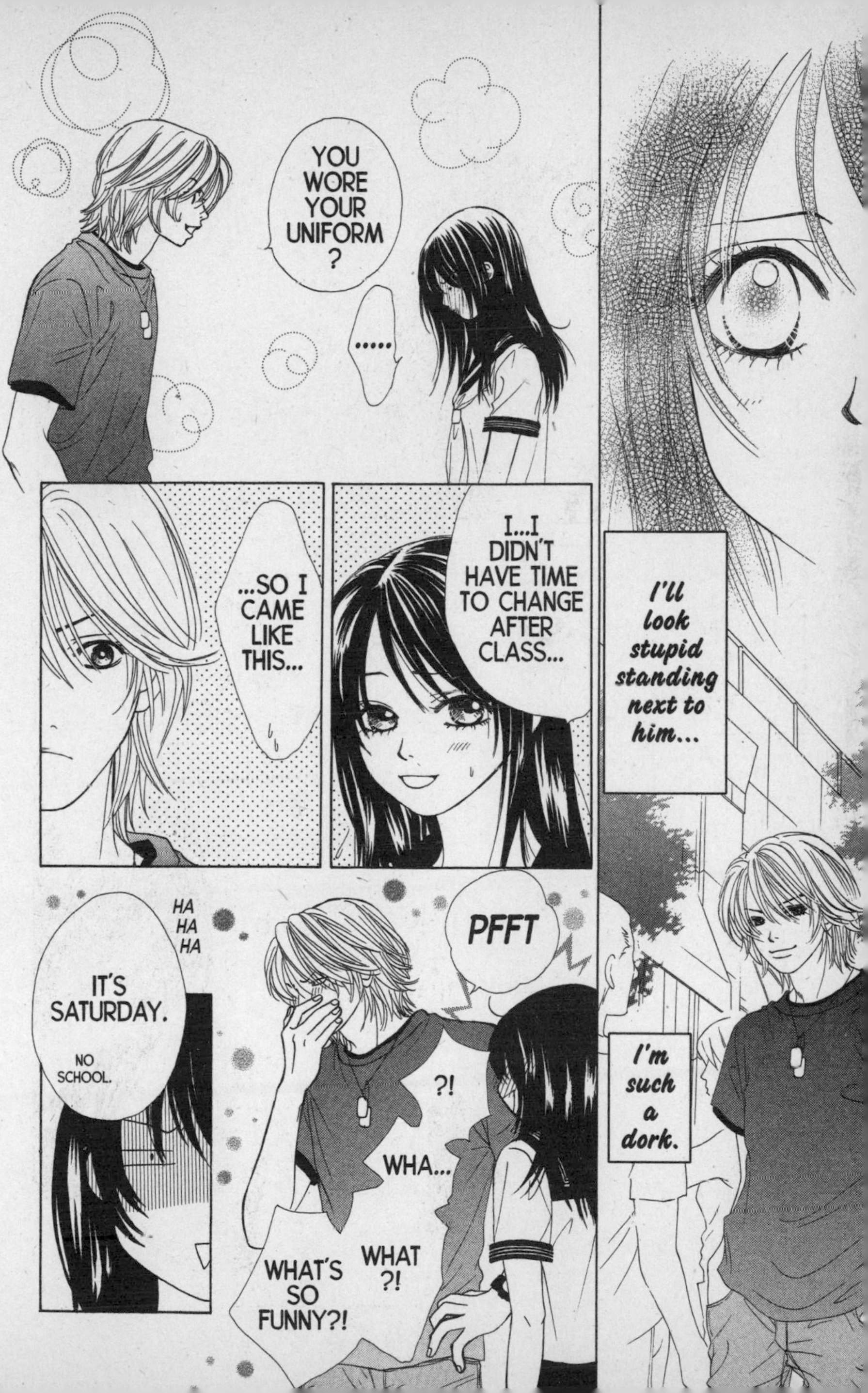
I'll look stupid standing next to him...
I'm such a dork.
YOU WORE YOUR UNIFORM?
.....
I...I DIDN'T HAVE TIME TO CHANGE AFTER CLASS...
...SO I CAME LIKE THIS...
PFFT
?!
WHA...
WHAT?!
WHAT'S SO FUNNY?!
HA HA HA
IT'S SATURDAY.
NO SCHOOL.

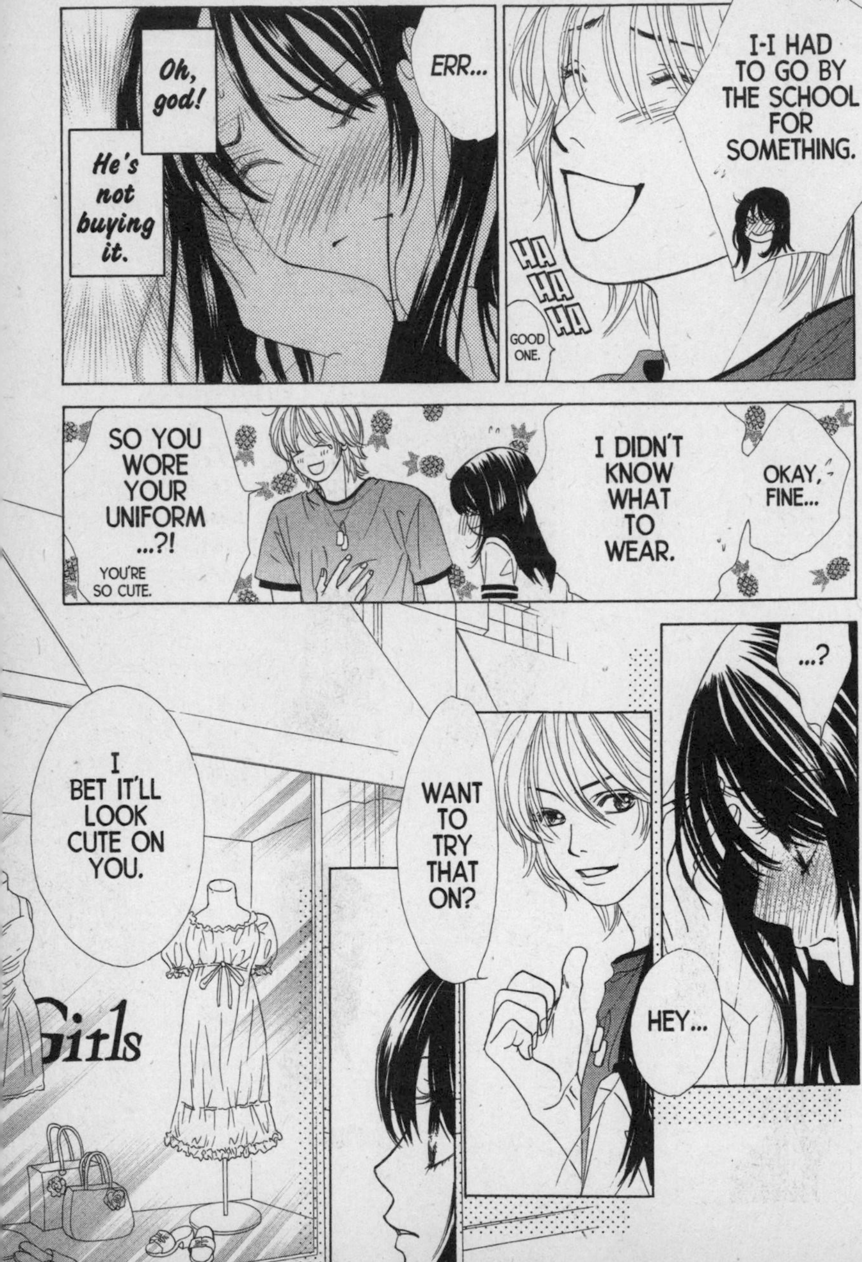
I-I HAD TO GO BY THE SCHOOL FOR SOMETHING.
HA HA HA
GOOD ONE.
ERR...
Oh, god!
He's not buying it.
OKAY, FINE...
I DIDN'T KNOW WHAT TO WEAR.
SO YOU WORE YOUR UNIFORM ...?!
YOU'RE SO CUTE.
...?
HEY...
WANT TO TRY THAT ON?
I BET IT'LL LOOK CUTE ON YOU.
Girls

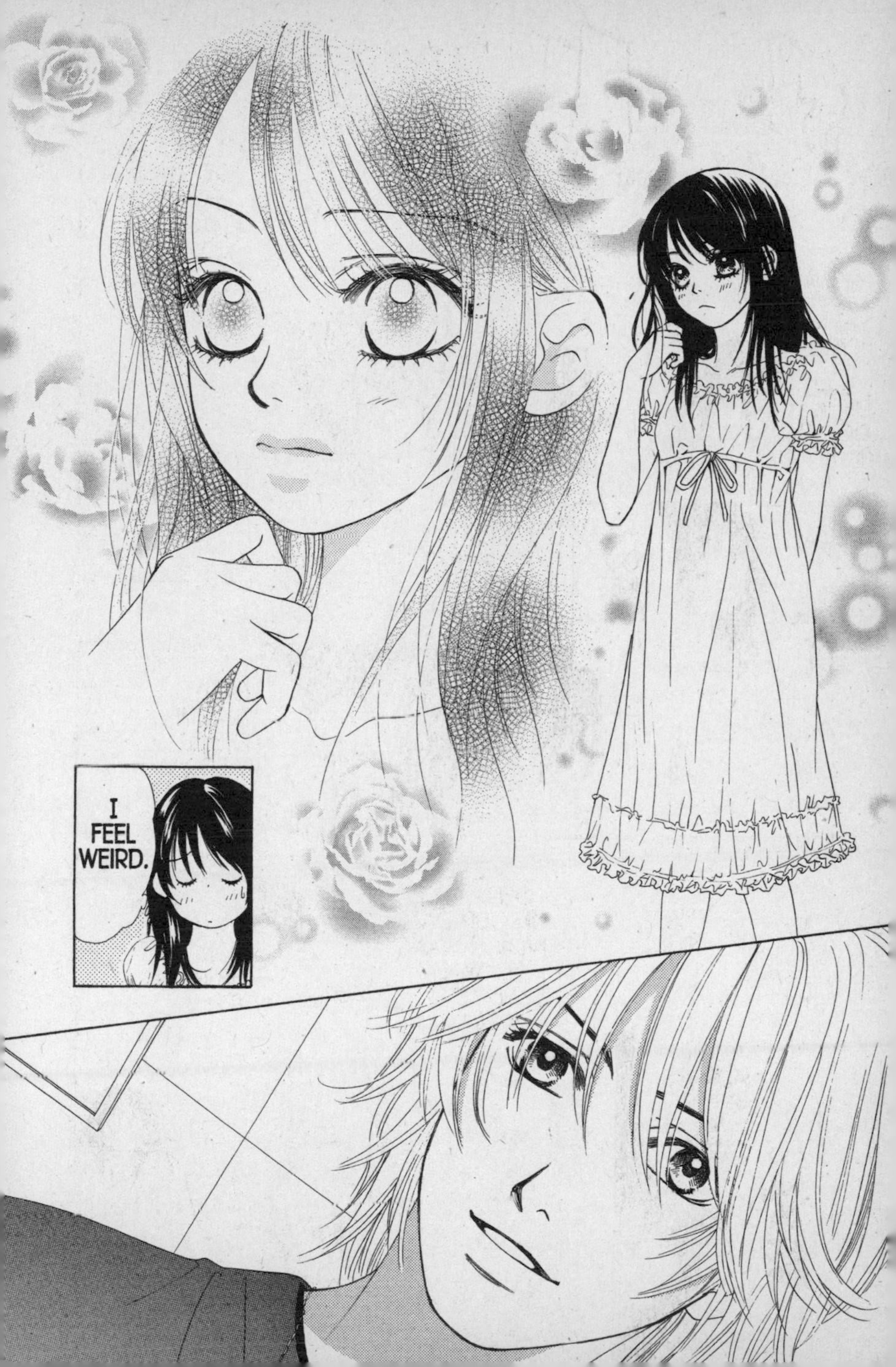
I FEEL WEIRD.

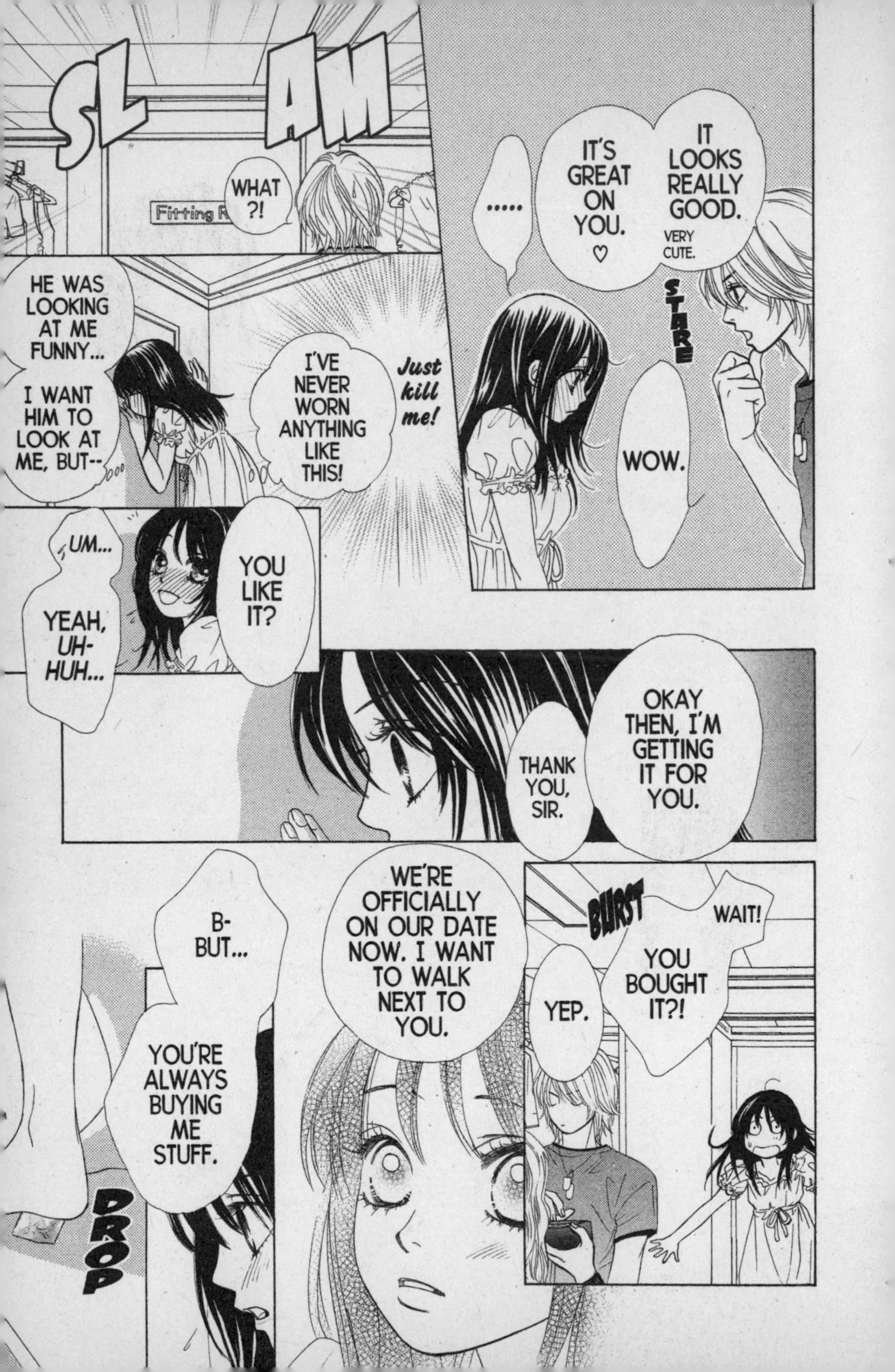
IT LOOKS REALLY GOOD.
VERY CUTE.
IT'S GREAT ON YOU. ♡
.....
STARE
WOW.
SL AM
WHAT?!
Fitting R
I'VE NEVER WORN ANYTHING LIKE THIS!
Just kill me!
HE WAS LOOKING AT ME FUNNY...
I WANT HIM TO LOOK AT ME, BUT--
YOU LIKE IT?
UM...
YEAH, UH-HUH...
OKAY THEN, I'M GETTING IT FOR YOU.
THANK YOU, SIR.
BURST
WAIT!
YOU BOUGHT IT?!
YEP.
WE'RE OFFICIALLY ON OUR DATE NOW. I WANT TO WALK NEXT TO YOU.
B-BUT...
YOU'RE ALWAYS BUYING ME STUFF.
DROP

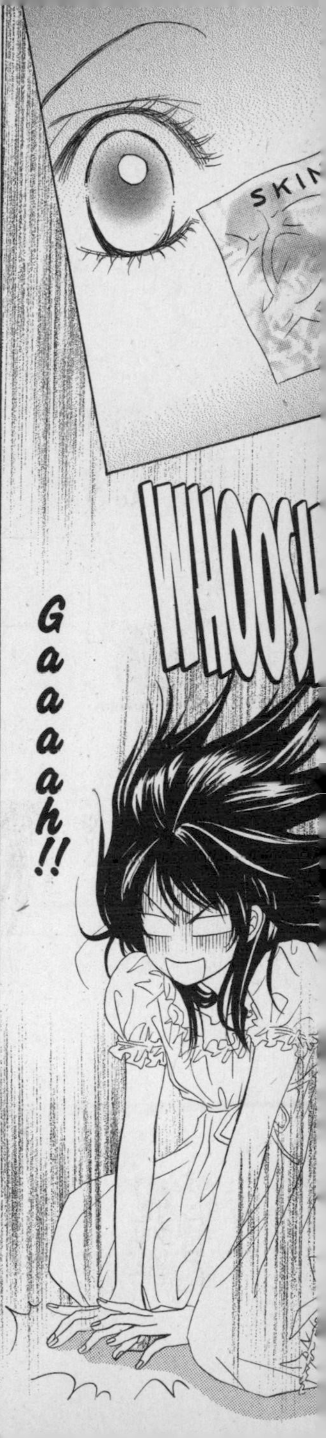
Gaaaaah!!

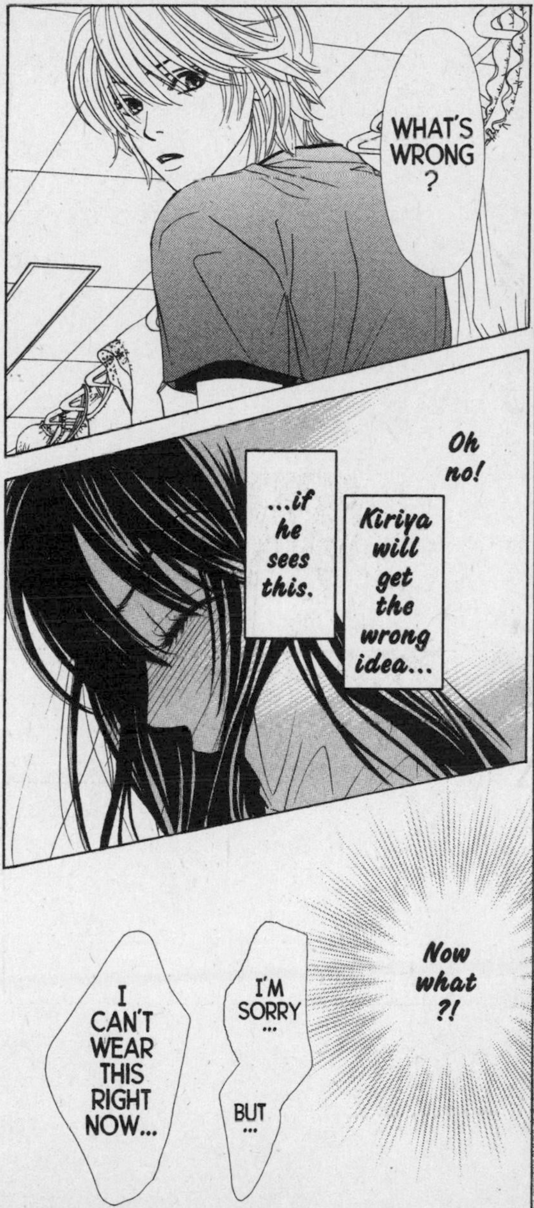
WHAT'S WRONG?
Oh no!
Kiriya will get the wrong idea...
...if he sees this.
Now what?!
I'M SORRY...
BUT...
I CAN'T WEAR THIS RIGHT NOW...

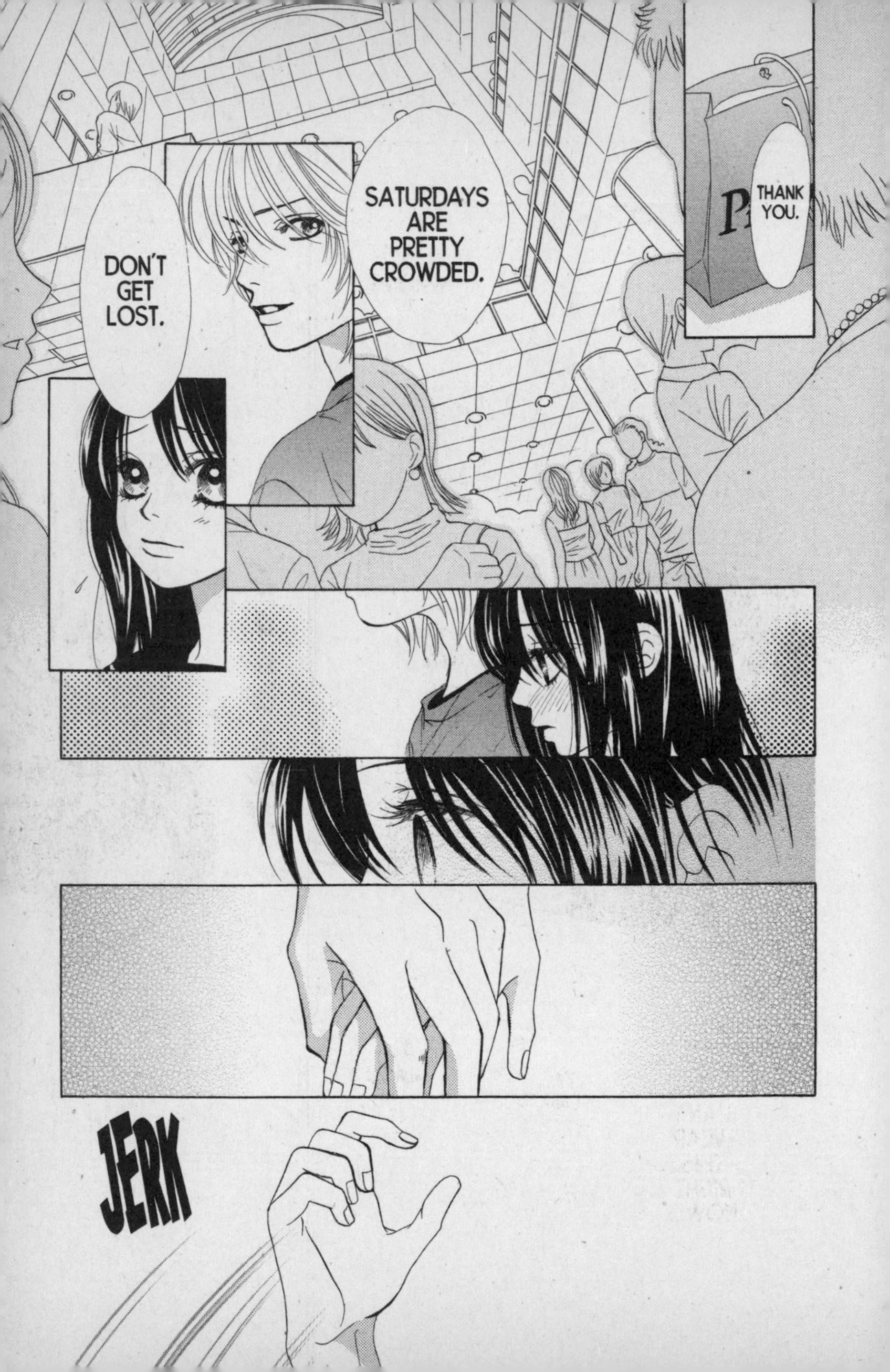
THANK YOU.
SATURDAYS ARE PRETTY CROWDED.
DON'T GET LOST.
JERK

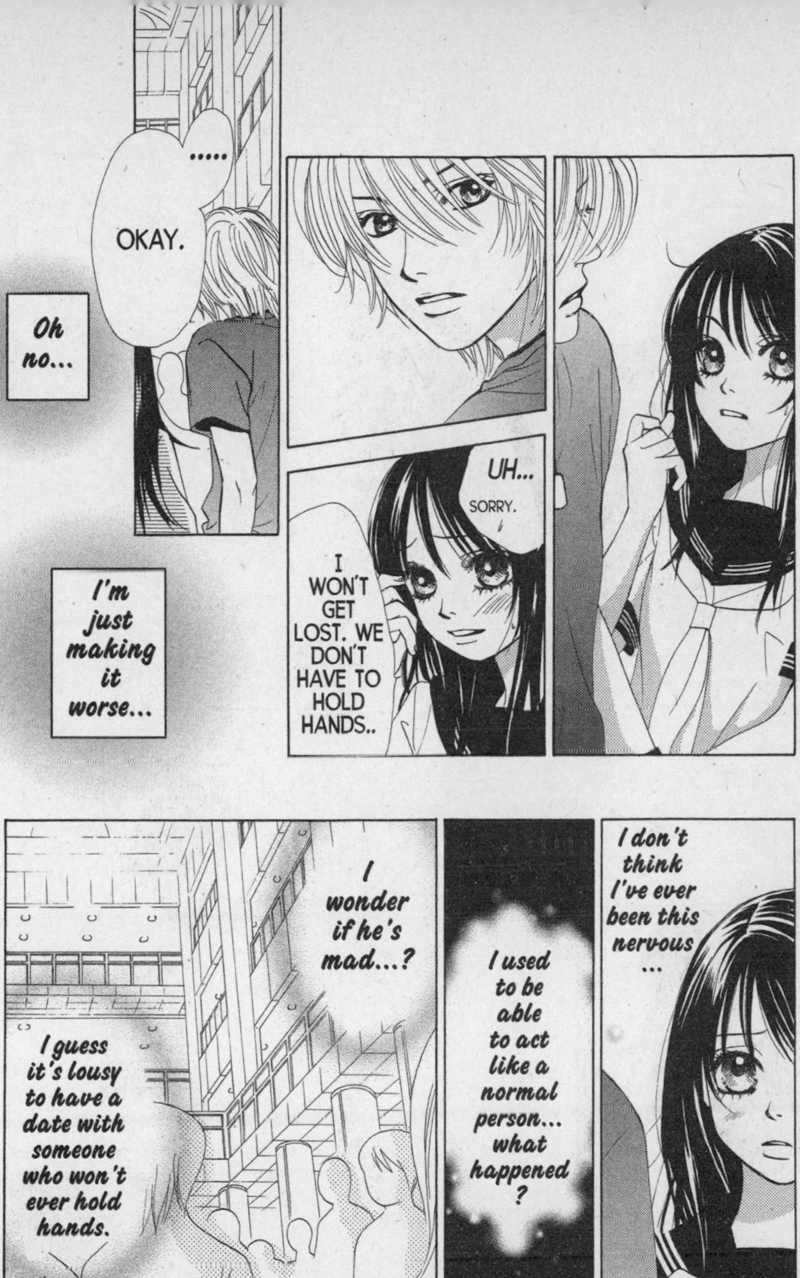
UH...
SORRY.
I WON'T GET LOST. WE DON'T HAVE TO HOLD HANDS..
.....
OKAY.
Oh no...
I'm just making it worse...
I don't think I've ever been this nervous ...
I used to be able to act like a normal person... what happened ?
I wonder if he's mad...?
I guess it's lousy to have a date with someone who won't ever hold hands.

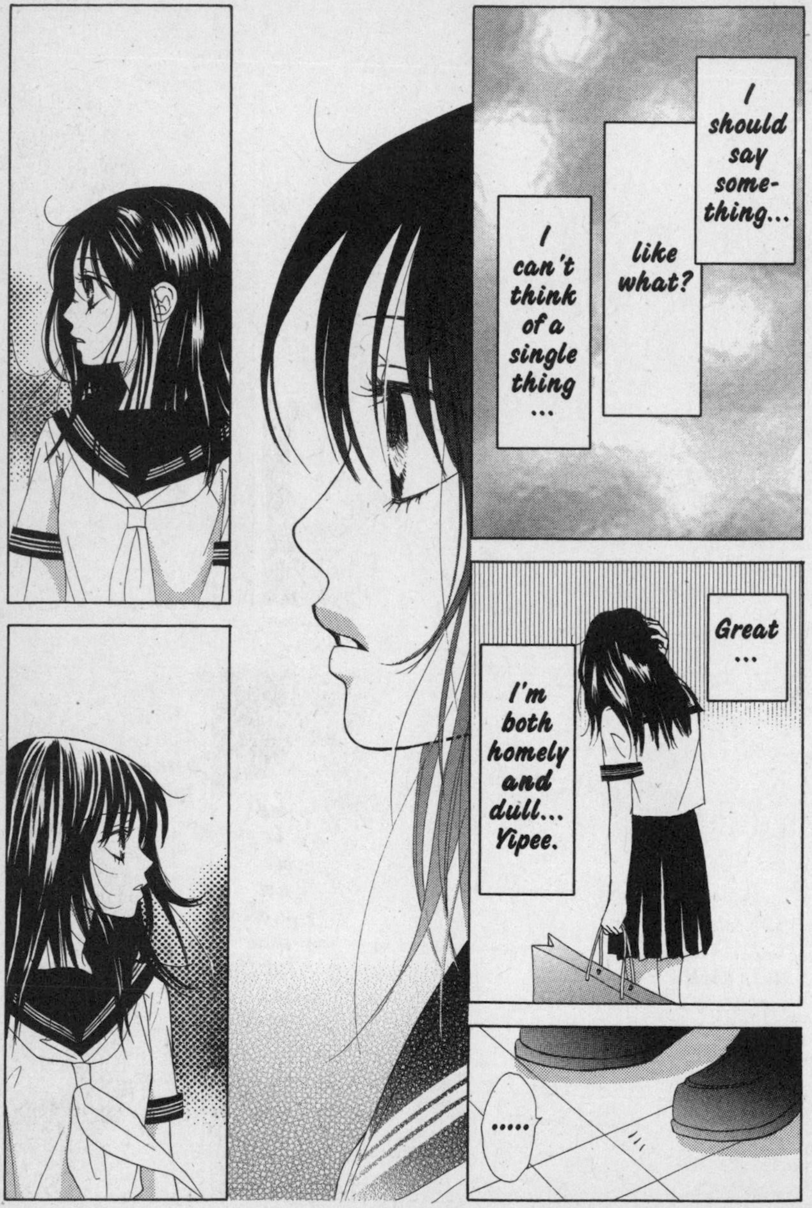
I should say some-thing...
like what?
I can't think of a single thing...
Great...
I'm both homely and dull... Yipee.
.....

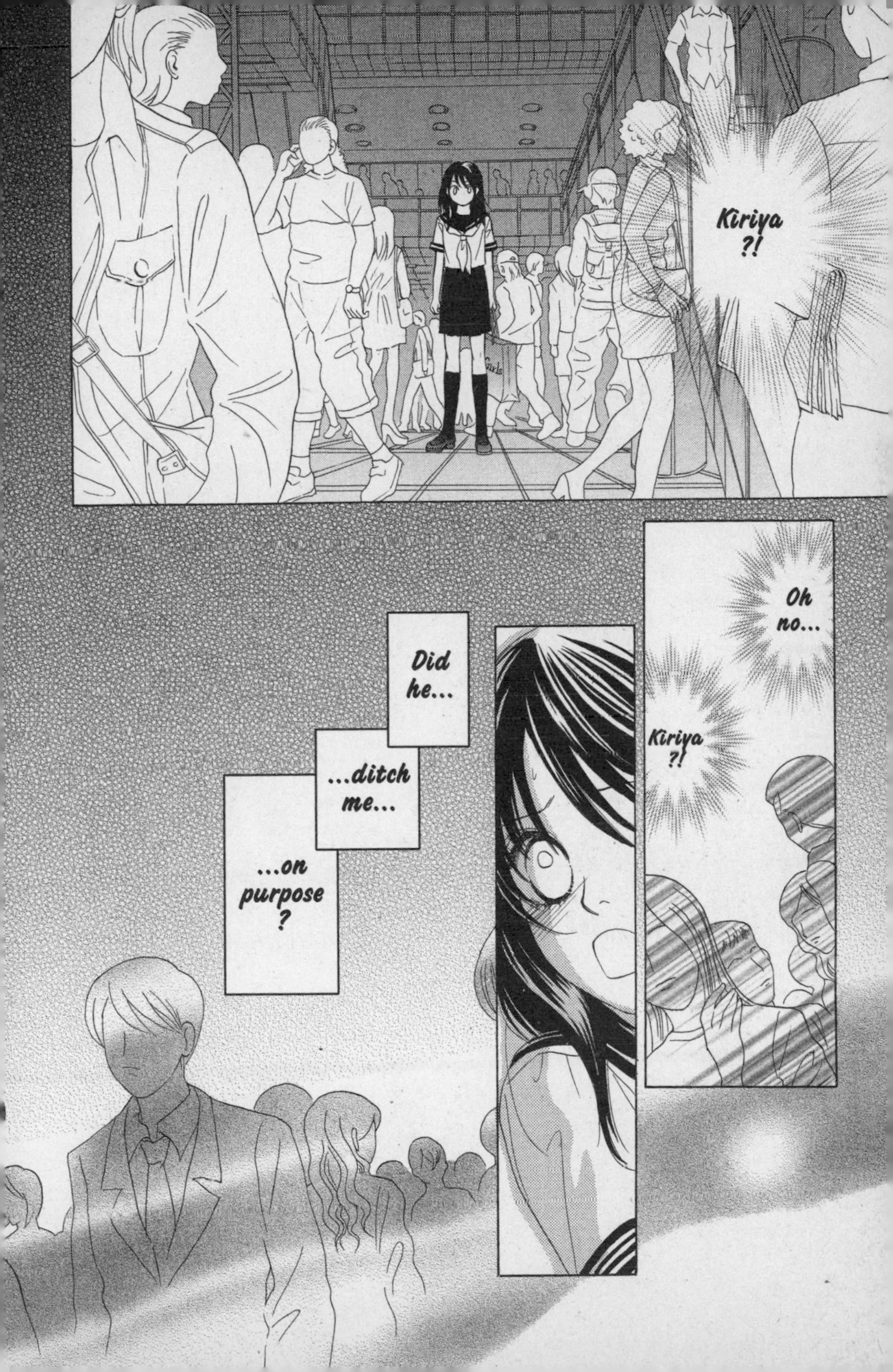
Kiriya ?!
Oh no...
Kiriya ?!
Did he...
...ditch me...
...on purpose ?

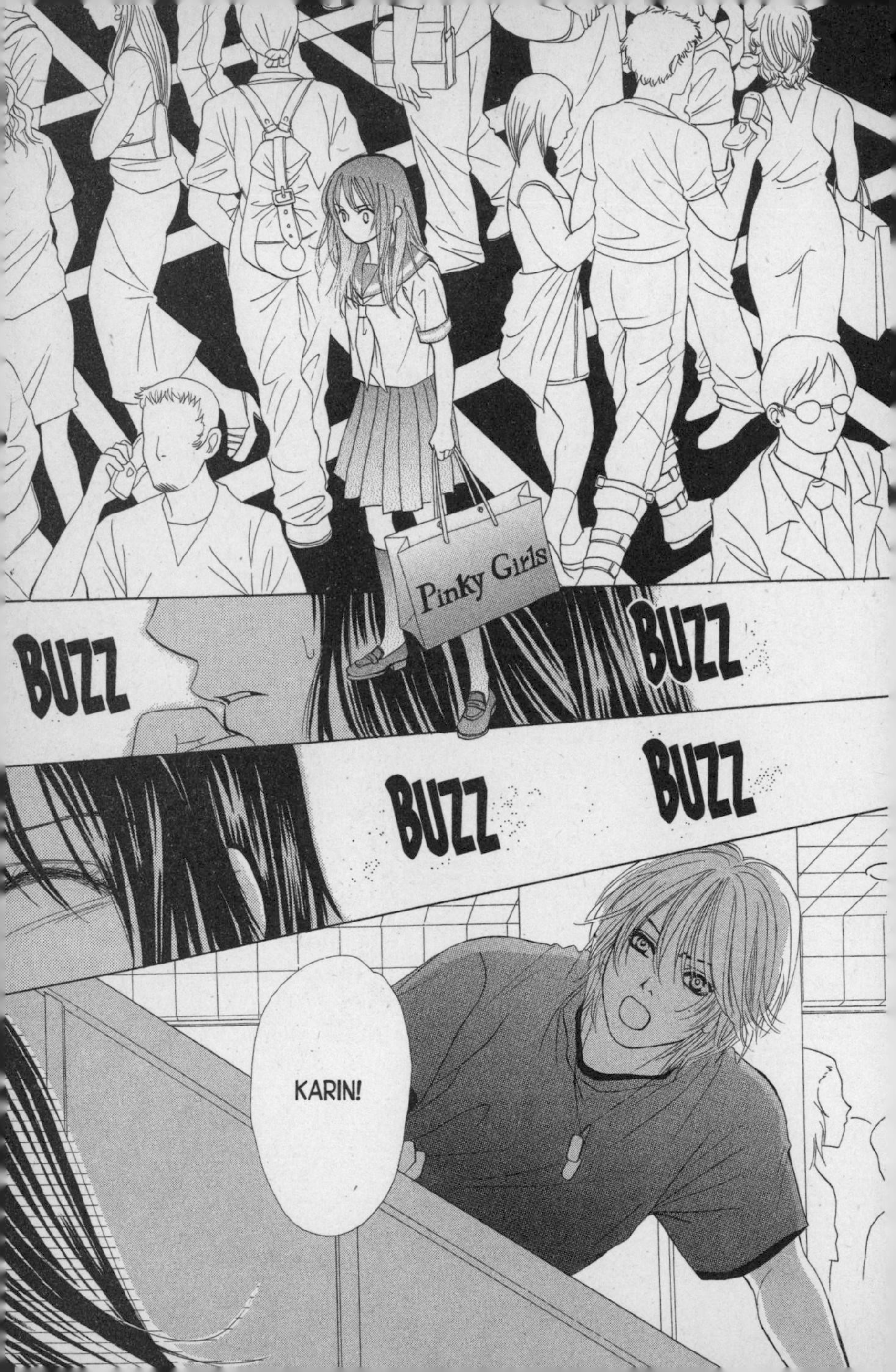
Pinky Girls
BUZZ
BUZZ
BUZZ
BUZZ
KARIN!

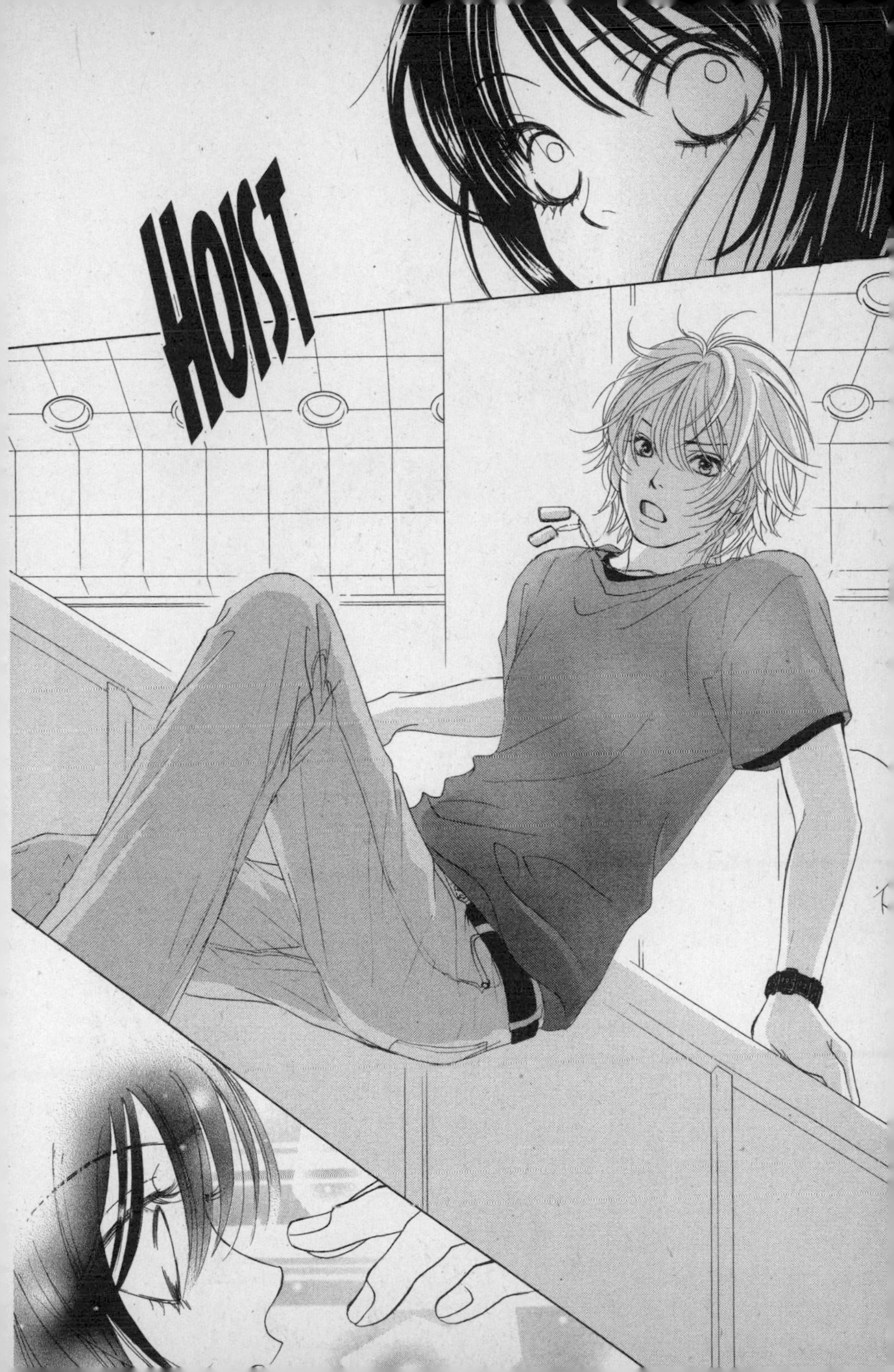
HOIST

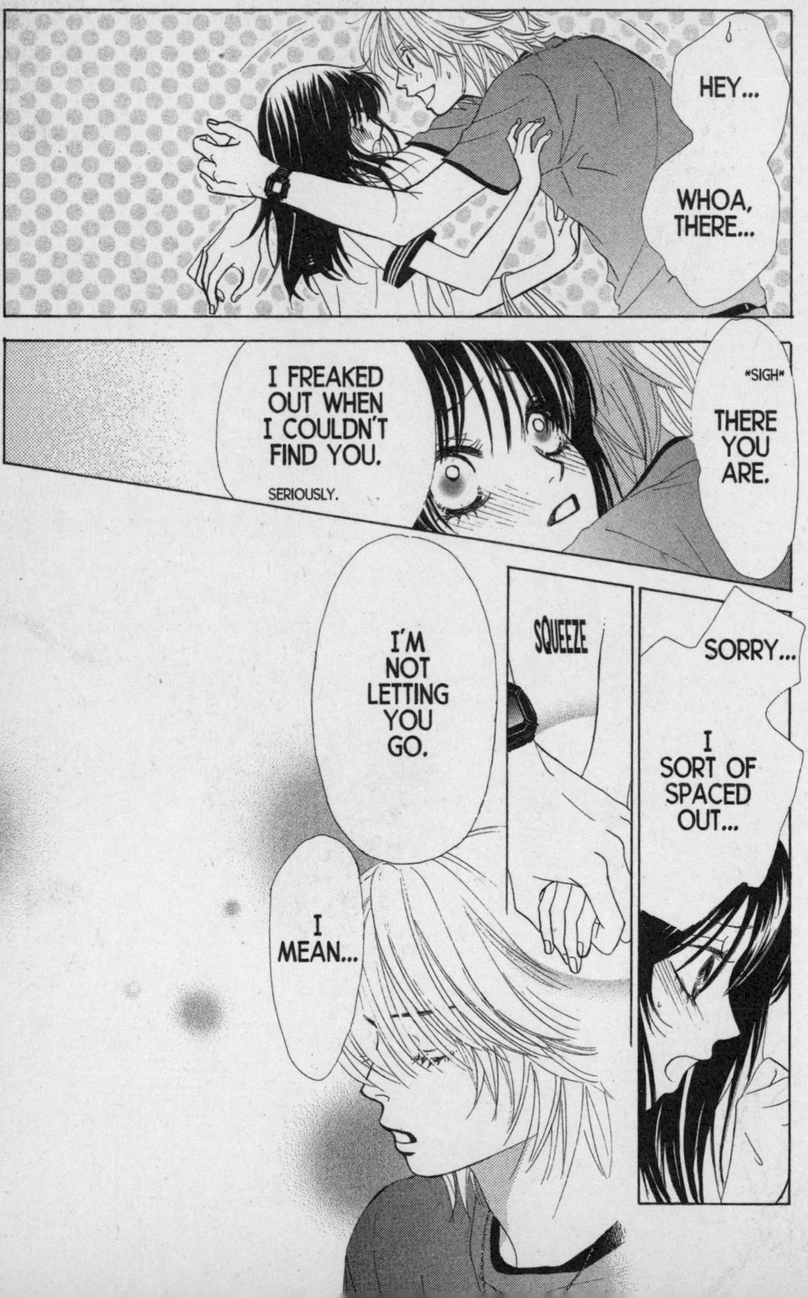
HEY...
WHOA, THERE...
SIGH
THERE YOU ARE.
I FREAKED OUT WHEN I COULDN'T FIND YOU.
SERIOUSLY.
SORRY...
I SORT OF SPACED OUT...
SQUEEZE
I'M NOT LETTING YOU GO.
I MEAN...

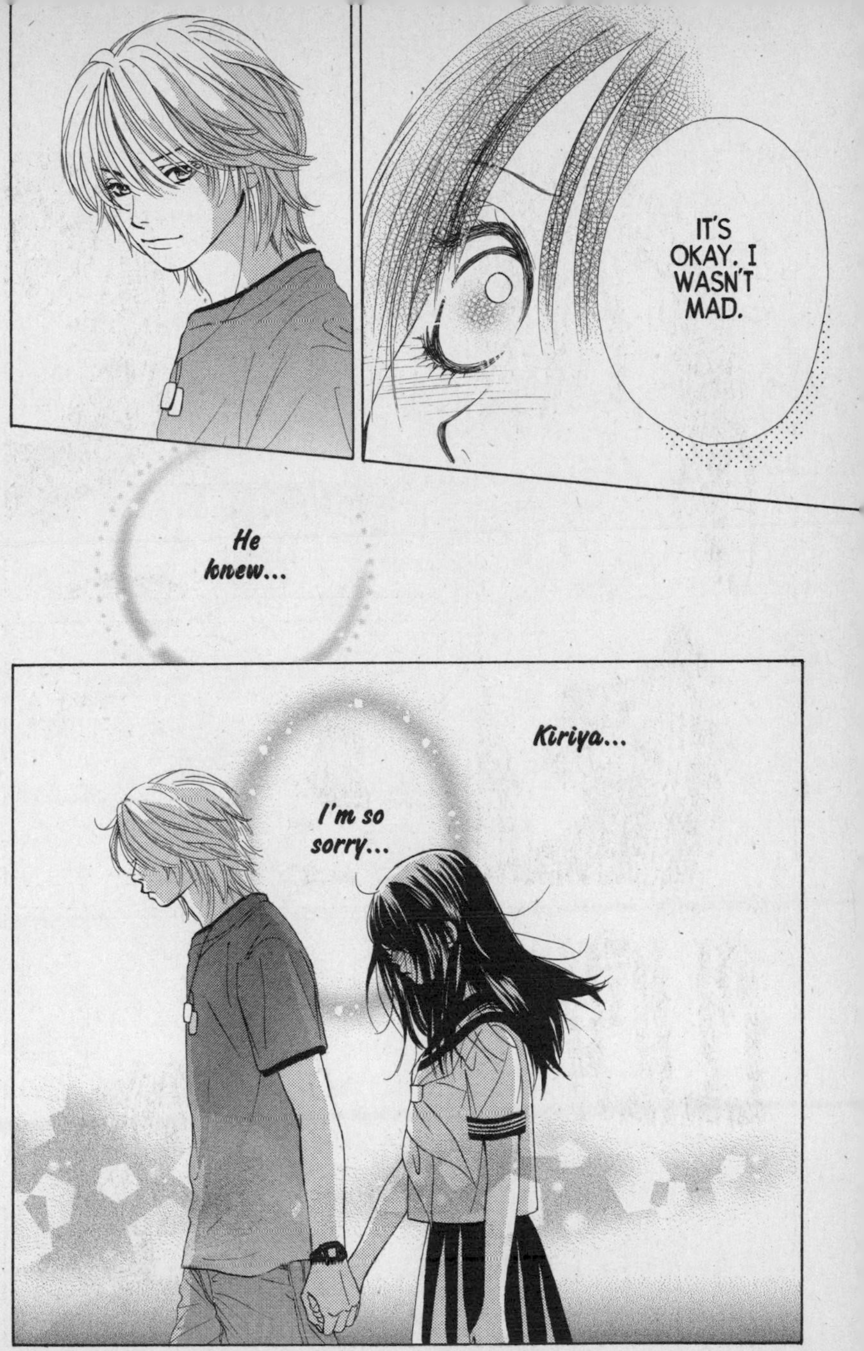
IT'S OKAY. I WASN'T MAD.
He knew...
Kiriya...
I'm so sorry...

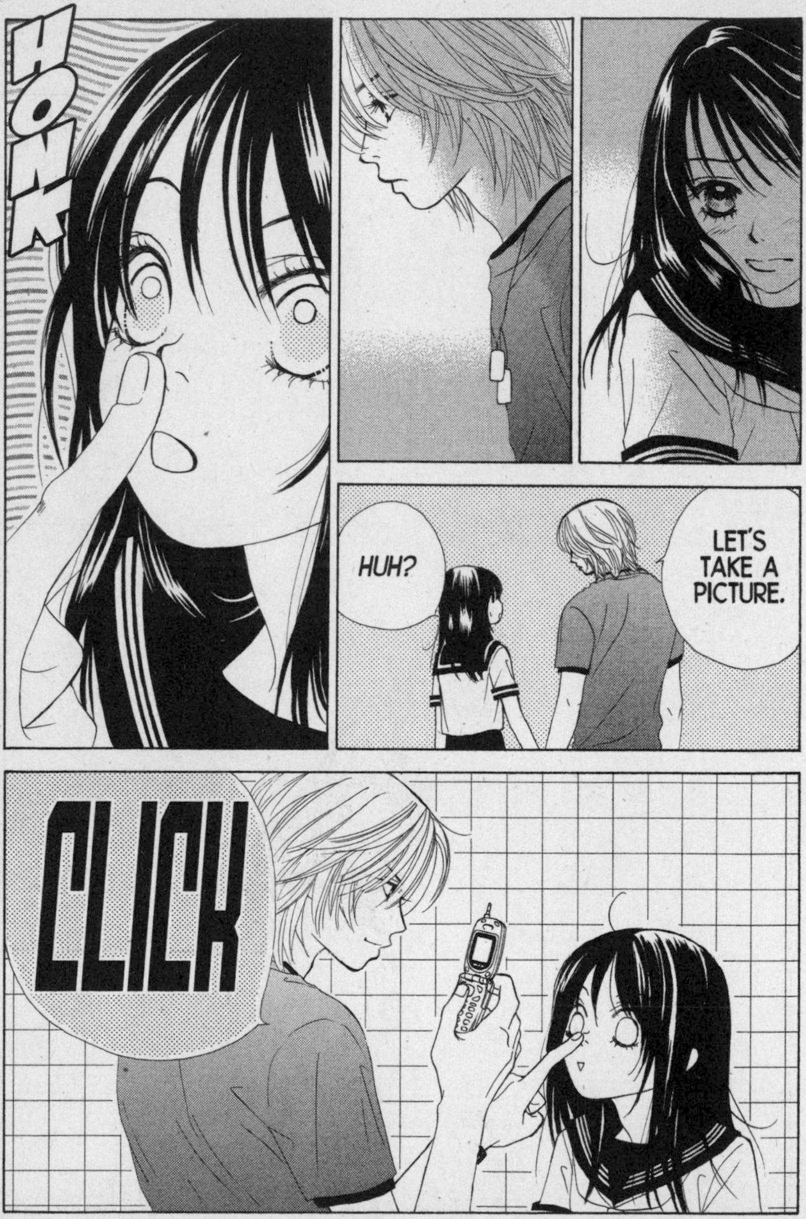
LET'S TAKE A PICTURE.
HUH?
HONK
CLICK

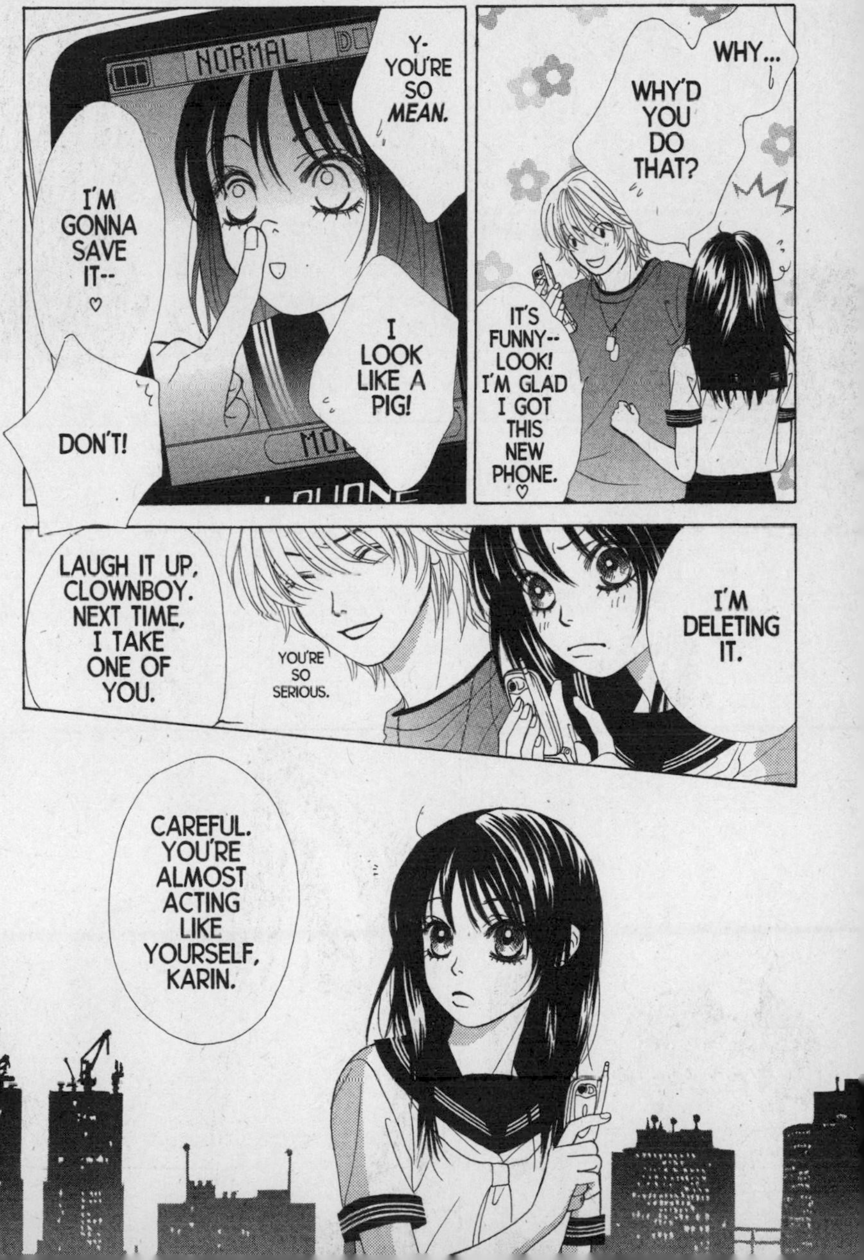
WHY...
WHY'D YOU DO THAT?
IT'S FUNNY-- LOOK! I'M GLAD I GOT THIS NEW PHONE. ♡
Y-YOU'RE SO *MEAN.*
I LOOK LIKE A PIG!
I'M GONNA SAVE IT-- ♡
DON'T!
I'M DELETING IT.
YOU'RE SO SERIOUS.
LAUGH IT UP, CLOWNBOY. NEXT TIME, I TAKE ONE OF YOU.
CAREFUL. YOU'RE ALMOST ACTING LIKE YOURSELF, KARIN.

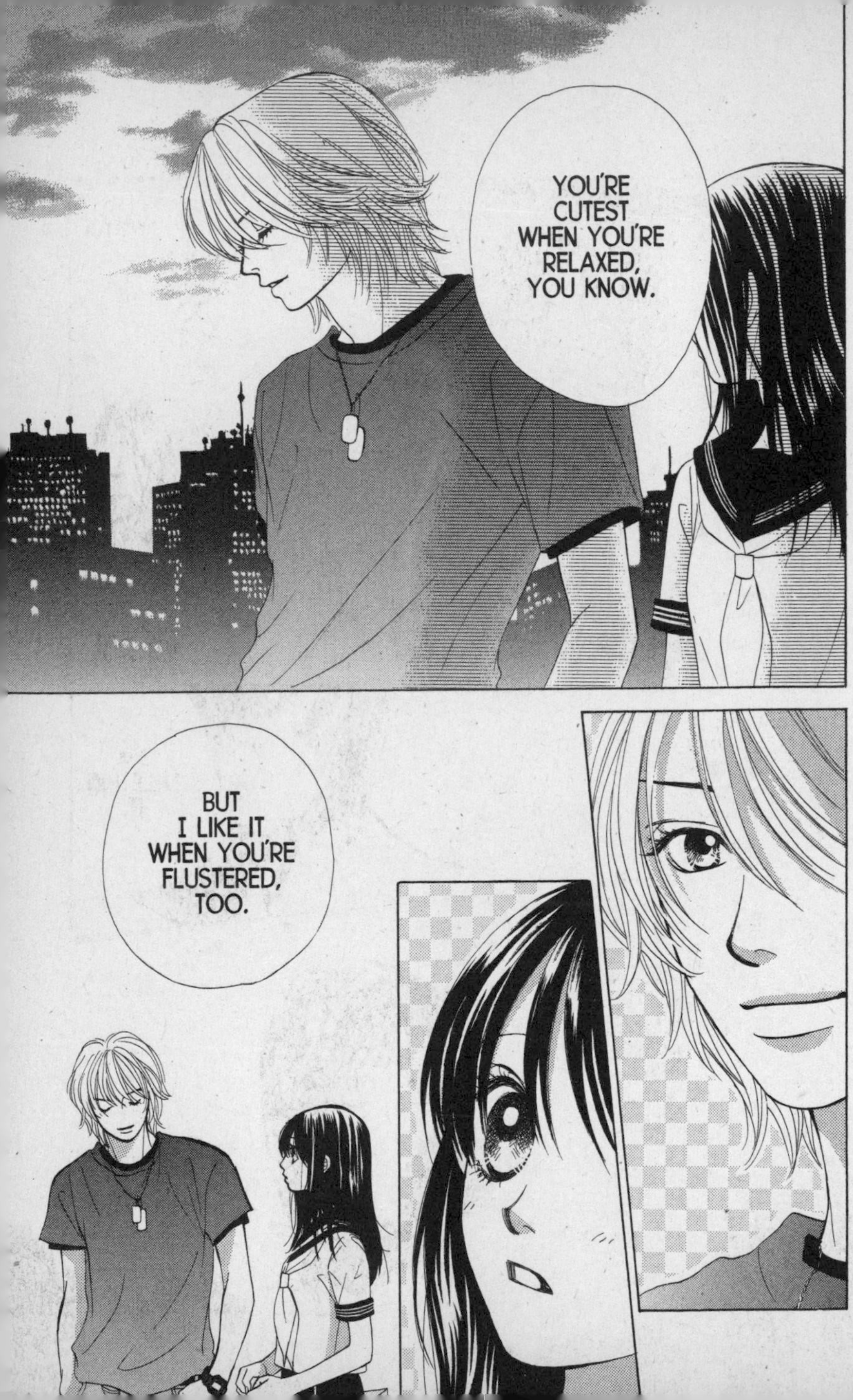
YOU'RE CUTEST WHEN YOU'RE RELAXED, YOU KNOW.
BUT I LIKE IT WHEN YOU'RE FLUSTERED, TOO.

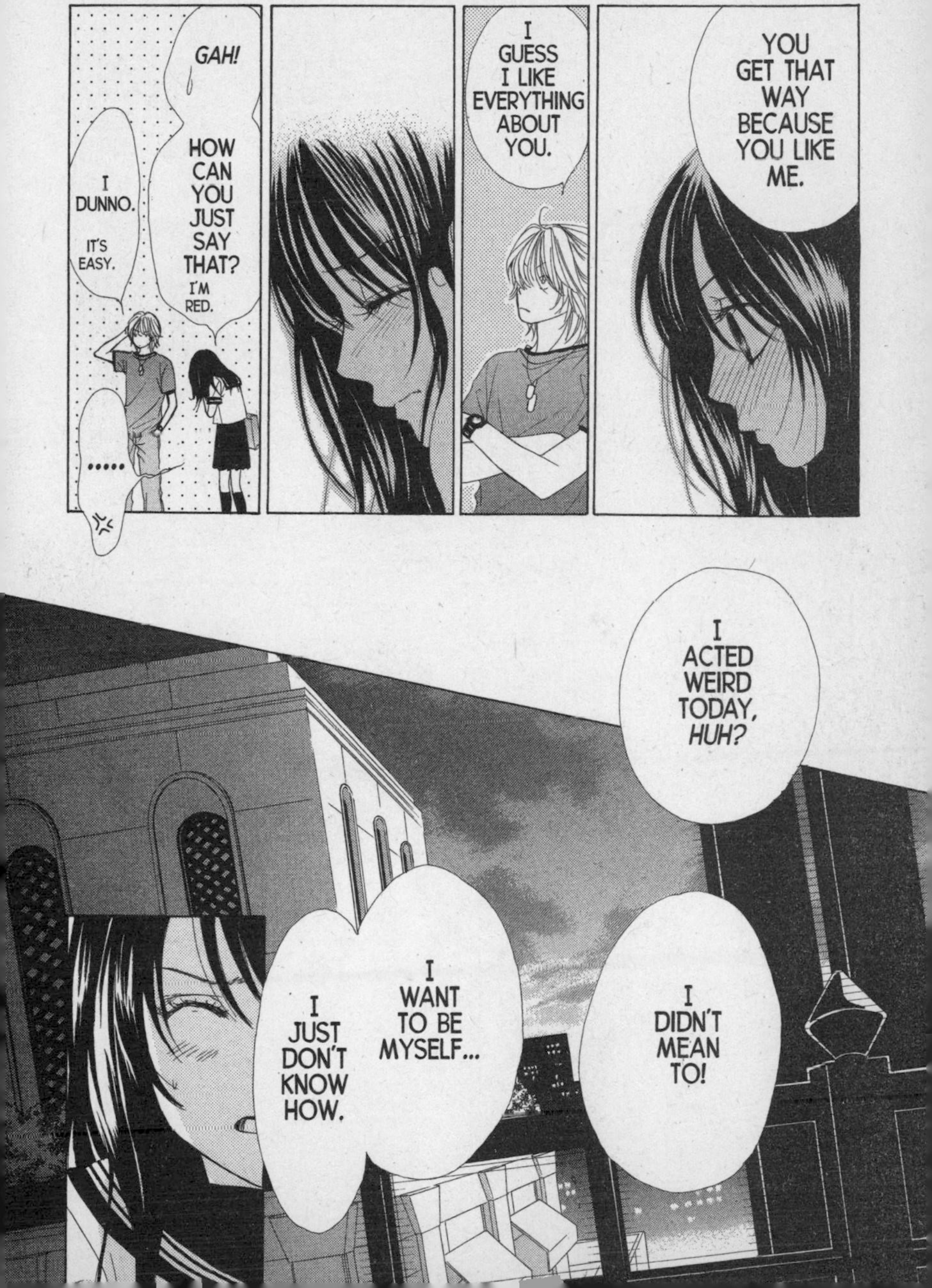
YOU GET THAT WAY BECAUSE YOU LIKE ME.
I GUESS I LIKE EVERYTHING ABOUT YOU.
GAH!
HOW CAN YOU JUST SAY THAT?
I'M RED.
I DUNNO.
IT'S EASY.
......
I ACTED WEIRD TODAY, HUH?
I DIDN'T MEAN TO!
I WANT TO BE MYSELF...
I JUST DON'T KNOW HOW.

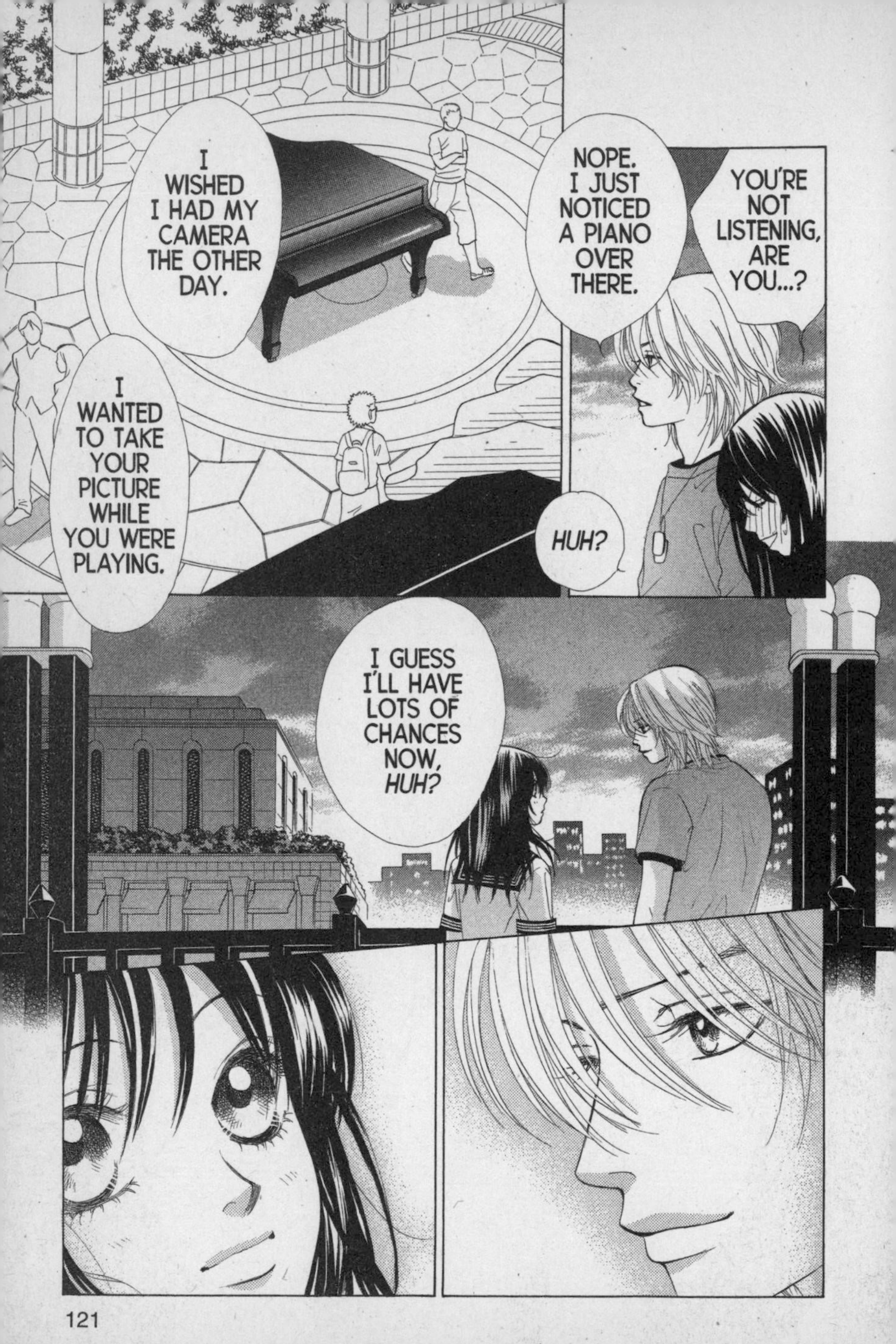
YOU'RE NOT LISTENING, ARE YOU...?
NOPE. I JUST NOTICED A PIANO OVER THERE.
HUH?
I WISHED I HAD MY CAMERA THE OTHER DAY.
I WANTED TO TAKE YOUR PICTURE WHILE YOU WERE PLAYING.
I GUESS I'LL HAVE LOTS OF CHANCES NOW, *HUH?*

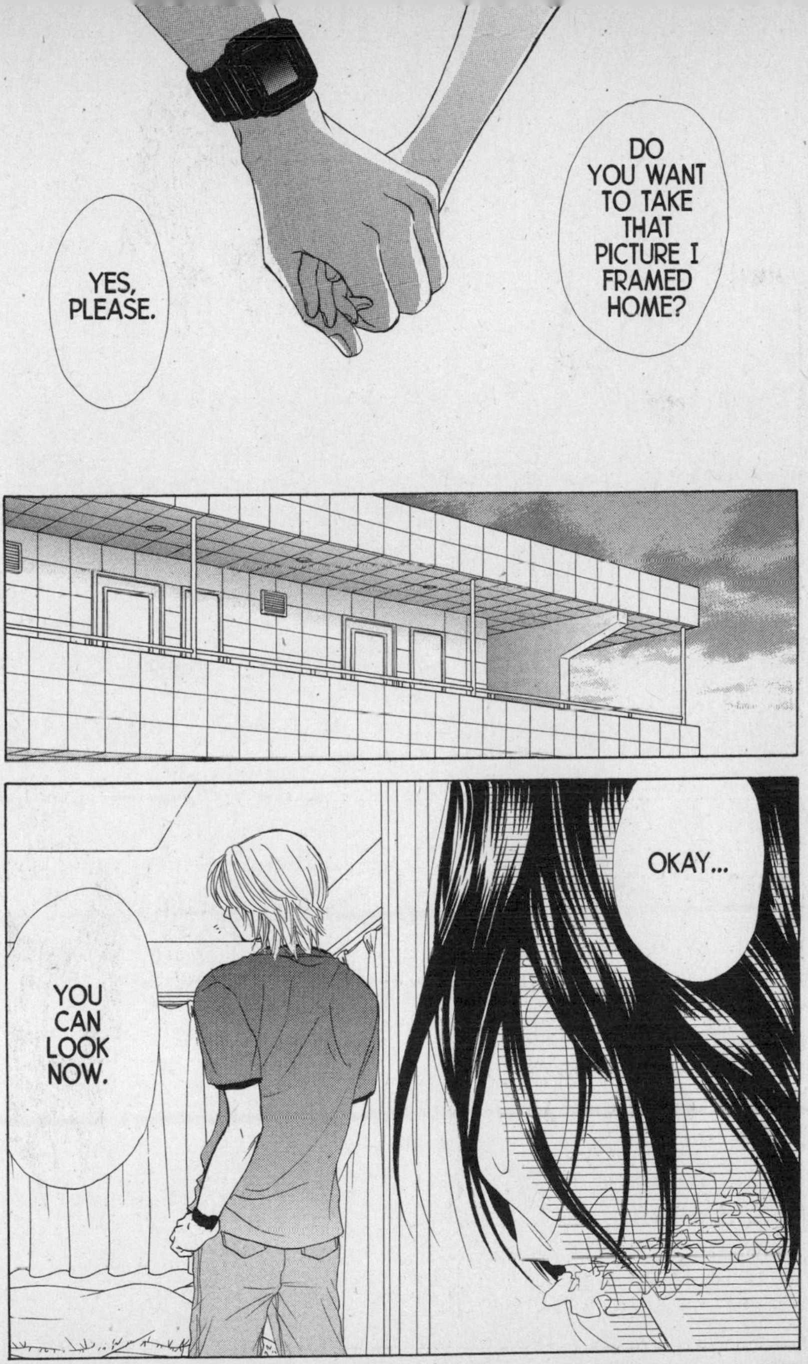
DO YOU WANT TO TAKE THAT PICTURE I FRAMED HOME?
YES, PLEASE.
OKAY...
YOU CAN LOOK NOW.

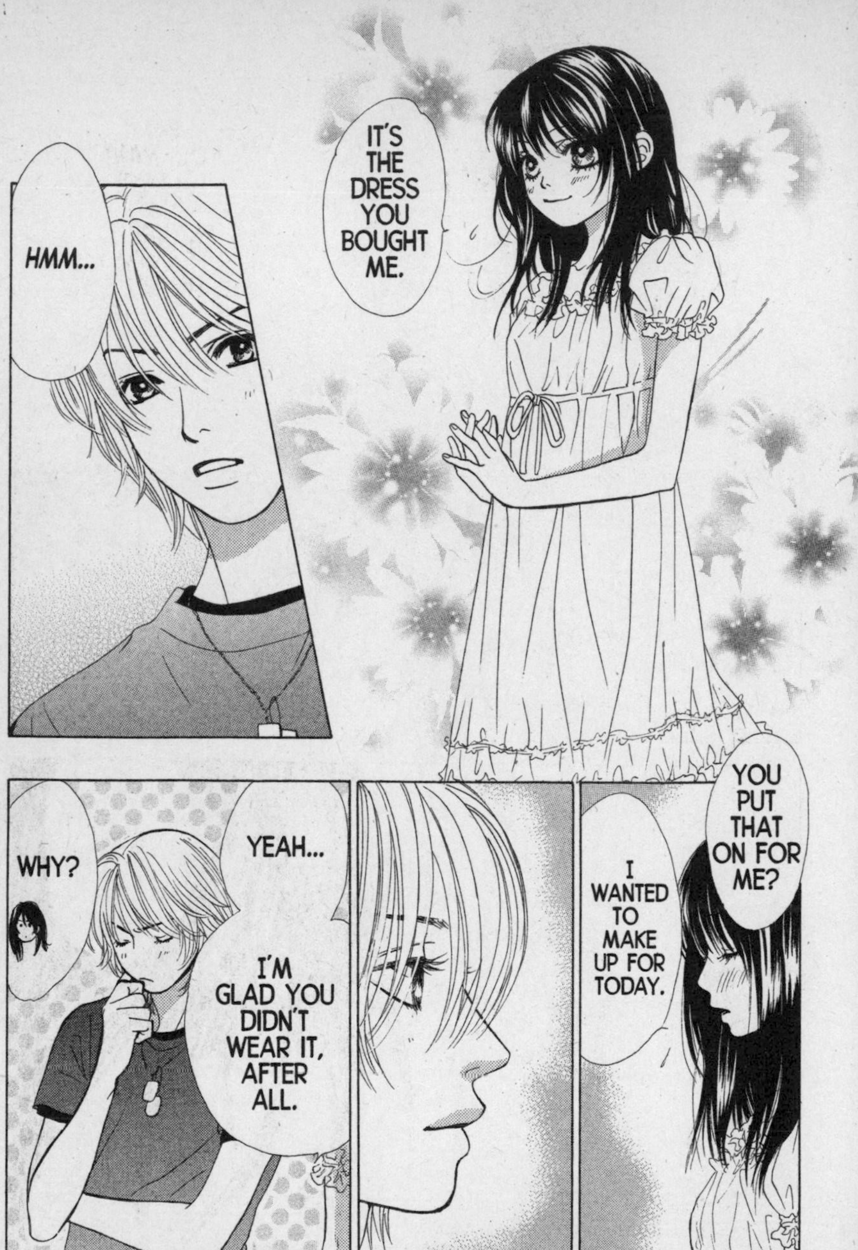
IT'S THE DRESS YOU BOUGHT ME.
HMM...
YOU PUT THAT ON FOR ME?
I WANTED TO MAKE UP FOR TODAY.
YEAH...
I'M GLAD YOU DIDN'T WEAR IT, AFTER ALL.
WHY?

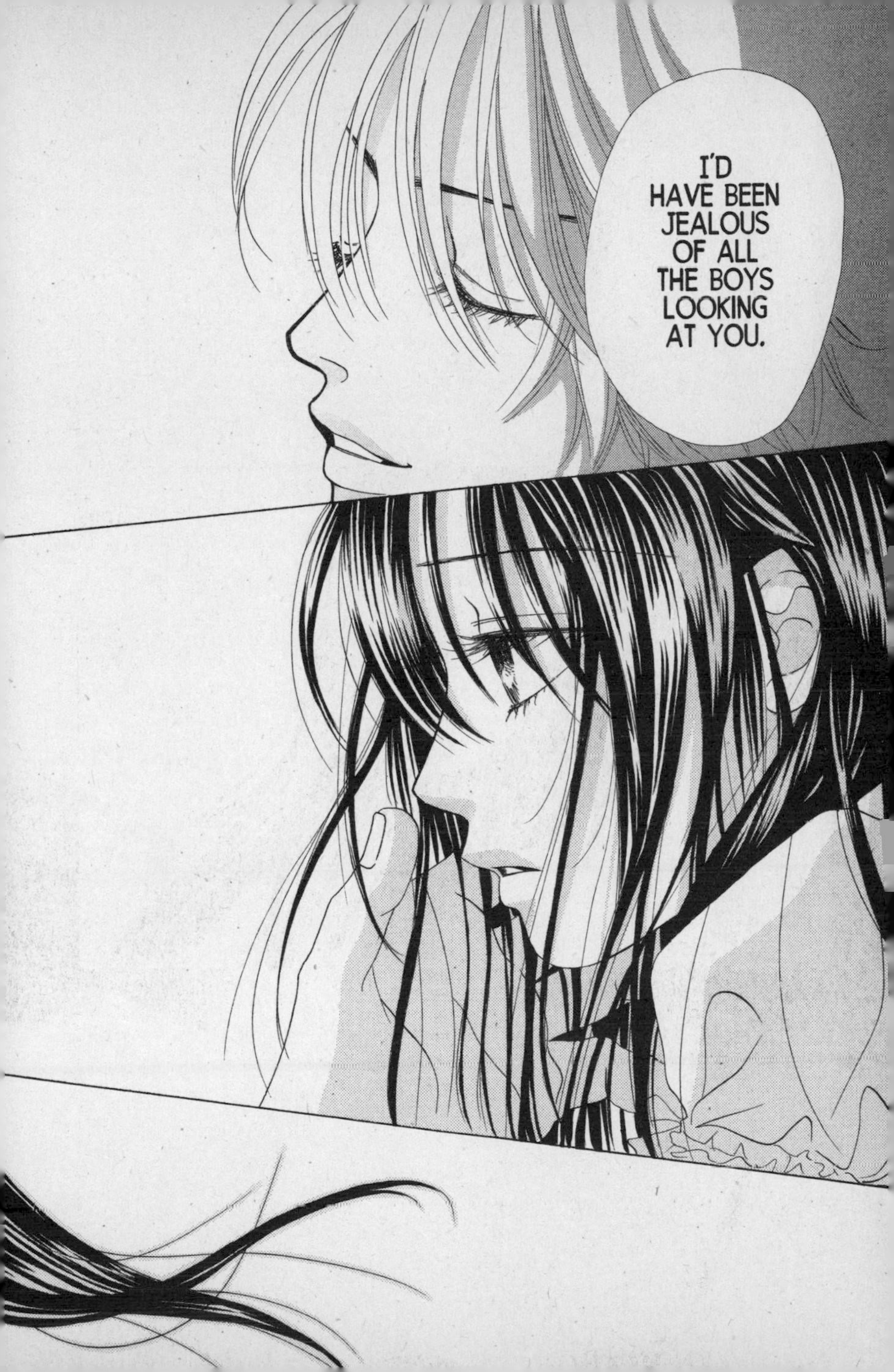
I'D HAVE BEEN JEALOUS OF ALL THE BOYS LOOKING AT YOU.

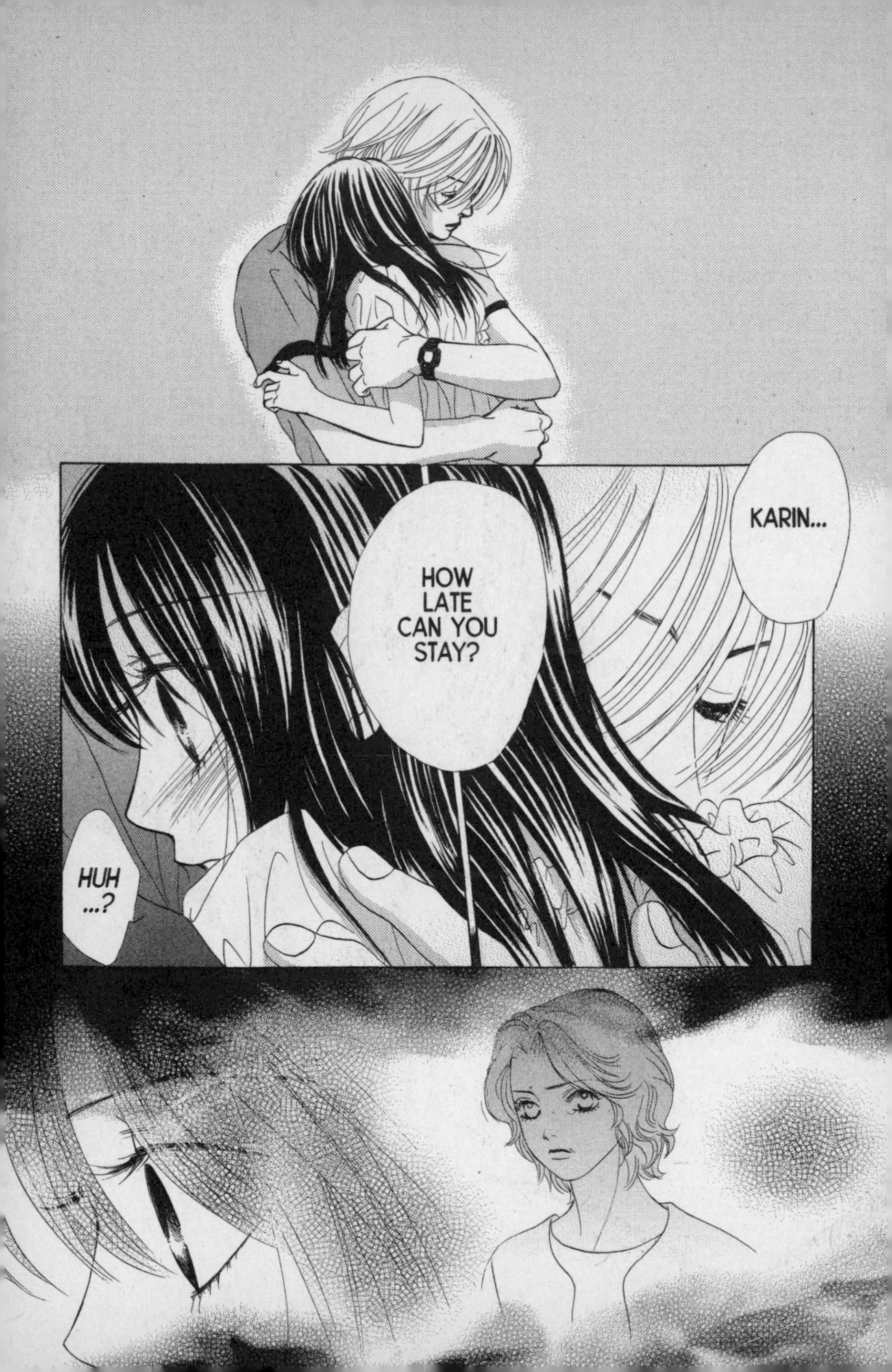
KARIN...
HOW LATE CAN YOU STAY?
HUH ...?

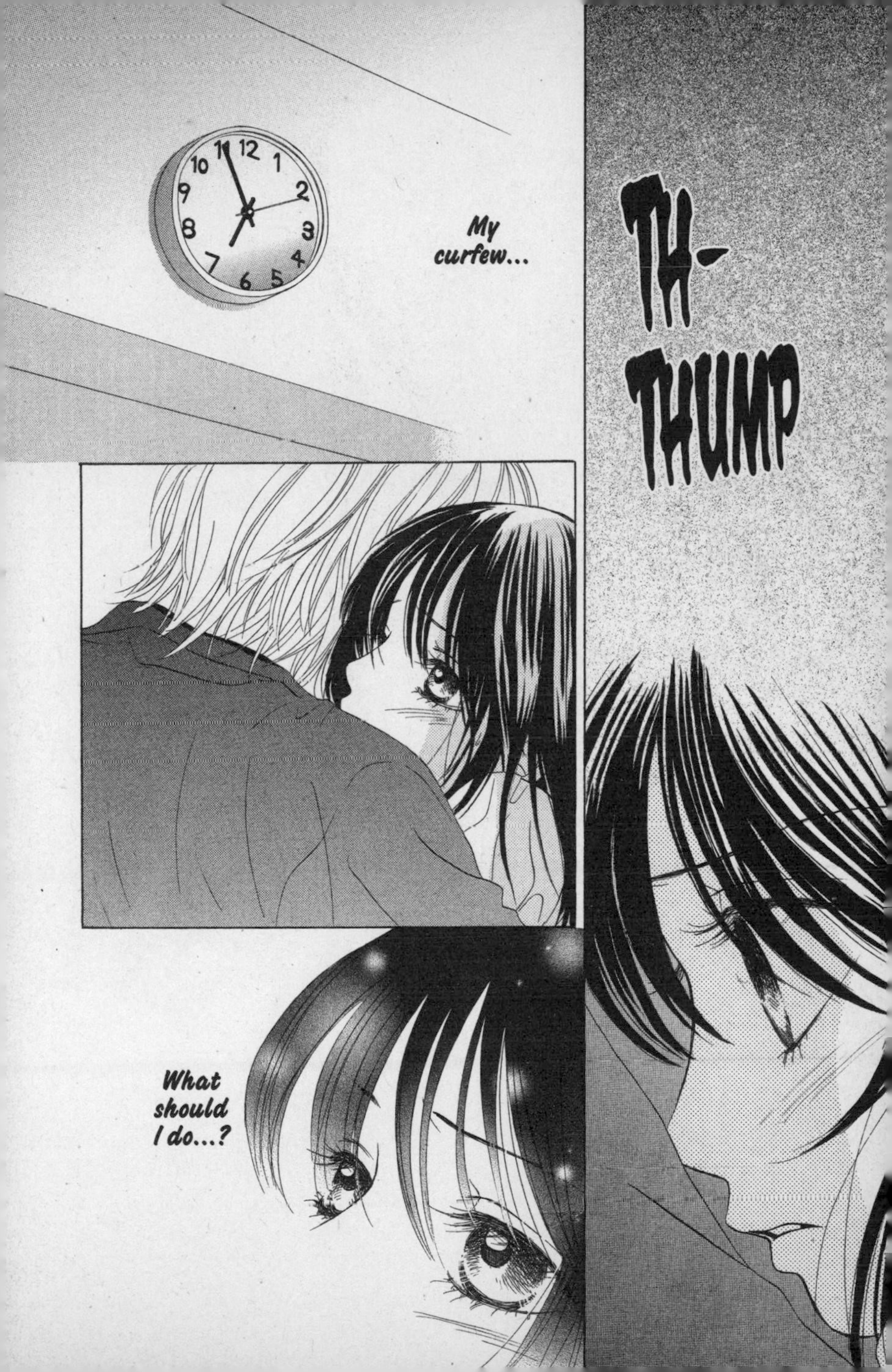
TH-THUMP
My curfew...
What should I do...?

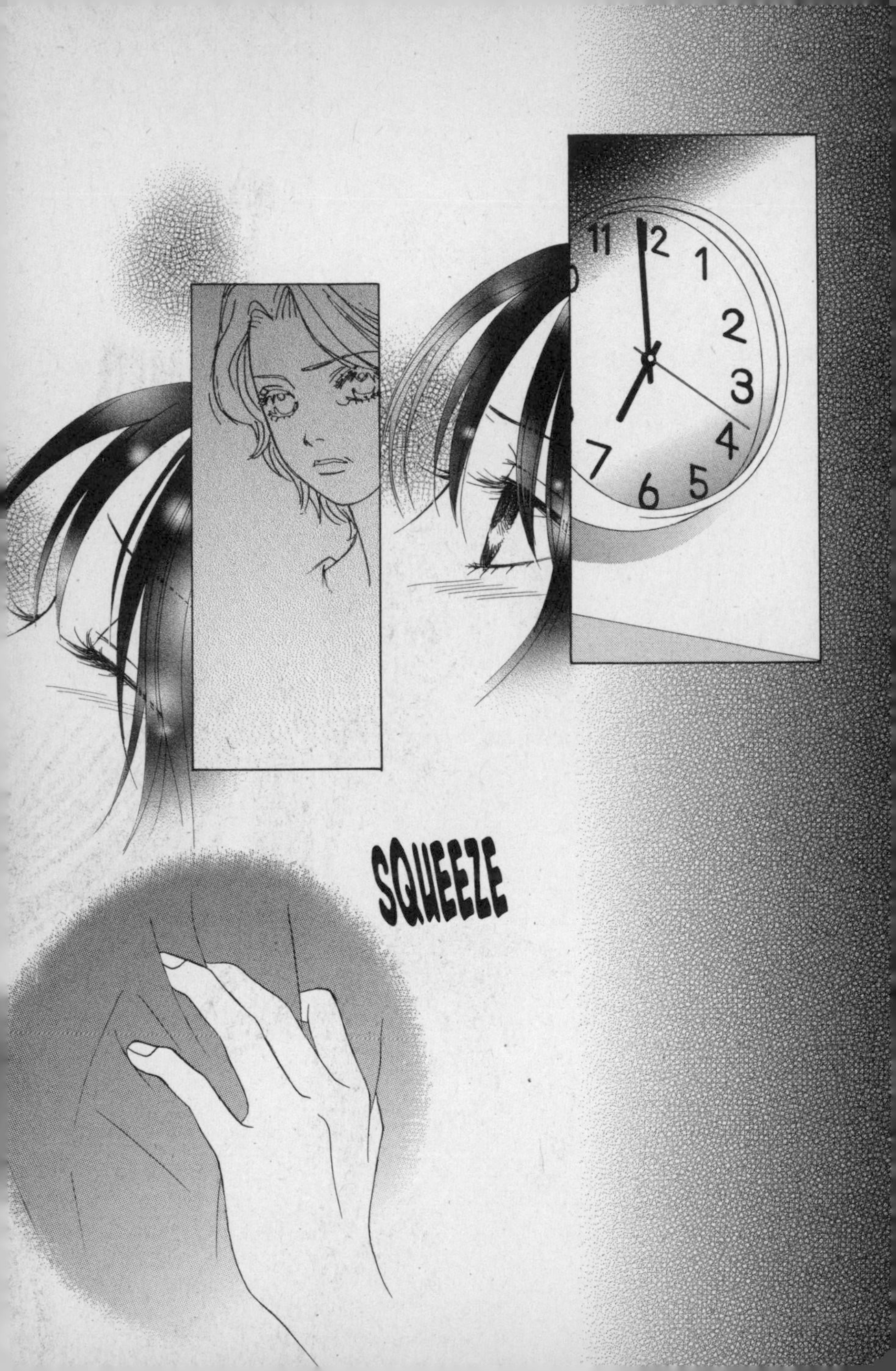
SQUEEZE

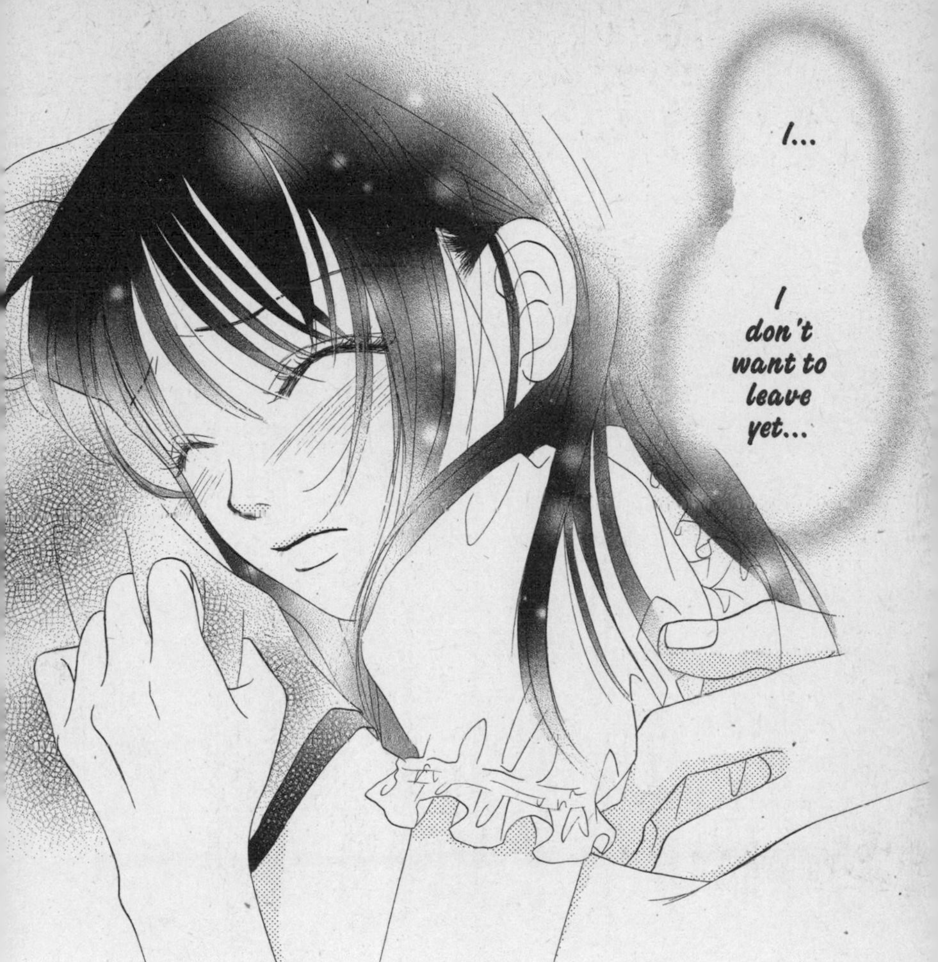
I...
I don't want to leave yet...

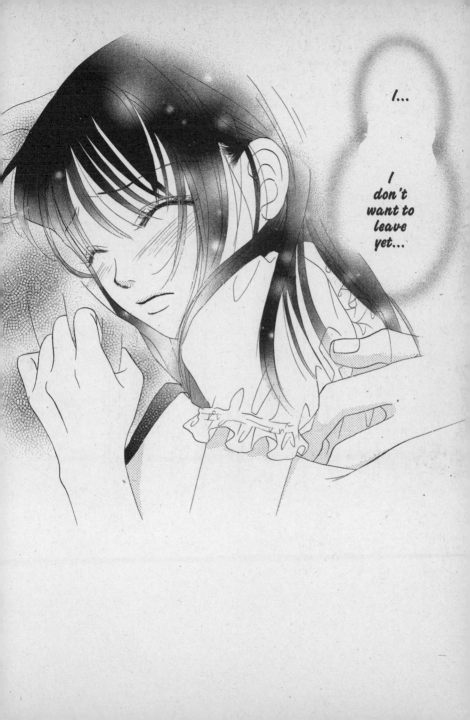

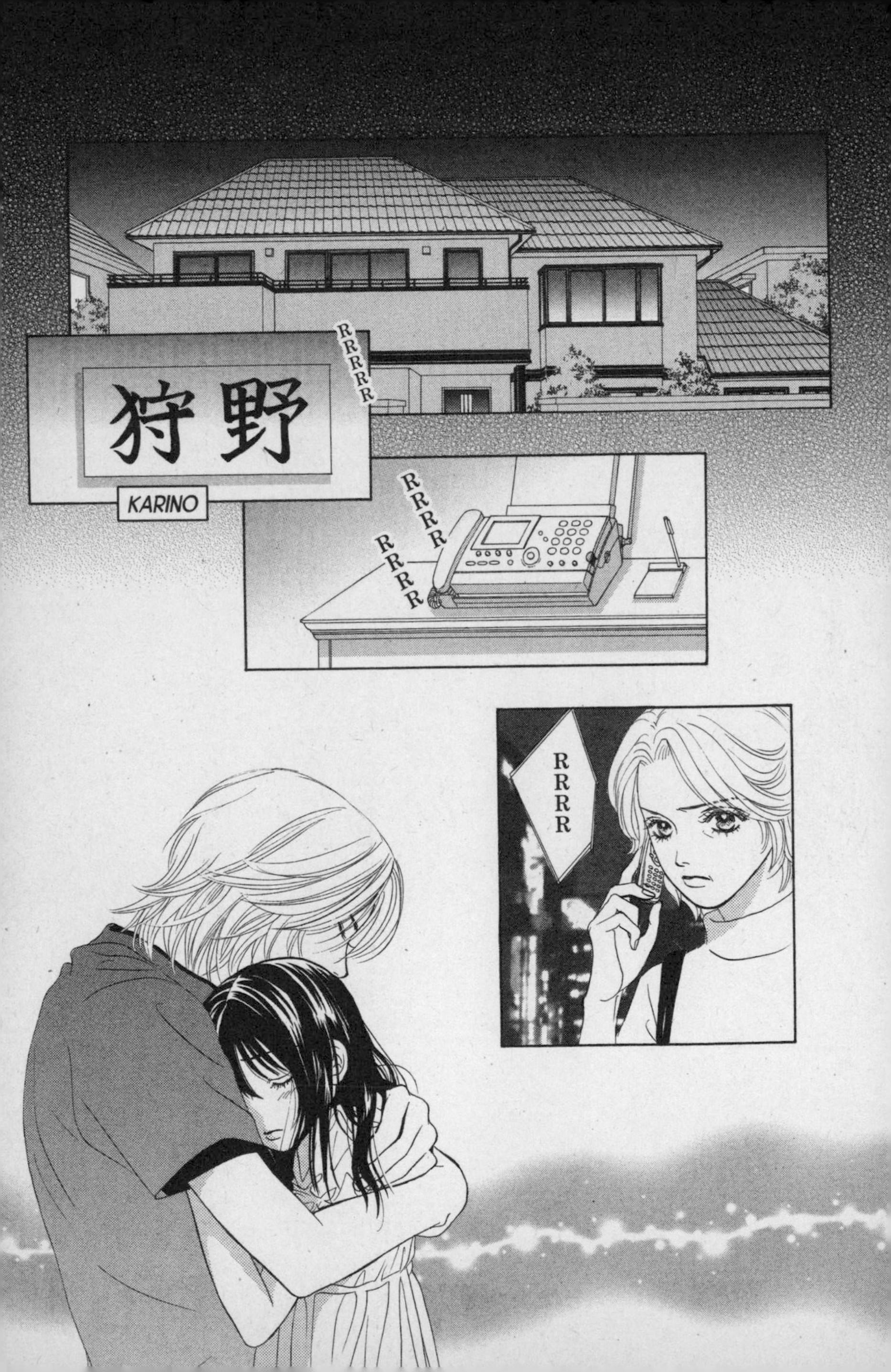

RRRRR
狩野
KARINO
RRRR
RRRR
RRRR

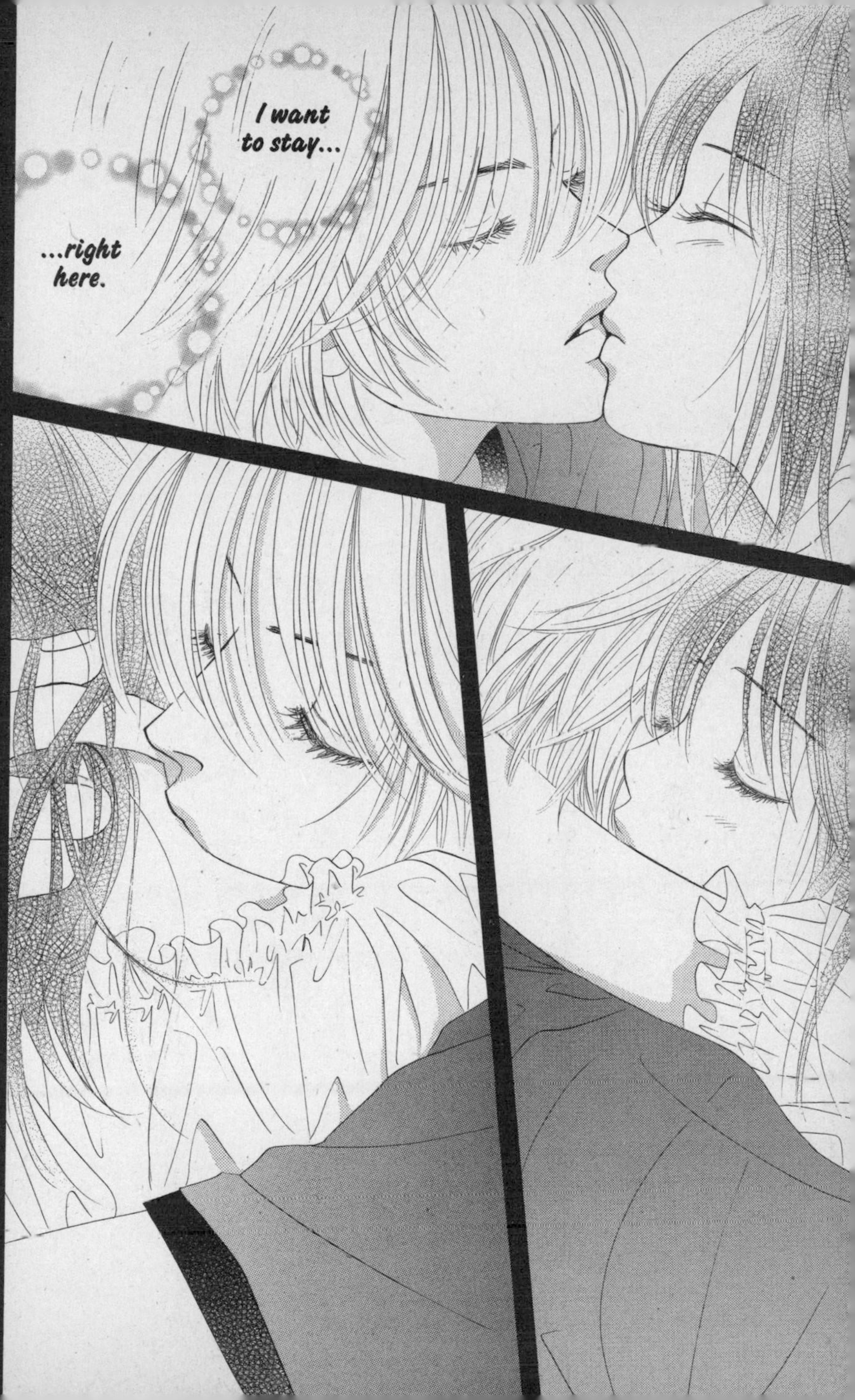
I want to stay...
...right here.

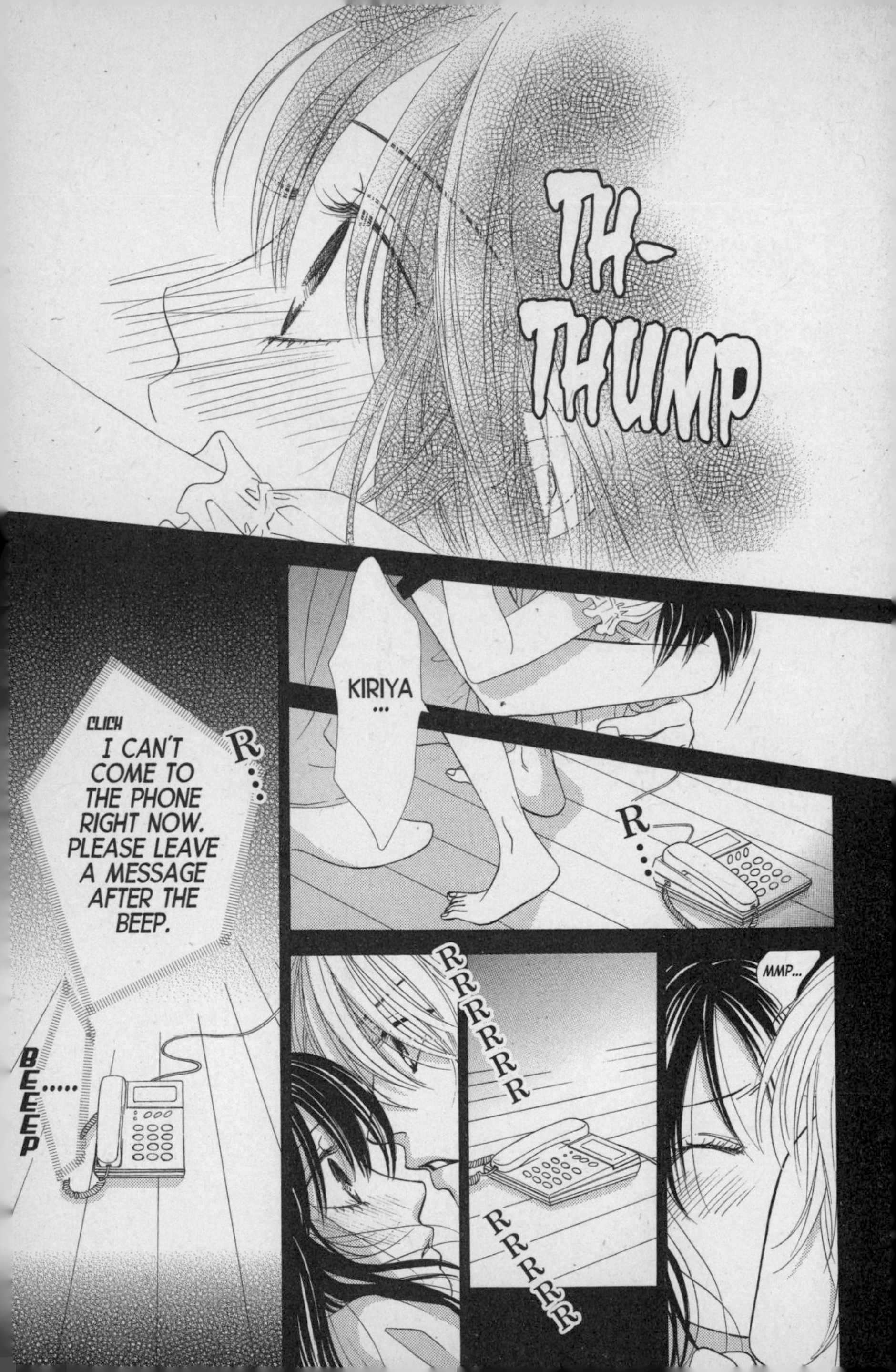
TH-THUMP
KIRIYA...
R...
MMP...
RRRRRR
RRRRR
R...
CLICK
I CAN'T COME TO THE PHONE RIGHT NOW. PLEASE LEAVE A MESSAGE AFTER THE BEEP.
BEEEP.....

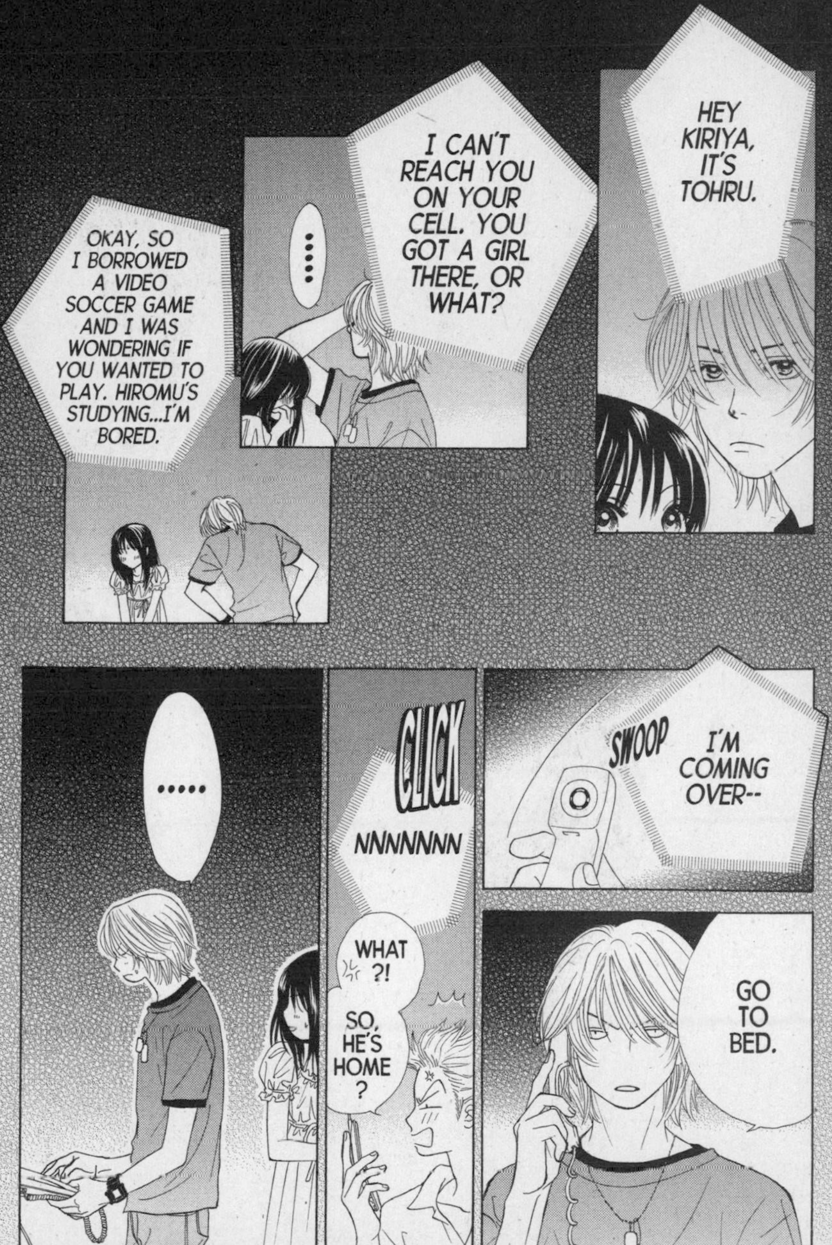
HEY KIRIYA, IT'S TOHRU.
I CAN'T REACH YOU ON YOUR CELL. YOU GOT A GIRL THERE, OR WHAT?
.....
OKAY, SO I BORROWED A VIDEO SOCCER GAME AND I WAS WONDERING IF YOU WANTED TO PLAY. HIROMU'S STUDYING...I'M BORED.
SWOOP
I'M COMING OVER--
GO TO BED.
CLICK
NNNNNNN
WHAT ?!
SO, HE'S HOME ?
.....

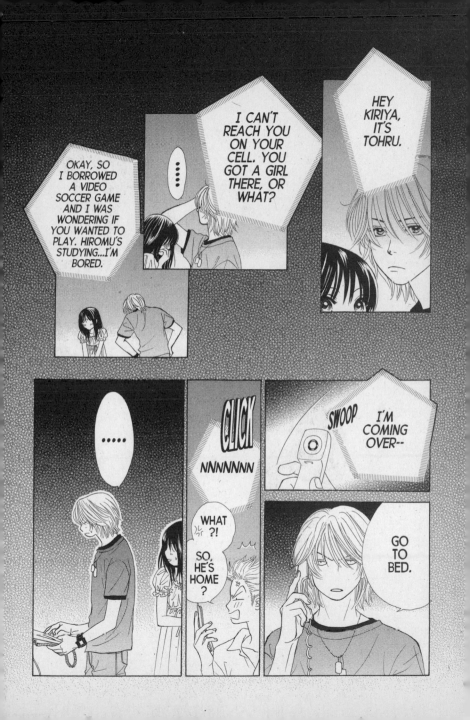

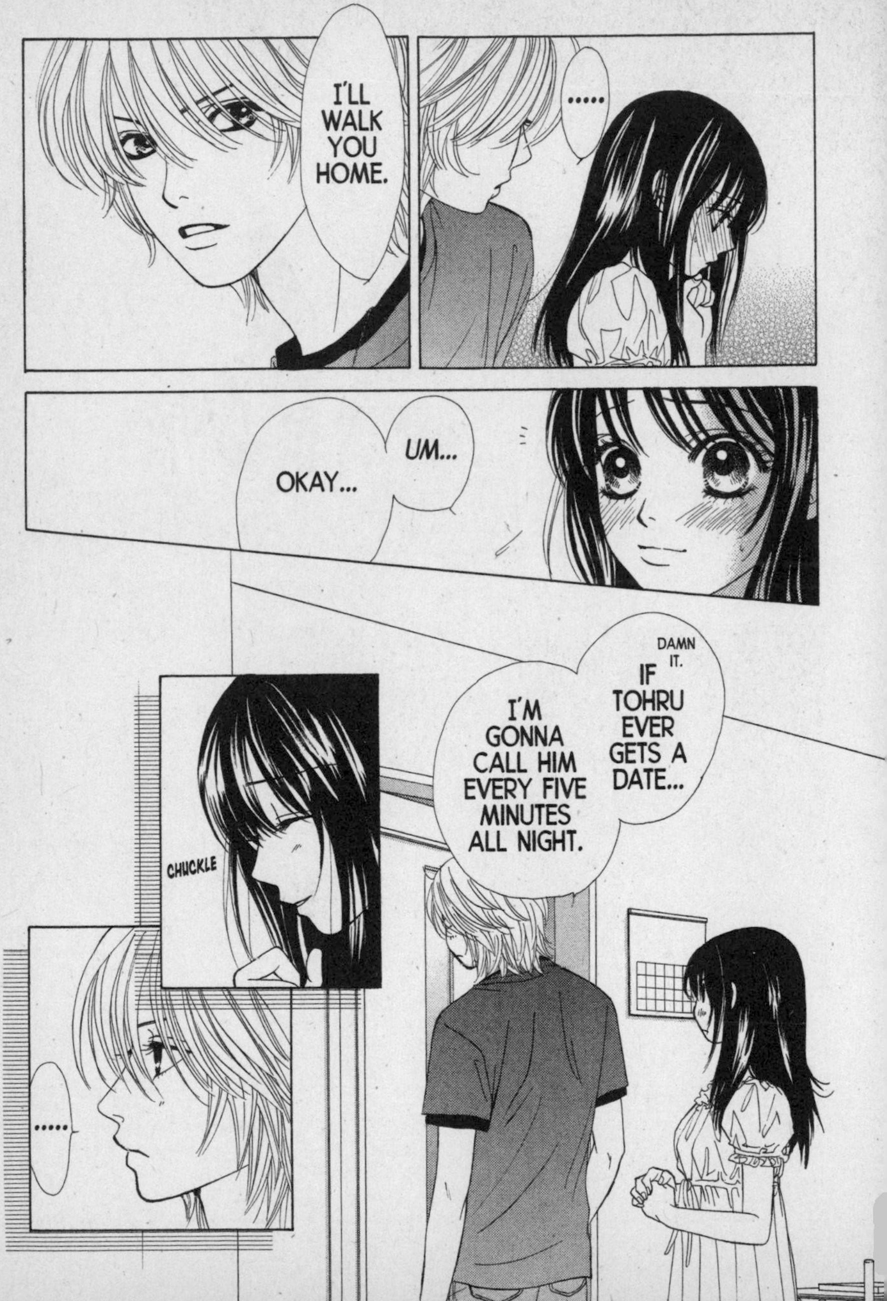
.....
I'LL WALK YOU HOME.
UM...
OKAY...
DAMN IT.
IF TOHRU EVER GETS A DATE...
I'M GONNA CALL HIM EVERY FIVE MINUTES ALL NIGHT.
CHUCKLE
.....

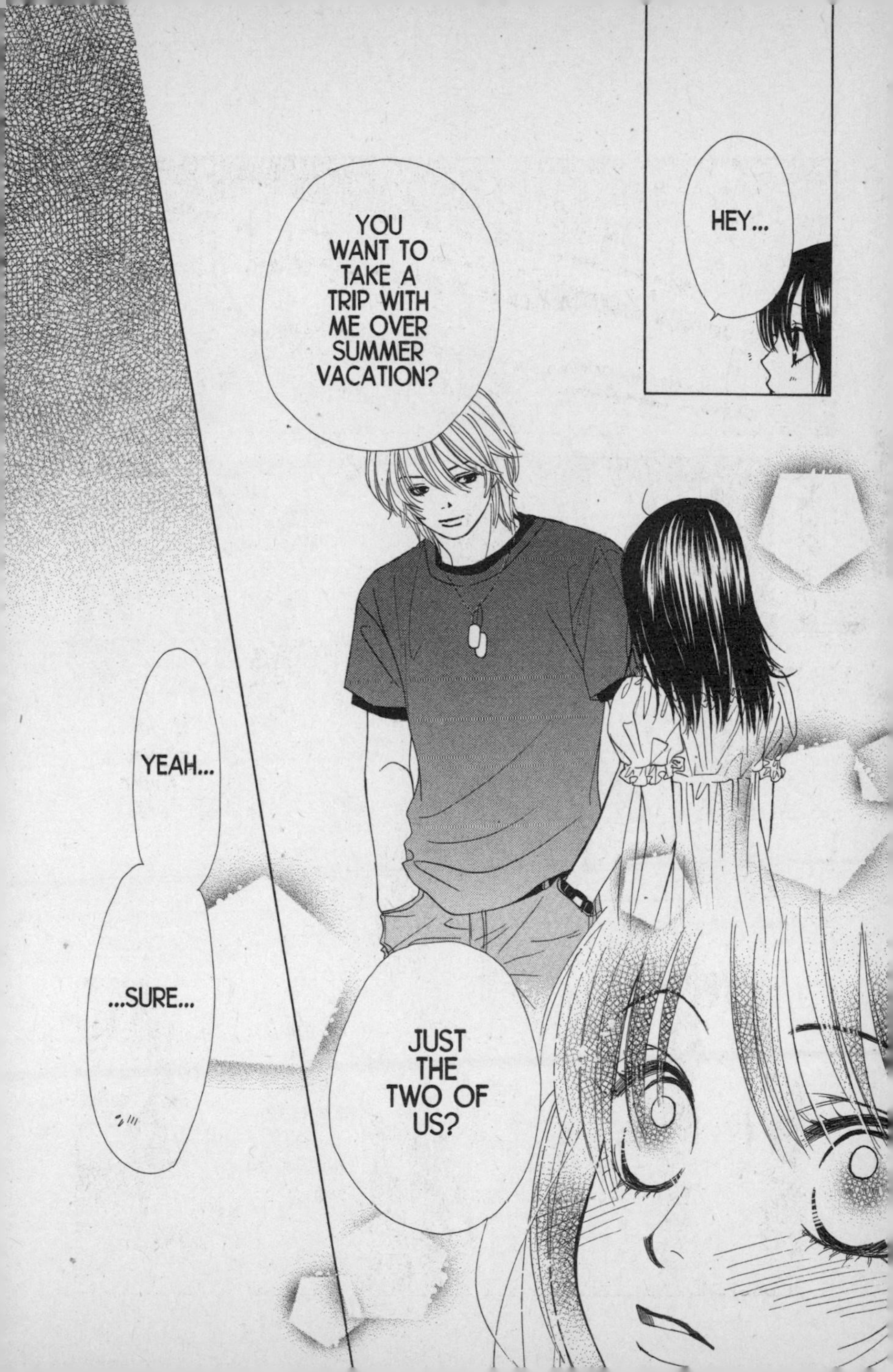
HEY...
YOU WANT TO TAKE A TRIP WITH ME OVER SUMMER VACATION?
JUST THE TWO OF US?
YEAH...
...SURE...

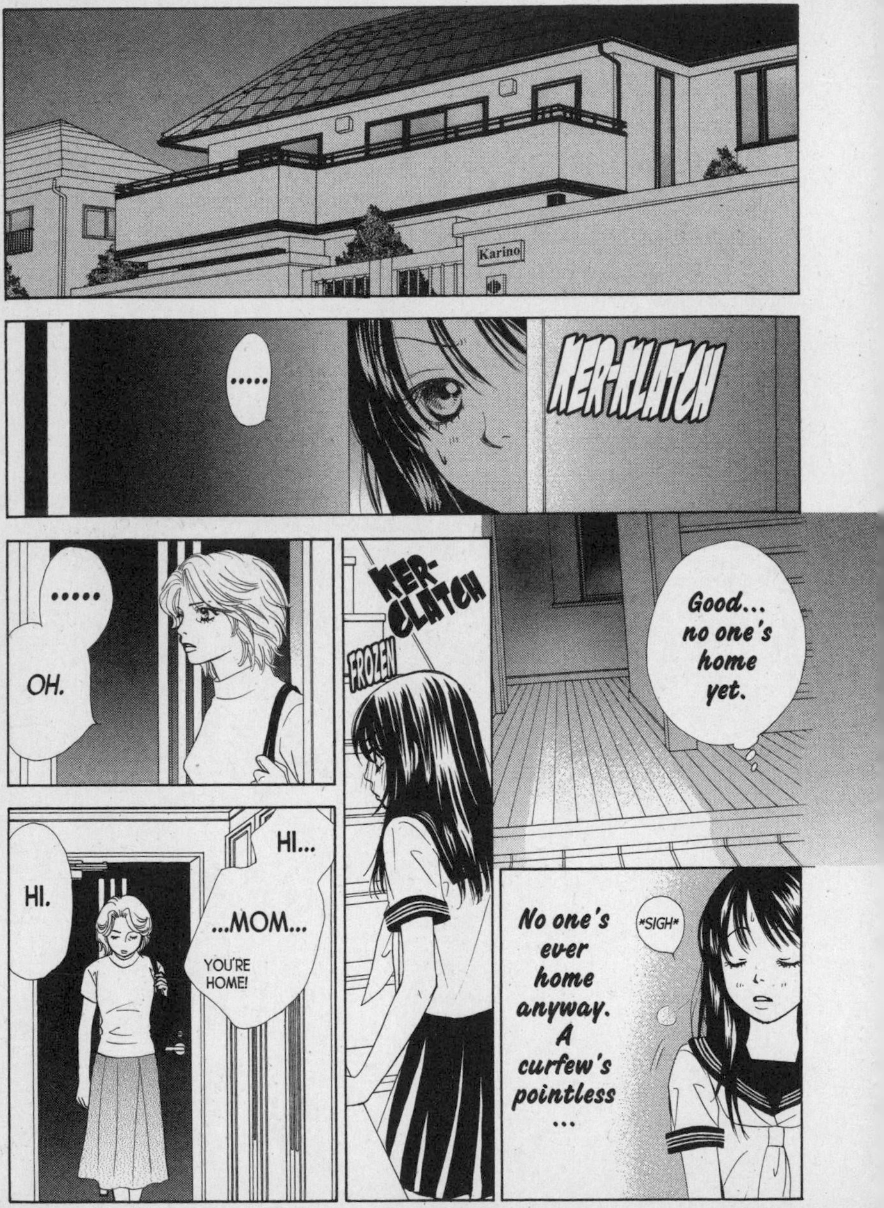
Karino
KER-KLATCH
......
Good... no one's home yet.
No one's ever home anyway. A curfew's pointless...
SIGH
KER-CLATCH
FROZEN
......
OH.
HI...
...MOM...
YOU'RE HOME!
HI.

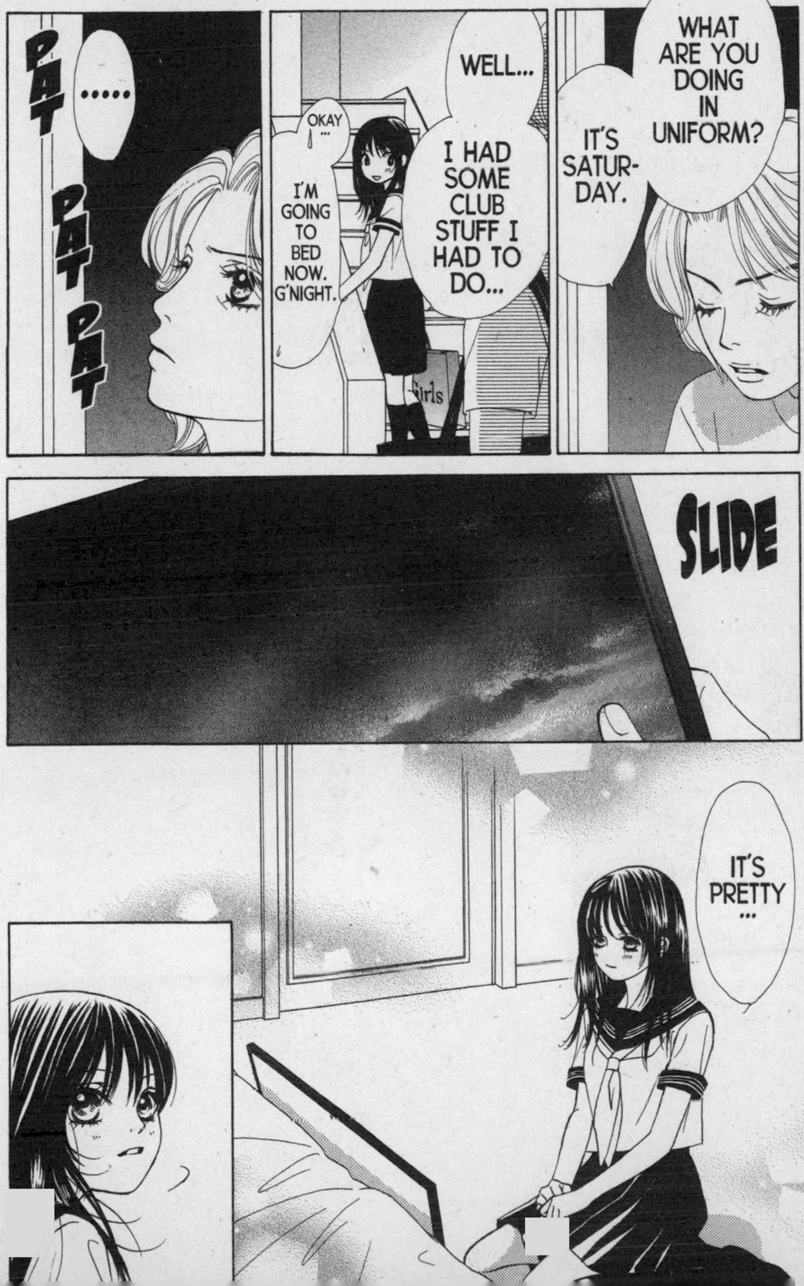

WHAT ARE YOU DOING IN UNIFORM?
IT'S SATUR-DAY.
WELL...
I HAD SOME CLUB STUFF I HAD TO DO...
OKAY ...
I'M GOING TO BED NOW. G'NIGHT.
......
PAT PAT PAT PAT
SLIDE
IT'S PRETTY ...

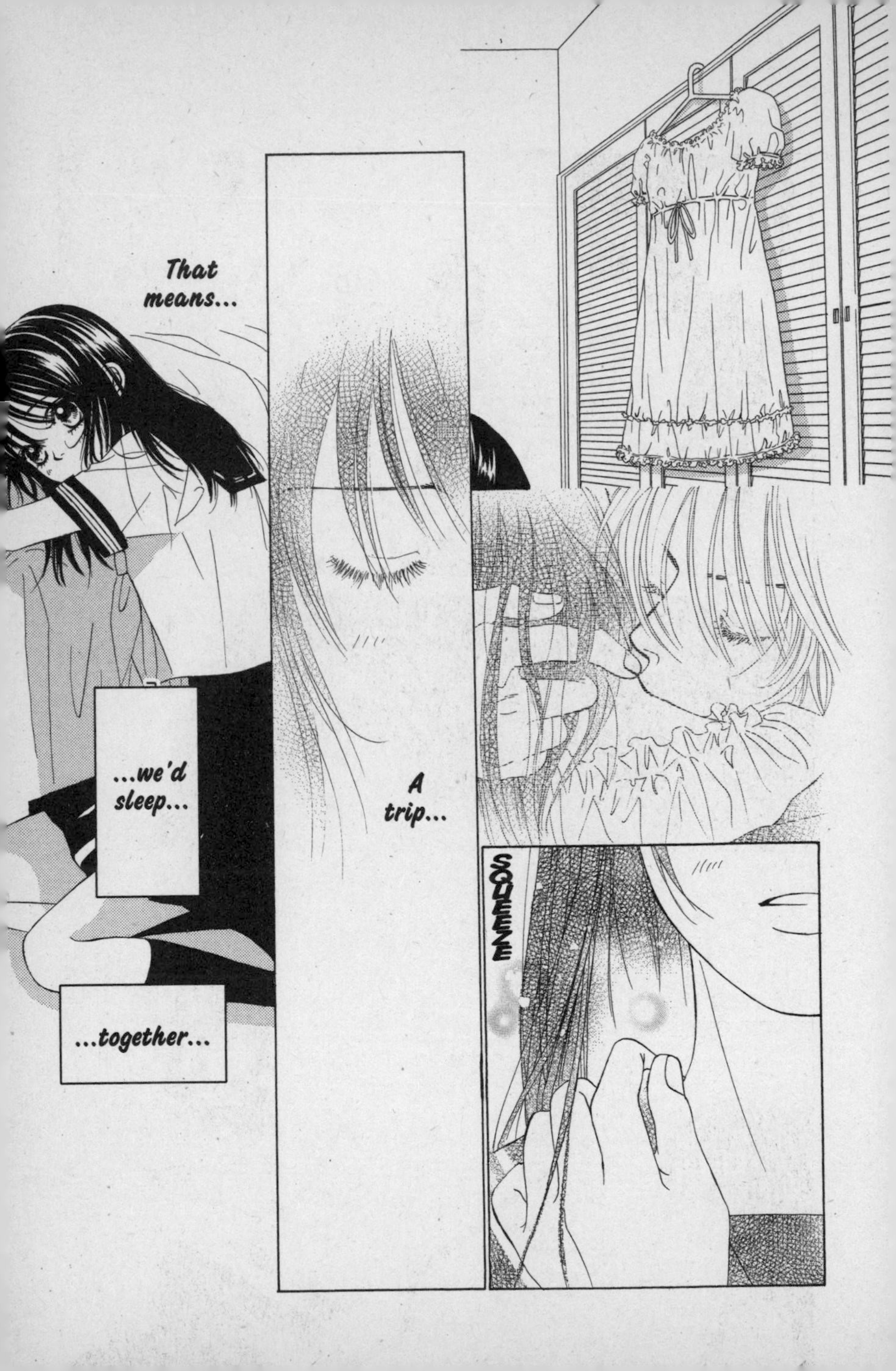
SQUEEZE
A trip...
That means...
...we'd sleep...
...together...

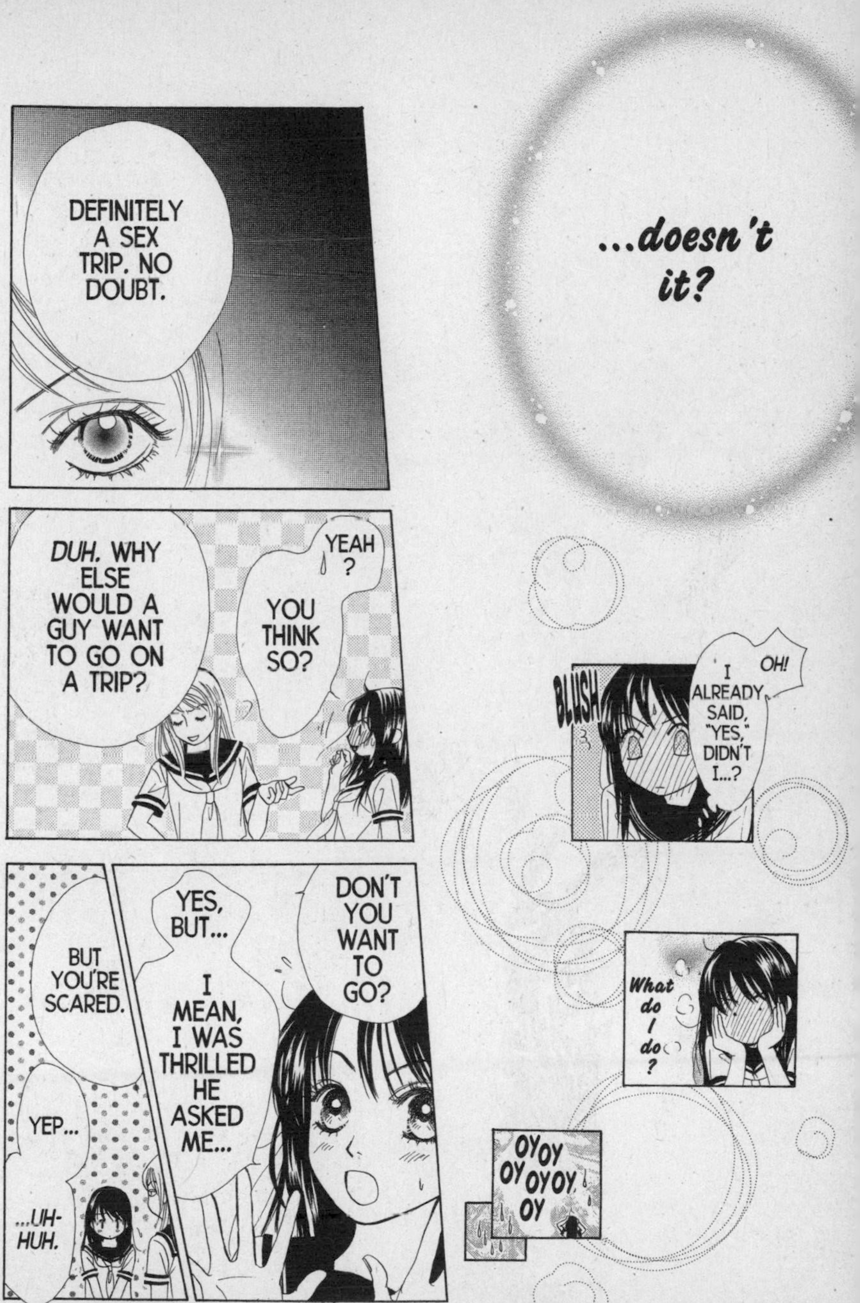
...doesn't it?
BLUSH
OH!
I ALREADY SAID, "YES," DIDN'T I...?
What do I do?
OYOY OYOYOY, OY
DEFINITELY A SEX TRIP. NO DOUBT.
YEAH?
YOU THINK SO?
DUH. WHY ELSE WOULD A GUY WANT TO GO ON A TRIP?
DON'T YOU WANT TO GO?
YES, BUT...
I MEAN, I WAS THRILLED HE ASKED ME...
BUT YOU'RE SCARED.
YEP...
...UH-HUH.

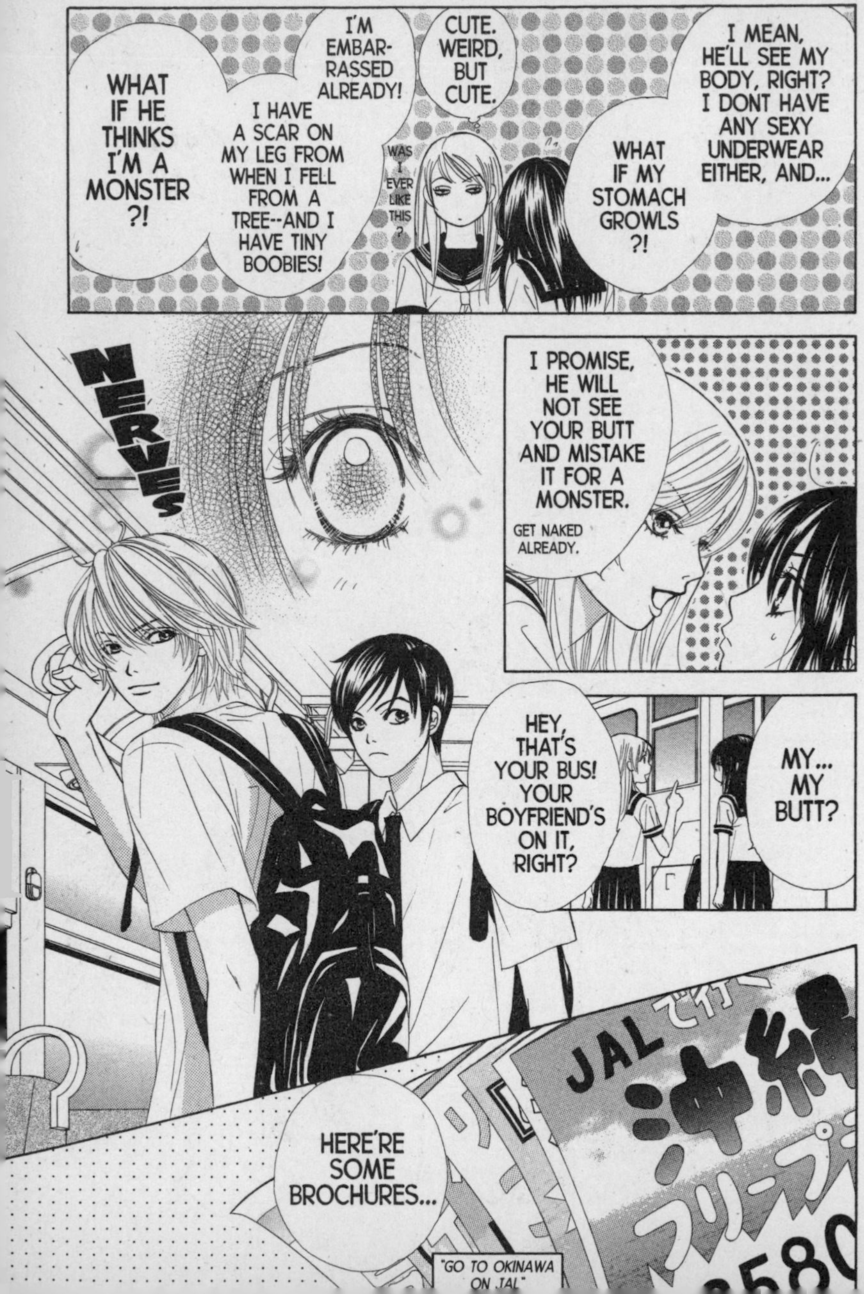
I MEAN, HE'LL SEE MY BODY, RIGHT? I DONT HAVE ANY SEXY UNDERWEAR EITHER, AND...
WHAT IF MY STOMACH GROWLS ?!
CUTE. WEIRD, BUT CUTE.
WAS I EVER LIKE THIS ?
I'M EMBARRASSED ALREADY!
I HAVE A SCAR ON MY LEG FROM WHEN I FELL FROM A TREE--AND I HAVE TINY BOOBIES!
WHAT IF HE THINKS I'M A MONSTER ?!
I PROMISE, HE WILL NOT SEE YOUR BUTT AND MISTAKE IT FOR A MONSTER.
GET NAKED ALREADY.
MY... MY BUTT?
HEY, THAT'S YOUR BUS! YOUR BOYFRIEND'S ON IT, RIGHT?
NERVES
JAL
HERE'RE SOME BROCHURES...
"GO TO OKINAWA ON JAL"

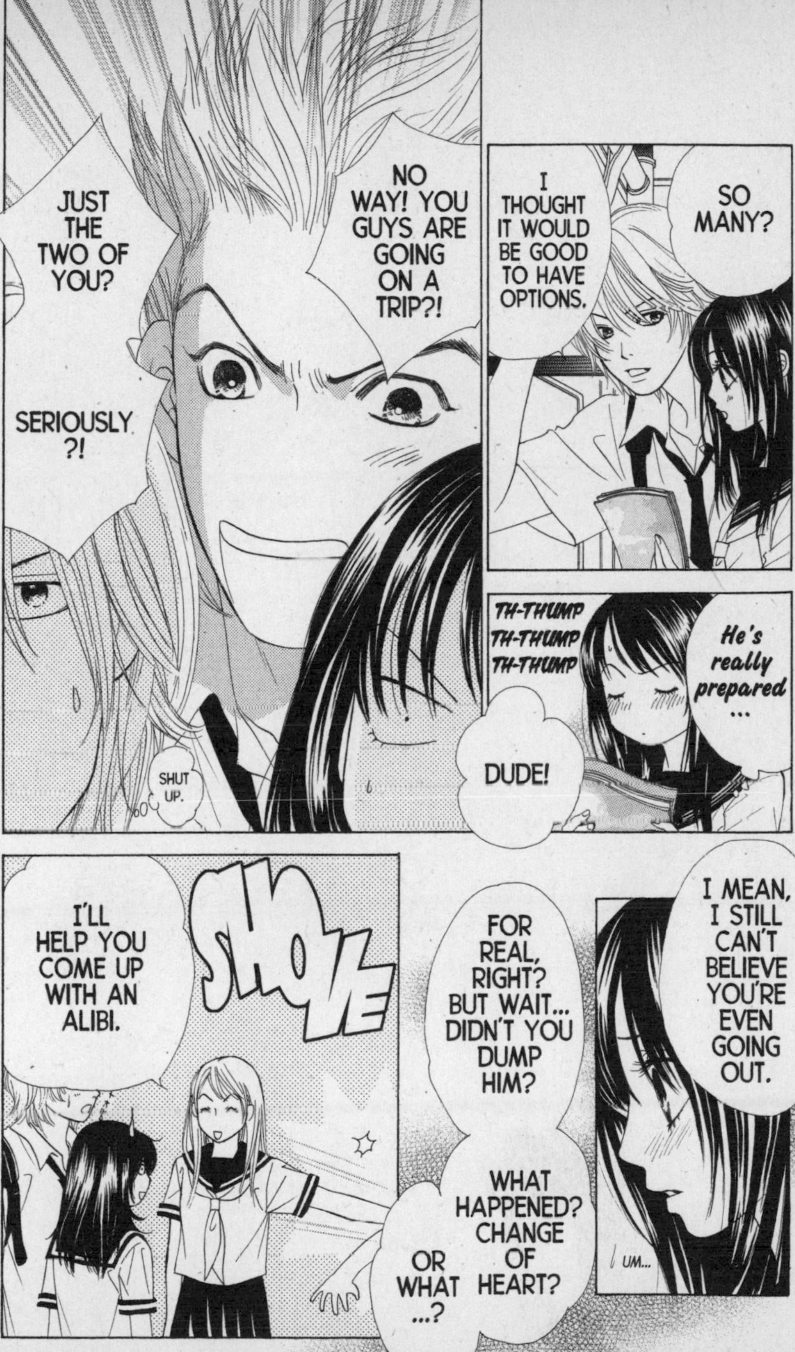
SO MANY?
I THOUGHT IT WOULD BE GOOD TO HAVE OPTIONS.
TH-THUMP TH-THUMP TH-THUMP
He's really prepared...
DUDE!
NO WAY! YOU GUYS ARE GOING ON A TRIP?!
JUST THE TWO OF YOU?
SERIOUSLY?!
SHUT UP.
I MEAN, I STILL CAN'T BELIEVE YOU'RE EVEN GOING OUT.
UM...
FOR REAL, RIGHT? BUT WAIT... DIDN'T YOU DUMP HIM?
WHAT HAPPENED? CHANGE OF HEART? OR WHAT...?
SHOVE
I'LL HELP YOU COME UP WITH AN ALIBI.

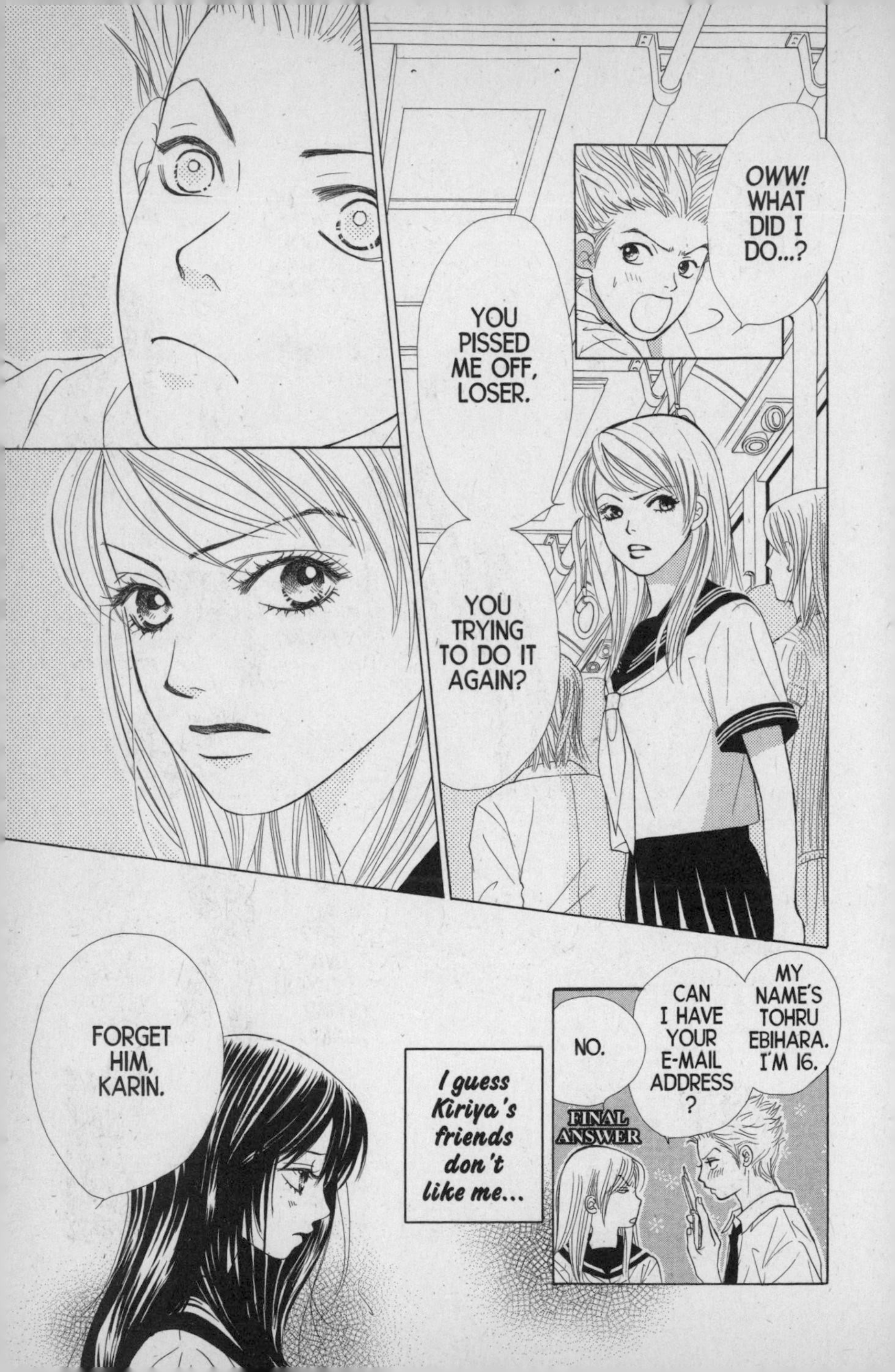

OWW! WHAT DID I DO...?
YOU PISSED ME OFF, LOSER.
YOU TRYING TO DO IT AGAIN?
MY NAME'S TOHRU EBIHARA. I'M 16.
CAN I HAVE YOUR E-MAIL ADDRESS ?
NO.
FINAL ANSWER
I guess Kiriya's friends don't like me...
FORGET HIM, KARIN.

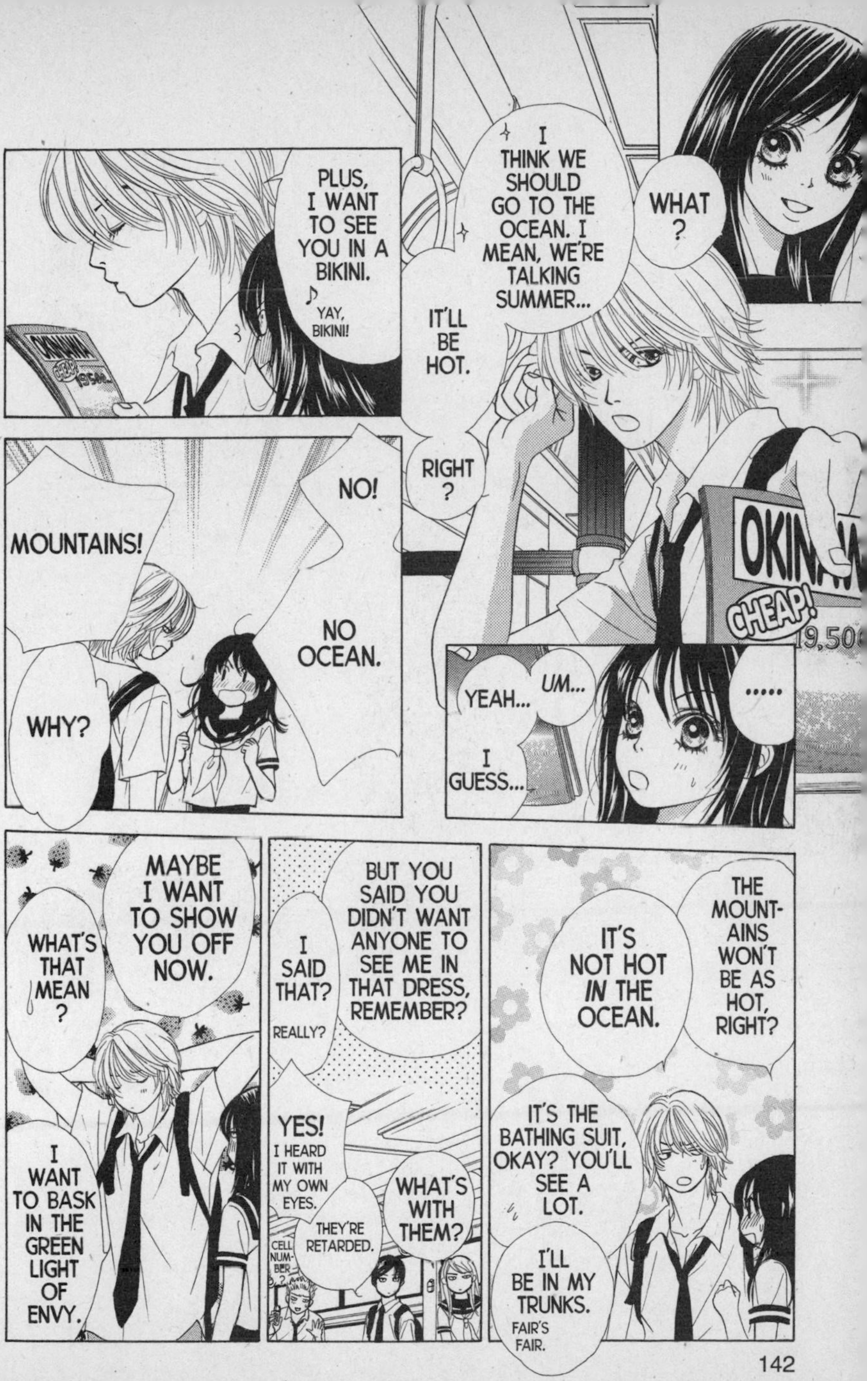
WHAT?
I THINK WE SHOULD GO TO THE OCEAN. I MEAN, WE'RE TALKING SUMMER...
IT'LL BE HOT.
RIGHT?
CHEAP!
.....
UM...
YEAH...
I GUESS...
PLUS, I WANT TO SEE YOU IN A BIKINI. ♪
YAY, BIKINI!
NO!
NO OCEAN.
MOUNTAINS!
WHY?
THE MOUNTAINS WON'T BE AS HOT, RIGHT?
IT'S NOT HOT *IN* THE OCEAN.
IT'S THE BATHING SUIT, OKAY? YOU'LL SEE A LOT.
I'LL BE IN MY TRUNKS.
FAIR'S FAIR.
BUT YOU SAID YOU DIDN'T WANT ANYONE TO SEE ME IN THAT DRESS, REMEMBER?
I SAID THAT?
REALLY?
YES!
I HEARD IT WITH MY OWN EYES.
WHAT'S WITH THEM?
THEY'RE RETARDED.
CELL NUMBER?
MAYBE I WANT TO SHOW YOU OFF NOW.
WHAT'S THAT MEAN?
I WANT TO BASK IN THE GREEN LIGHT OF ENVY.

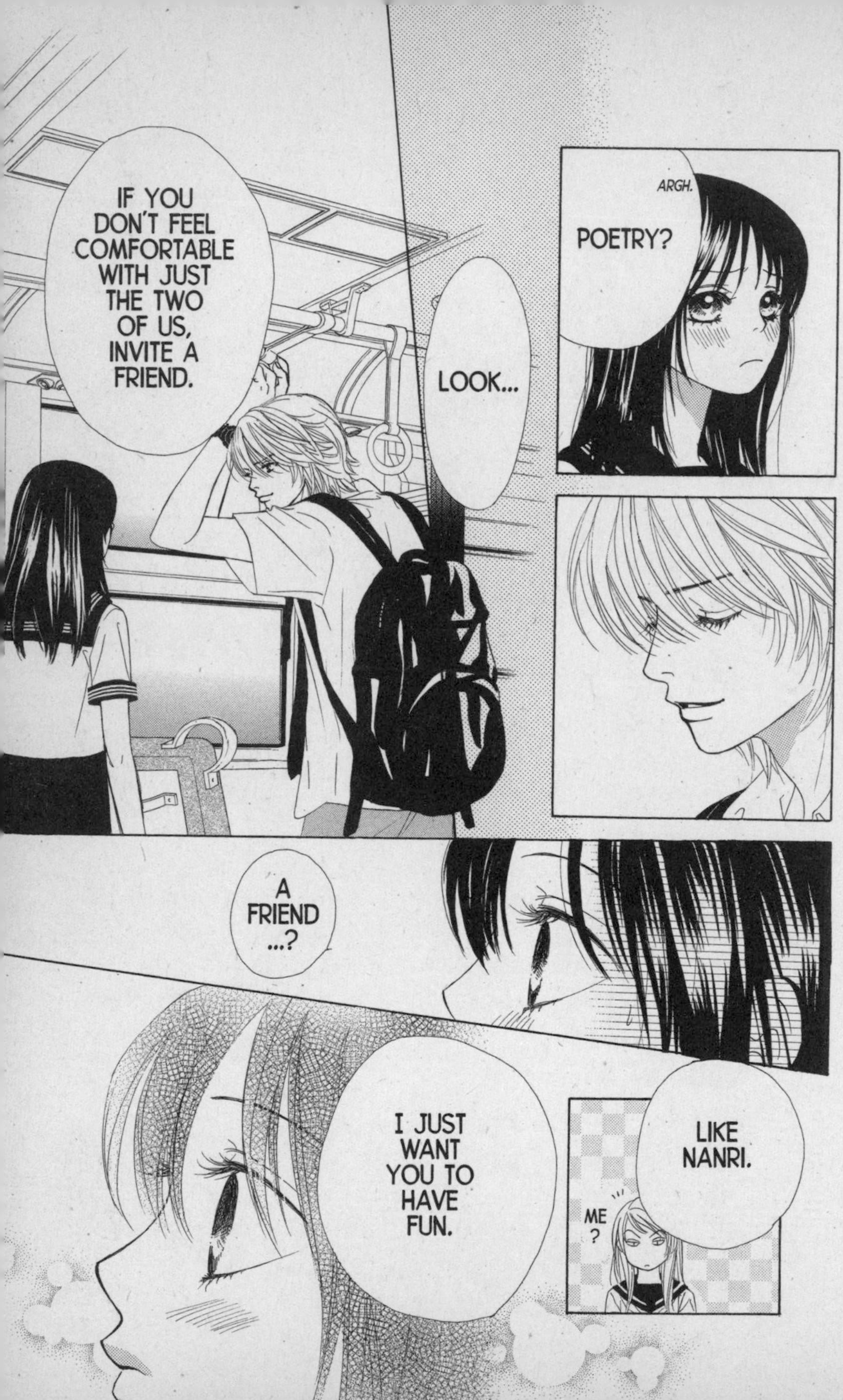
ARGH.
POETRY?
LOOK...
IF YOU DON'T FEEL COMFORTABLE WITH JUST THE TWO OF US, INVITE A FRIEND.
A FRIEND ...?
LIKE NANRI.
ME ?
I JUST WANT YOU TO HAVE FUN.

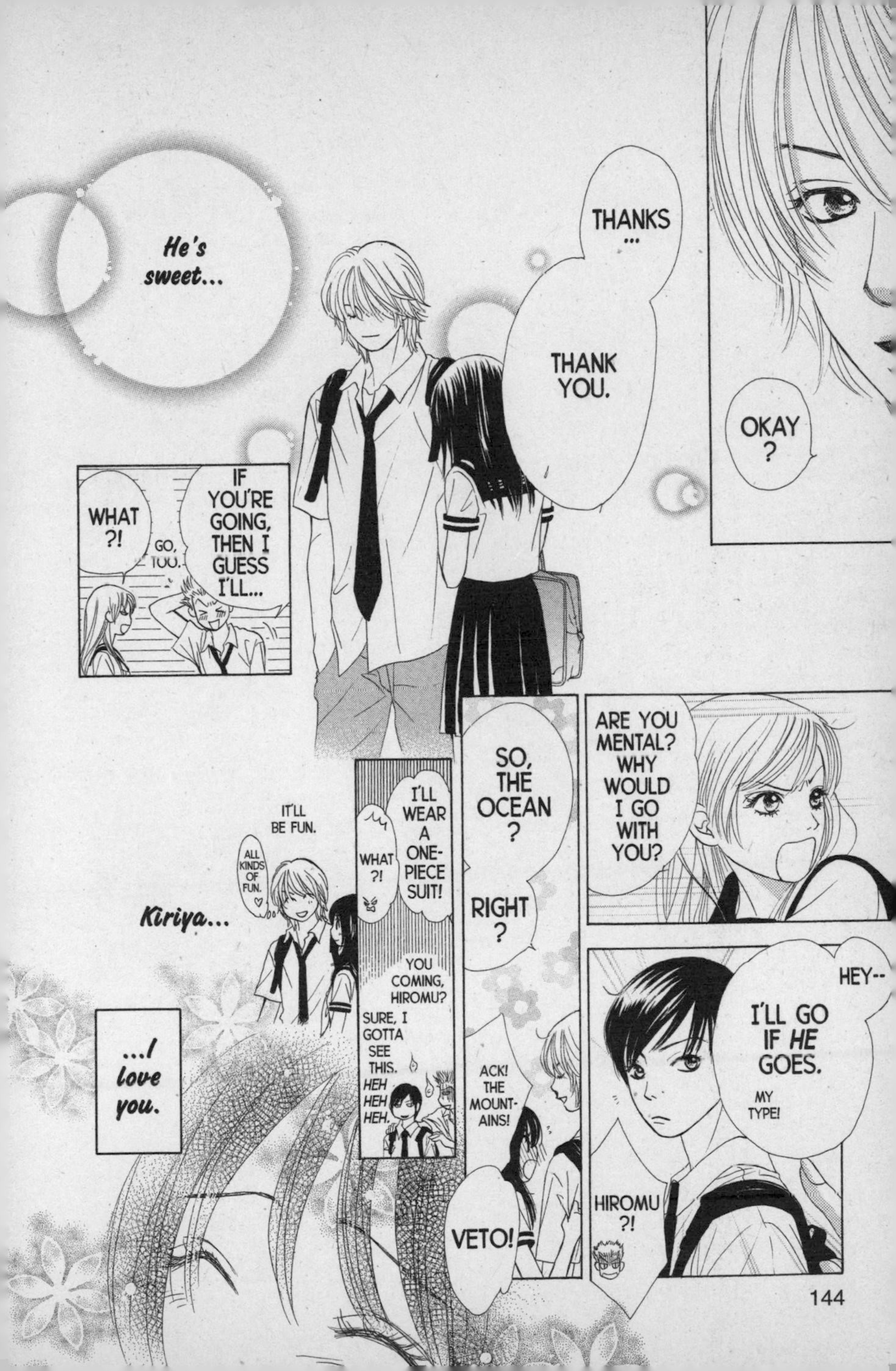
OKAY?
THANKS...
THANK YOU.
He's sweet...
IF YOU'RE GOING, THEN I GUESS I'LL...
GO, TOO.
WHAT?!
ARE YOU MENTAL? WHY WOULD I GO WITH YOU?
SO, THE OCEAN?
RIGHT?
I'LL WEAR A ONE-PIECE SUIT!
WHAT?!
IT'LL BE FUN.
ALL KINDS OF FUN.
Kiriya...
YOU COMING, HIROMU?
SURE, I GOTTA SEE THIS. HEH HEH HEH.
HEY--
I'LL GO IF HE GOES.
MY TYPE!
HIROMU?!
ACK! THE MOUNT-AINS!
VETO!
...I love you.

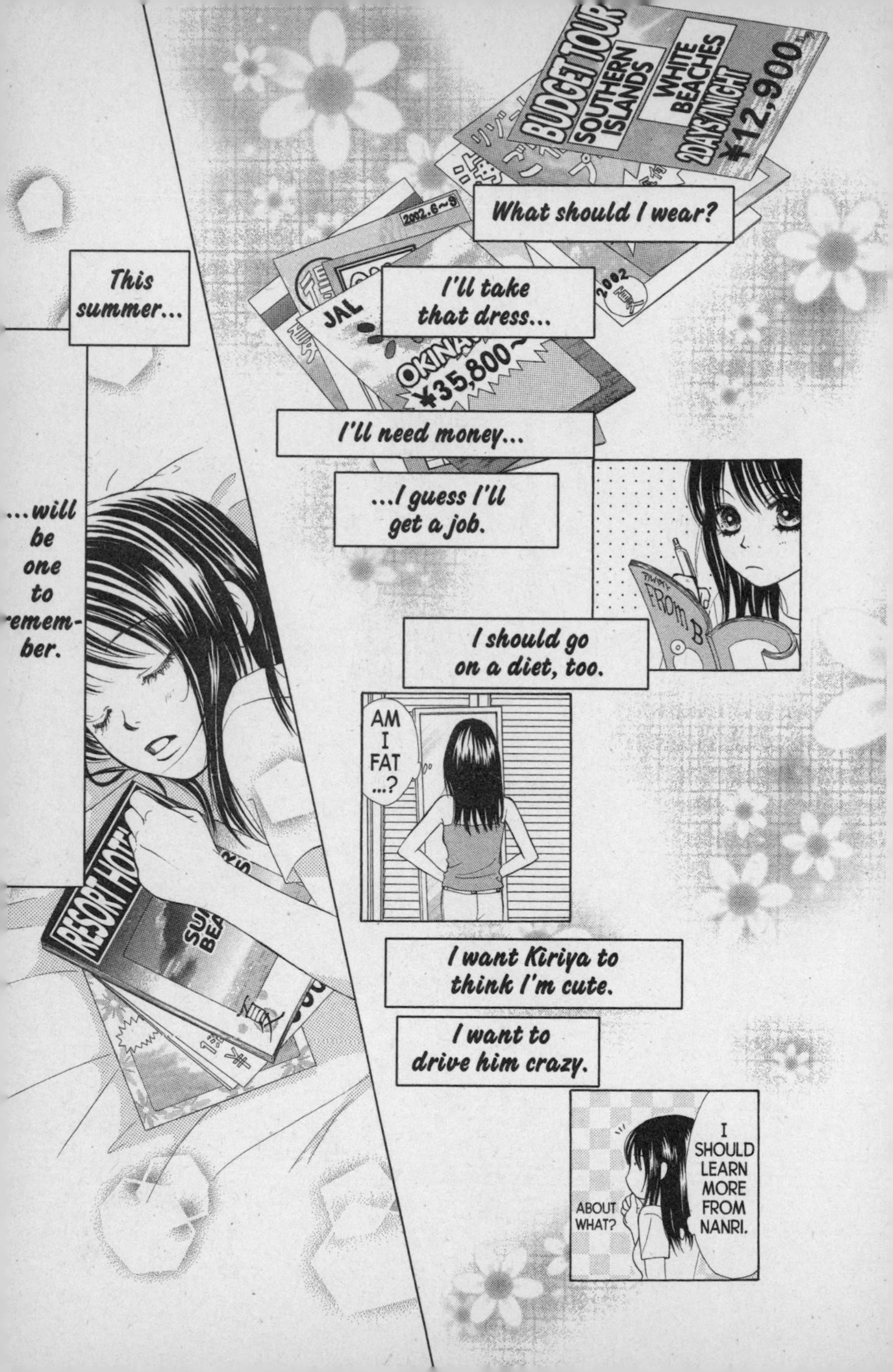

BUDGET TOUR
SOUTHERN ISLANDS
WHITE BEACHES
2DAYS 1NIGHT
¥12,900
What should I wear?
2002.6~9
2002
JAL
I'll take that dress...
¥35,800~
I'll need money...
...I guess I'll get a job.
FROM B
I should go on a diet, too.
AM I FAT ...?
I want Kiriya to think I'm cute.
I want to drive him crazy.
I SHOULD LEARN MORE FROM NANRI.
ABOUT WHAT?
This summer...
...will be one to remember.

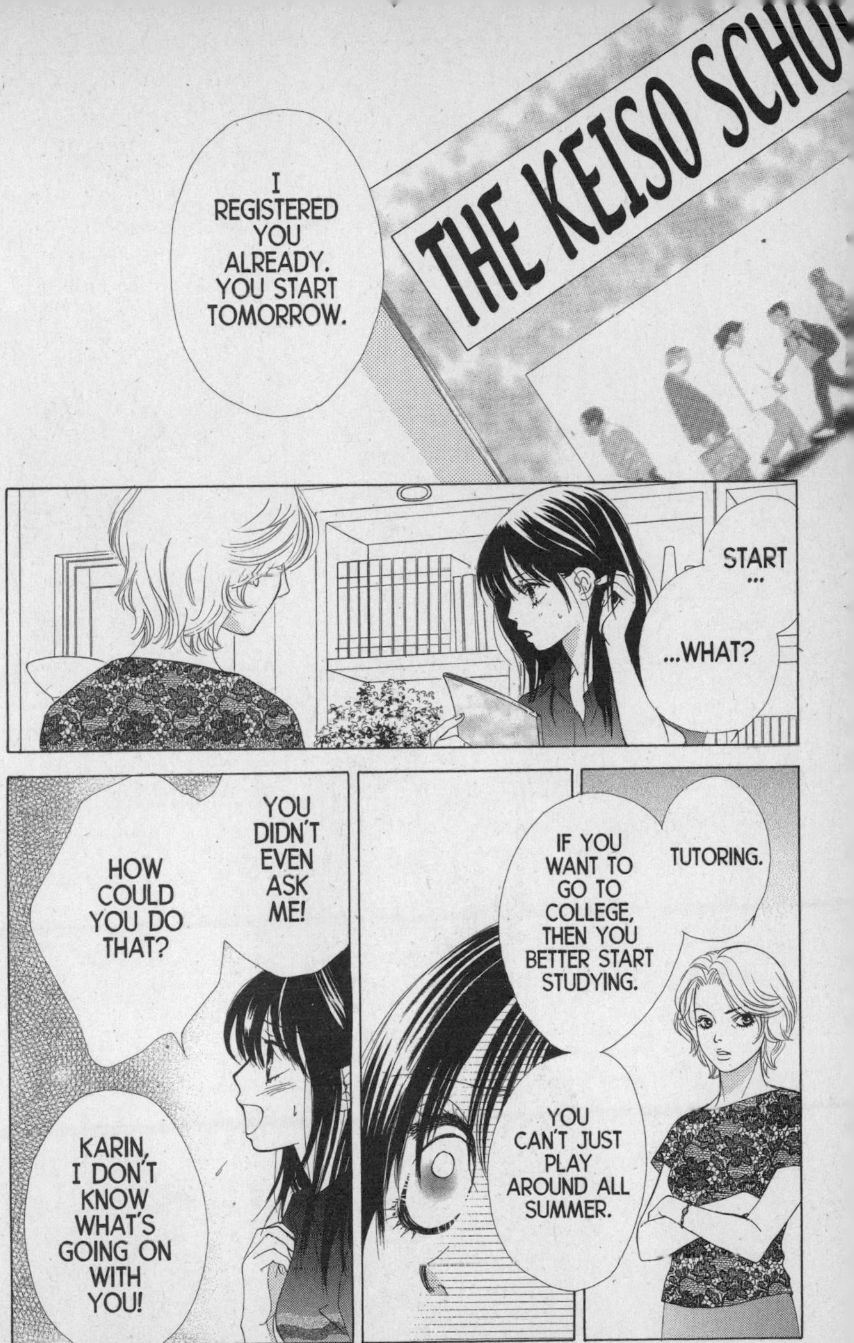
THE KEISO SCH
I REGISTERED YOU ALREADY. YOU START TOMORROW.
START ...
...WHAT?
TUTORING.
IF YOU WANT TO GO TO COLLEGE, THEN YOU BETTER START STUDYING.
YOU CAN'T JUST PLAY AROUND ALL SUMMER.
YOU DIDN'T EVEN ASK ME!
HOW COULD YOU DO THAT?
KARIN, I DON'T KNOW WHAT'S GOING ON WITH YOU!

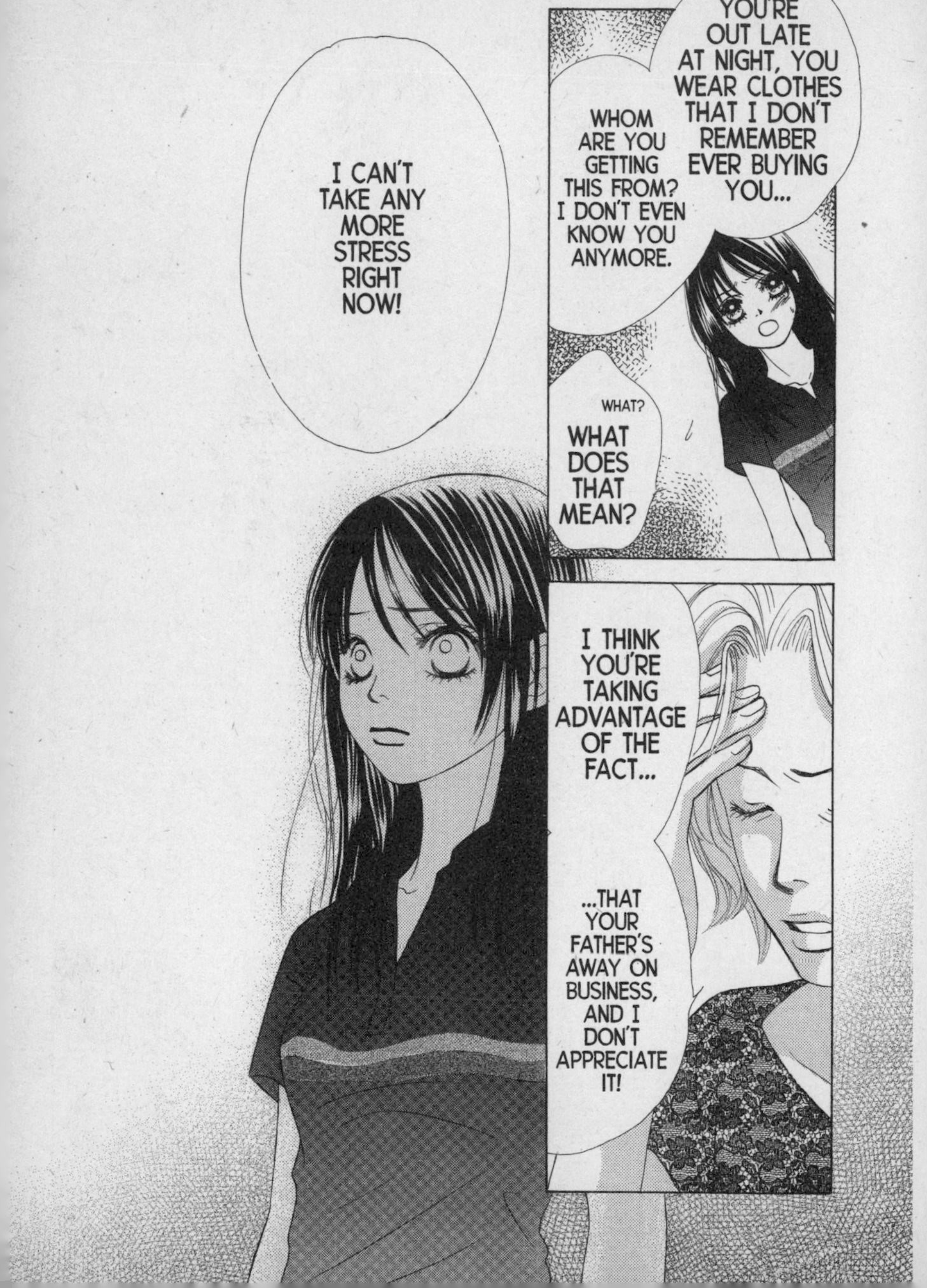
YOU'RE OUT LATE AT NIGHT, YOU WEAR CLOTHES THAT I DON'T REMEMBER EVER BUYING YOU...
WHOM ARE YOU GETTING THIS FROM? I DON'T EVEN KNOW YOU ANYMORE.
WHAT?
WHAT DOES THAT MEAN?
I THINK YOU'RE TAKING ADVANTAGE OF THE FACT...
...THAT YOUR FATHER'S AWAY ON BUSINESS, AND I DON'T APPRECIATE IT!
I CAN'T TAKE ANY MORE STRESS RIGHT NOW!

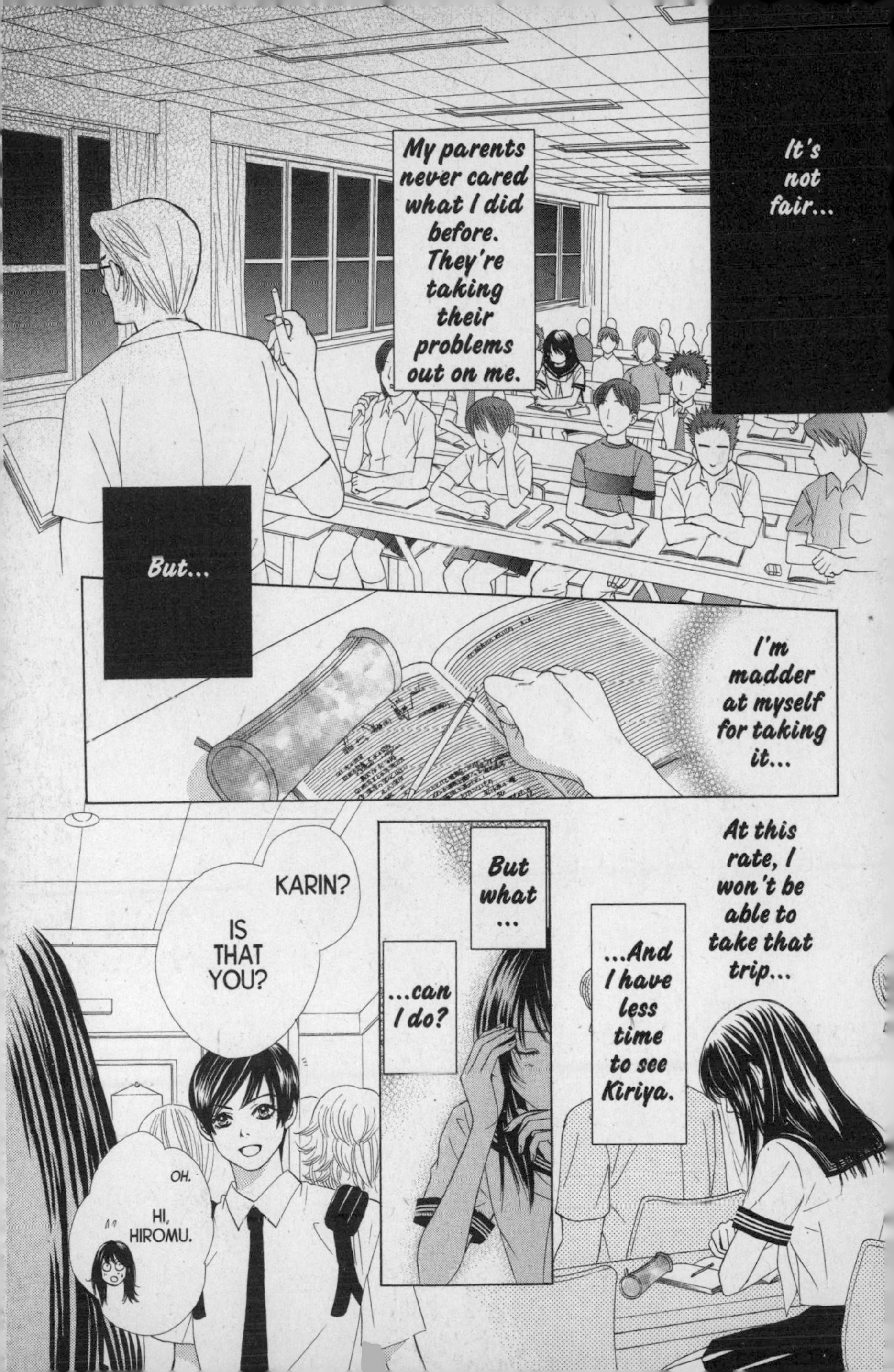
It's not fair...
My parents never cared what I did before. They're taking their problems out on me.
But...
I'm madder at myself for taking it...
At this rate, I won't be able to take that trip...
...And I have less time to see Kiriya.
But what...
...can I do?
KARIN? IS THAT YOU?
OH. HI, HIROMU.

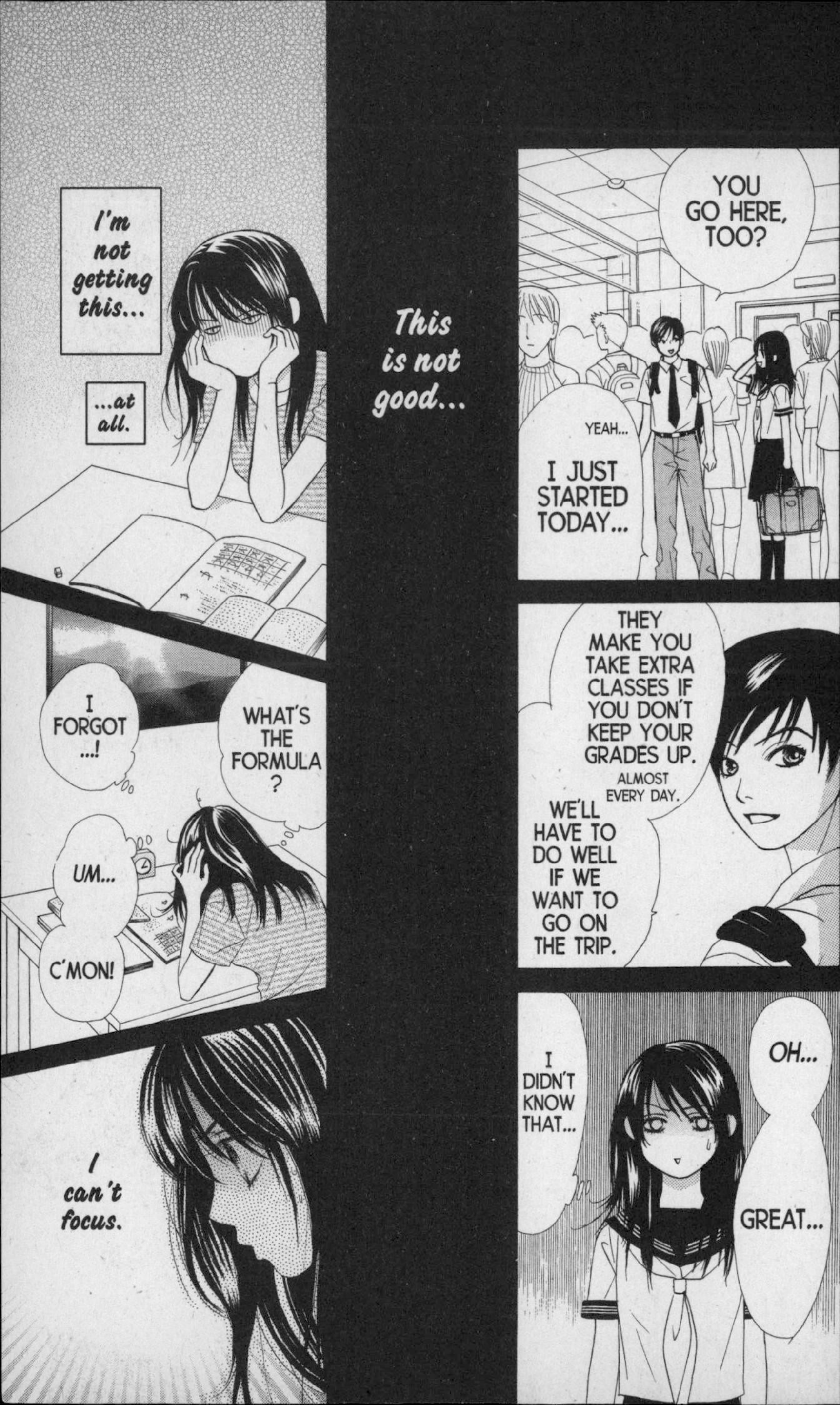
YOU GO HERE, TOO?
YEAH...
I JUST STARTED TODAY...
THEY MAKE YOU TAKE EXTRA CLASSES IF YOU DON'T KEEP YOUR GRADES UP.
ALMOST EVERY DAY.
WE'LL HAVE TO DO WELL IF WE WANT TO GO ON THE TRIP.
OH... GREAT...
I DIDN'T KNOW THAT...
This is not good...
I'm not getting this...
...at all.
WHAT'S THE FORMULA?
I FORGOT...!
UM...
C'MON!
I can't focus.

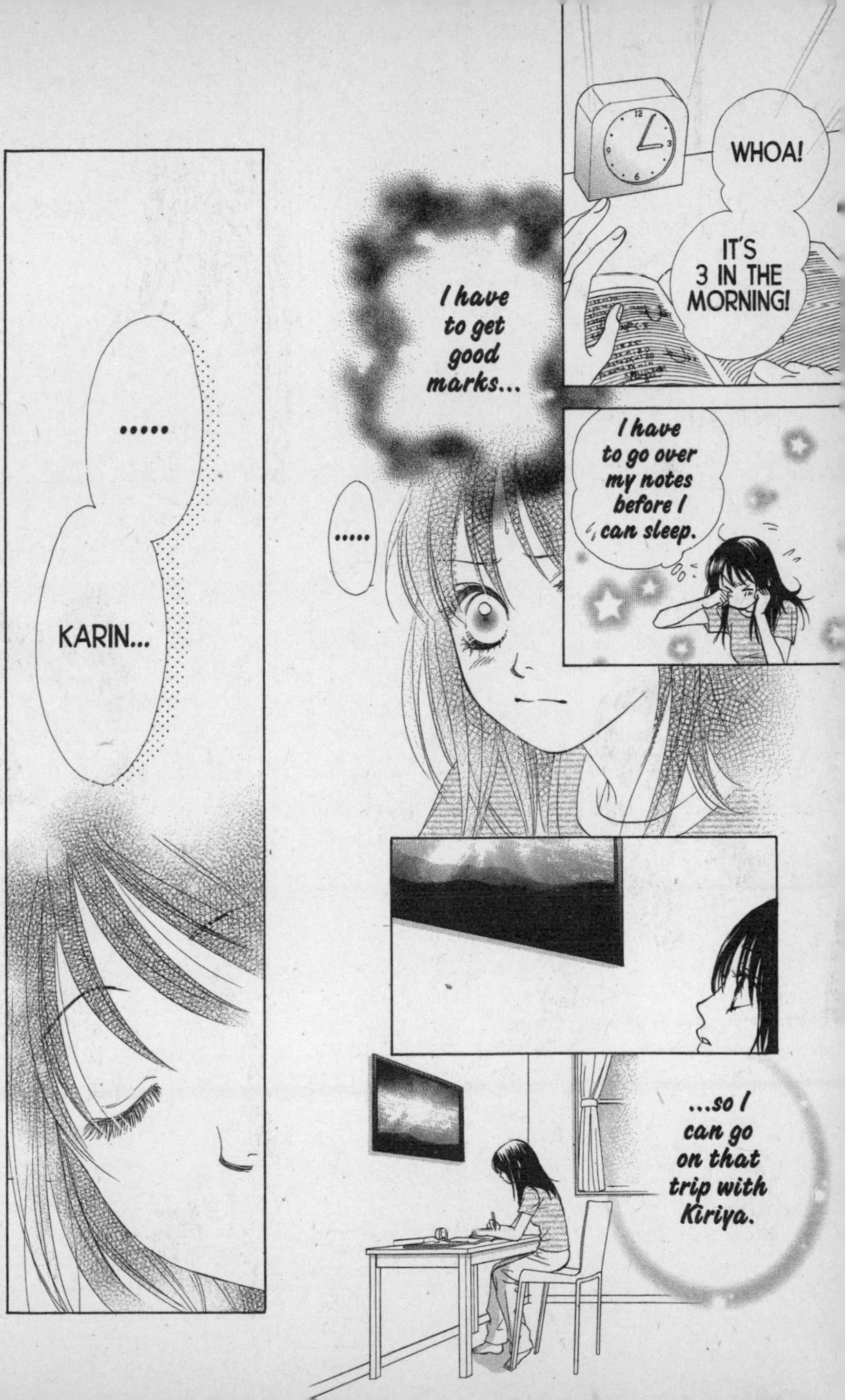
WHOA!
IT'S 3 IN THE MORNING!
I have to go over my notes before I can sleep.
I have to get good marks...
.....
...so I can go on that trip with Kiriya.
.....
KARIN...

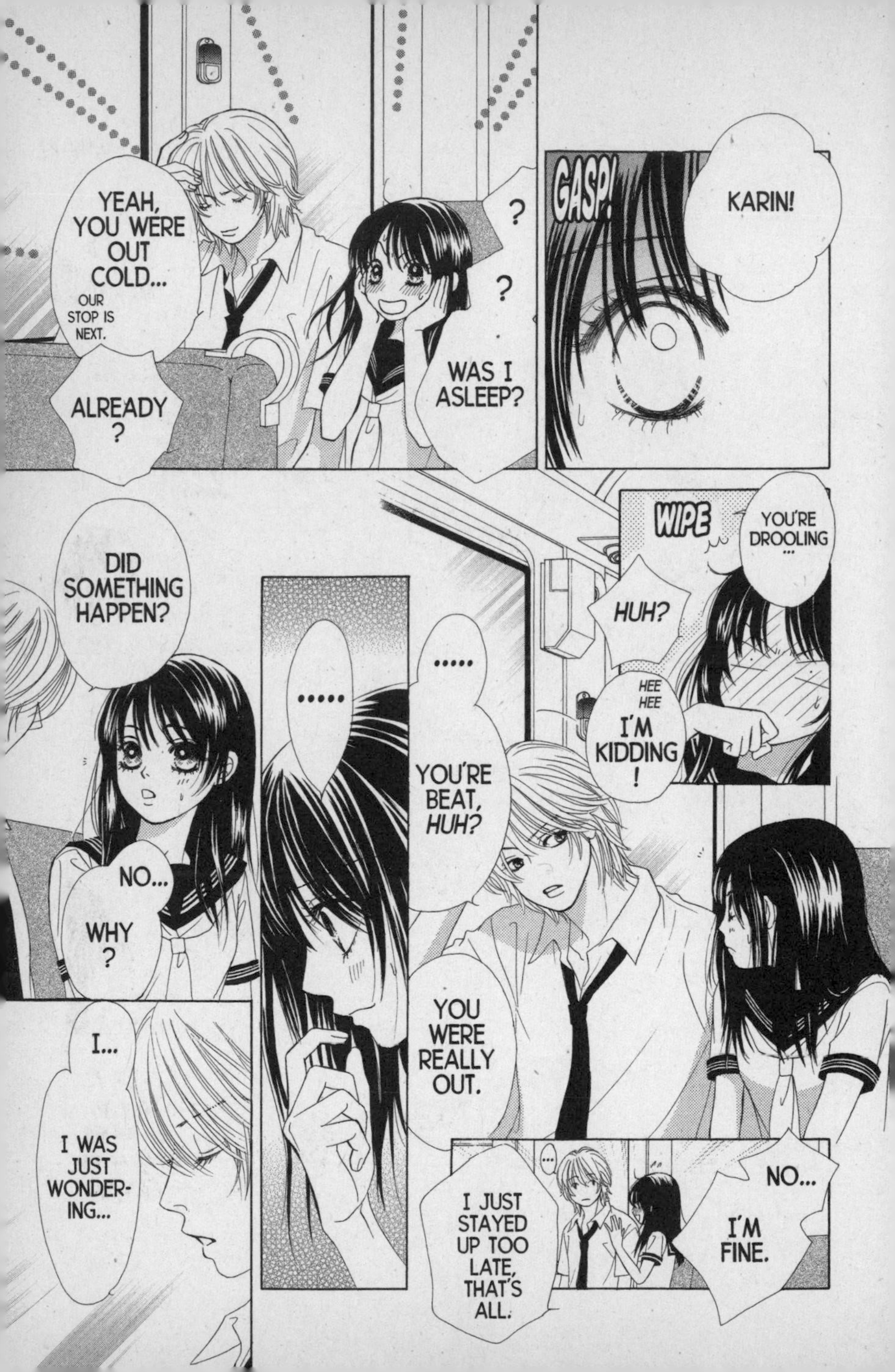
KARIN!
GASP!
?
?
WAS I ASLEEP?
YEAH, YOU WERE OUT COLD...
OUR STOP IS NEXT.
ALREADY?
YOU'RE DROOLING...
WIPE
HUH?
HEE HEE
I'M KIDDING!
.....
YOU'RE BEAT, HUH?
YOU WERE REALLY OUT.
.....
...
NO...
I'M FINE.
I JUST STAYED UP TOO LATE, THAT'S ALL.
DID SOMETHING HAPPEN?
NO...
WHY?
I...
I WAS JUST WONDERING...

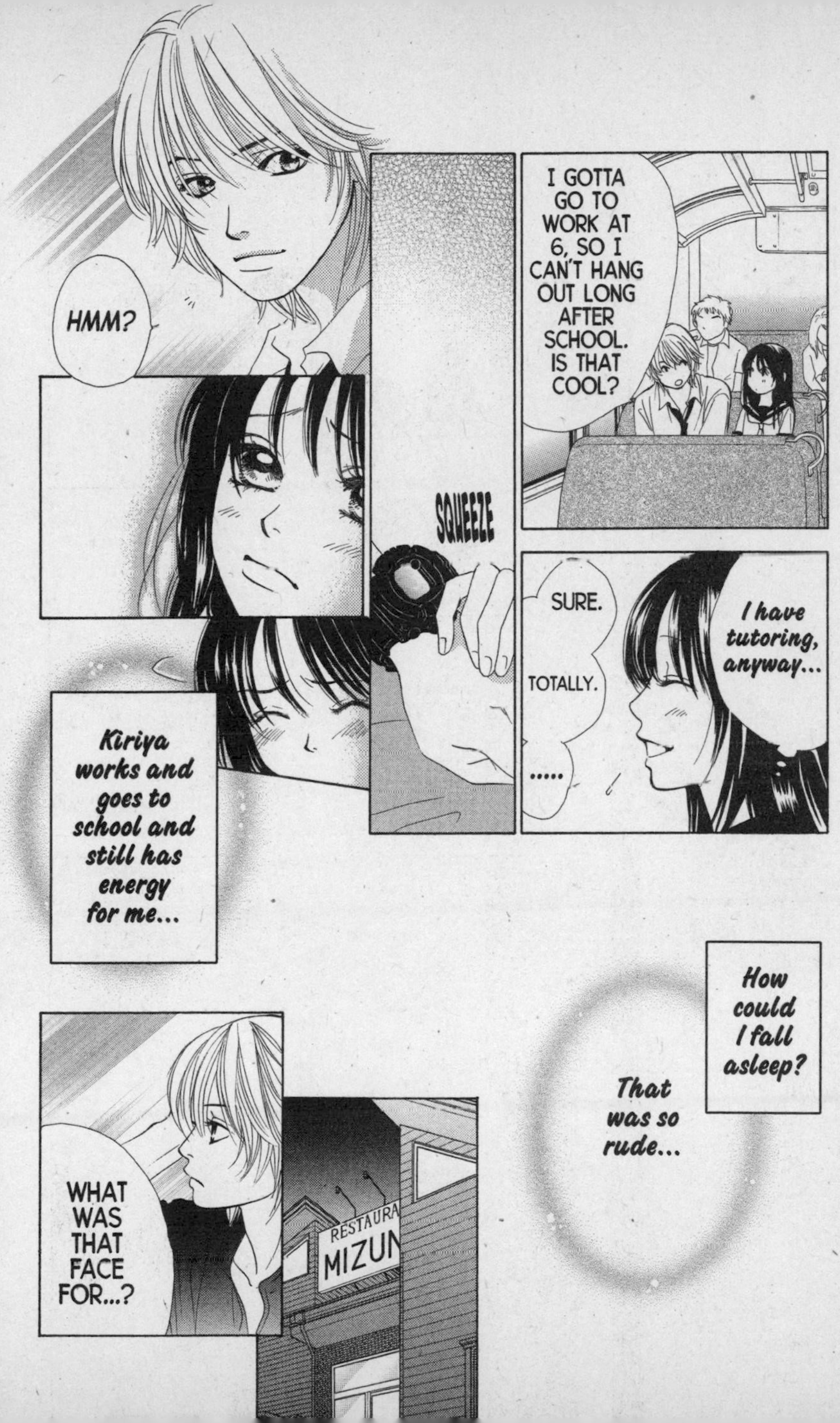
I GOTTA GO TO WORK AT 6, SO I CAN'T HANG OUT LONG AFTER SCHOOL. IS THAT COOL?
I have tutoring, anyway...
SURE.
TOTALLY.
.....
SQUEEZE
HMM?
Kiriya works and goes to school and still has energy for me...
How could I fall asleep?
That was so rude...
WHAT WAS THAT FACE FOR...?
RESTAURA
MIZUN

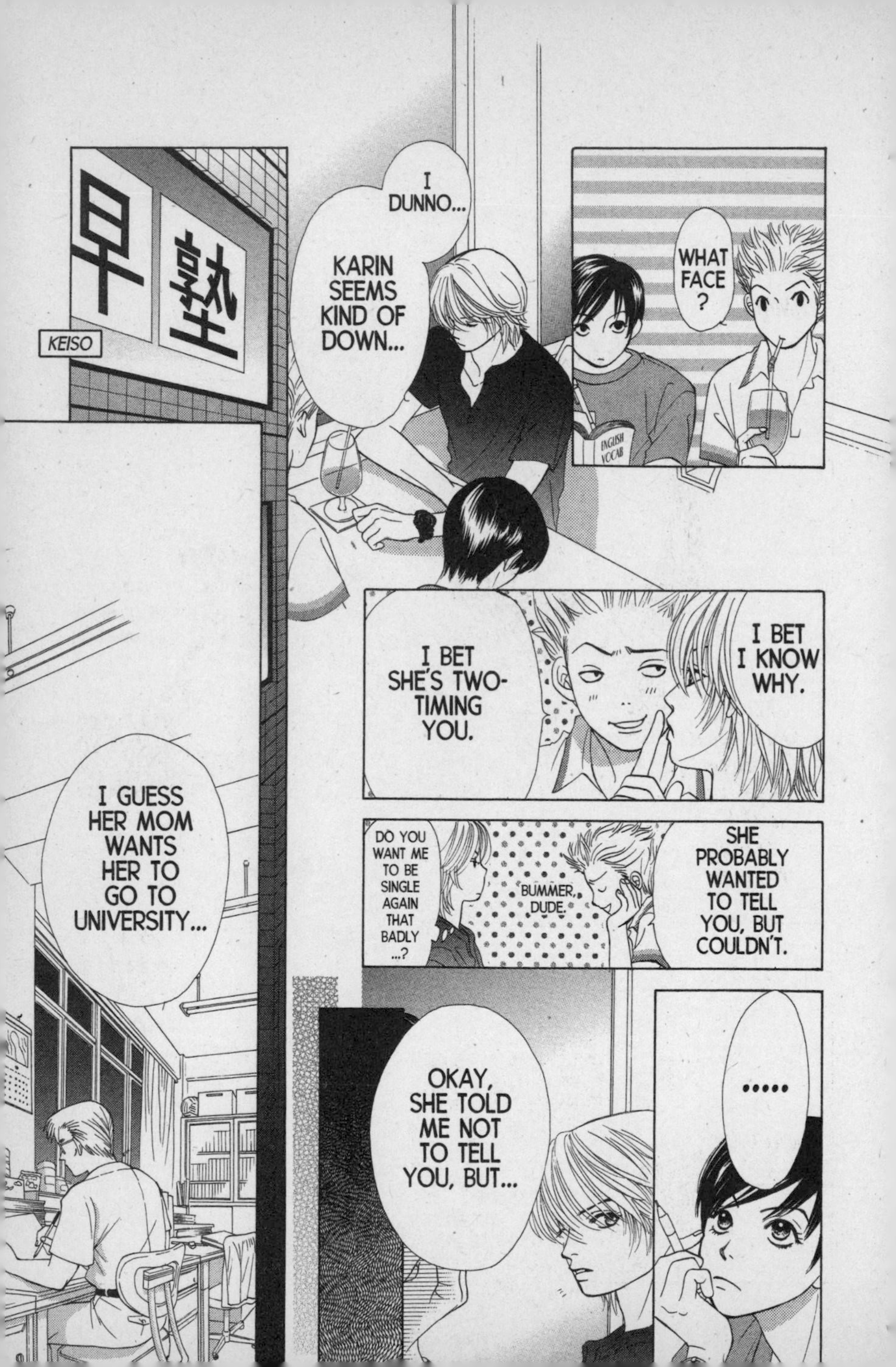
WHAT FACE?
I DUNNO...
KARIN SEEMS KIND OF DOWN...
I BET I KNOW WHY.
I BET SHE'S TWO-TIMING YOU.
SHE PROBABLY WANTED TO TELL YOU, BUT COULDN'T.
BUMMER, DUDE.
DO YOU WANT ME TO BE SINGLE AGAIN THAT BADLY ...?
.....
OKAY, SHE TOLD ME NOT TO TELL YOU, BUT...
早塾
KEISO
I GUESS HER MOM WANTS HER TO GO TO UNIVERSITY...

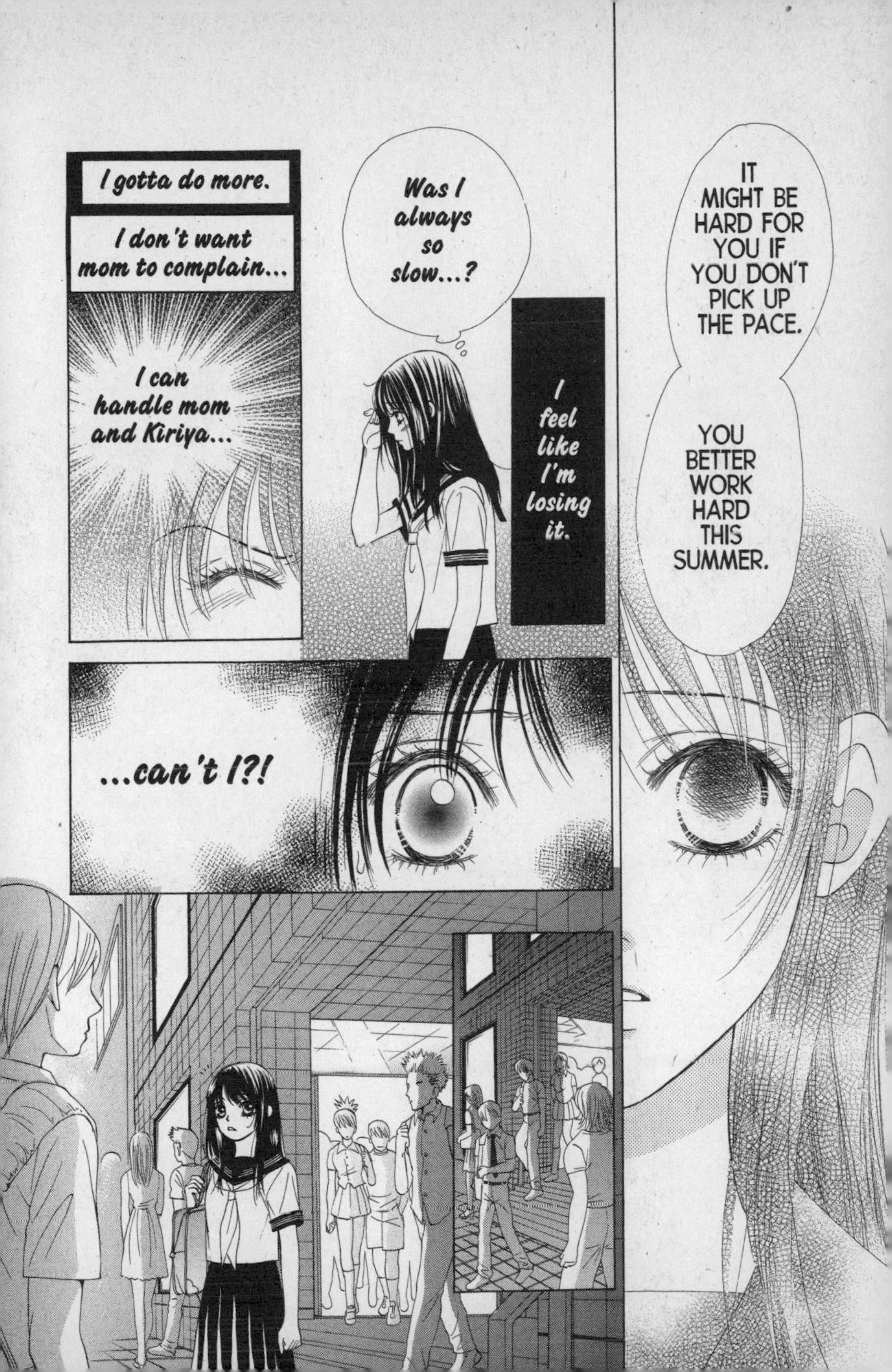
IT MIGHT BE HARD FOR YOU IF YOU DON'T PICK UP THE PACE.
YOU BETTER WORK HARD THIS SUMMER.
Was I always so slow...?
I feel like I'm losing it.
I gotta do more.
I don't want mom to complain...
I can handle mom and Kiriya...
...can't I?!

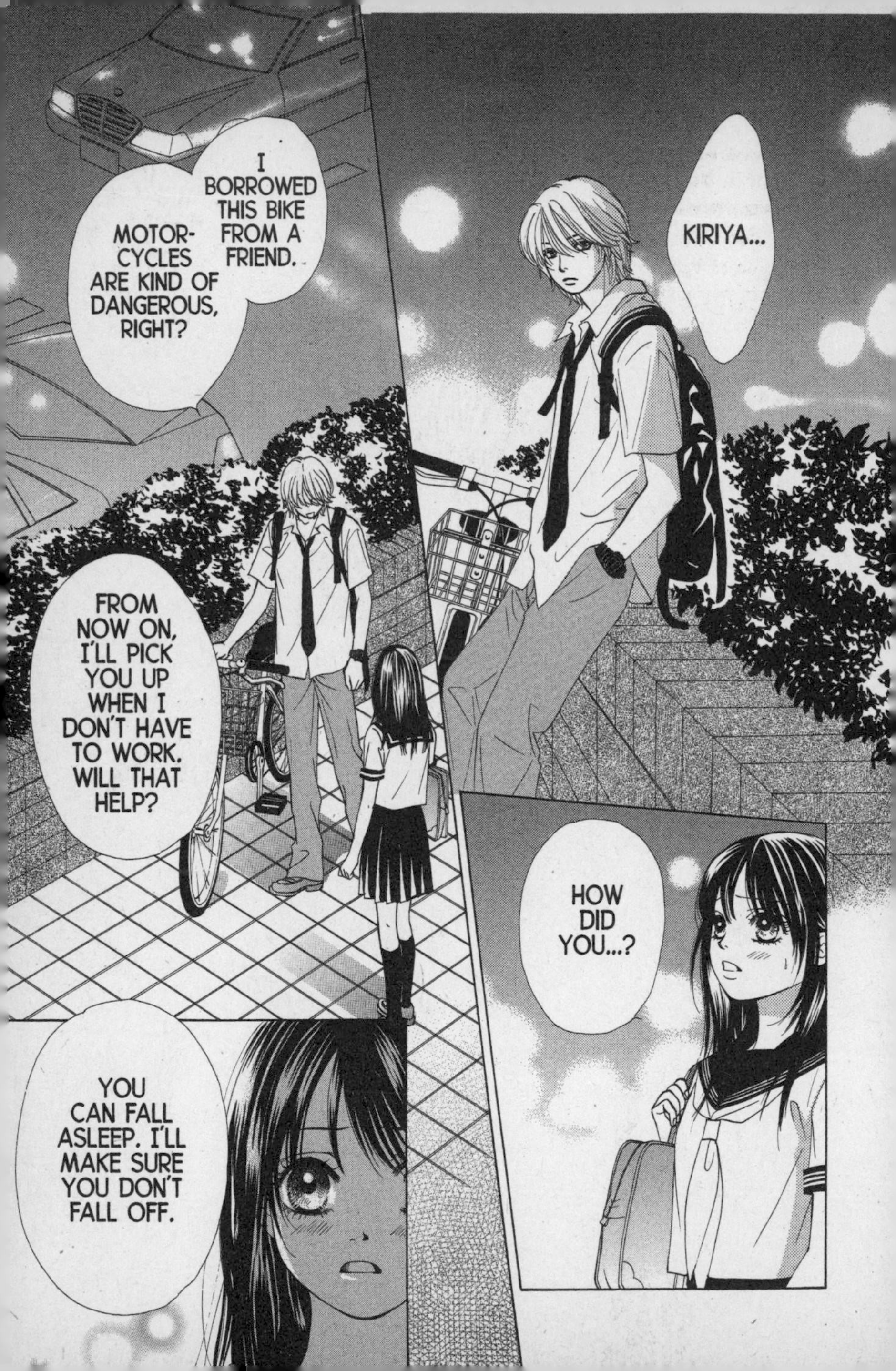
KIRIYA...
HOW DID YOU...?
I BORROWED THIS BIKE FROM A FRIEND.
MOTOR-CYCLES ARE KIND OF DANGEROUS, RIGHT?
FROM NOW ON, I'LL PICK YOU UP WHEN I DON'T HAVE TO WORK. WILL THAT HELP?
YOU CAN FALL ASLEEP. I'LL MAKE SURE YOU DON'T FALL OFF.

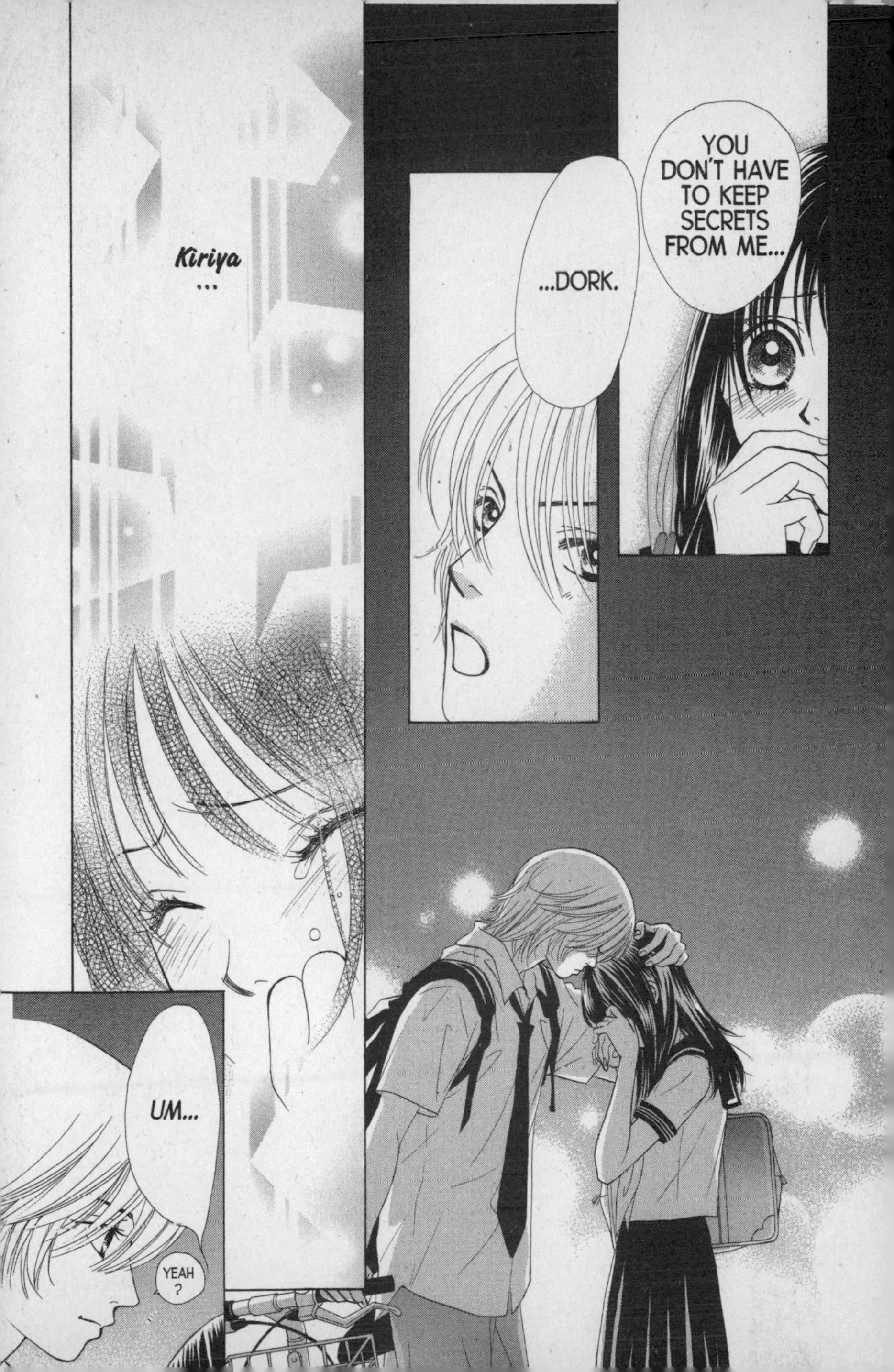
YOU DON'T HAVE TO KEEP SECRETS FROM ME...
...DORK.
Kiriya ...
UM...
YEAH ?

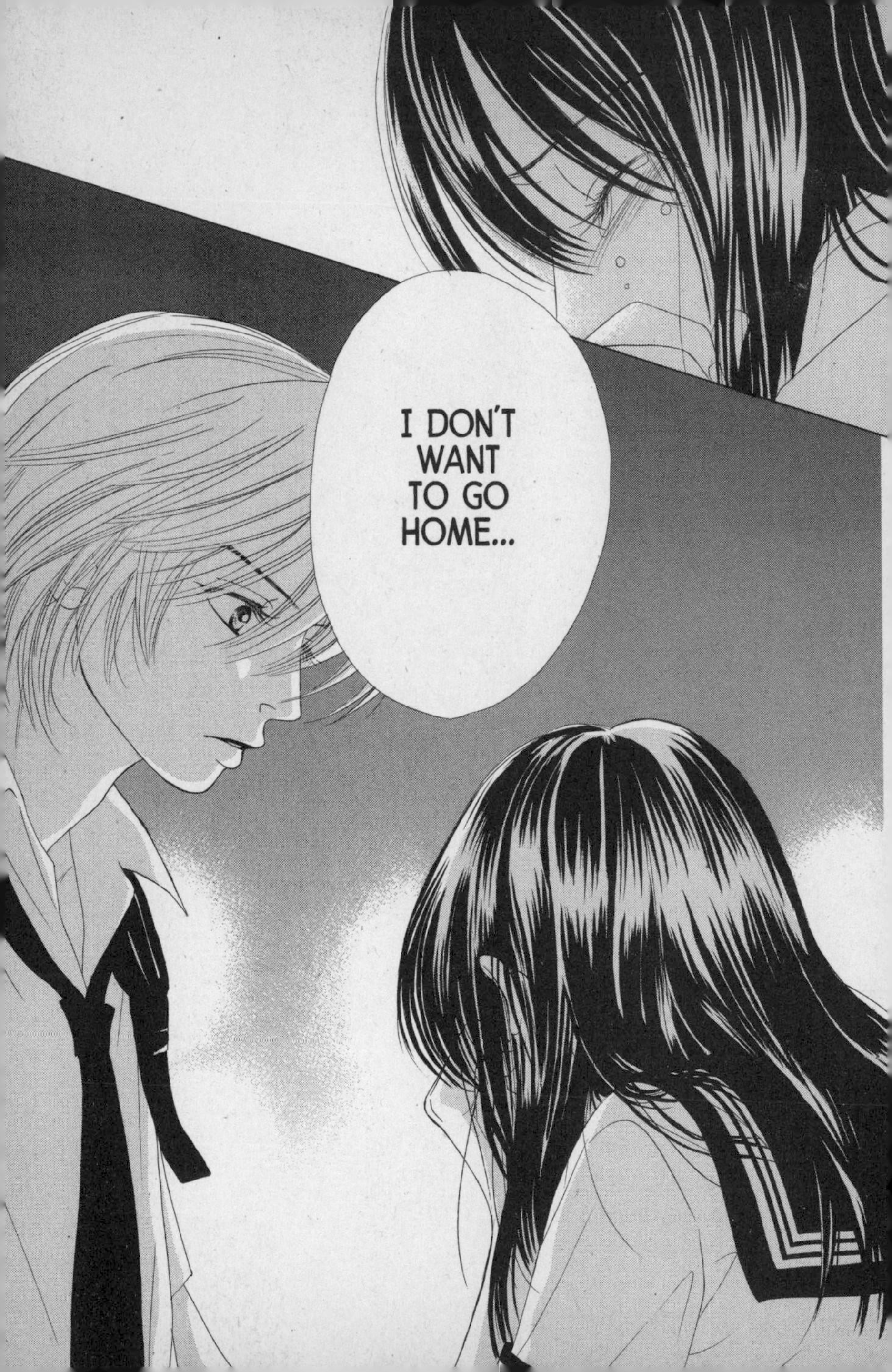
I DON'T WANT TO GO HOME...

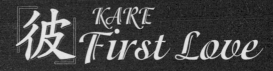

KARE
彼 First Love

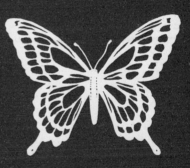

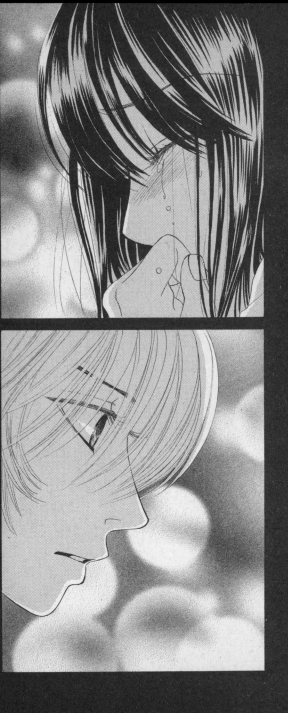

I don't want to go home...

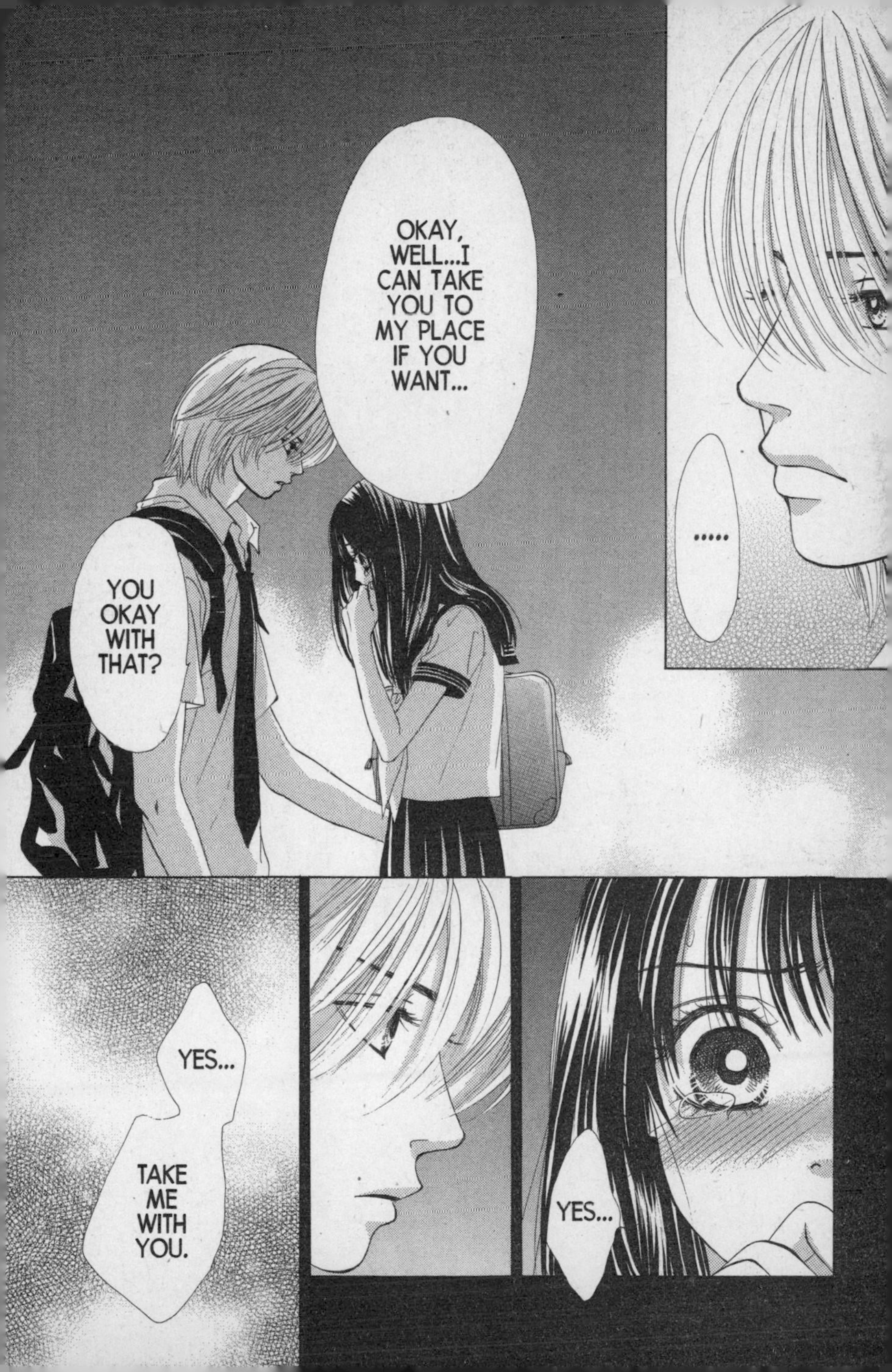
OKAY, WELL...I CAN TAKE YOU TO MY PLACE IF YOU WANT...
YOU OKAY WITH THAT?
.....
YES...
YES...
TAKE ME WITH YOU.

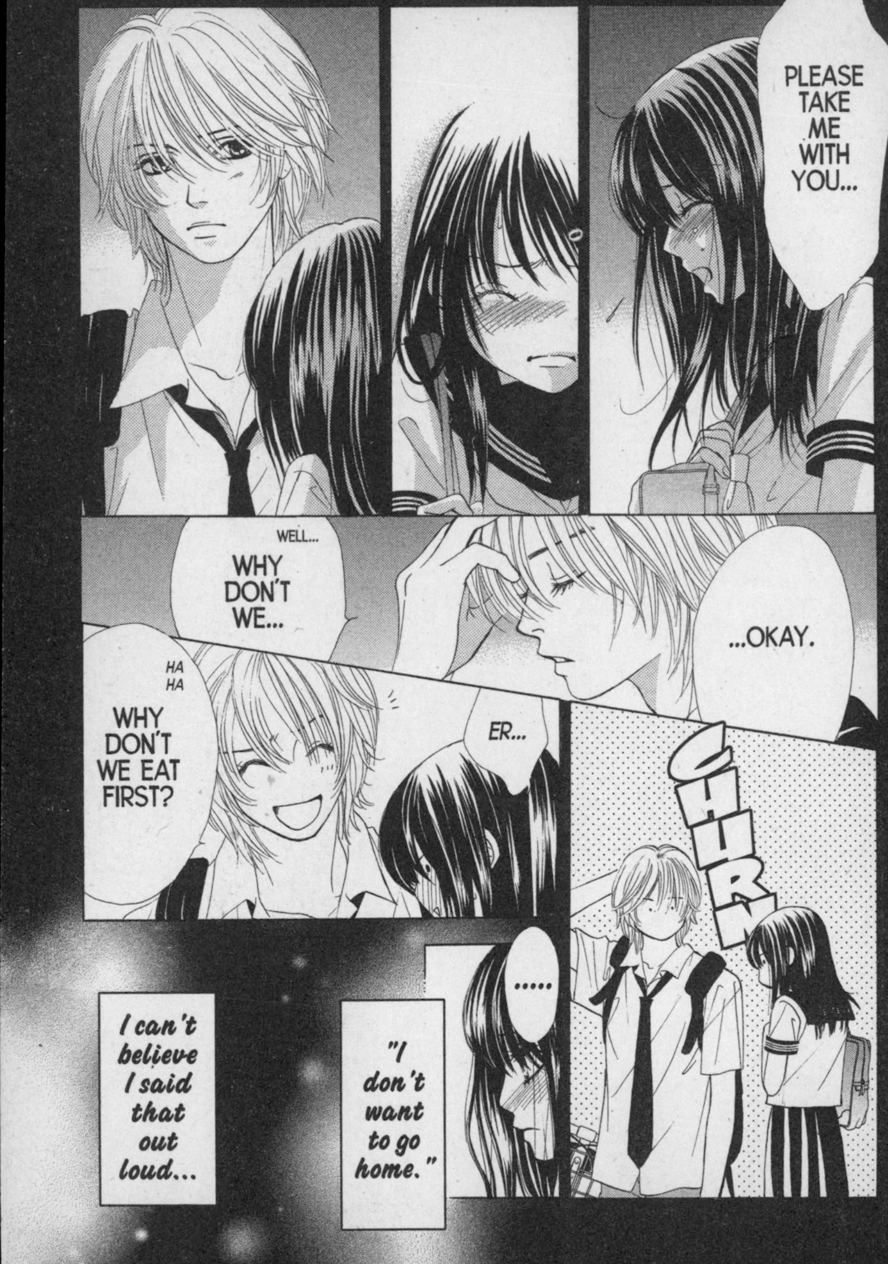
PLEASE TAKE ME WITH YOU...
...OKAY.
WELL... WHY DON'T WE...
CHURN
ER...
HA HA
WHY DON'T WE EAT FIRST?
......
"I don't want to go home."
I can't believe I said that out loud...

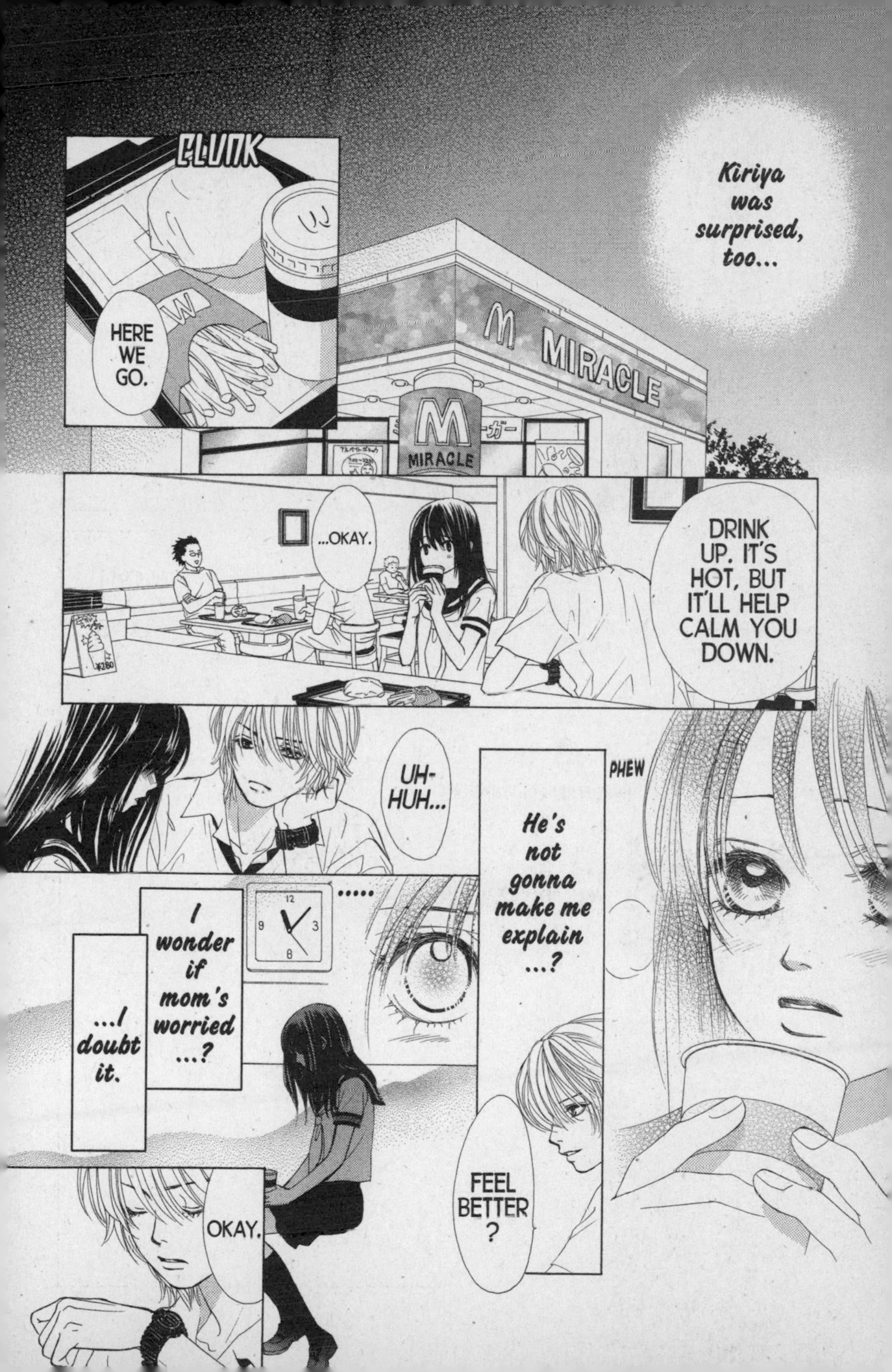
Kiriya was surprised, too...
M MIRACLE
M MIRACLE
CLUNK
HERE WE GO.
DRINK UP. IT'S HOT, BUT IT'LL HELP CALM YOU DOWN.
...OKAY.
PHEW
He's not gonna make me explain ...?
UH-HUH...
.....
I wonder if mom's worried ...?
...I doubt it.
FEEL BETTER ?
OKAY.

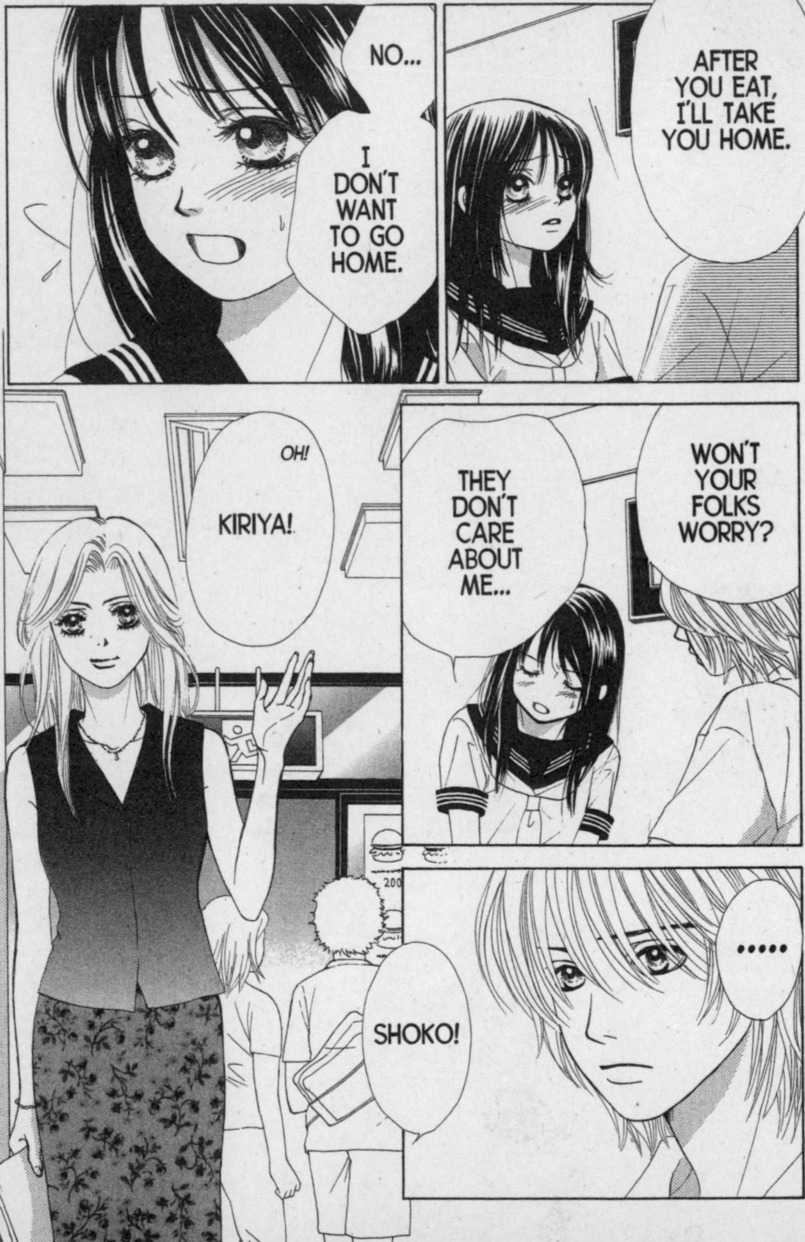
AFTER YOU EAT, I'LL TAKE YOU HOME.
NO...
I DON'T WANT TO GO HOME.
WON'T YOUR FOLKS WORRY?
THEY DON'T CARE ABOUT ME...
......
OH!
KIRIYA!
SHOKO!

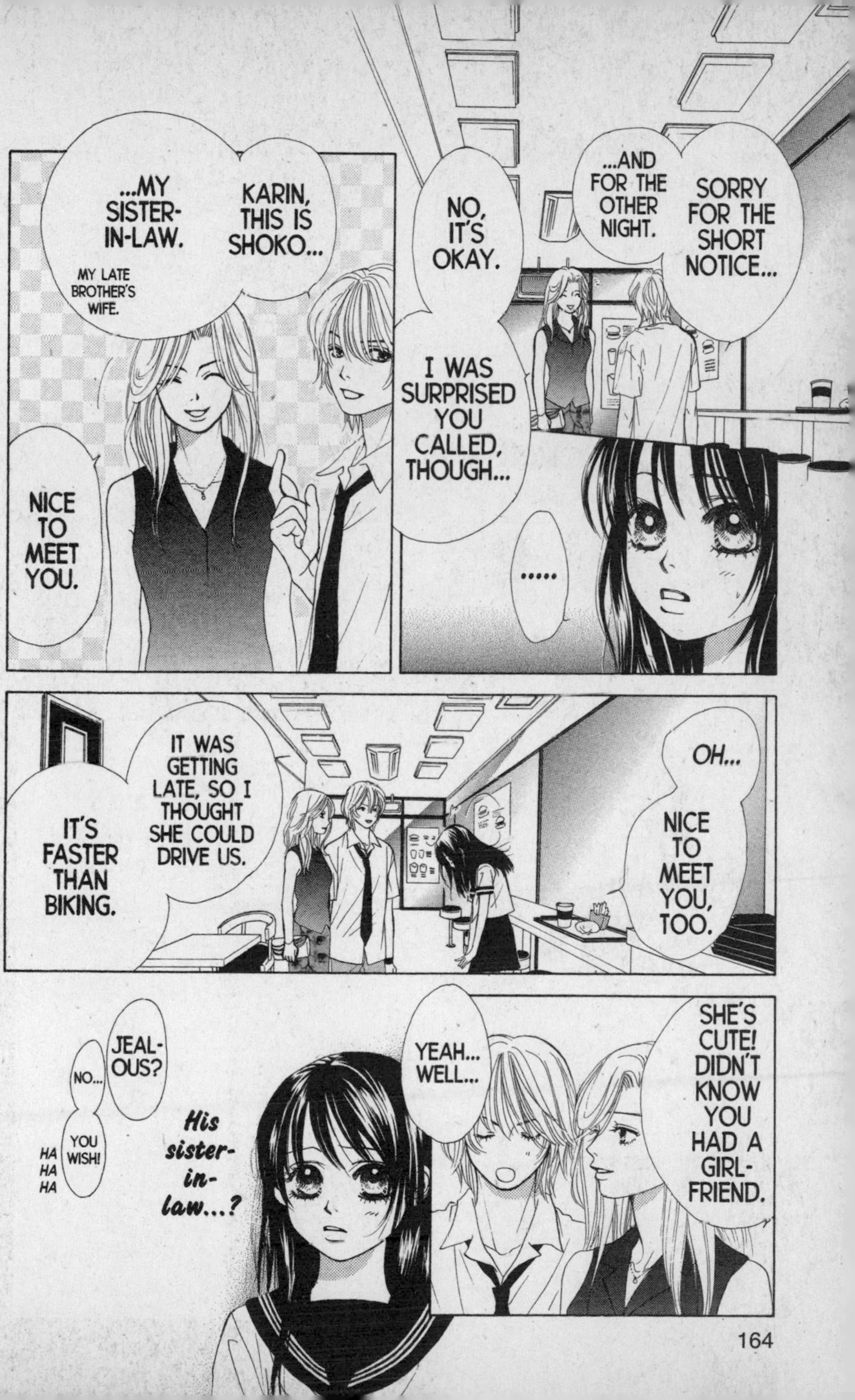

SORRY FOR THE SHORT NOTICE...
...AND FOR THE OTHER NIGHT.
NO, IT'S OKAY.
I WAS SURPRISED YOU CALLED, THOUGH...
.....
KARIN, THIS IS SHOKO...
...MY SISTER-IN-LAW.
MY LATE BROTHER'S WIFE.
NICE TO MEET YOU.
OH...
NICE TO MEET YOU, TOO.
IT WAS GETTING LATE, SO I THOUGHT SHE COULD DRIVE US.
IT'S FASTER THAN BIKING.
SHE'S CUTE! DIDN'T KNOW YOU HAD A GIRL-FRIEND.
YEAH... WELL...
His sister-in-law...?
JEAL-OUS?
NO...
YOU WISH!
HA HA HA

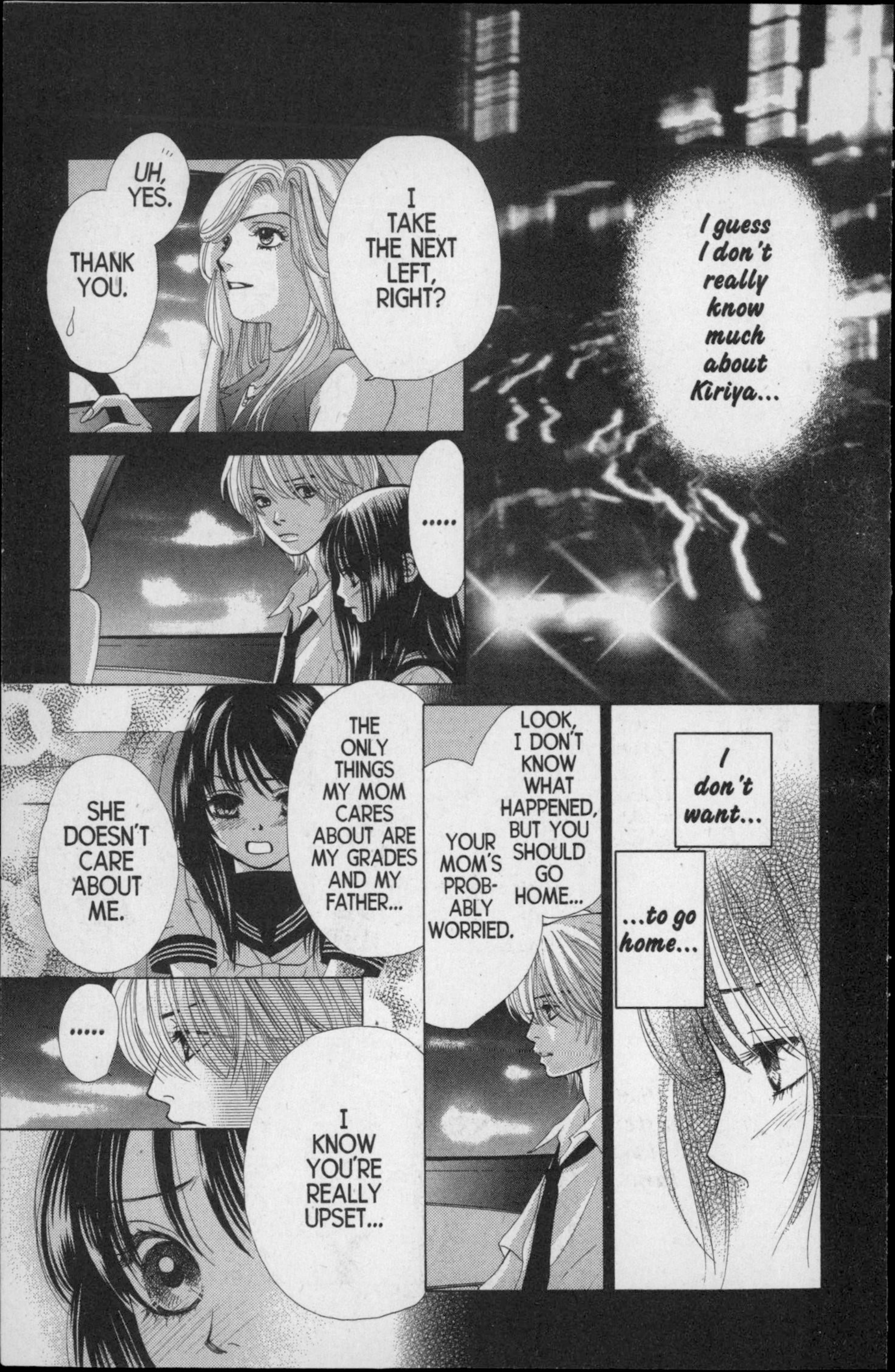
I guess I don't really know much about Kiriya...
I TAKE THE NEXT LEFT, RIGHT?
UH, YES.
THANK YOU.
......
I don't want...
...to go home...
LOOK, I DON'T KNOW WHAT HAPPENED, BUT YOU SHOULD GO HOME...
YOUR MOM'S PROB-ABLY WORRIED.
THE ONLY THINGS MY MOM CARES ABOUT ARE MY GRADES AND MY FATHER...
SHE DOESN'T CARE ABOUT ME.
......
I KNOW YOU'RE REALLY UPSET...

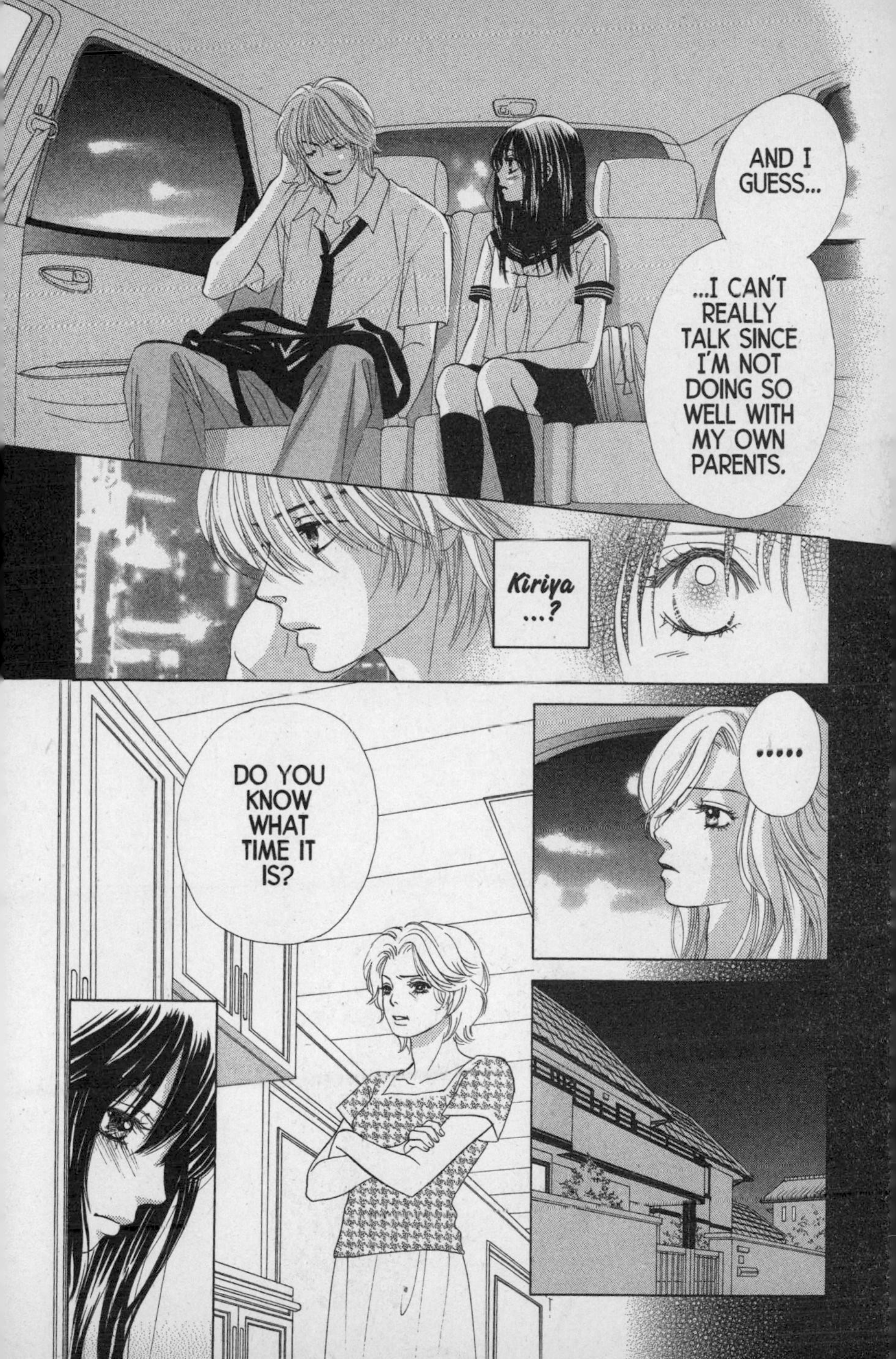
AND I GUESS...
...I CAN'T REALLY TALK SINCE I'M NOT DOING SO WELL WITH MY OWN PARENTS.
Kiriya ...?
.....
DO YOU KNOW WHAT TIME IT IS?

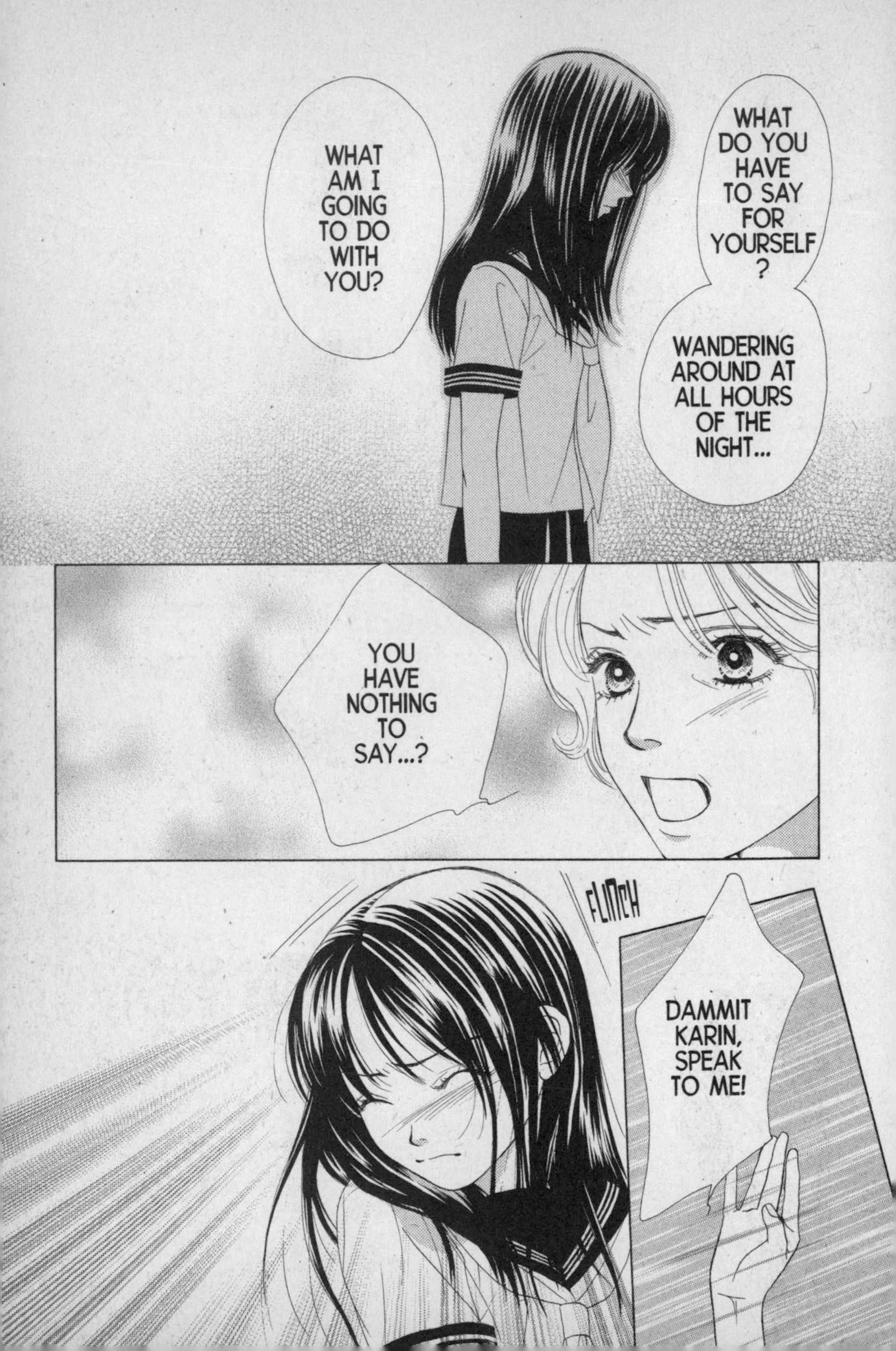
WHAT DO YOU HAVE TO SAY FOR YOURSELF?
WANDERING AROUND AT ALL HOURS OF THE NIGHT...
WHAT AM I GOING TO DO WITH YOU?
YOU HAVE NOTHING TO SAY...?
FLINCH
DAMMIT KARIN, SPEAK TO ME!

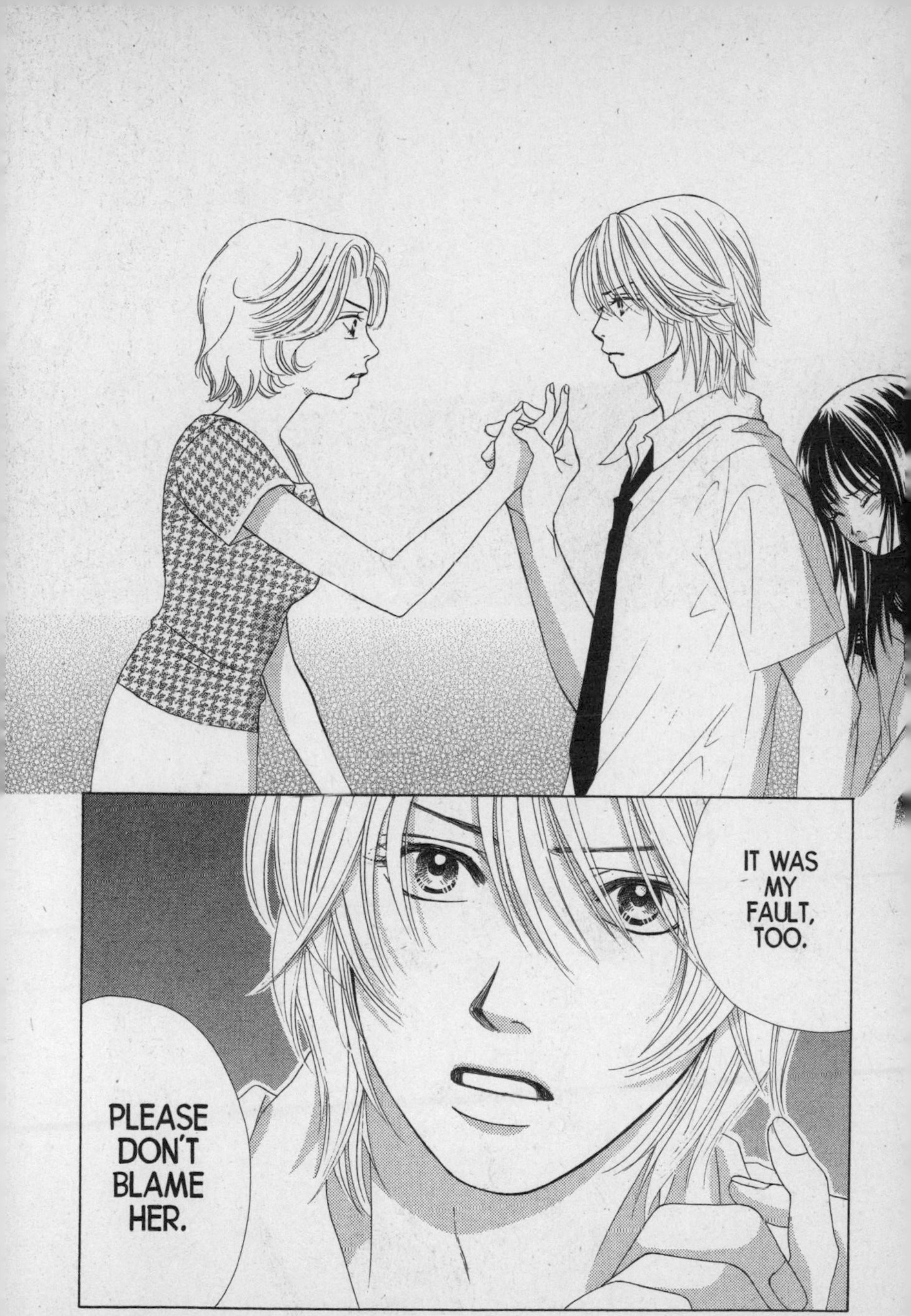
IT WAS MY FAULT, TOO.
PLEASE DON'T BLAME HER.

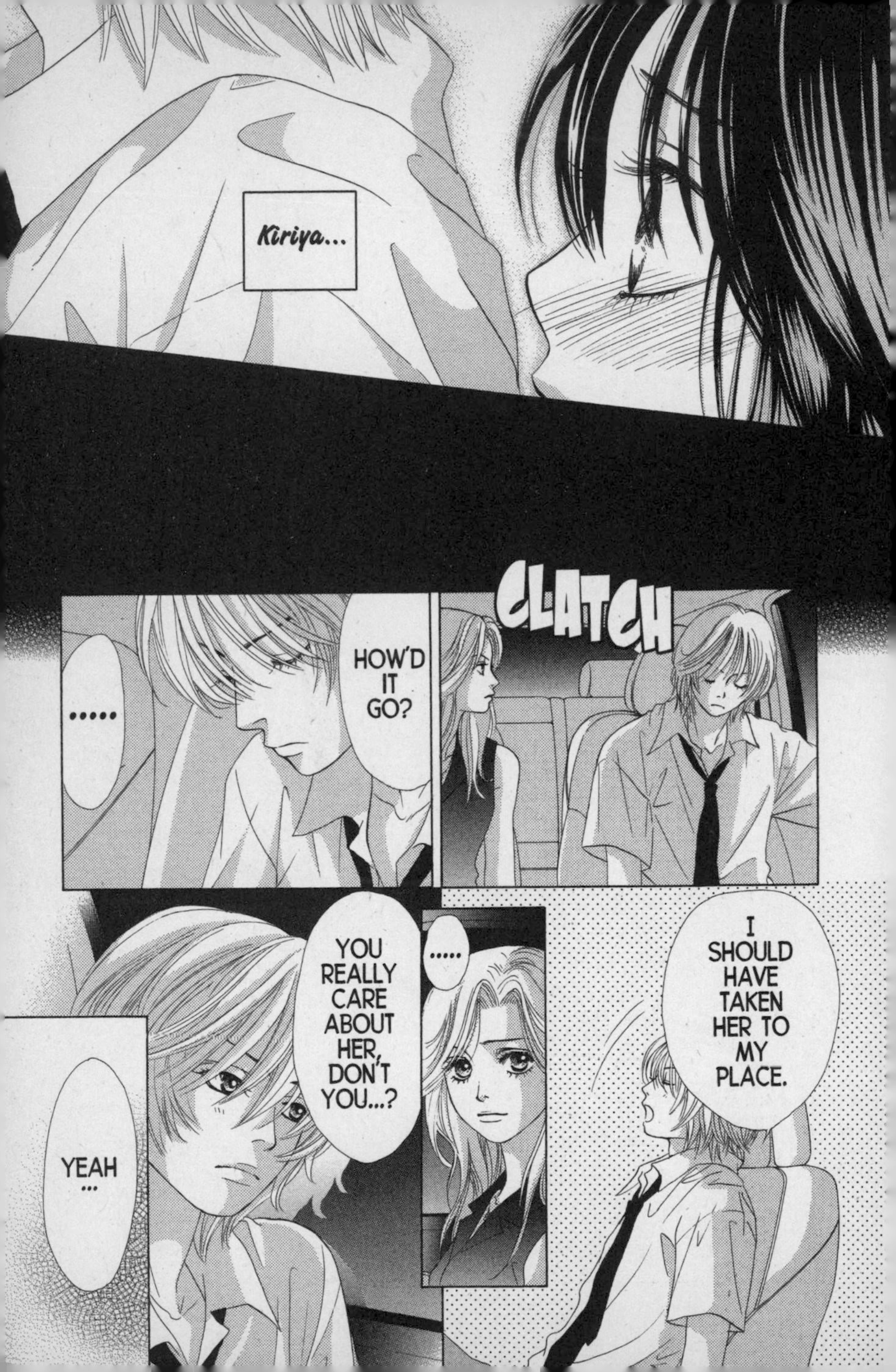
Kiriya...
CLATCH
HOW'D IT GO?
......
I SHOULD HAVE TAKEN HER TO MY PLACE.
......
YOU REALLY CARE ABOUT HER, DON'T YOU...?
YEAH ...

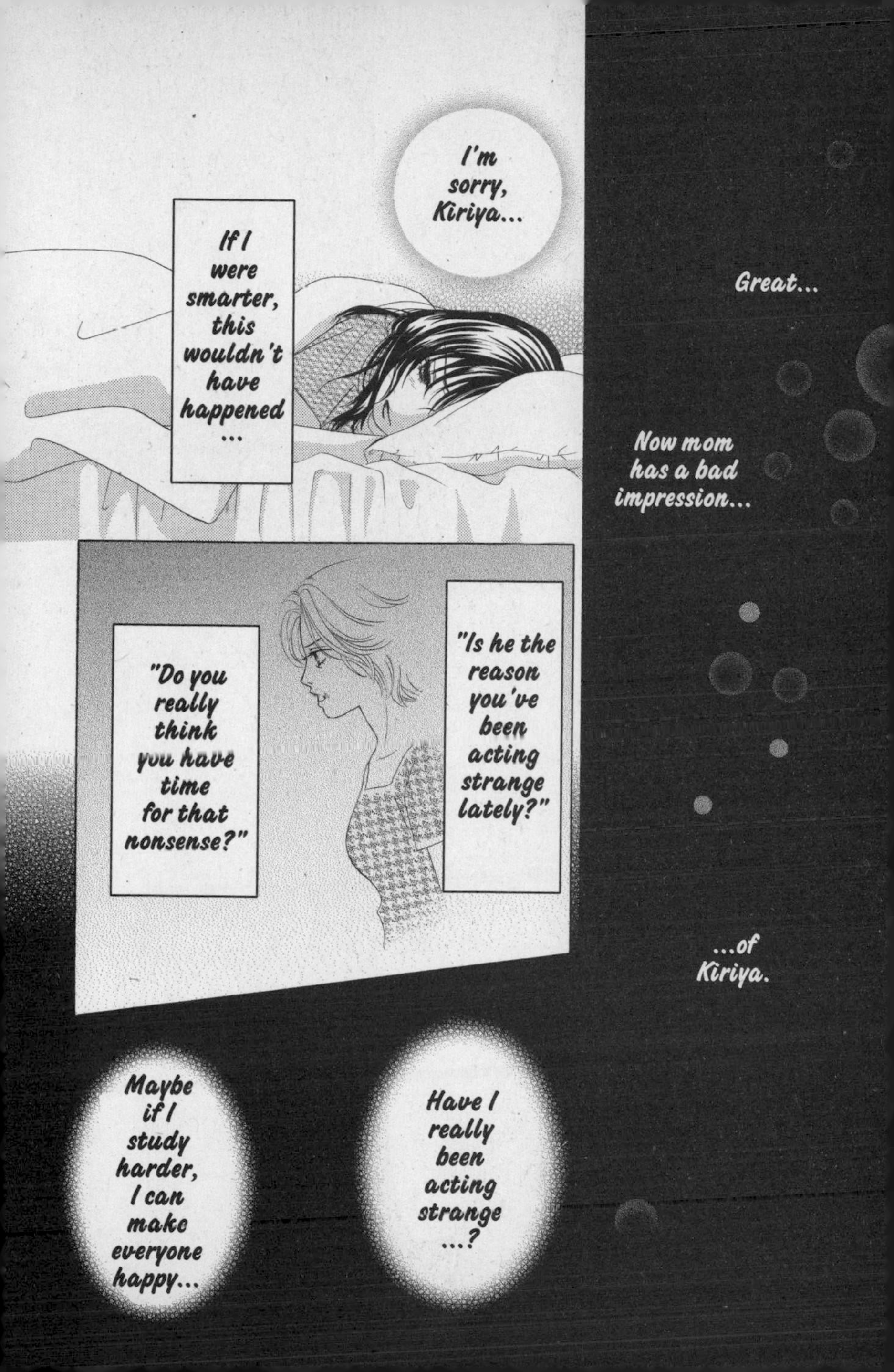
Great...
Now mom has a bad impression...
...of Kiriya.
I'm sorry, Kiriya...
If I were smarter, this wouldn't have happened...
"Is he the reason you've been acting strange lately?"
"Do you really think you have time for that nonsense?"
Have I really been acting strange...?
Maybe if I study harder, I can make everyone happy...

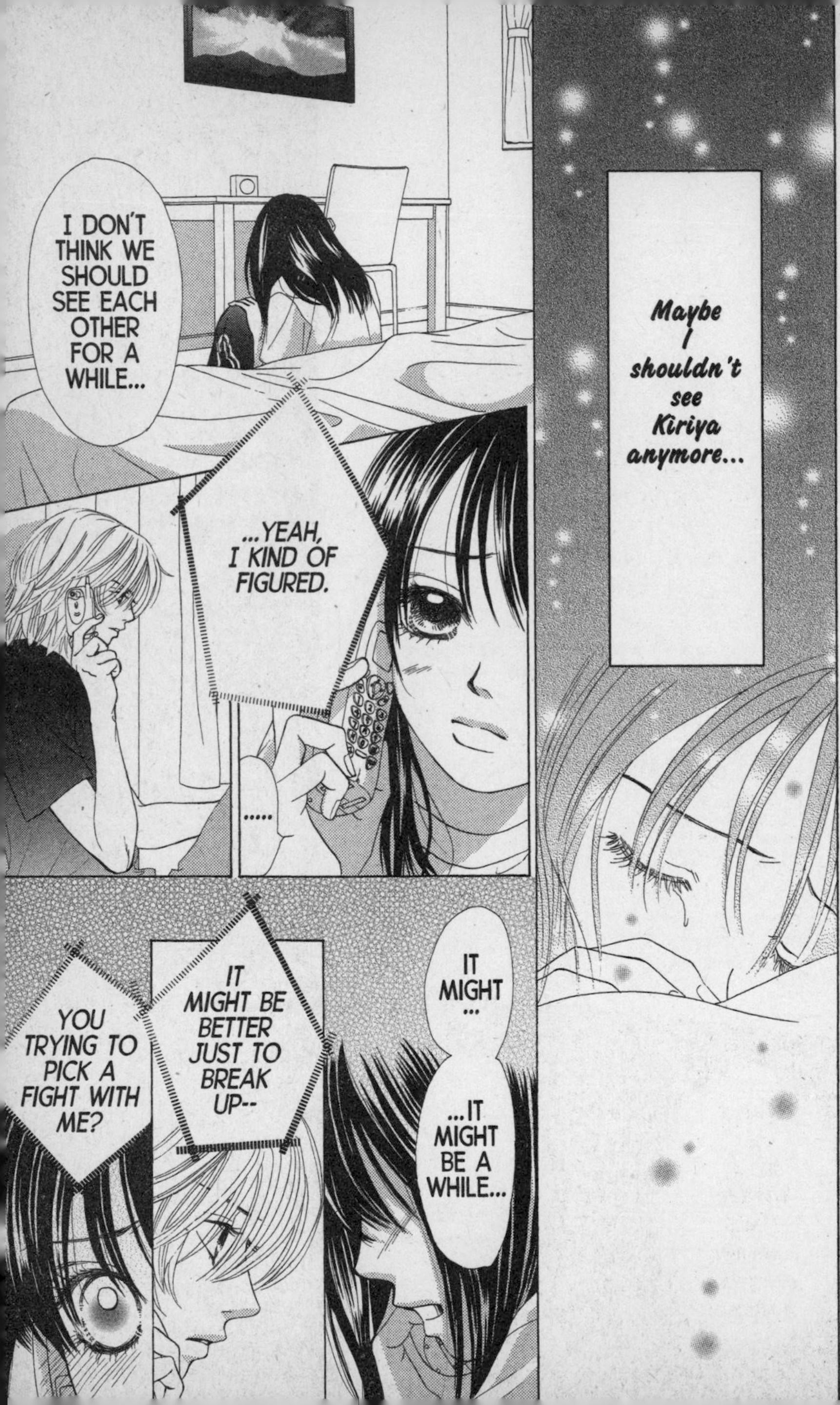
Maybe I shouldn't see Kiriya anymore...
I DON'T THINK WE SHOULD SEE EACH OTHER FOR A WHILE...
...YEAH, I KIND OF FIGURED.
.....
IT MIGHT...
...IT MIGHT BE A WHILE...
IT MIGHT BE BETTER JUST TO BREAK UP--
YOU TRYING TO PICK A FIGHT WITH ME?

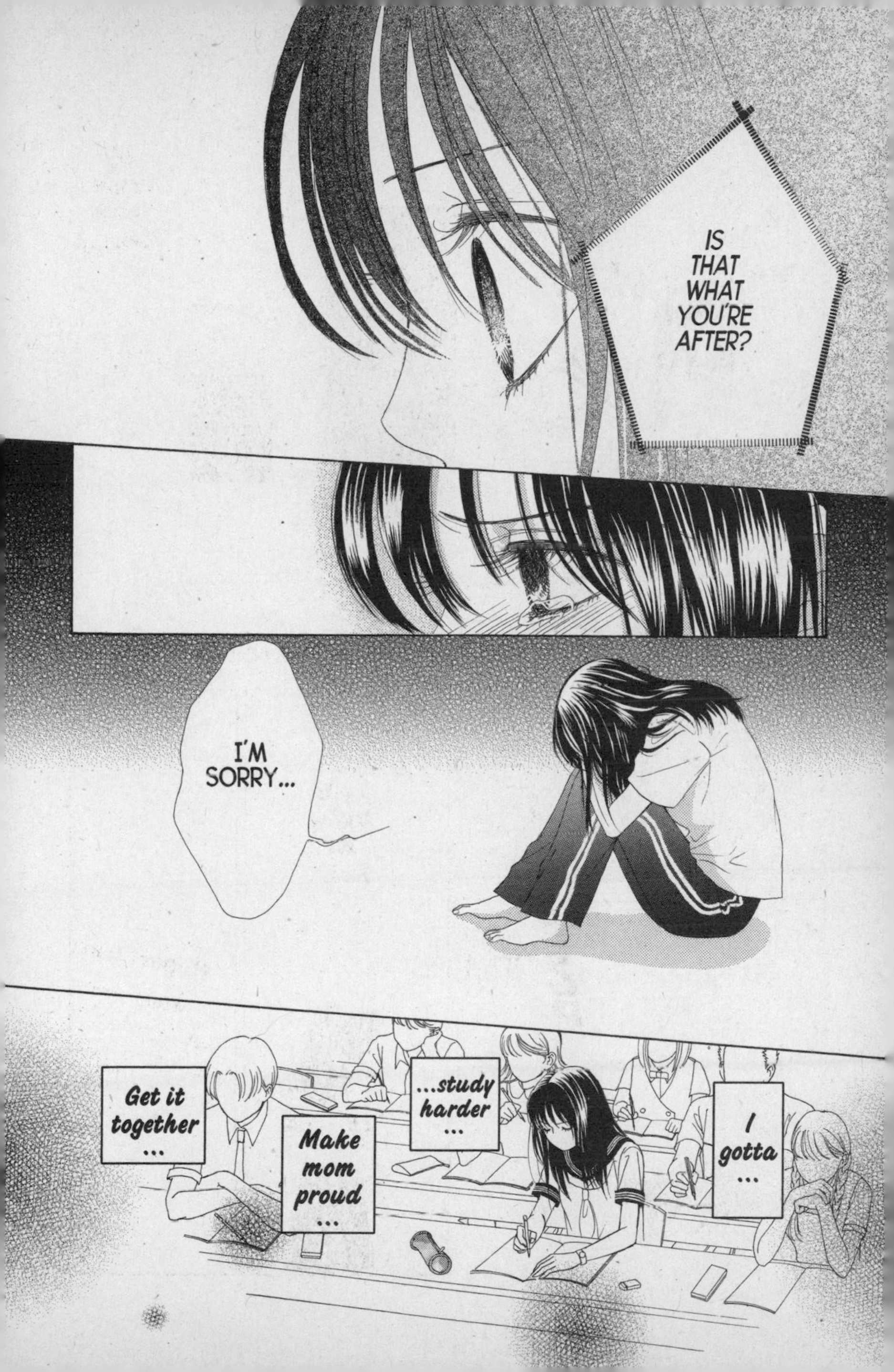
IS THAT WHAT YOU'RE AFTER?
I'M SORRY...
I gotta...
...study harder...
Make mom proud...
Get it together...

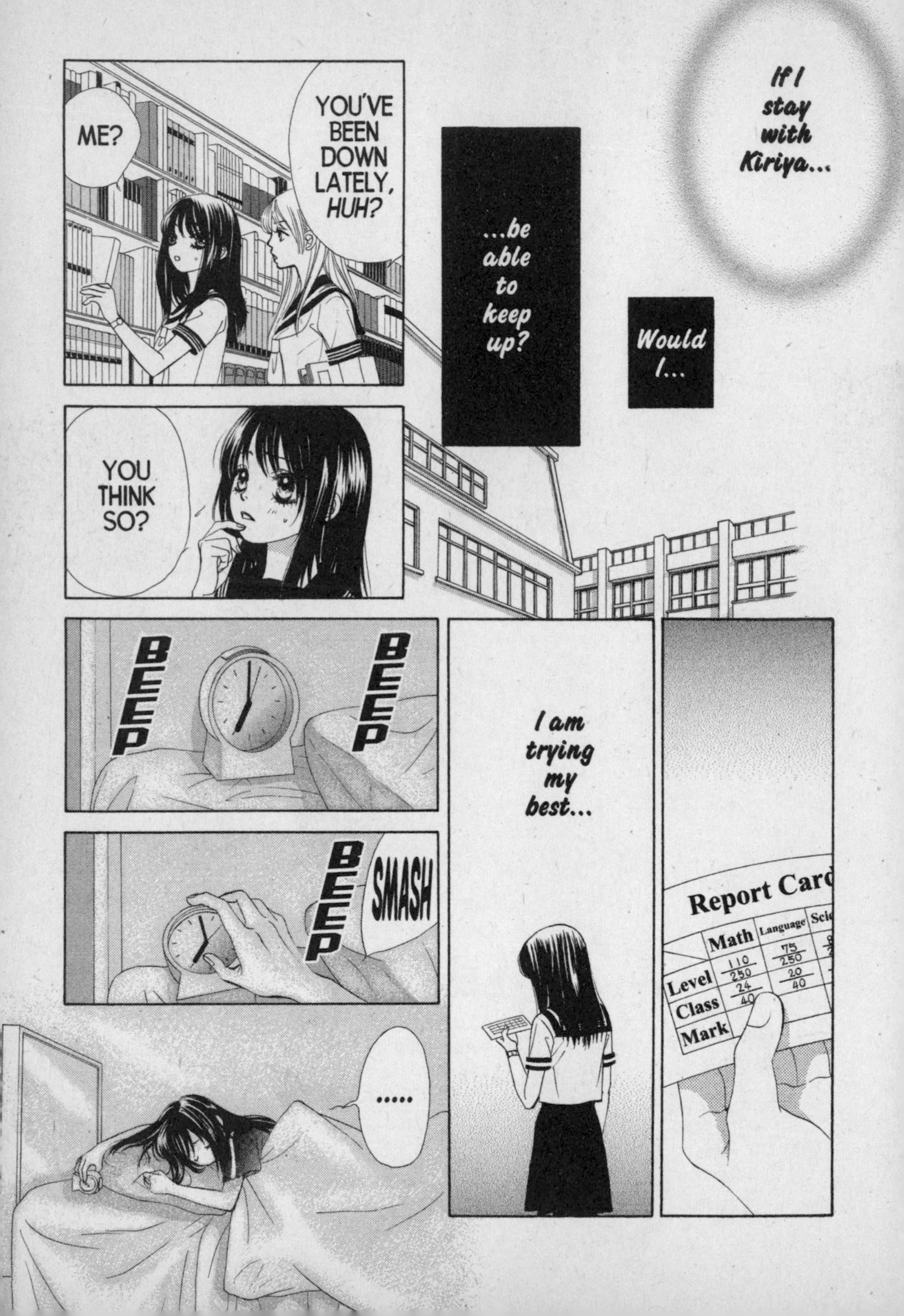
If I stay with Kiriya...
Would I...
...be able to keep up?
YOU'VE BEEN DOWN LATELY, HUH?
ME?
YOU THINK SO?
Report Card
Math
Language
Level
Class
Mark
110
250
24
40
75
250
20
40
I am trying my best...
BEEP
BEEP
BEEP
SMASH
.....

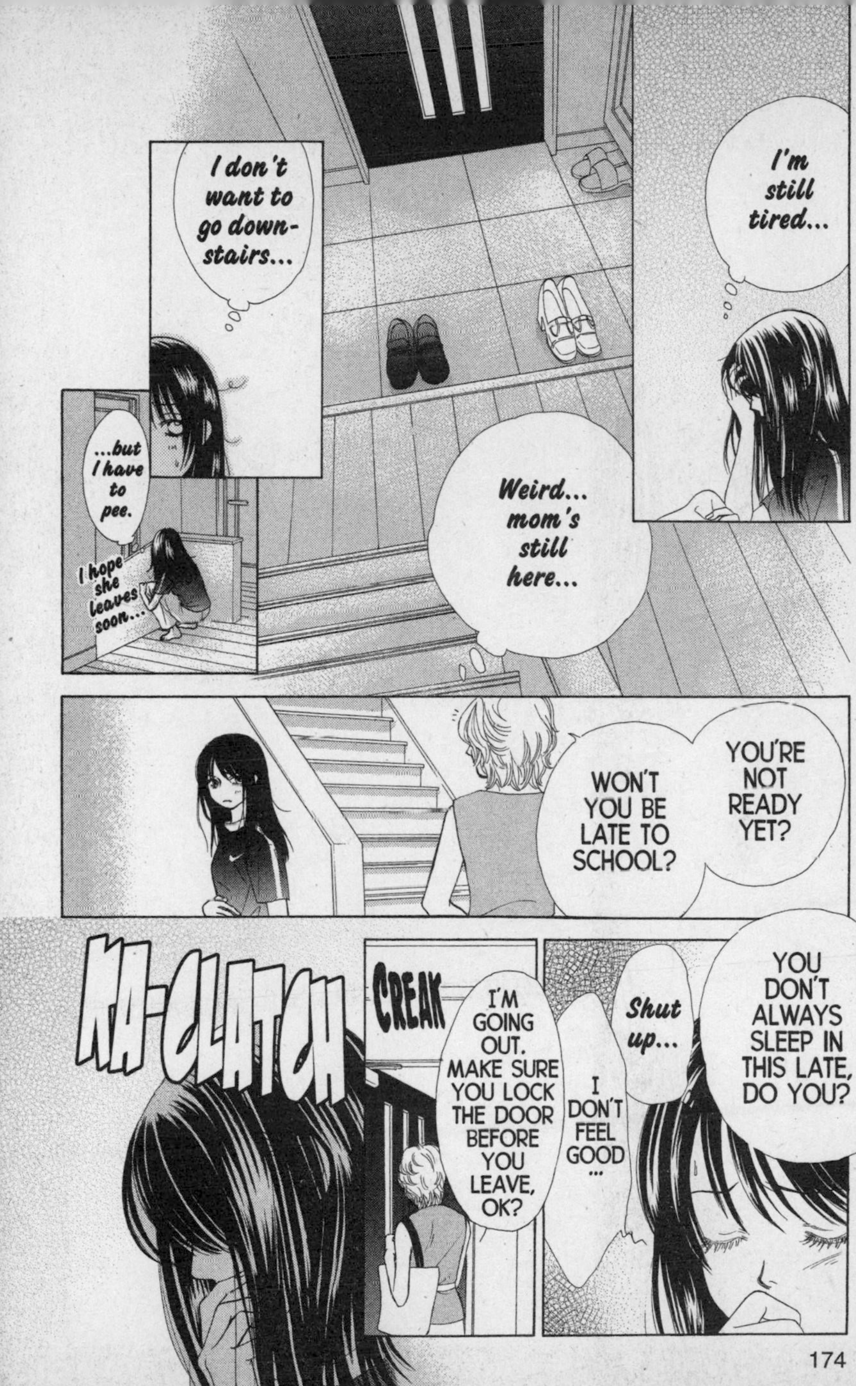
I'm still tired...
I don't want to go down-stairs...
...but I have to pee.
I hope she leaves soon...
Weird... mom's still here...
YOU'RE NOT READY YET?
WON'T YOU BE LATE TO SCHOOL?
YOU DON'T ALWAYS SLEEP IN THIS LATE, DO YOU?
Shut up...
I DON'T FEEL GOOD ...
I'M GOING OUT. MAKE SURE YOU LOCK THE DOOR BEFORE YOU LEAVE, OK?
CREAK
KA-CLATCH

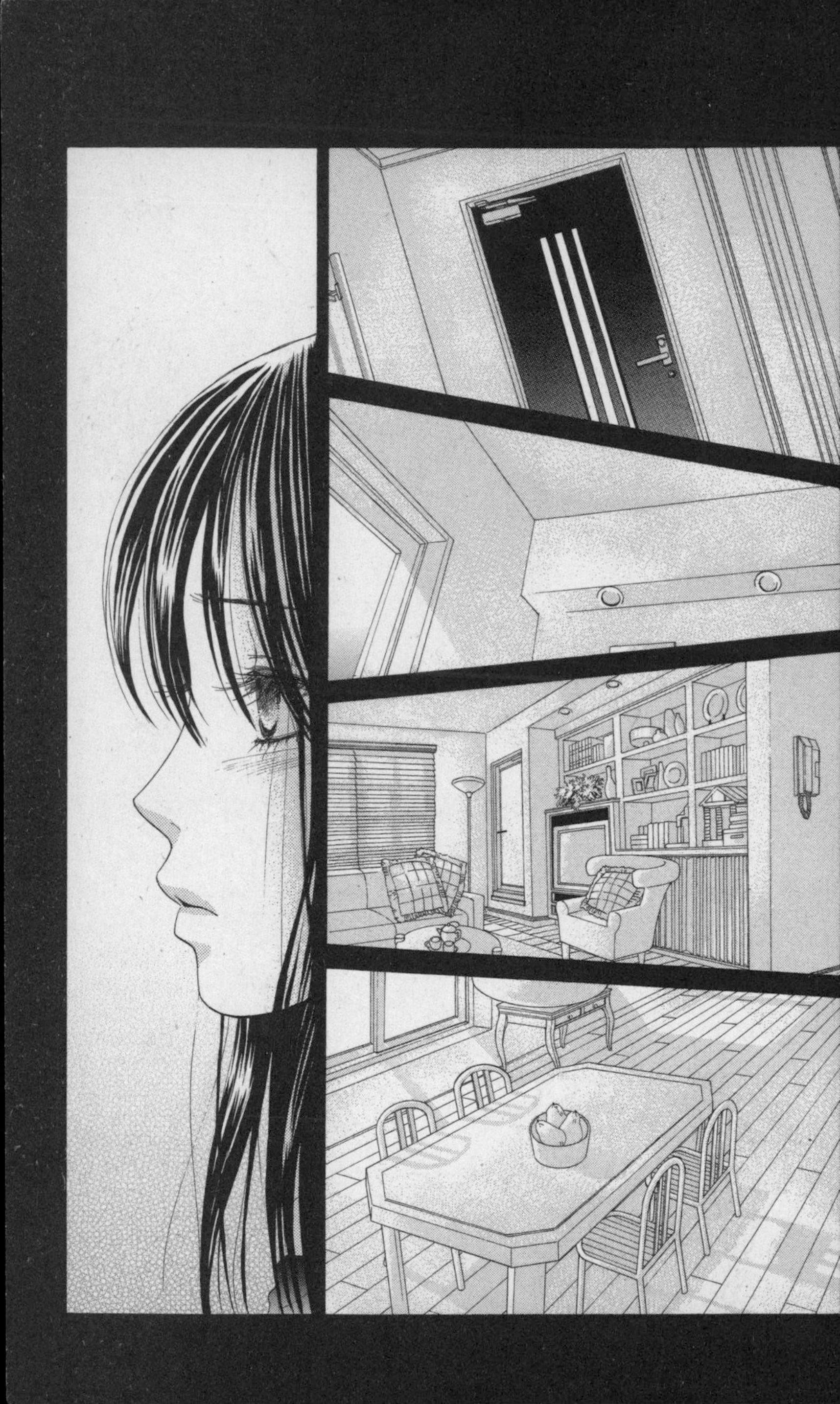

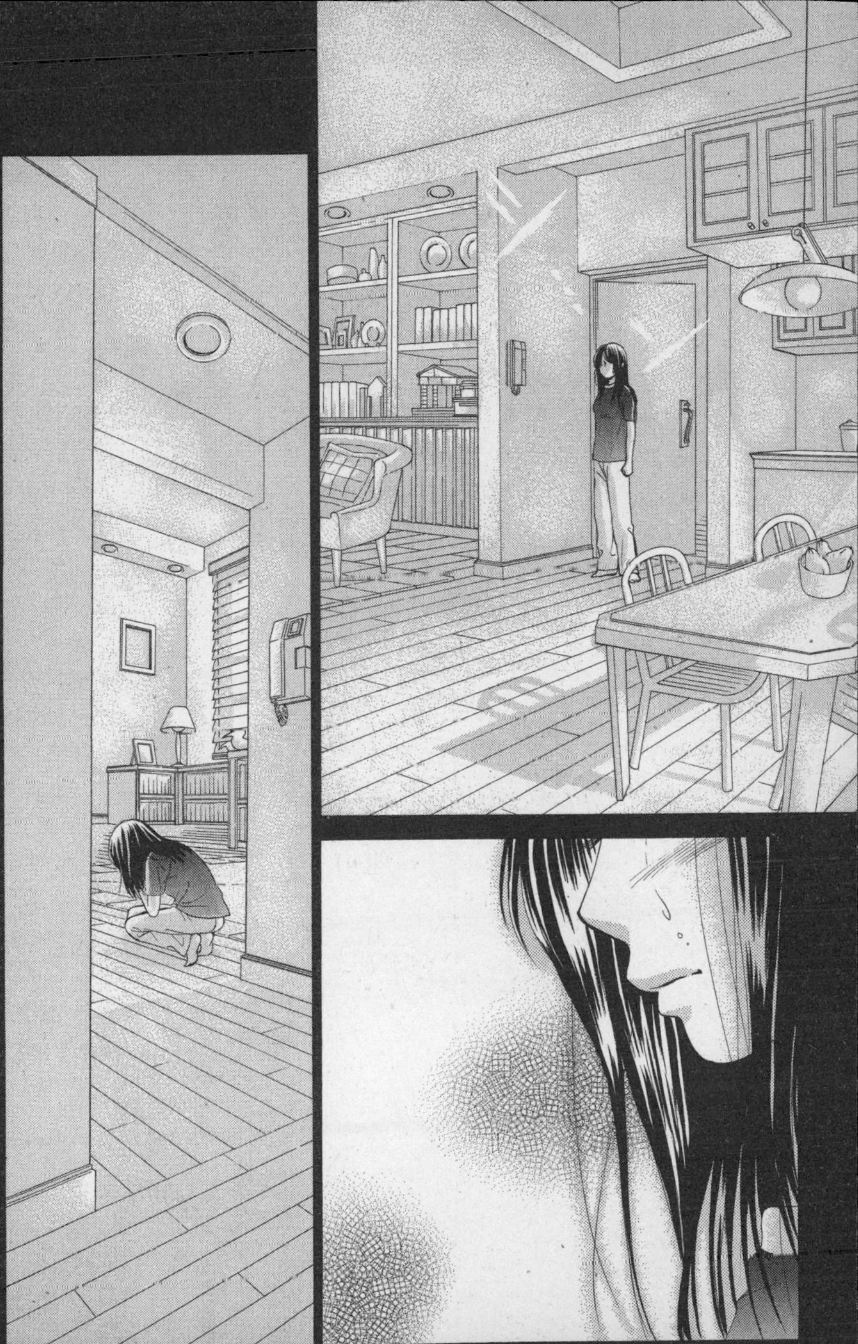

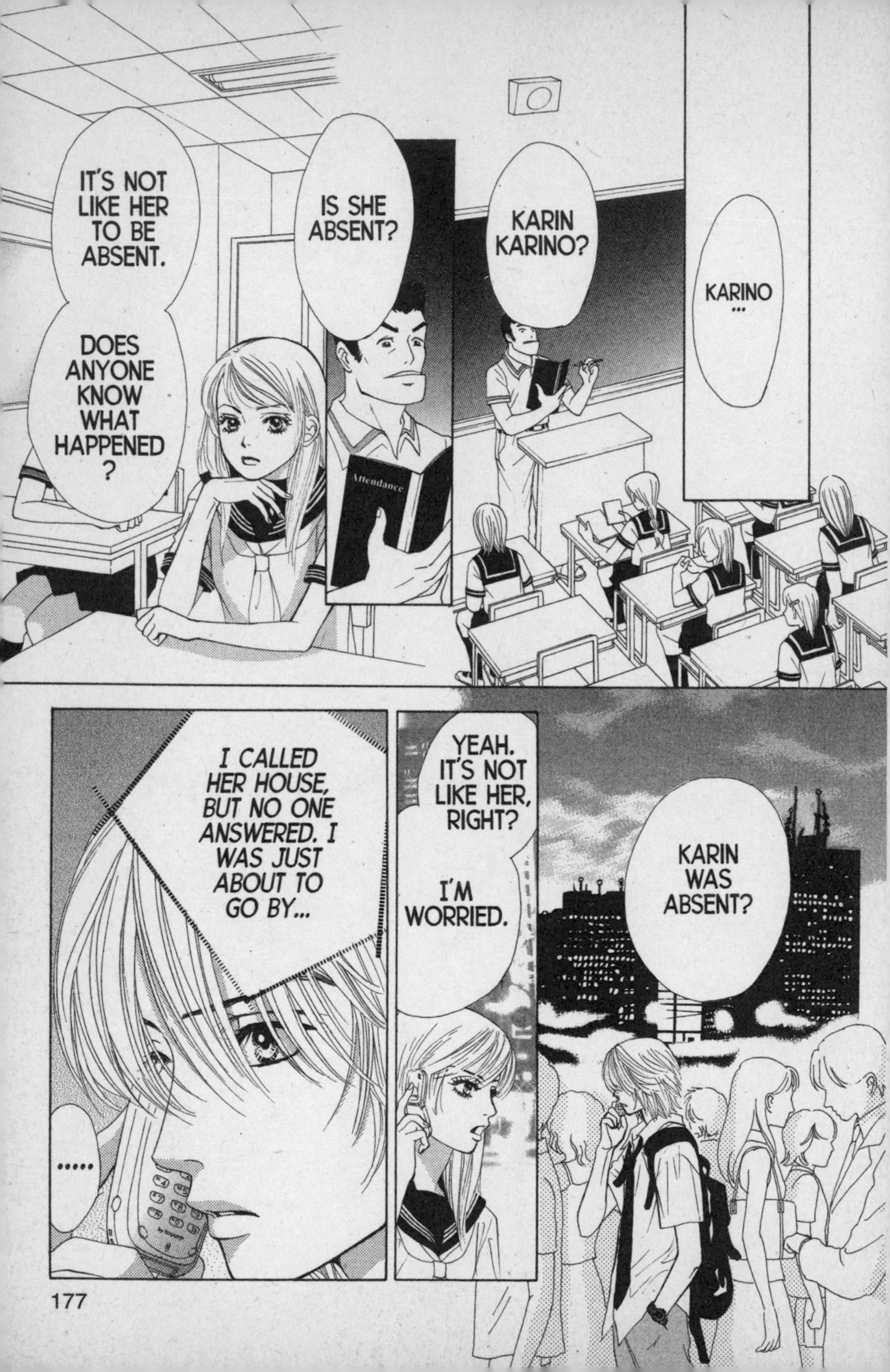
KARINO ...
KARIN KARINO?
IS SHE ABSENT?
IT'S NOT LIKE HER TO BE ABSENT.
DOES ANYONE KNOW WHAT HAPPENED?
Attendance
KARIN WAS ABSENT?
YEAH. IT'S NOT LIKE HER, RIGHT?
I'M WORRIED.
I CALLED HER HOUSE, BUT NO ONE ANSWERED. I WAS JUST ABOUT TO GO BY...
.....

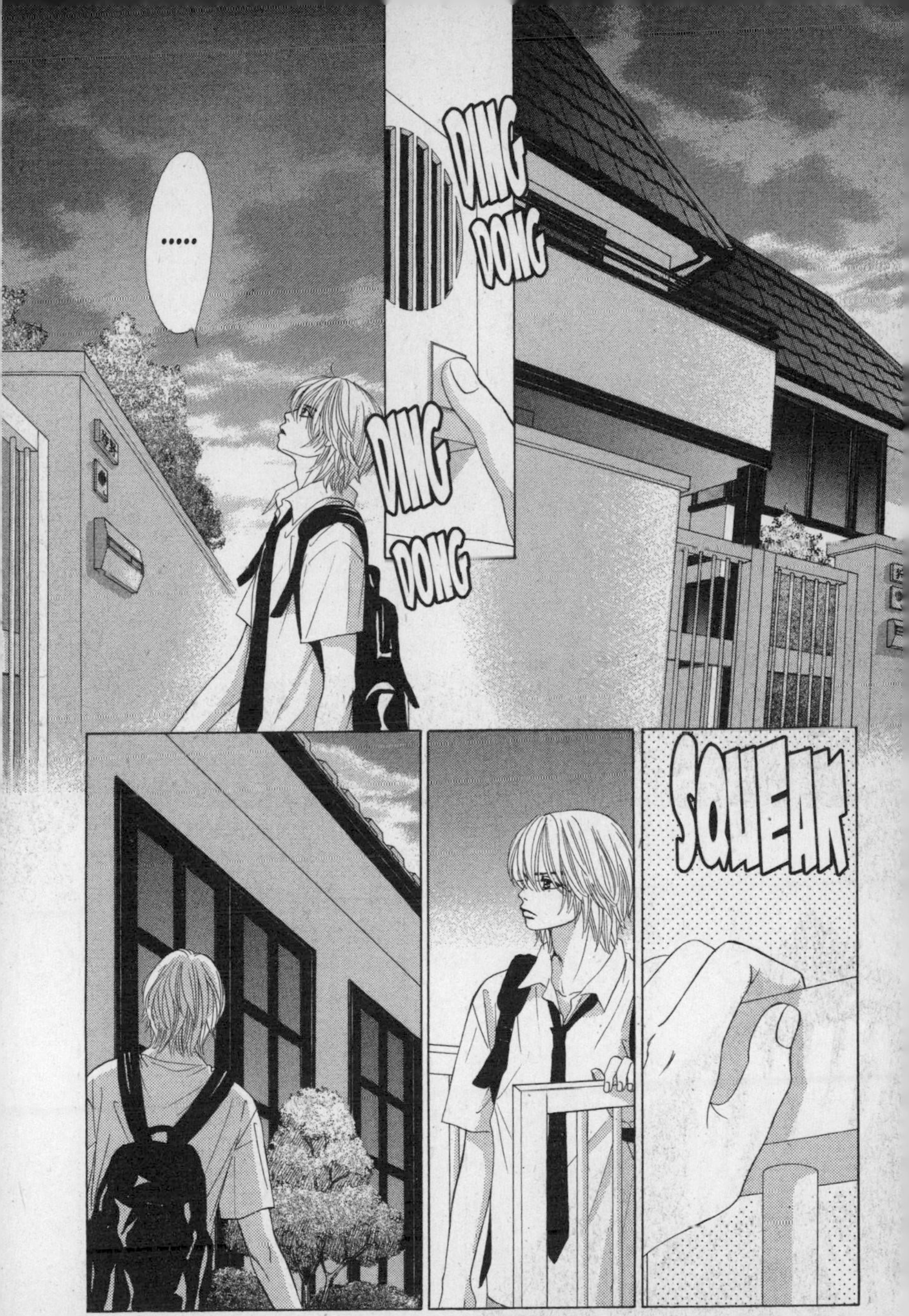

DING DONG
DING DONG
......
SQUEAK

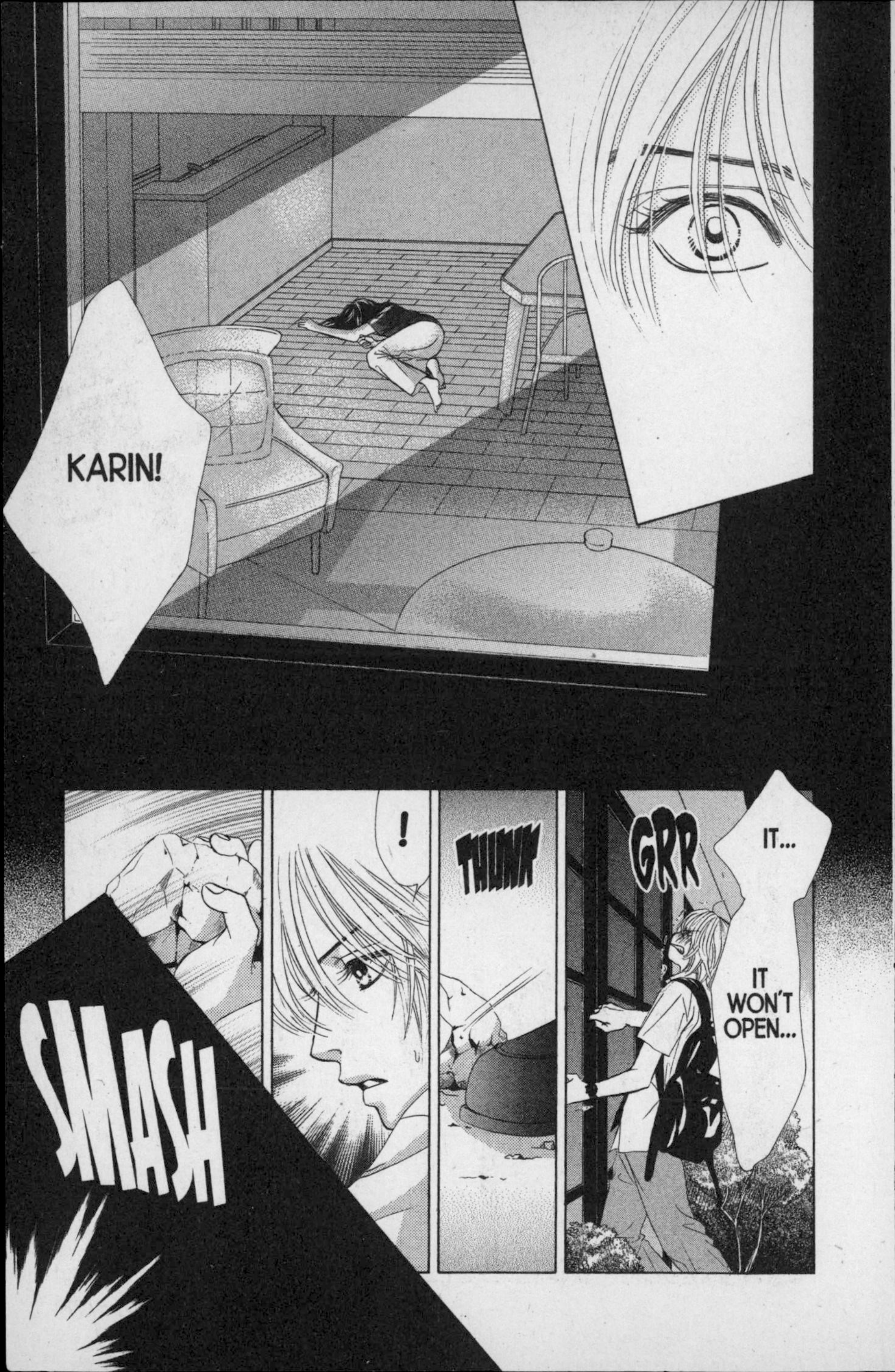
KARIN!
IT... IT WON'T OPEN...
GRR
THUNK
!
SMASH

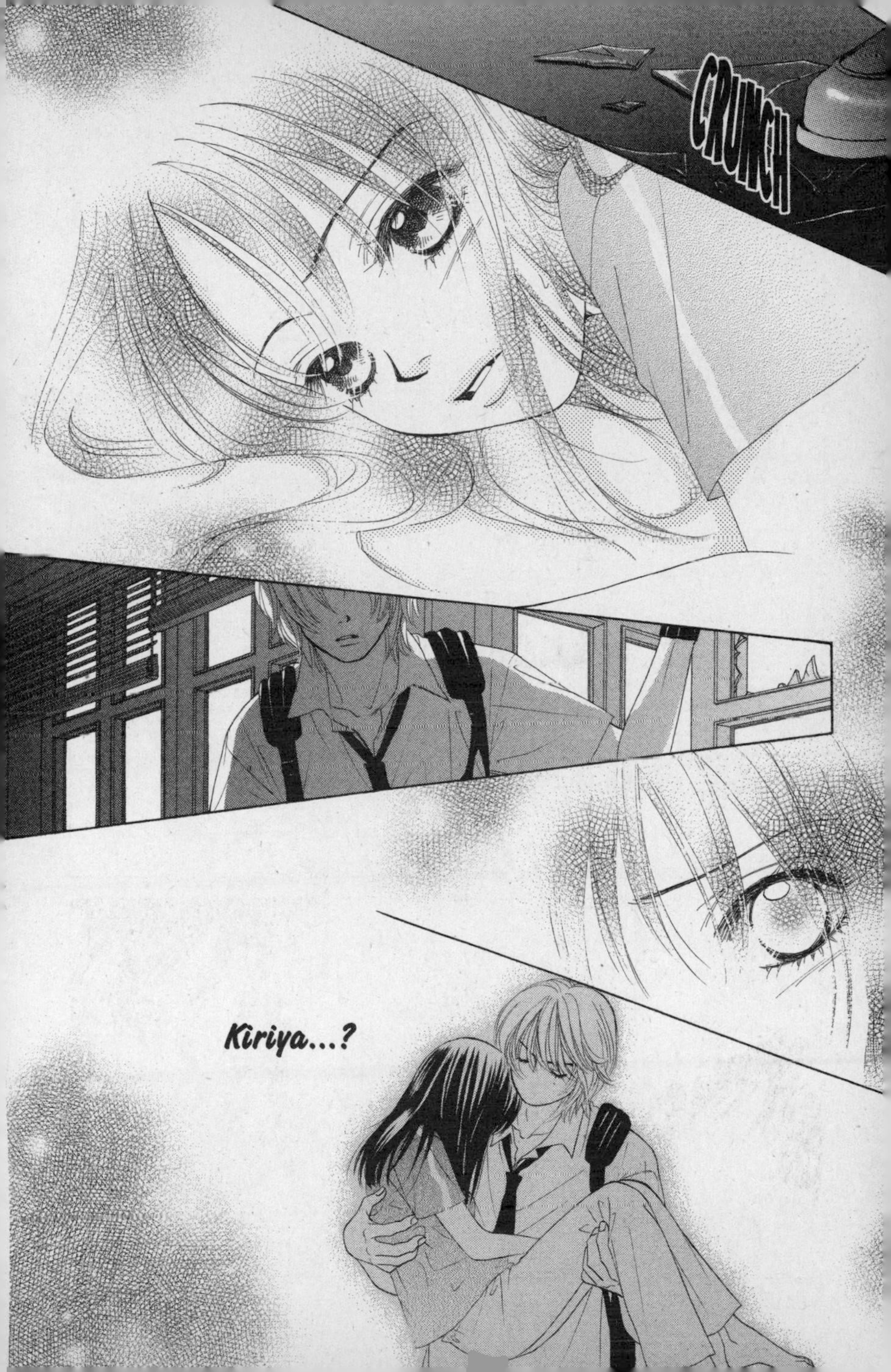
CRUNCH
Kiriya...?

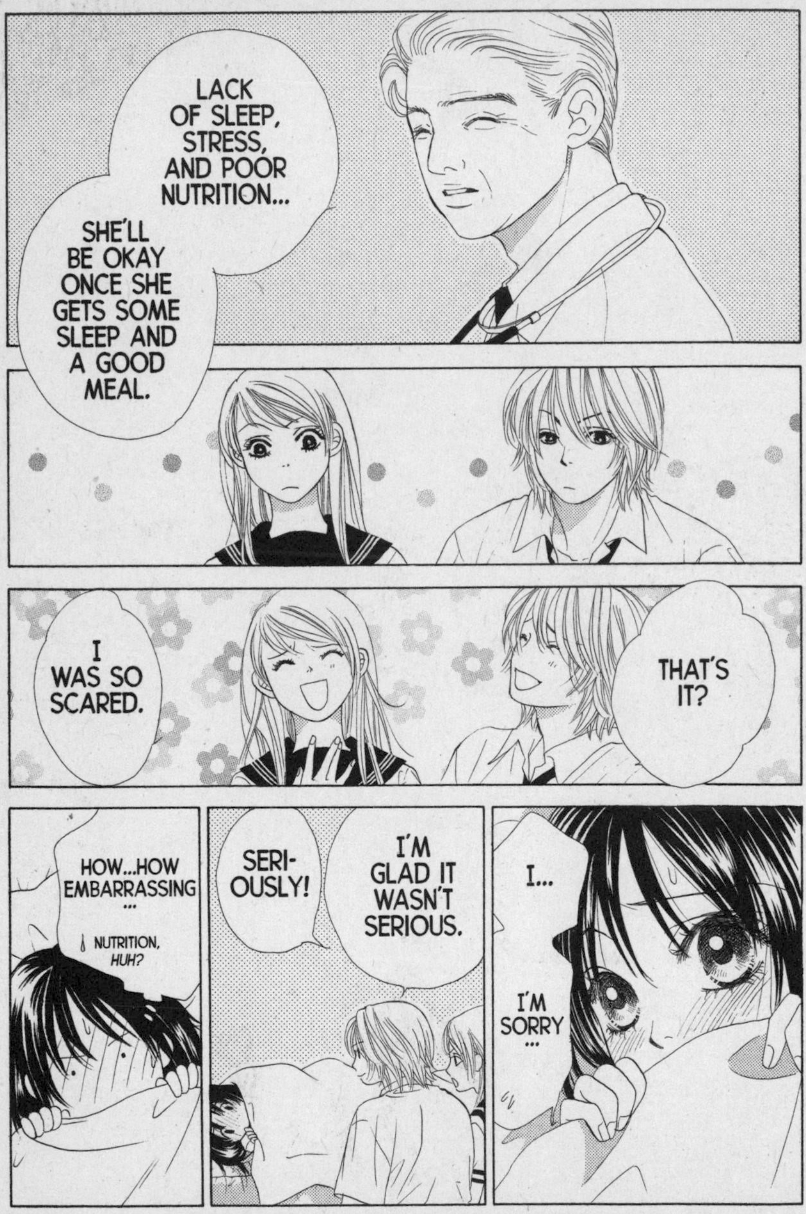
LACK OF SLEEP, STRESS, AND POOR NUTRITION...
SHE'LL BE OKAY ONCE SHE GETS SOME SLEEP AND A GOOD MEAL.
THAT'S IT?
I WAS SO SCARED.
I...
I'M SORRY...
I'M GLAD IT WASN'T SERIOUS.
SERI-OUSLY!
HOW...HOW EMBARRASSING...
NUTRITION, HUH?

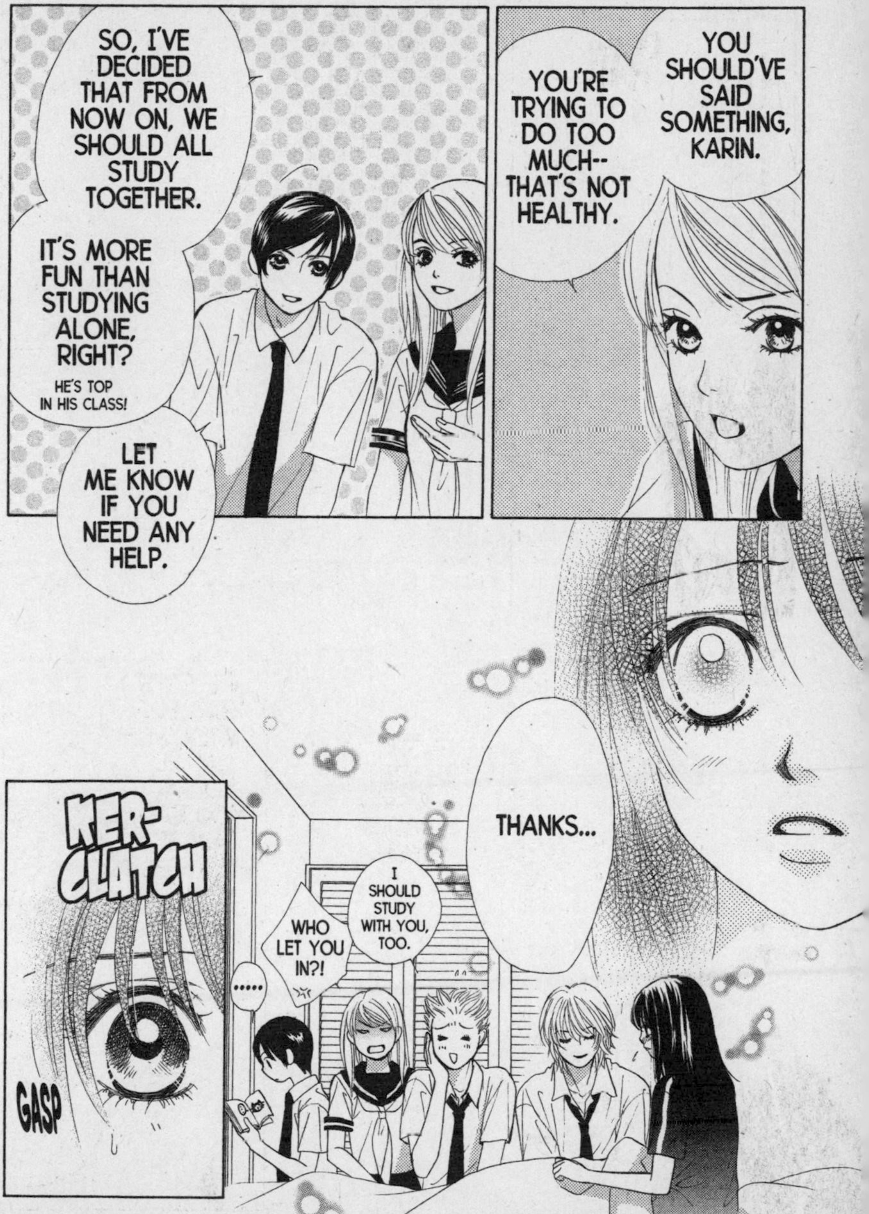
YOU SHOULD'VE SAID SOMETHING, KARIN.
YOU'RE TRYING TO DO TOO MUCH-- THAT'S NOT HEALTHY.
SO, I'VE DECIDED THAT FROM NOW ON, WE SHOULD ALL STUDY TOGETHER.
IT'S MORE FUN THAN STUDYING ALONE, RIGHT?
HE'S TOP IN HIS CLASS!
LET ME KNOW IF YOU NEED ANY HELP.
THANKS...
I SHOULD STUDY WITH YOU, TOO.
WHO LET YOU IN?!
......
KER-CLATCH
GASP

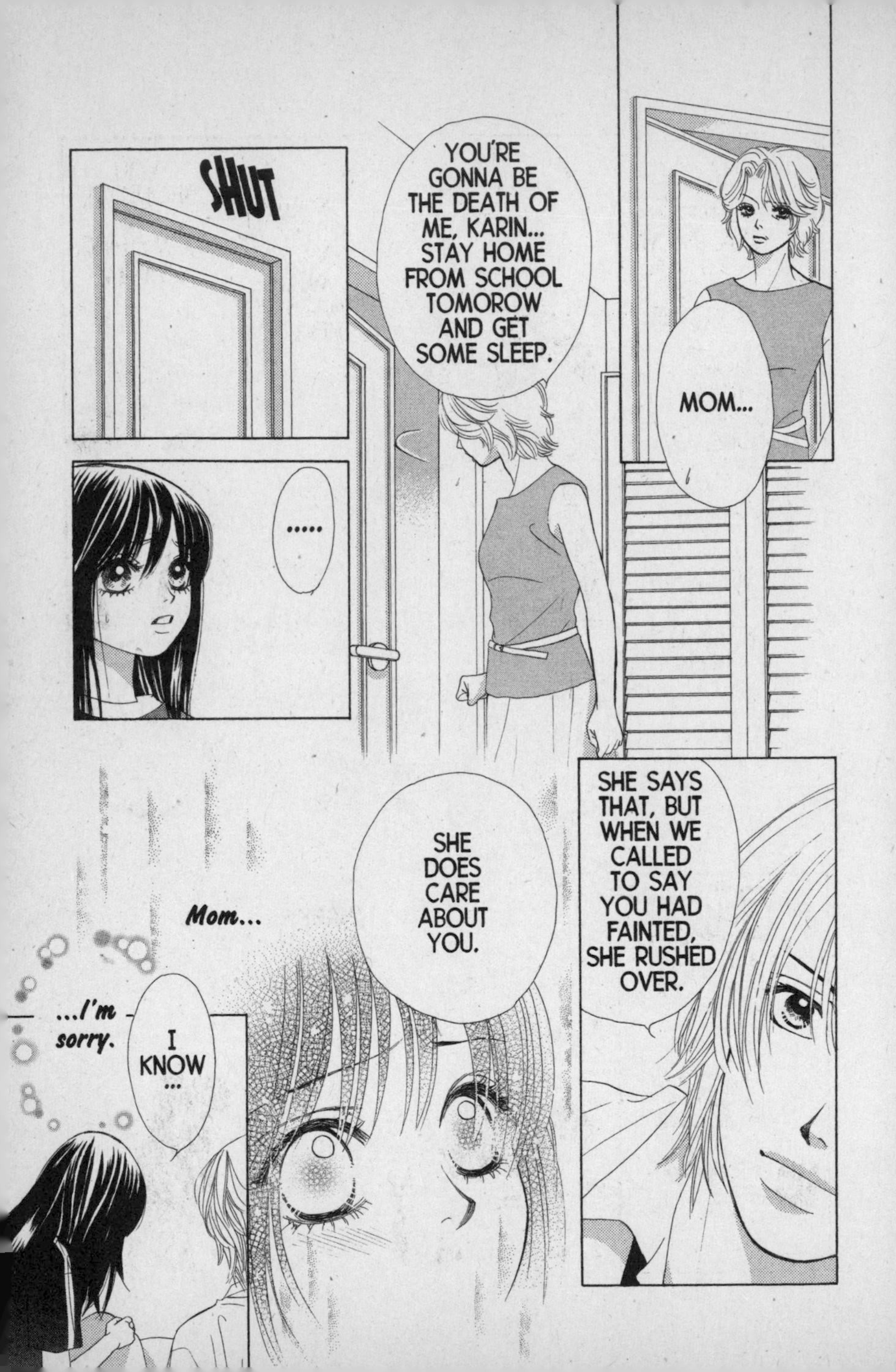
MOM...
YOU'RE GONNA BE THE DEATH OF ME, KARIN... STAY HOME FROM SCHOOL TOMORROW AND GET SOME SLEEP.
SHUT
......
SHE SAYS THAT, BUT WHEN WE CALLED TO SAY YOU HAD FAINTED, SHE RUSHED OVER.
SHE DOES CARE ABOUT YOU.
Mom...
I KNOW ...
...I'm sorry.

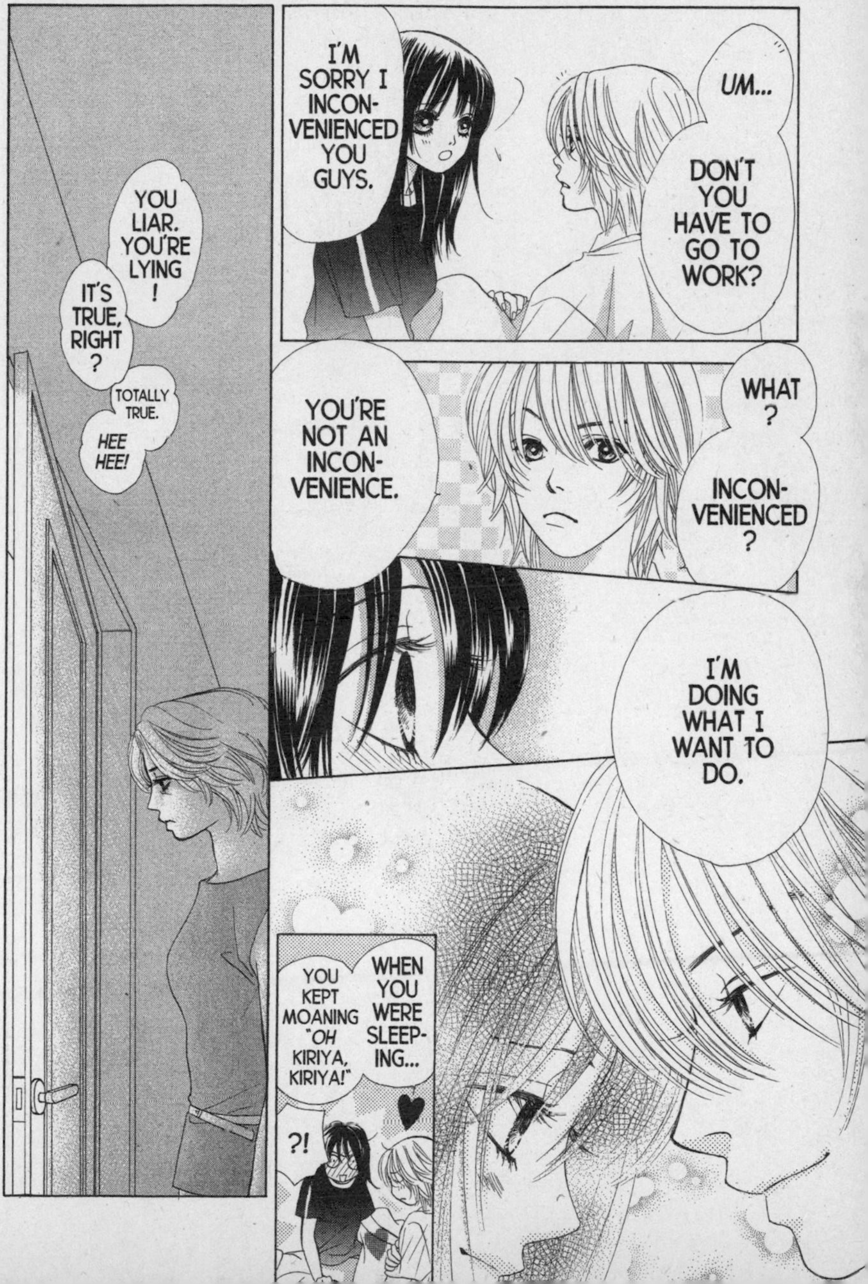
UM...
DON'T YOU HAVE TO GO TO WORK?
I'M SORRY I INCONVENIENCED YOU GUYS.
WHAT?
INCONVENIENCED?
YOU'RE NOT AN INCONVENIENCE.
I'M DOING WHAT I WANT TO DO.
WHEN YOU WERE SLEEPING...
YOU KEPT MOANING "OH KIRIYA, KIRIYA!"
?!
YOU LIAR. YOU'RE LYING!
IT'S TRUE, RIGHT?
TOTALLY TRUE.
HEE HEE!

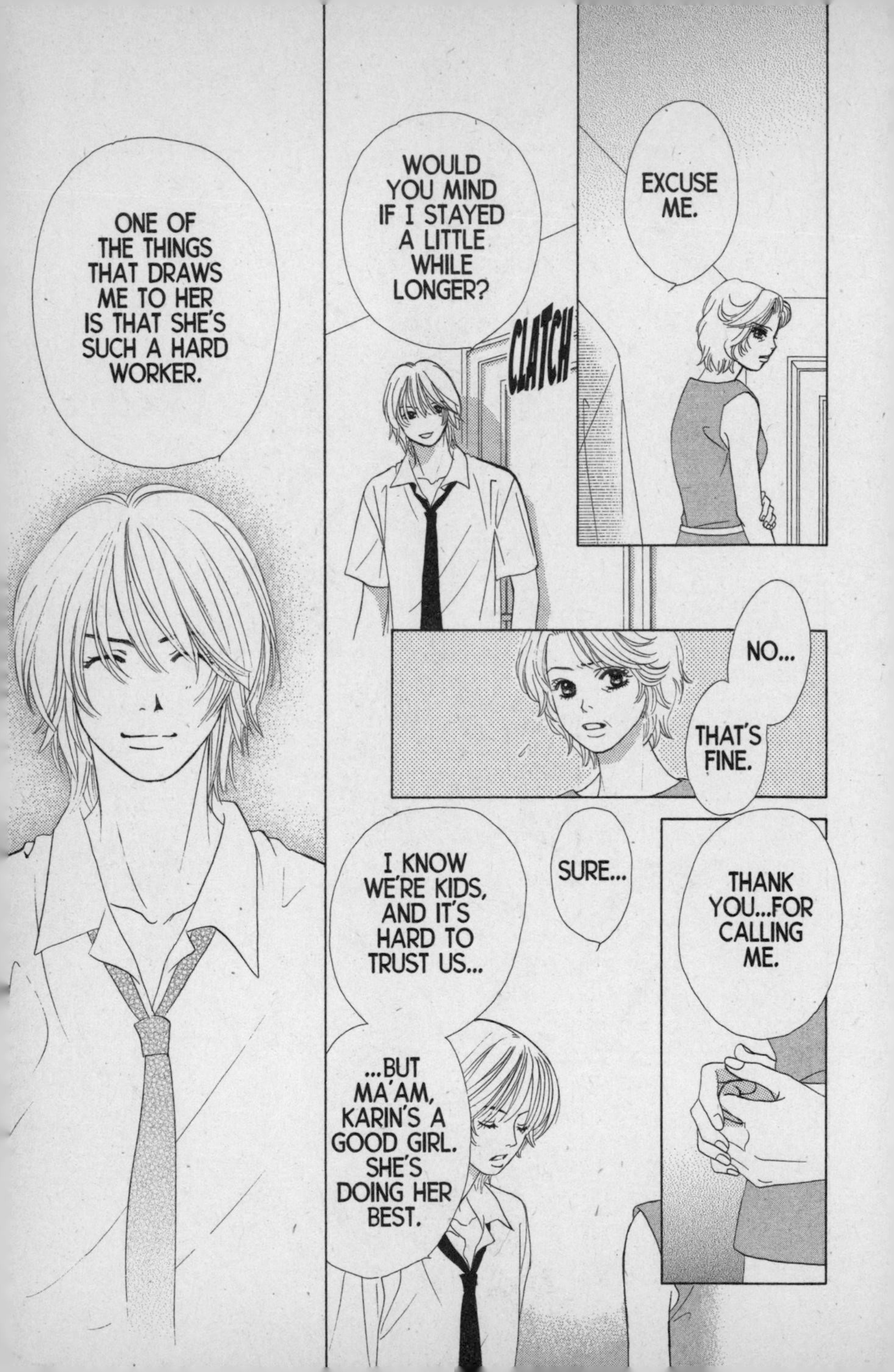
EXCUSE ME.
WOULD YOU MIND IF I STAYED A LITTLE WHILE LONGER?
CLATCH
NO...
THAT'S FINE.
THANK YOU...FOR CALLING ME.
SURE...
I KNOW WE'RE KIDS, AND IT'S HARD TO TRUST US...
...BUT MA'AM, KARIN'S A GOOD GIRL. SHE'S DOING HER BEST.
ONE OF THE THINGS THAT DRAWS ME TO HER IS THAT SHE'S SUCH A HARD WORKER.

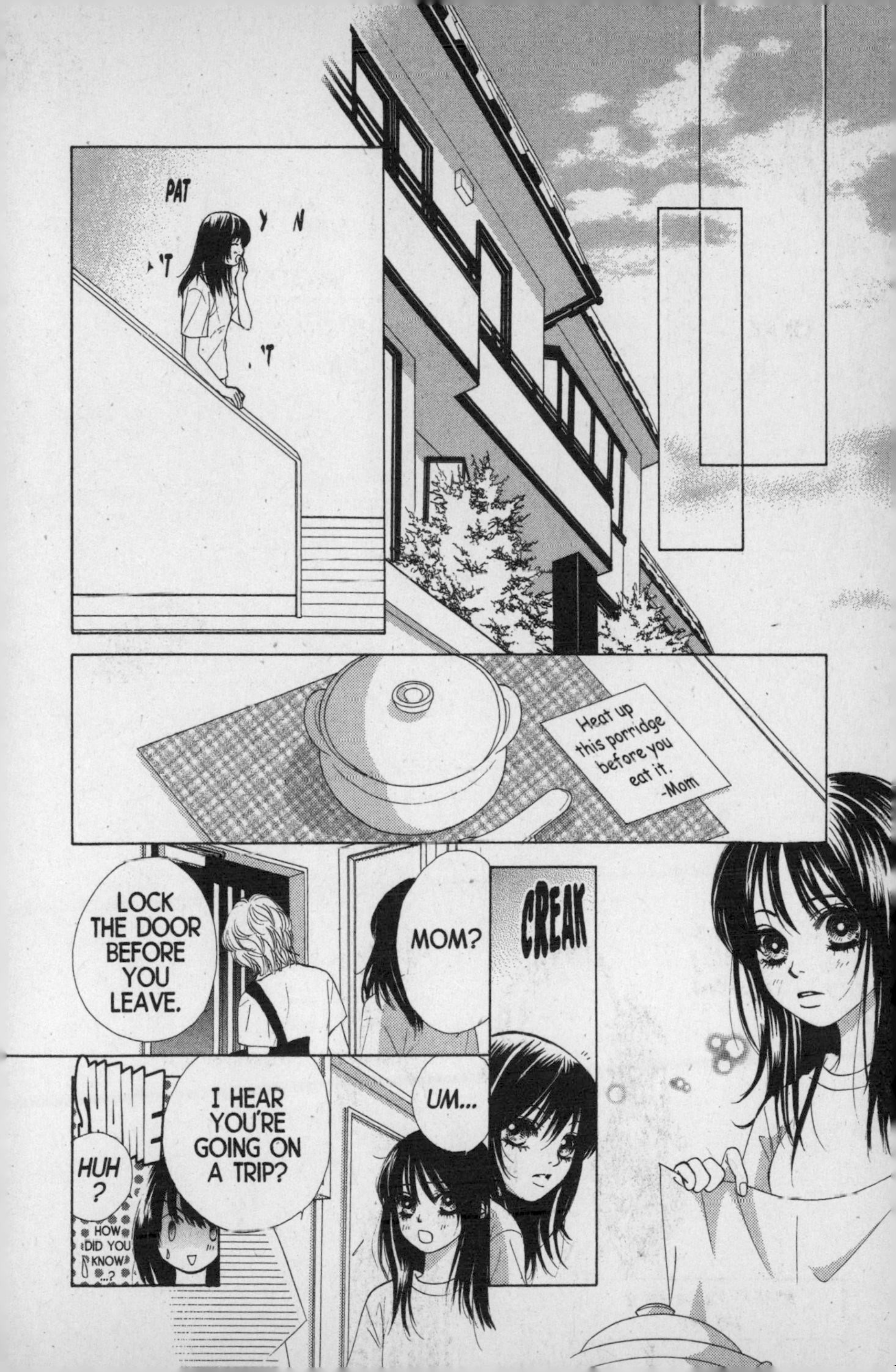
PAT
Heat up this porridge before you eat it.
-Mom
CREAK
MOM?
LOCK THE DOOR BEFORE YOU LEAVE.
UM...
I HEAR YOU'RE GOING ON A TRIP?
HUH?
HOW DID YOU KNOW...?

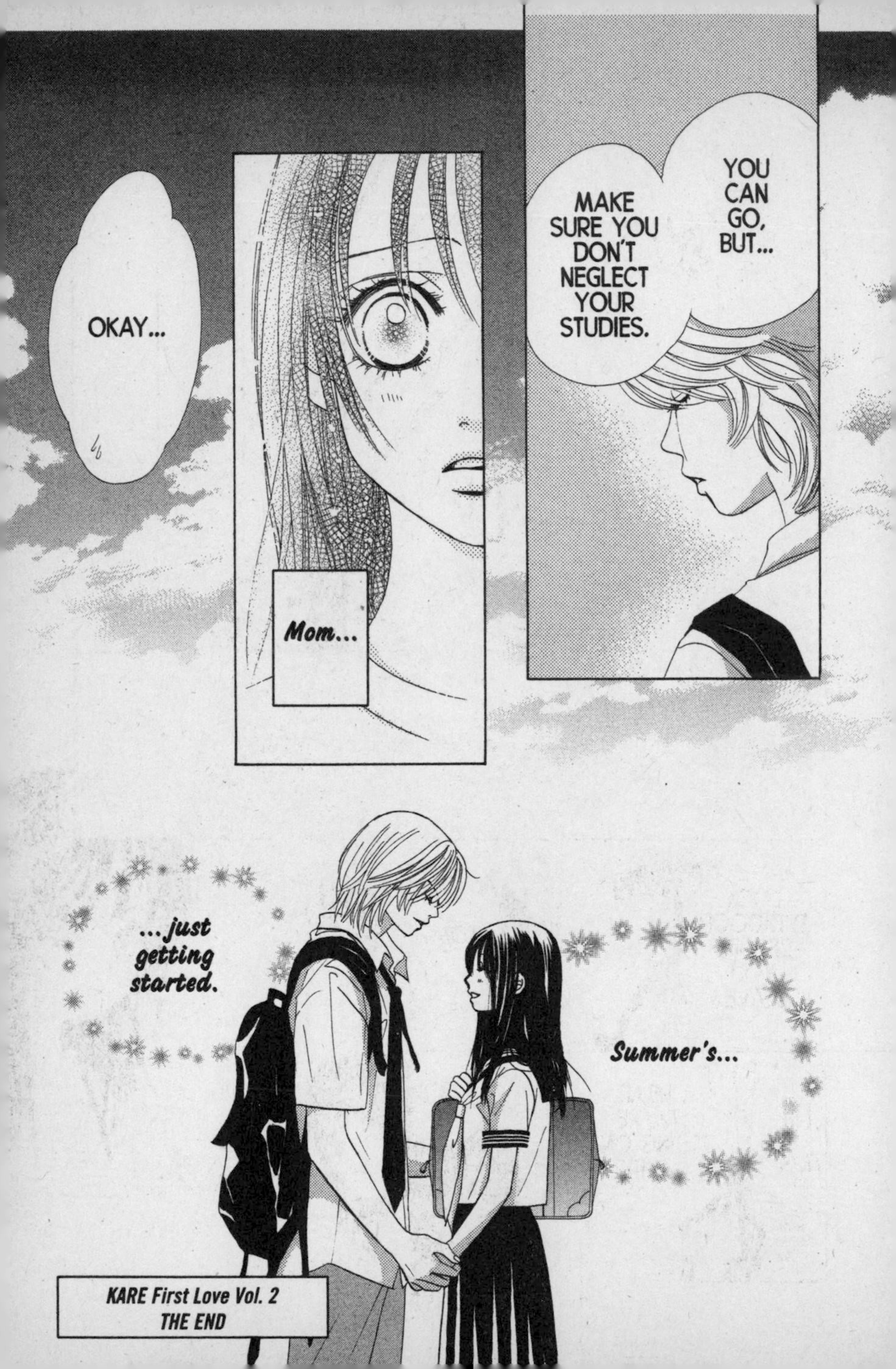
YOU CAN GO, BUT...
MAKE SURE YOU DON'T NEGLECT YOUR STUDIES.
Mom...
OKAY...
Summer's...
...just getting started.
KARE First Love Vol. 2
THE END

Kaho Miyasaka
official site

Love＊Factory

http://www.k-miyasaka.com/

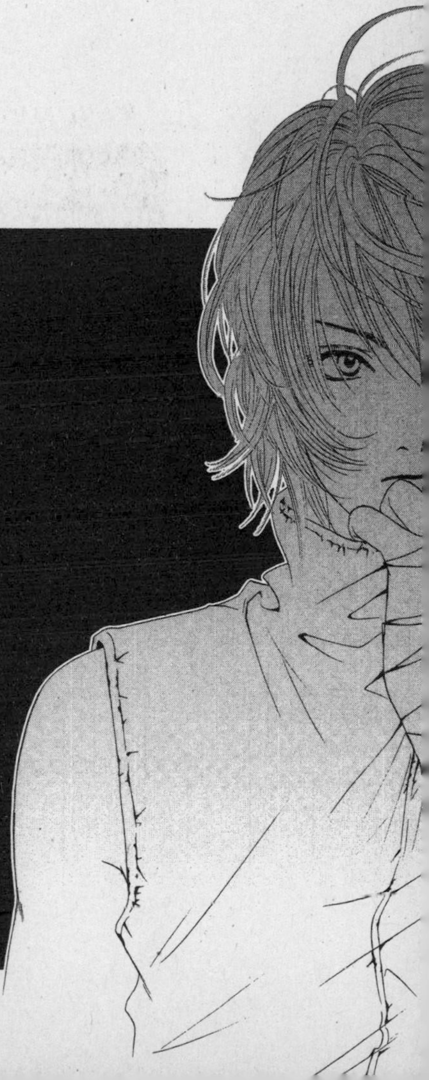

Message From the Author

I really had a hard time with the cover illustration of Kiriya for this volume. I accidentally splashed ink on his face when I was almost done, and I cried as I was forced to redo the whole thing. Not only that— this was on the day of the deadline. Anyway, I'm glad I got it in on time.

— Kaho Miyasaka

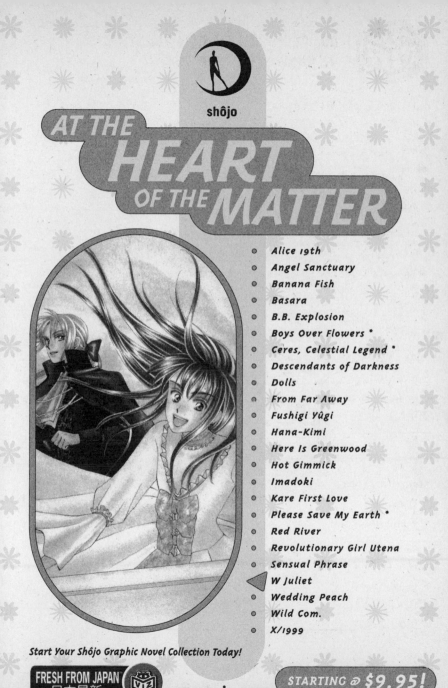

COMPLETE OUR SURVEY AND LET US KNOW WHAT YOU THINK!

☐ Please do NOT send me information about VIZ products, news and events, special offers, or other information.

☐ Please do NOT send me information from VIZ's trusted business partners.

Name: _____

Address: _____

City: _____ **State:** _____ **Zip:** _____

E-mail: _____

☐ Male ☐ Female **Date of Birth** (mm/dd/yyyy): ___/___/___ (Under 13? Parental consent required)

What race/ethnicity do you consider yourself? (please check one)

☐ Asian/Pacific Islander ☐ Black/African American ☐ Hispanic/Latino

☐ Native American/Alaskan Native ☐ White/Caucasian ☐ Other: _____

What VIZ product did you purchase? (check all that apply and indicate title purchased)

☐ DVD/VHS _____

☐ Graphic Novel _____

☐ Magazines _____

☐ Merchandise _____

Reason for purchase: (check all that apply)

☐ Special offer ☐ Favorite title ☐ Gift

☐ Recommendation ☐ Other _____

Where did you make your purchase? (please check one)

☐ Comic store ☐ Bookstore ☐ Mass/Grocery Store

☐ Newsstand ☐ Video/Video Game Store ☐ Other: _____

☐ Online (site: _____)

What other VIZ properties have you purchased/own? _____

_____

How many anime and/or manga titles have you purchased in the last year? How many were VIZ titles? **(please check one from each column)**

ANIME	MANGA	VIZ
☐ None	☐ None	☐ None
☐ 1-4	☐ 1-4	☐ 1-4
☐ 5-10	☐ 5-10	☐ 5-10
☐ 11+	☐ 11+	☐ 11+

I find the pricing of VIZ products to be: **(please check one)**

☐ Cheap ☐ Reasonable ☐ Expensive

What genre of manga and anime would you like to see from VIZ? **(please check two)**

☐ Adventure ☐ Comic Strip ☐ Science Fiction ☐ Fighting

☐ Horror ☐ Romance ☐ Fantasy ☐ Sports

What do you think of VIZ's new look?

☐ Love It ☐ It's OK ☐ Hate It ☐ Didn't Notice ☐ No Opinion

Which do you prefer? **(please check one)**

☐ Reading right-to-left

☐ Reading left-to-right

Which do you prefer? **(please check one)**

☐ Sound effects in English

☐ Sound effects in Japanese with English captions

☐ Sound effects in Japanese only with a glossary at the back

THANK YOU! Please send the completed form to:

VIZ Survey
42 Catharine St.
Poughkeepsie, NY 12601

All information provided will be used for internal purposes only. We promise not to sell or otherwise divulge your information.